# DEDICATION

For my wife Nicola.

# DIRTY

ROBERT WHITE

ISBN: 10: 1492794368
ISBN-13: 978-1492794363

# CONTENTS

# ACKNOWLEDGMENTS

Firstly, I must point out that this book is in no way auto-biographical.

Although like the main protagonist here, I did patrol the streets of Preston in 1981 and continued to do so for fifteen years, I was fortunate enough never to encounter police officers or lawyers like some depicted in these pages.

Indeed, my experiences were the total opposite. I was lucky enough to work alongside some of the bravest men and women I have ever met.

Yes, police officers are human and suffer the same failings as all reading this, but I am proud to say I found the vast majority of officers to show great integrity and compassion in their daily lives.

The early 1980's cast a dark shadow over the north of England and people turned to crime for any number of reasons. Therefore, I would also comment that not all criminals would be off my Christmas card list.

Some however, should rot.

I would like to thank my wife for her unrelenting support and guidance during the writing of this novel. Writers will concur that it is a lonely business and without Nicola, this novel would never have been published.

Robert White.

# JUST ANOTHER DAY

David Stewart stopped walking and listened. His steady footsteps and rustling uniform made it difficult to detect the exact cause of the tinkling noise he was sure he'd heard two or three streets away.

Was it a drunk kicking a stray bottle or a window breaking?

A lone dog barked. And there was silence again.

The copper pushed his gloved hand deep into his overcoat, and removed a Maglight.

He inspected it, checked it worked, even though he knew it did, and headed for the alley that would take him toward the suspicious noise.

His beat, Callon Estate, was notorious.

When it was built by the Local Authority in the mid fifties, it had housed hundreds of mill workers that sweated their bollocks off for a pittance. David Stewart figured that maybe they were the 'good times' for Callon. Those jobs were long gone. In fact,

Thatcher's current Government was in no mood to give in to the unions, and most of the houses he walked by were home to the unemployed.

On Callon, the black economy reigned.

As if to rub salt in the wounds of the jobless occupants, the once vibrant factory buildings on Dundonald Street still loomed derelict over the rows of dilapidated housing. Chain-link fences and barbed wire surrounded the old mill. Various councils had made vain attempts to keep the kids out. But the gangs that roamed Callon, some as young as five years old, found their way in, and stole or vandalized anything of value. Holes appeared in the fences faster than they were repaired. It was a playground in everything but name.

The estate had been gaining a reputation for the last five years and, despite Moor Nook, Grange Park and Avenham already fighting it out for shit hole of the 'eighties, Callon was as dismal and dangerous an area of Preston Lancashire you would want to come across.

Dave had followed the mysterious glassy sound through the back alleys and walked slowly along Nevett Street. One lone street-lamp was left intact, which was of little help. His new Maglight was needed more to avoid the numerous dog turds, kids' toys, and various bits of burnt out Ford Cortina, rather than find the errant thief or drunk responsible for the noise that had disturbed him.

He stood perfectly still and watched the white frost of his warm breath disappear into the chilled night. Once again there was silence. He pushed the backlight button and checked his near new digital watch.

0207hrs 9th March 1981.

Dave pointed his torch at his Doc Martins and checked for dog shit.

Katie's place, warmth and a brew were in order.

He surveyed his beat with his own working class eyes. The semi-detached, rendered houses were grey and doleful. Large patches of damp formed on the gables, giving the homes a camouflage effect in the half-light.

He noticed the odd bedroom curtain twitch as he paced slowly to his destination. Coppers never went unnoticed on this estate, no matter what the time.

Occasionally he came across a well-maintained garden, probably the home of some retired couple who had lived on the estate all their lives and refused to move.

It reminded him of his own scheme over the Pennines in South Yorkshire. His family home had been little different. Dave's mother and father had been fiercely house-proud, despite the desperate conditions that surrounded them. The poverty Arthur Scargill promised to remove was still present, and Thatcher, together with Norman Tebbit and his infamous bike, was looking to make it worse.

Much worse.

Dave felt the early morning chill despite his heavy uniform, and turned up the collar of his overcoat. He was unsure if it was the cold, or the memories of Barnsley that made him shiver.

Severn House was what Dave's father referred to as an 'old folks home.' Insanely, the Council had built the Sheltered Housing Village smack bang in the centre of Callon. Katie worked the night shift and was the saviour of all wet, cold and pissed off policemen. David Stewart fitted that bill perfectly.

She made the most glorious hot buttered toast and tea. More importantly to Dave, she was a friendly face on a beat where coppers were as popular as a fart in a space suit.

Rumour had it that at one time Katie gave the odd passing copper a little more than tea and toast, but to Dave, who was still four hours from the end of a twelve hour foot patrol, the tea and company, would be just fine.

At the time of its construction the community project was a novel design, with thirty or so one-bedroom semi bungalows, each with a small garden, surrounding a warden's house in the centre. Each house had direct contact with the warden by alarm twenty-four hrs a day. An emergency cord was situated in every room; if any of the elderly residents had a problem, they could pull the little orange handle and the warden would come to their aid. That was okay when the place was built. What the Council hadn't banked on, was the rapid demise in both the moral and financial condition of society surrounding the poor old dears come the present day.

The elderly residents had major problems when they left their front door. If they didn't have the luxury of a car, the nearest bus stop was ten minutes walk if you were good on your pins.

Not good on the Callon Estate.

As Dave approached, he studied the Warden's house and saw the telltale light burning in the rear. Katie was up and about. Dave could taste the hot sweet tea already.

The young policeman knocked lightly on the back door of the residence. Seconds later, he heard the shuffle of feet. There was a brief pause as Katie checked the spy hole in the door.

“Only me, Katie!”

Dave shone his torch at himself to aid her. He could see his breath again, and figured he looked like something from the new Halloween movie he’d just seen on video.

After various locks and bolts had been undone, Katie opened the door and Dave gave his very best smile. Her dark hair was tied back to reveal a round, once very pretty face, devoid of make-up.

She drew heavily on a Dunhill which, in Dave’s experience, seemed to be permanently fixed in the corner of her mouth and had caused a deep wrinkle on that side.

“Can’t be too careful, love,” she said, exhaling smoke over him. “The little bastards on this estate never sleep. They’d rob the pennies from a dead man’s eyes, they would.”

Katie was Preston born and bred, but like many of the town’s residents, was descended from Irish stock. The town of Preston had been a trading post for hundreds of years, and the sea link between Preston and Dublin was only dwarfed by its big sister twenty-three miles away in Liverpool. Katie had family in all three cities.

Divorced, much to her father’s disapproval, and approaching fifty, she was still an attractive woman. With a little help from Max Factor, she still managed to turn a few heads in the local pubs around the town, even if the heads were a little thin on top these days.

She wore a dark blue overall, which Dave noticed was a little too tight at the chest. A pair of pink fluffy slippers completed the picture.

“Get y’self inside, lad. It’s bloomin’ freezin’ tonight.”

She closed the door behind Dave, re-applied two of the four locks, and rubbed her hands briskly to warm them.

Dave loped into the lounge, removed his heavy uniform overcoat, and made himself comfortable in a much worn, all enveloping armchair.

“All quiet, Katie?” he asked, knowing the answer.

“Aye, so far, I’m not countin’ any chickens just yet though.”

Katie turned and made for the kitchen, her slippers making shuffling noises on the recently bleached linoleum floor. Dave listened to the familiar household sounds and, minutes later, she returned with the obligatory tea and toast.

“These evil little villains round here will be the death of me, Dave.” Katie sat down heavily on an even more dog-eared sofa. “We’ve had three bungalows done over in the last week; all in the early hours. My residents are terrified.”

“Yeah, I heard someone is active.” Dave bit into his toast. It tasted heavenly. Simple things for a simple guy, he thought.

Katie smiled at the young officer; his use of the jargon she had heard used by older, more experienced officers amused her.

“You’re starting to sound like an old hand, Dave. We only get the new ones, y’know, the sprogs, on this patch.”

Dave looked a little hurt, but it was true. Only the younger officers got Callon as a foot patrol beat. The more experienced coppers avoided it like the plague.

“I’ve nearly two years in now, Katie.”

She manoeuvred her matronly figure behind Dave and ruffled his hair, in a vain attempt to flirt.

“You’re a baby. Eat your bloody toast.”

He did as ordered, and bit into the hot buttered slice.

Dave’s police radio burst into life. The young officer put down his toast and listened. He waited for the transmission to end and then answered his control room.

“239, I’m five away, over.”

A violent domestic dispute had started on the estate. Dave was just a minute’s walk from the house.

“I’m gonna have to go, Katie, sounds like some poor lass is getting the sharp end of the stick from her old man again.”

Domestic violence made up much of Dave’s night shift duties. It was a dangerous job, most murders were domestic related. Dave had heard many stories of how even the battered wife had turned on the visiting copper as soon as he’d attempted to arrest her husband. Domestics were time consuming and very often, a waste of that time. If a woman made a statement of complaint against her husband, it was usually withdrawn the next day. The ‘new men’ being talked about in the papers didn’t live on Callon.

Katie helped Dave on with his coat, which was still damp from the cold moisture in the night air. She could have been a mother sending a child to school. She studied him for a moment as he pulled on leather gloves.

Well over six feet, strong and muscular, with dark features that undoubtedly made him very popular with the ladies. He had a hardness about him, and Katie thought that he had acquired it a little too soon for his years. What was he? Twenty-five? Yes, she remembered his birthday last month. Not yet out of his probation, and she had already seen the scars of street brawls on his face. In fact, the star shaped scar just below his right eye had been with him from day one.

Had he not been a copper, this one could have gone the other way. She'd seen it all before. After all, she was a Callon girl.

Katie pecked Dave's cheek. "You be careful, sweetie."

She smiled, and for a brief moment, saw a flash of a grin come to the young policeman's face. She thought he needed to smile more. He was a deep soul.

"I'll be back if I can." Dave gestured toward his half-eaten snack. "And I'll try to keep an eye on the bungalows tonight n'all."

Katie stood at the window and watched the handsome young man stride out into the darkness. She rubbed the back of her neck and spoke ruefully to herself.

"Hmm, if you were twenty years younger, girl!"

William Henry Bailey was cold. He touched his face with his fingers and he didn't feel a thing. That was a sure sign of brass monkey weather. After a few beers in the park with the lads, and a dab of whizz from Sheila Mellor on Bidston Street, who Billy reckoned was a deffo shag on the next visit, he'd crawled through one of the many holes in the fencing that let him inside the old mill on Dundonald Street.

Sitting inside the derelict shell of a rotting building, instead of being in the bedroom of the lovely Sheila, Billy was ruing his luck. If he had the cash for a few tins and a pack of fags he'd be in there.

The last thing he needed was to risk another job so soon after the last one. The pigs were bound to be sniffing around. But he had to do it, there was just no choice. He was skint.

The old walls were covered in graffiti, and the ambient light played tricks. The freezing night was full of noises that made Billy's head turn, his eyes searching the shadows.

As usual, the boy was shitting himself. Just before a job, the fear always came over him.

The cold wasn't that much of a problem, he could piss the cold. He was used to it. There had been no gas in Billy's house all winter. Since his mam had done one with that taxi driver from up Greenlands, his old man had gone clean off it and there hadn't been gas or leccy since. His house was no warmer than the mill.

The cold was one thing, but his fear was different. Some burglars said they got off on the buzz of a job. They felt alive, the adrenaline flying through their bodies as they broke the window or forced that door.

Billy didn't get off at all, and he hated feeling scared. It wasn't allowed. Fear was a weakness and you never, ever, admitted weakness to anyone.

He'd done three of the old fogies' bungalows inside a week. They were easy pickings, and he was long past caring that the old farts were often inside, shitting their pants at the sound of him rummaging around in their smelly little rooms. Even if they did wake up, they were too shit scared to do anything, and to Billy all fear, no matter how warranted, was weakness.

He looked at his watch. It wasn't nicked; it was bought and paid for. You didn't wear knock-off gear, because if you got a pull from the pigs and the guy had half a brain, you were fucked. Besides, if you were Billy Bailey and lived on the Callon, you got pulled regular.

It was 4am.

Billy needed that cash and quick. Tomorrow was Friday, the weekend, time to go out on the pull and sink a few beers. Not just a four-pack of knock off cans from Patel's shoved down your neck on the park, but to a pub or two. Maybe he could even go dancing to a club if he dragged enough out of that tight bastard Cliff, the local fence.

Tonight though, despite the fear, he was feeling lucky. He'd done a walk-by of the old girl's house that afternoon. He always did it in the daytime because if he got a pull, he could make any old excuse to the coppers.

He smiled to himself as he recalled checking out a job a few days back. A new, young beat copper had seen him. Billy knew him by name. He knew most of Preston Nick by name, including the CID.

"I'm lookin' for me cat, PC Swindles. I'm goin' straight now, y'know." It was a lame excuse. Billy knew the copper couldn't prove any different. So, he got turned over and they kept him waiting as usual. So what? They had nothing. Fuck all. Billy was a clever boy when it came to the streets, ask anyone on the Callon.

On the day's walk-by, a quick snoop in the front window of the bungalow had revealed a new looking telly and what looked to Billy like an antique clock on the mantle. Put them together with the gold ring he still had to weigh in from last night's job, and he could have a good weekend.

He checked his pockets for his Marigolds. Billy didn't carry anything else. No torch or tools; the Marigolds could be easily hidden. Billy liked that.

If you got a pull with a tool, you could get lifted for 'going equipped.' Billy's brother Mick got pinched on his way to a job with a torch and screwdriver. He got six months in Walton jail for his trouble. Some people never listened, and his Mick was one of them.

Billy was different. Billy was clever. He was a bodily pressure man. Using his powerful frame to push open locked doors had made him good money the last two years. He never kicked a door in. The coppers could match your trainers to any mark left on the door. No, Billy simply pushed his way through like the day he was born.

If waiting in the mill was bad, the walk to the job was worse. Billy had to look cool, just in case some nosy pig got close. How many times had Billy just walked right by a copper on the way to a job? Oh yes, clever boy, Billy.

Tonight though, it seemed Billy had no need to worry. His luck was holding firm. Although he had no way of knowing it, the only man in the area was Dave Stewart, who was trying, in vain, to reconcile the differences of man and wife four streets away.

The youth strolled, almost strutted, touching the rubber gloves in his pocket once in a while to see they were still there.

He did a quick recce of the little bungalow. Everything looked cool. There was a breeze that would hide any noise he made, and the back garden was surrounded by a mature hedge to keep him hidden. Billy pulled on the Marigold washing-up gloves, and walked the few steps to the back door. All the woodwork of the house was the original softwood from when it was built, and despite having a recent coat of paint, it was rotten. He hummed a tune in his head to try and calm himself. Shakin' Stevens, This Ole House, it was new out.

His heart was pounding in his chest as he fought with his fear, and Billy was convinced that it could be heard streets away.

He leaned his bulky frame into the door. The youth was very proud of his body and couldn't resist looking at his biceps as he put pressure on the lock. At nineteen, he had worked out in the best gyms in the country courtesy of HMP. You couldn't leave at the end of the session and the showers were cold, but the good side was, you didn't pay and you met some really good lads in there that knew a thing or two about going on the rob.

The door was stronger than it looked. He brushed his blond hair from his eyes, held his breath and applied more pressure. The frame made an almost inaudible popping sound and gave way. To Billy, it was a redwood falling.

Billy quickly stepped back and concealed himself behind a dustbin. As he crouched down, he noticed it had a brick on the lid and smelt of disinfectant.

"Tidy old sod," he thought. If the old codger had heard the door go, then now was the time. So, he had to wait and shake.

A full five minutes went by and nothing happened. Billy had to remind himself to breathe. He gripped his knees, his position near foetal. Was it the cold breeze that made his hands tremble? Each step to the now open door was loud enough to wake the dead. With one foot into the tiny kitchen, his blood raced, his pulse was deafening. Careful, Billy;

No pots in the sink. *A place for every thing and everything in its place,* he thought.

The door from the kitchen led into a small hallway. From there, Billy could see two other doors, one to the lounge, the other to the bedroom. He knew the layout; all the bungalows were identical. He could smell fresh paint, mixed with the odour of old people. He looked to the bedroom and saw he had a big problem; the door was wide open and Billy could see the old crone snoring not ten feet away from where he stood, holding his breath.

Almost on tiptoe, Billy stepped into the lounge. His prize was just seconds away from him. He moved the clock first and it made a clanging sound.

"What are you doing?" A shaky, but loud, elderly female voice came from behind him.

Billy couldn't believe his ears; the wizened old cow was up!

"Get out of my house!" There was no fear in the old voice.

Billy intended to do just that but not before he had got at least some of what he'd come for. He turned to face the old lady.

Her pure white hair was held firmly in place by large pink plastic rollers, which made her head look far too big for such a petite frame. He stood over a foot taller than her. He looked down at the frail soul, and pointed toward the bedroom.

"Go back to bed you, silly old cow," he hissed. "If you wake the neighbours, I'll break your fuckin' jaw."

Billy had known his own Gran. Granma Davey, his mother's mother. She hadn't been like this old bird, though. She'd been a big woman with pendulous breasts that she would push your head into at every drunken opportunity. A loud old tart she was. Always smelled of aniseed.

"Back to bed, I said."

Then he saw it. No! Fuck no! The little orange alarm handle, dangling from a length of cord. He'd heard about the alarm system in the bungalows, but never actually seen it on his previous outings. Worse still, the silly cow was almost in reach of it. Her left hand was just steps from the cord.

The old lady was going for it.

Billy's voice was evil; "Don't even fuckin' think about it, grandma."

Courage had never been lacking for the elderly lady. After surviving two world wars, a foul-mouthed youth wasn't going to frighten her. She moved a step closer to the cord.

Billy reached for her wrist, it was all going wrong, everything was slowing down, his strength was waning, he was in a dream. He had to stop her before it was too late.

He lunged at the woman.

Even through his gloves, the old girl's skin was ice to him. He could feel her bones under it, the muscles, emaciated by age. What remained seemed wrapped in cold thin gauze.

She was easy to manoeuvre. Billy must have been twice her weight. He just shifted his bulk onto his left foot, and pulled.

The old lady spun like a top until she made contact with a nearby armchair, which caused her to lose her balance. Her arms flailed. She grabbed at Billy in an attempt to steady herself. Billy simply shoved her backward.

"Fuck off," he spat.

She gave a low moan as she hit the floor, but Billy didn't hear. He was running. He ran faster and harder than he had for a very long time. He didn't stop until he reached the mill gates again.

Back at the bungalow Elsie lay immobile, staring toward the alarm cord. She had been so close.

Her legs were pretty numb. Something was wrong with them, and she felt pain, a sharp pain in her hip, and the cold was troubling her, even though the heating was on.

She wasn't worried though, as Malcolm, her eldest, would be round just after breakfast, and he would sort this mess out for her. Meanwhile, she needed to sleep. As Elsie lost consciousness, she wondered if she had paid her paper bill.

Billy got his breath back at the mill gates, just as Elsie May Townsend, eighty-three years old, widow, mother of two and grandmother of eight, lay dead on her perfectly vacuumed living room floor . . .

Billy shook. It wasn't the cold, either. His powerful legs were gone, and his head felt like it would explode. He gulped in deep breaths of crisp night air, and waited for his heart to change from its thunderous beat to the normal steady pace.

Finally, he got his wish and was left in his own shaken silence. Scared, unable to move, like a rabbit in a snare.

He'd been inside the perceived safety of the dark mill for over an hour. Surely the old woman would have called the coppers by now? They would have been to the house and they'd be all over the estate like a rash.

Could she give a description of him? Maybe not, the old bat was probably half blind anyway, and it was dark. Just the same, he was Billy Bailey and even if she could only give them, '*Young, stocky, blond and wearing a biker jacket,*' it could be enough. If he got a pull on the way back to his house, it could mean a lengthy visit down at the local nick, and that was out of the question. He didn't need that shit. He was never going to jail again. He was far too clever for that.

*Yeah*, he thought, *give it another half an hour, let the coppers fuck off, then a quick walk home while it's still dark and no one is the fuckin' wiser.*

Another set of tired legs were not half a mile away from the drama.

Having settled the domestic between the couple from hell in Great Townley Street, PC Dave Stewart was resigned to spending the final two hours of his shift rattling the door handles of the few remaining shops on the estate. Someone had recently added to the graffiti on the late night shop shuttering. A new swastika and '*Pakis go home*' in multi-coloured spray paint had appeared since his last tour. The fact that the Indian shopkeepers had probably never even dreamed of visiting Pakistan, other than to fight over the disputed land of Kashmir, made no difference. To the residents of Callon, if you were Asian, you were a Paki.

Dave checked the time, decided enough was enough, and a new spring came to his step as he turned to make the mile long walk back to Preston nick.

A half-hour stroll, type up the 'drunk and disorderly' file from last night's lock-up, and it would be time for much needed bed.

He walked past Callon Primary school, which was in remarkable shape for a change. A full fifty percent of the windows were intact, and the football posts seemed operational.

He looked across the pitch, saw movement, and his tiredness left him in an instant. A tall, blond, bulky figure walked briskly toward him.

Dave recognised Billy from twenty yards away. He'd had a couple of dealings with the family since his arrival on the Callon estate, and remembered the lad as a nasty piece of work.

Billy had his head down. He was re-living his botched job. He didn't see the copper until it was much too late. With only seconds to spare his senses came to life, he spotted his enemy, but he was fucked.

Billy knew he had been recognised. He couldn't run, it would look bad, besides he was too cool for that. Then he remembered his gloves. The fuckin' Marigolds were still in his pocket. In all the excitement, he'd forgotten to ditch them.

Calmly and as deftly as possible, Billy pulled the gloves from his leather biker jacket, and let them fall to the ground behind him as he walked the last yards.

Dave Stewart, on the other hand, was checking that the handcuff pouch on his belt was unclipped and the cuff readily available. His last encounter with Bailey had been a violent one, and he was in no mood to take chances so far from backup. He felt the flush of adrenaline readying his body. Fight or flight. The darkness of the playing-field was enough to hide Bailey's discreet drop, Dave didn't notice. The gloves were gone.

The two young men stood opposite each other on the winter mush of the school grounds. Violence beckoned both players, but this was no game with rules and a ball of any shape.

Dave's voice was quiet but confident. His training told him to stay casual, even if he felt anything but.

"Out late, Billy?"

Bailey eyeballed him and walked squarely into Dave's personal space. His breath visible, even in the half light.

"Why don't you fuck off and leave me be."

Billy hoped that some front would do the trick. He recognised the copper and didn't think it could work, but it had to be worth a try. He considered the nosey twat might be unnerved by his surroundings and Billy's ever growing rep, so he carried on.

"I didn't know they'd started the Y.T.S. for pigs now."

Dave was neither unnerved nor surprised by his subject's manner. Every cheap face acted tough. He'd seen real hard men at work back in Leeds, witnessed it first hand. This lad was playing at it.

As far as Dave could see, Bailey's attitude was a good excuse to give him a slap. Teach him a lesson. They were well and truly alone. No witnesses.

Dave's tone remained flat calm, but there was menace there and Bailey could almost taste it.

"Keep talking, Billy." Stewart checked the field, no-one in sight or earshot as far as he could see.

"You fancy a tear-up with a copper, then?

Billy felt some of his confidence drain, but held firm.

"Might do, yeah. Why? You think you can take me, do ya?" You wouldn't be so fuckin' brave if it was just me 'n you without that uniform of yours."

Billy was doing his best to be his cool self, but he didn't like this guy, not one little bit. He just needed to get the two hundred yards to his front door and fuck this night off.

The copper was straight to the point.

"Billy, I'm gonna turn you over whether you like it or not, don't give me the hard man routine, let's have a quick search of your pockets and you can be on your way. Know what I'm sayin'? What's it to be? I do my job, or do you get a fuckin' slap?"

Billy held Stewart's gaze like a boxer at a weigh-in.

This copper knew fuck all about the old dear, or the cuffs would have been out by now. He had nothing on him. Billy was clever. See? Let the twat do his check. He was clean as a whistle.

He stepped a pace back and held out his palms.

The pig grinned at him, and it wound him up.

"239 to control, over," Stewart spoke into the radio whilst Billy did his best to look bored, and inspected his fingernails.

The communications room replied and Dave spoke clearly into his set, "Yes, PNC check wanted, on William Henry Bailey, nineteen years, male, white, six feet two."

"You're wasting your time, mate. I'm whiter than white. Paid all my fines off last month when I did my last job!" Billy put on his best *'fuck you'* smile especially for Dave, his confidence growing by the minute. He was a powerfully built young man with white-blond hair and piercing blue eyes. His jacket, which was the latest style a la Duran Duran, probably cost more than Dave's best suit. How Bailey paid for it was another matter. Dave didn't give a fuck.

Bailey held his arms out to the side, resigned to a search, and let the copper root in his pockets. He knew he had fuck all on him, so he just stared straight at the pig and smiled. As Stewart leaned in, Bailey spoke into his ear.

"I know where you live, pal."

Dave Stewart had spent his youth on an estate just like Callon across the border in South Yorkshire. Been there, bought the T-shirt. For families like the Baileys, lies, just like larceny, were the family business.

He stepped back, and felt himself clench his fists.

"Well you must drop in sometime and empty my bins."

"239?" The radio crackled.

Dave regained his composure.

"Receiving, over."

Instead of the control room he had expected to hear, it was the voice of another section officer, Andy 'Armless Dunn. 'Armless had been Dave's Tutor Constable when he first arrived at Preston nick. He had been allocated Dave as his 'sprog' for five weeks, before he was let loose on the unsuspecting general public.

Andy was the shift van driver. If there was a prisoner to bring to the nick, or any rough stuff going on, he hated to miss out.

Some of the new style senior officers, the men and women brought through the ranks via some university and later Bramshill College, thought Andy a little over-zealous, but they, like every bobby on the shift, were glad to see 'Armless if the shit hit the fan.

"Where are you, Dave?" questioned 'Armless.

"I'm on the Callon, Andy, on the primary school playing fields."

"Can you speak?"

Dave turned the P.R. down so Bailey was unable to hear the radio conversation.

"Go ahead."

"Just watch yourself with this one, Dave, I'm on my way. He can get a bit naughty."

Dave allowed himself a smile; he could hear the van engine racing in the distance and could imagine Andy's determination not to be too late.

"Roger that."

Billy was getting restless. "What the fuck is going on, dickhead?"

Dave couldn't hide a smile. "Just waiting for your check, Billy. Calm down."

"No, I won't fuckin' calm down. I've 'ad enough now. This is fuckin' harassment. I'm gonna complain about this, you tosser. I'll have my brief on this, just you see."

"239?" the radio crackled.

This time it was the control room.

"239 receiving."

"Outstanding Arrest Warrant on one William Henry Bailey, for non-payment of fines, power of arrest, over."

Dave Stewart looked at Bailey. He never came quietly, but that suited Dave Stewart just fine. He didn't like the guy one bit.

"You gonna come nice and easy, Billy? You should pay those fines of yours."

Bailey set himself. Dave could see the muscles in his neck and shoulders swell. Billy's eyes glazed over, it was always the same for him. He clenched his teeth. His fists were now solid balls of bone and muscle. He had no intention of going to the station, and he would fight anyone to avoid it.

"Fuck you."

The young policeman wasn't about to take chances. Dave dropped his right shoulder and sent a punch to Bailey's left kidney. He delivered it with all his weight. It was more practiced than any of his colleagues could ever know.

The moment the punch connected, Stewart brought up his left hand to Bailey's throat. He took hold of his windpipe between thumb and forefinger, slid his left leg behind Bailey's and expertly dropped him to the ground.

Bailey was choking now. The fall to the ground had knocked the air from his body, and he was unable to breathe as the policeman had cut off his supply.

Dave Stewart spoke into the ear of the slowly asphyxiating Bailey, his mouth so close that Billy felt hot spittle on his lobe, "No…fuck you Bailey, you're nicked."

In all the excitement, Dave had failed to see his colleague saunter casually over to the scene of the trauma. He looked directly at the struggling youth pinned on the grass below.

'Armless was a monster of a man. No spring chicken, but definitely not one to be messed with.

His young trainee seemed in perfect control of the situation, but there was one small problem. Dave just may kill his prisoner if he didn't let go in the next few seconds.

Andy thrust his hands into his pockets. His still, thick Glaswegian accent cut the air in two.

"Ye don't seem to need me anymore, David," Andy said playfully, "and you have no fuckin' idea how much that upsets me."

Armless, was born and bred a Scot. He'd been a military man before joining Lancashire Constabulary nine years earlier, and it still showed. He coughed into his hand theatrically and added less jovially, "I think the wee lad's had enough now, pal."

Dave released Bailey, who promptly spewed his last meal on the wet grass.

He stood and brushed part of a field from his uniform. "Hello, 'Armless, I see you're slowing down, leavin' the young lads t'do all the work."

"I'll still give you a run for your money, you cheeky wee shite," said the older man. Dave looked Andy up and down. He had the appearance of a half-savage pit bull terrier squeezed into a police uniform, and Dave believed every word he said.

Armless picked up the now deflated Bailey in one huge fist, carefully avoiding the pool of vomit at his feet. He handcuffed him and led him to the waiting van.

As he slammed the door closed, he turned and shouted to Dave, "Aye, an' just for your cheek, lad, you can walk back to the nick."

Dave was devastated.

"Awe come on, Armless, I've just done a twelve on foot."

Any protest fell on the ears of a man who had spent the last eighteen years teaching lessons to mortals from both sides of the fence.

“Bloody typical,” said Dave, to no-one in particular, as he picked up his helmet, gloves and torch that had fallen to the ground in the struggle.

He checked the state of his uniform in the half light. The knees of his trousers were covered in damp green grass stains, and his coat looked like the local football team had used it to clean their boots.

“Another bloody report,” he mused. The police service was like any other government department and if you wanted them to dry-clean your kit, they wanted a report as to how you got dirty.

Dave examined his new torch for damage, and found none. He pushed it back in his pocket and stretched himself. He was knackered but despite his aching back, and the gloom of the playing field, something caught his eye. Some fifteen feet from the scene of his brief struggle with Bailey, he saw something.

He stepped closer and shone his Maglight at the stray objects.

A pair of pink coloured washing up gloves lay on the grass.

Dave was young in service, but he knew that some burglars used washing up gloves in their crimes. The gloves allowed them to pick up small items with better dexterity than woollen or leather. They also stretched halfway up your forearm, therefore eliminating the chance of leaving a partial palm print, the downfall of many criminals in the past.

Billy had previous for burglary.

Bingo.

He collected the gloves and put them in his pocket. As soon as he got to the nick, it was a two minute job to book them into the crime store and leave a note for the early CID officers. They could perhaps have a word with Bailey about them.

Dave walked from the scene, sliding on the cold wet grass of the playing field, and made his way back onto the estate. The first signs of dawn were forcing the night sky away from above the town. People were beginning to awaken. Milk floats buzzed by, and paperboys were delivering the news of the day on their bikes. He reached the main road and paced for several minutes until a familiar structure towered into view. Preston prison, one of Her Majesty's more elderly institutions, seemed in far better shape than most of his beat. The Victorian brick walls were newly pointed, and the massive wrought iron gates freshly painted. It seemed ironic to Dave that the town's dishonest citizens got preference over some of its honest. He watched as a prison van entered the confines of the jail, and wondered how many of Bailey's kind he would encounter over the coming years. He imagined it would be quite a few.

Preston Police Station was built in 1969, after the old Borough force out-grew the previous one close to the Crown Court on Earl Street. It stood six stories high. The basement held the cellblock and the charge office. Dave made his way downstairs to sort his prisoner.

The Rules of Arrest stated, that the arresting officer must relate the circumstances of that arrest to the charge office Sergeant.

He, in turn, then either accepted the arrest as lawful, or, threw out your man. This process was a daunting task for a young officer on his first few arrests. A charge office sergeant was a fearsome breed. If you cocked up, not only would the sergeant in charge bollock you until your ears bled, but your whole shift would give you shit for weeks to come. The piss-taking was always worse.

On this occasion though, Dave knew it was a straightforward job. The warrant for Bailey's non-payment of fines would be in a drawer in the charge office. Just slap the warrant in front of the sergeant, tell him the time, date and place of the lock-up, and bugger off home for some much needed kip.

Dave did just that.

As a local milkman discovered the body of an eighty-three year old female, the pair of Marigold washing up gloves, worn by her killer, were still in PC239 David Stewart's uniform jacket pocket.

# TROUBLE

His telephone was ringing.

David Stewart was living a deep dark dream, a running dream, lots of doors that wouldn't give, his heavy legs chasing the invisible but haunting foe just inches away in the next room.

What was that sound?

His telephone was ringing.

Dave eyed the ten year old trim-phone with blurred suspicion.

Only three people knew his number, and the persistence of the caller meant someone was either very pleased or very pissed off. He stretched out a very tired arm, and lifted the receiver.

"Hello."

"PC Stewart?"

The voice was male and businesslike.

"Yes," he replied, clearing his throat and with it his head.

It was the nick calling, as he could hear the activity of the control room in the background. What he didn't recognise was the voice on the end of the line.

"Ah, good, you're awake. This is Detective Inspector Williams. I'm sorry to disturb you so early, but I understand you were the foot patrol officer on Callon estate last night."

Dave swallowed hard. It was not good news. If a detective of any kind was ringing you at home when you were eighteen months into your police service, it was bad.

To have a detective inspector ringing meant only one thing.

"Yes, sir, that's correct."

The man's voice was solemn but there was friendliness in there, a manner any doctor would have been proud of at his bedside.

"There has been an incident that we need to talk to you about, David."

Dave was confused if not a little worried. What the fuck had he done? An incident? That could mean anything.

"OK, sir. What is it?"

The Inspector's tone stayed level. He had a smooth southern Irish accent that was intent on putting Dave at ease, but did exactly the opposite.

"Why don't you pull your trousers on now and nip to the station, so we can have a chat?"

"Now?"

"Let's say half an hour, David."

The Inspector put down the telephone in its cradle and swung around in his chair to face the Superintendent.

"The lad's on his way, sir."

Williams fished in his top pocket for his fags. His watery blue eyes darted around the room, ensuring he was out of earshot of any comms operators.

"He'll be shittin' himself when he gets here."

The Super drained the last of his coffee from a mug with the words '*The Boss*' printed on it. He grimaced at the dreadful chicory taste.

"Good, when he gets here bring him straight to my office. He'll be shitting it then."

Dave sat on the end of his bed. He scratched his head and yawned. A narrow strip of daylight shone through a gap in his curtains and it played host to thousands of dancing specs of dust. The dust came from the bare floor, and the bare floor was there because Dave was skint.

Shit like this, he did not need.

A quick check of his watch revealed he had been in bed for two hours. He silently cursed all coppers and stretched himself, an action which made him shiver. He pulled on a tatty dressing gown and walked to the bathroom. His constabulary house was in poor repair but it had just been fitted with a new avocado coloured suite as part of a long-term renovation plan by the force. The wall tiles remained in shit state, but were apparently on the list.

Dave showered, shaved and dressed before walking downstairs. He rarely used the lounge, and boxes of gear, unopened from the day he'd moved in, still sat in front of an ancient gas fire. His job and his erratic shift patterns, together with regular trips to his parents, meant there was little time for home-making.

He never had company. That mostly suited Dave. He was a man who enjoyed his own.

It was 10.30 am, he was knackered and to add insult to injury, as he left the house it started to piss down. Dave took the bus to the nick, as daytime parking close by was fraught with danger. In just shy of a year, his car had attracted seven parking tickets and four large scratches in the streets around Lawson Street. So, he forced himself to take public transport, which consisted of a Zippy bus which ran every thirty minutes. He also planned to cycle, when he could afford a bike of course.

The bus was eight minutes late, and by the time he stood in the parade room of Lawson Street nick he positively dripped.

Feeling half asleep, he surveyed the space where every shift started. It was a very drab affair. Rows of desks littered with paper all faced a podium, where the section sergeant would give the duties of the day.

Sitting at his favorite desk was Andy Dunn. Andy obviously hadn't been home since the nightshift ended. He had the look of a man who needed his bed, but was writing a report instead.

Andy had a reputation of being a ladies' man, and he'd had the misfortune to have been chatting up one of the new female probationers outside the front door of the nick when the body of Elsie May Townsend had been discovered. His shift was over, but when he heard the news he walked back inside and started again. It was something that many busy section officers did all too often. Andy was in his sixteenth hour of duty, and the old brain cells had started to fail him.

He rubbed his square jaw, scratching at his shadow beard, and pulled himself together.

"Lady called Townsend has been found dead in one of the old folks' bungalows on the Callon." Andy's face wore a troubled mask, his tone matter of fact. "Looks like a break-in, gone wrong like. The panic button was pressed about half seven. Forensics are out there now."

Dave was dog-tired, but his brain was working just fine. He nodded.

"You spoke to Katie? She'll be gutted."

Armless shook his head. "Aye, yer right, but no, not yet, pal, I'm gonna nip over in a wee while, before I go home."

Dave was inexperienced, but he knew why he'd been called in.

As if to batter the truth home, Andy immediately confirmed Dave's thoughts. "CID thinks your Billy boy has a bit of flavour to him, and they want to know the full circs of the lockup.

Apparently the back door was the point of entry. No tools used, and bodily pressure is William Bailey's favourite M.O. as I recall."

Dave was racking his brains. He was trying to recount every detail of the arrest. He shook his head.

He spoke absently to himself. "Can't be him. Can't be, he was so fuckin' cool."

He looked at Andy, and regained some of his composure.

"He didn't even expect the warrant, mate. He was convinced he was walking."

Before Andy could answer, the scenes of crime team shuffled into the room. The four men and one woman all sported white paper suits, worn to avoid cross contamination. The suits made them look like slightly crumpled astronauts.

The eldest of the four men recognised Andy Dunn. He walked over, hand outstretched.

"Fuck me, Armless, you still bustin' heads and workin' seven on two off?"

"It's better than carrying some poor fucker's stomach contents round in a jar," Andy joked, and lit a cigarette in the strictly non-smoking parade room. He exhaled slowly, and pointed towards the evidence bags on the floor.

"So, what have you guys come up with?"

The scenes of crime guy unzipped his paper suit. He was a balding, slightly overweight man in his forties, and wore a rather unkempt moustache that partially hid a set of rotten teeth.

He ignored Andy's question for a moment, and gestured toward the packet of Embassy on the desk. Andy reluctantly offered, and joked, "Still a tight bastard, I see?"

The S.O.C.O gave a small laugh and lit up.

"I'm tryin' to give up. The wife would kill me if she could see me now."

"Well, now you've managed to scrounge a fag, yer gonna tell me about the job?" Andy pressed.

"Oh err... yeah, not a lot, Andy. A few fibres on the door frame, but whoever did the deed was wearing Marigolds. There's rubber glove marks everywhere."

Dave Stewart was close to a chair, and it was a good job. The S.O.C.O. saw Dave flop.

"You all right, lad? You look like you've seen a ghost."

"Yeah...I'm fine."

Dave was all but fine. He mumbled partly to himself and partly to the room, "I'm just here to get my kit. There's a Detective Inspector Williams wants to see me."

He stood, nodded towards Andy Dunn and left the room, his legs like jelly. The walk to the locker room was hell. The legal problems of producing evidence not properly recorded at the time of discovery were all too apparent to him. It was something you had drilled into you at the training college. Property is trouble. Pick it up. Book it in, and whatever you do don't just stick it in your locker. He was in the shit. As a probationary constable you could be sacked for just about anything, and this was a lot more than just anything. Dave, and his extended family, could not afford him to lose this job.

He walked into the cluttered locker room. Wet uniforms were hanging haphazardly wherever the owners could find space, and made the room smell musty and older than its years. Row upon row of tall grey metal containers stood to attention, every one holding secrets only their possessors knew.

Dave thought about the very large skeleton in his. He fumbled for his key, and managed to work it into the lock on the third attempt. He took out his soiled uniform coat and gingerly felt inside the pockets. His hand brushed the cold rubber of the gloves, and he shivered. He hadn't dreamed about them. They were as real as he. This was a waking nightmare and he couldn't escape it.

The gloves lay in his hand. Innocent household items instantly transformed into evil tools of crime. He felt bile rise within his gut, and he swallowed hard. Dave took three deep breaths.

He studied the gloves. In his heart he instantly knew Bailey was responsible. It was too much of a coincidence. Right place, right time right MO. He had no choice. He had to come clean and take the consequences.

Dave took the lift to the second floor where all the CID offices were located. The elevator seemed to take an age to the young constable. He knew the layout of the floor. One turn left, and second door on the left. Dave stood in the doorway of the Detective Inspector's office and could feel his legs shake.

"Ha! PC Stewart, good."

The Inspector was in his late forties, maybe early fifties. A shock of unkempt hair simply protruded from his head, and was pure silver. He gave the impression of never visiting a professional barber. Seemingly, the Inspector didn't possess a comb or declined to use one. Williams was also a chain smoker, a heavy drinker and divorced for the second time. He wore a shirt that Dave presumed had been ironed once, but not recently. He was the scruffiest senior officer that Dave had ever seen. Despite that, Williams had an easy joviality about him that made him popular amongst all ranks, and considering he was Detective Chief Superintendent John McCauley's right hand, that was no mean feat.

Williams pretended to finish what he was doing as he spoke.

Dave noticed it and it made him shiver.

"We're going straight to see the boss. He wants to clear this job up on the Callon, A.S.A.P. and he thinks your little scuffle with Mr. Bailey's youngest last night may just be the break we are looking for."

Williams stopped shuffling random papers and looked Dave in the eye.

"OK, son?"

"Yes, sir." Dave could think of no more to say.

Williams pushed a fag into his mouth and rummaged for a light.

"Now don't be intimidated by the old man, now." He found some matches and took a large drag, breathing cigarette smoke over Dave. "His fuckin' bark is only half as bad as his fuckin' bite."

Dave thought Williams sounded like Jimmy Cricket but didn't get the joke. The Inspector thought it was hilarious, and howled at his own quip all the way to John McCauley's door.

Dave thought that his legs would give way. He heard the Inspector give a courteous knock on the door.

"Come."

"This is PC Stewart, boss." The Inspector sat on a small sofa to the left of McCauley's large desk, without being asked.

Dave merely stood to attention in the middle of the office floor. He thought the office would have been bigger. It all looked very basic. A few trimmings made it almost personal to the man it housed. There were a few rugby trophies on a table and some framed commendations on the wall, but no family pictures on the desk. None of it mattered, because the one thing you couldn't take your eyes off was John McCauley.

His mere presence was daunting. Dave wanted a way out. There was none.

John McCauley had been a police officer for twenty-two years. He was old school. The chances of further career development for him were, frankly, nil. The days of hands-on bosses were quickly disappearing, and this particular officer's hands had been on far too many people for the liking of any politically minded Chief Constable.

He was a racist, a sexist, a womaniser, a bully and the most productive detective the force had come up with in years. As a result of the latter, he had been forgiven his many sins.

Dave noticed that McCauley's fingernails were cut short and

seemed unusually shiny. They didn't fit the remainder of the man. It wasn't that he seemed untidy; just the opposite. Crisp white shirt, L.C.C.C. tie perfectly knotted, number 2 crew, scrubbed and starched from top to toe. Nevertheless, something about him just wasn't right. Dave couldn't put his finger on it. He was sure of one thing, though. This was one scary son of a bitch.

Most of McCauley's men in his close knit team feared him and loved him in equal amounts. Dave definitely fell into the former category.

The Chief didn't bother to look up from a report on his desk. His tone was almost secondary.

"Where the fuck have you been, Stewart?"

"Sir?"

McCauley's eyes left his paper, and the young officer wished they had remained where they were. As dark as the devil's own, his iris was so close to the colour of his pupil, it gave the recipient of his glare a view of a void. A black abyss of bitterness stared straight at you. It cut straight into Dave, and he felt his pulse rate quicken further.

The Chief had never considered elocution part of the ladder to success, and still boasted a broad Lancashire accent.

"If the first question is too difficult for you, lad, how the fuck did you get in this job?"

Dave decided not to answer and to ride out the initial storm. McCauley sat back in his swivel chair and made a pyramid with his fingers. His top lip curled slightly as he spoke. It gave the impression of constant irritation.

"Not a fuckin' university poofter, are you?"

"No, sir."

"Thank fuck for small mercies. What did you do before you came to lower the tone of our wonderful police force then, Stewart?"

Dave had been everything. Before he left school, he'd had three jobs at once. Two paper rounds and working the pop wagon on a Saturday. From then, he'd laboured on motorways, worked nightclub doors and stacked shelves. His father had been injured in a pit accident at Grimethorpe in 1977, money was always tight.

Jobs in Barnsley had been few and far between, and Dave had done some things for people he'd rather forget. It earned a crust, but wasn't always legal. He decided to flower.

"I was a security guard, sir."

The Chief spat his words out like a machine gun.

"Well, you're not working for fuckin' Group Four now, son, and I expect you to get here in less than two fuckin' hours."

By the end of the sentence, McCauley was purple.

"Sorry, sir."

Dave watched the Chief's mood change with almost psychotic precision.

He became instantly businesslike and leaned forward over his desk, the movement pushing up the sleeves of his shirt. Dave decided that McCauley had the hairiest forearms he had ever seen.

“What can you tell me about William Henry Bailey?”

Dave felt his knees start to tremble again and hoped it wasn’t visible. There was no going back now.

“I arrested Bailey on the playing fields on Callon primary school this morning about six o’clock. He was coming from the direction of the old mill. I figured that he would have been up to no good, so I stopped him, gave him a check and he came back as wanted on warrant, sir.”

Mackay’s eyes pierced Dave again. “The boy has a reputation of being a hard man. Did he put up a fight?”

“He got a bit naughty for a while, more verbal than anything, sir.”

Mackay looked Dave up and down, a trace of sarcasm in his voice, “You look like a pretty boy to me, son. Bet you were shouting for help before he said boo to your goose.”

Dave looked to the Inspector for support, but got none. Williams just smoked and looked dishevelled.

“I used the necessary force, sir.”

“Fuck necessary force,” Mackay bellowed. ”The thieving twat should be in the casualty if he had a go at a copper.”

The Chief then turned to Williams, who sat unruffled by the whole thing. He was opening his second packet of Marlboro, and picking dried cornflakes from his suit trousers.

“What do you say, Clive?”

The Inspector seemed happy to have removed the last piece of his wayward breakfast, and slowly nodded. His Irish brogue seemed accentuated in the presence of his boss.

“Oh aye, casualty. There’s no excuse for hittin’ a copper now, is there?”

McCauley calmed again, riding his emotional rollercoaster. The little double act wasn’t wasted on Dave, but he was too shit scared to care. “All right, Stewart, what else can you tell us about our little housebreaker?”

Dave knew the moment of truth had arrived. Everything he had worked for the last eighteen months now hung in the balance. The thought of returning to Yorkshire, jobless and humiliated, was a daunting prospect. He swallowed hard and took the plunge.

“I think Bailey may have been carrying rubber gloves just before I locked him up, sir.”

Even Williams sat up at this remark, spilling ash on his already stained trousers.

The Chief, though, took on the guise of a volcano about to explode.

His voice was truly menacing, “And what fuckin’ rubber gloves are these then?”

Dave shifted slightly, and produced the gloves from his pocket. He felt like Oliver asking for more. McCauley stood, and for a moment, Dave thought he was going to attack him. Instead, a torrent of abuse flowed from the man. Every expletive Dave had ever heard and a few more besides were launched in his direction. Spittle sprayed over him as the man ranted and raved.

Suddenly, the senior detective snatched the gloves from Dave's still outstretched hand, and handed them to the Inspector.

With a change of voice and character that would give most psychologists enough material for a prize-winning paper, McCauley wiped his mouth and said, "Sit the fuck down, sonny."

William Henry Bailey was not a happy soul. Something was wrong but he couldn't think what. He had been unceremoniously dumped in a drunk cell on his arrival at the nick. That was normal, he'd been booting off as usual, and they were used for 'difficult' prisoners.

He'd been sharing with some sad student type who had been busted for trying to sell half an ounce of bush to an undercover drug squad officer in the college bar. That too was normal.

However, it was now well past noon and he hadn't been put in front of the beak yet. All fines offences were normally heard early in the day, not late on, and he had been moved to a cell on his own. When he was given a mattress and blanket, he knew it was fuckin' bad news.

"What's goin' on, boss?" Billy was trying to get the attention of a copper who was walking the corridor of the block on cell duty. Billy called the twats '*boss*,' as it made them feel important. It was the best he could do. He couldn't bring himself to call any copper '*officer*' or '*sir*.'

"You'll have to wait and see, Billy," said the plod. "We're very busy today."

Billy sat down on his bunk, away from the small hatch in the cell door. The stench of the block filled his nostrils. A mixture of unwashed feet and misused drains. He looked around him at the pale green painted walls. To his horror, he saw his own name scratched into the plaster. It had been painted out, but it was there.

*'Billy was 'ere Aug 1978'*

Billy had been 'ere' all too often. He had first been arrested at age twelve. It was the usual, shoplifting, how most started. Then it was nicking pushbikes, and sellin' 'em to the Pakis on Deepdale. Billy broke into his first house at thirteen, and never looked back. Nine further arrests and four periods in young offenders' institutions did little to slow him down.

Each time he got caught, he learned. Each time in nick, he learned even more.

*I bet they got nothin' on me*, he thought, *just tryin' to shit me up. I never got a touch from the old birds house, wore my gloves n'all.* Billy knew how clever he was. They would never get him again. He lay back, closed his eyes and, unbelievably, slept. The noise of the cells around him powerless to disturb the disturbed.

Dave Stewart, on the other hand, could not have slept if his life had depended on it. After explaining the full story of the Marigold glove find to Superintendent John McCauley, he was ordered home and told to return at 7p.m. for duty as normal.

He was in deep shit, and Mackay had left him without any hint of his future.

Beside himself, he thrust his hands into damp pockets and marched toward his bus stop. He checked his watch and found he had a ten minute wait. The rain was hammering down, and he lowered his head and hunched his shoulders against the heavy drops.

A car horn made him jump.

"Want a lift, mate?"

Once again, Dave was very glad to see Andy Dunn. He slid into the passenger seat of the warm, dry car.

"Cheers, 'Armless."

"You look a little pissed off," said Andy with a smile, "Even for a Yorkshireman."

Andy pulled out into traffic. The two men drove in silence for a while until Dave felt like he would burst.

"I know you've had no kip, Armless, but do you fancy a quick jar? I need a word."

Andy looked across at his prodigy, who was fast looking like a drowned rat.

"You payin'?"

Dave had to smile. "Aye, I suppose."

It was a short drive. The Black Bull was a real ale pub just outside the centre of town. It was popular with the local constabulary for several reasons. First, the landlord didn't let the shit in. Second, the beer was pure nectar, and third, the barmaids were buxom and friendly. It was rumored Andy was romantically attached to one of the said barmaids, but Armless was prone to wander, and Dave took little notice of gossip.

The two very tired policemen sat together in deep conversation in the corner of the taproom. The oak paneled walls were stained with years of tobacco smoke. Brass fittings and paintings, which had seen drinkers born and buried, adorned the walls. Not one voice was raised above a murmur.

Lucy was indeed Andy Dunn's latest bird. She knew all about his reputation with the girls, and what all those girls said about him, but she didn't care. Andy Dunn was her kind of man, and even if he hadn't realised it yet, she was the only woman for him.

Lucy also knew something was up, as neither Armless, dirty bastard that he was, nor young Dave, had taken the piss or made a dirty joke since they came in.

Unaware he was being observed by the lovely Lucy, Dave had finished his story and his second pint.

"So that's about it, Andy. What do you think will happen?"

"That's a tough one, laddie. If it had been mysel', I'd've kept quiet like and dumped the fuckin' things at a later date."

"Andy! We're talkin' murder here. An old woman is dead. Even you haven't got that cynical."

Armless finished his beer. "I have, pal. I tell you this. Ye look out for yersel' in this game."

He waved his empty toward the bar.

"Where are the gloves now, then?"

"Forensics got 'em. Apparently you can sometimes get fingerprints from the inside of a rubber glove, but it's touch and go."

Andy shrugged. "You're just gonna have to wait this one out, lad. McCauley is a real hard case. He's old school, you know? Still believes you can beat a confession out of anyone. He won't think twice about throwing you to the wolves if things don't go his way, let me tell you. On the other hand, if he gets a confession from Bailey, he may just forget all about you."

Lucy walked over to the table, dropped a full pint in front of Andy and collected their empties. She turned to the bar.

"Hey, juicy!" Armless shouted.

Lucy turned again.

"Great tits!"

Detective Sergeant Pierce was forty-eight, astute and well qualified.

He was the divisional forensic expert. The security of his job was now in doubt. A new idea coming from Whitehall was to civilianise his kind of task.  When the time came for the hatchet to fall on Pierce's forensic job, he had every intention of developing a bad back and retiring to Benidorm.

For now though, he sat in front of another dinosaur, John McCauley.

The Chief liked Pierce. He had been a keen rugby player in his day, and had worked with McCauley when he was a sectional CID Inspector.

"What's the script then, Piercie?"

Pierce was comfortable in the surroundings of the boss's sparse office. He'd spent many hours poring over serious crime scenes there, and just as many drinking Irish whiskey.

Peirce knew there was no need to beat around the bush.

"Well, boss, there are no usable prints inside the gloves."

Before McCauley could speak, Pierce put up his hands.

"Wait now, boss, before you go off on one. Our boy, Bailey, was definitely wearing them. It's just we've not enough for court. We've got twelve separate matches found on a print inside the gloves, making it virtually impossible not to be William Henry Bailey's fingerprint, but you know as well as I do, that sixteen matches are required to produce them to the judge. Therefore, as an expert witness, I can't testify that Bailey had been wearing the gloves. In fact I couldn't even mention the print existed."

The Chief frowned at this technicality, but he knew Pierce was right.

The Sergeant had more to offer.

"We have some good news; the right-hand glove has an abrasion on the fingertip of the index. We made an impression of it and compared it to the glove marks found at the murder scene."

Pierce smiled, and waited for his moment.

"The fucker matches perfectly, boss."

Mackay carefully examined the two 8"x10" blow up photographs Pierce had produced of the glove marks.

"Can we put this to the jury, Piercie?"

The Sergeant shrugged. "It's not an exact science, boss, but any jury with decent eyesight can see the match. It's not a fingerprint, but it's fuckin' close."

Mackay rubbed his chin. His mind was working overtime. He had Bailey, and no doubt, the little fucker had killed old Elsie Townsend. He had the gloves and the evidence Sgt. Pierce had dropped on his desk, but how could he put Bailey with those gloves in a court of law?

He dropped the forensic photographs onto his well-organised desk.

Pierce read his mind.

"We have to persuade Bailey to admit he had them on his person in interview."

McCauley was planning. "We might just already be able to do just that, Piercie."

The Chief lifted the telephone to his ear. "Clive, when that boy Stewart turns in, get him back up here."

Pierce left the office. McCauley was up to something. He'd known him long enough to know that. Pierce didn't want the details. It was bound to be dodgy and he wasn't hanging around to find out. His pension wasn't that far away after all.

Dave returned to the station as instructed at 6.20p.m., ready for yet another twelve-hour tour. Manpower was a problem across the section, and overtime was on offer. Dave was in no position to turn it down. Armless had dropped him at his house after their heart to heart in The Bull. He knew he should sleep, but couldn't.

Instead, he went for a run and did a punishing weight routine in the Police Training School gym that backed onto his house. His head felt clearer after the exercise. He had to face facts; he'd fucked up. He wasn't the first, and wouldn't be the last. It was a question of taking the lumps and getting on with it.

With this thought in his mind, he'd arrived feeling a little better.

Within minutes, the sight of Clive Williams shuffling long the corridor in Dave's direction meant things quickly deteriorated. Clive looked even more disheveled than on their previous meeting. He had obviously eaten again since breakfast and was wearing half the meal on his shirtfront. From the smell of him, Dave noted, it had also been a liquid lunch.

"David," chirped Clive, swinging an arm around Dave's shoulders and simultaneously revealing a body odour problem.

"Yes, sir?"

“The boss wants you in the office right away.”

Williams motioned Dave to follow, and the same feelings of dread came over him.

Once in the office, Dave was more than slightly surprised. McCauley had his jacket off, sleeves rolled up and a five o’clock shadow. A Jameson’s bottle and two glasses adorned the desk.

“Dave!” McCauley’s pleasant, almost jovial manner was more unnerving than his previous psychotic bawling. “Have a seat, boy. We need to talk again.”

Dave gingerly sat in a chair that was a good six inches lower than the Chief Superintendent’s. Clive Williams took up his previous position on the small sofa and commenced his one-man attempt at the chain-smoking record. Williams knew the script by heart and was ready to play his part in the game if needed.

The boss put his elbows on the table, and made his favourite pyramid shape with his fingers.

“I’m going to be straight with you, Dave,” began the Chief. There was absolutely nothing straight about this little scenario. McCauley was simply warming to a task he’d played out many, many times.

“This afternoon, I was ready to make the one call needed to have you drummed out of the constabulary, son.” He opened his palms. “Then I thought, well, we all make mistakes. You are young in service and should be getting a pat on the back for good police work. Instead, here we are putting you through the wringer.”

Dave started to feel much better.

“We are all in the same job, Dave,” McCauley turned to Williams. “Right, Clive?”

Clive exhaled, nodding furiously. “Hmm.”

McCauley leaned forward slightly and made an imaginary globe shape with his hands. “The police service, CID, Uniform, Drug Squad, Traffic, all want the same thing. We’re all grafting our nuts off for one purpose. You know what that thing is, Dave, don’t you?”

The boss didn’t wait for a reply; he was on a roll.

“Justice, Dave, the one thing we all want.” McCauley pointed a perfect nail. “This is where you can help us, my lad.”

The detective smiled, and revealed a set of yellowing, crooked teeth. He didn’t smile often and this false enterprise reminded Dave of Jaws in James Bond. The smile disappeared as quickly as it came, and the Chief continued.

“We have a young boy downstairs in the cells. The lad you arrested last night, William Henry Bailey. The lad is on the point of shitting himself because he’s a killer, Dave. The vicious little bastard murdered that defenceless old lady. He knows what he’s done and he knows he will pay for it. Our job,” McCauley made a circle with his forefinger, “is to prove it.”

The detective lifted the whiskey bottle and poured two generous shots.

“He will confess his crime, Dave. Be certain of that. We have a team of interrogators here, to match any in the country. But we don’t want some smart-arsed barrister getting him off on a technicality, now do we?”

Dave felt himself shaking his head in agreement.

McCauley picked up a glass and downed the contents in one. He sat back in his chair, eyes firmly fixed on the young copper. He had interviewed thousands of suspects in his time, murderers, rapists, and every type of low life imaginable. David Stewart was a mere probationary constable. He was just a boy from a depressed area of South Yorkshire, father unemployed, mother near alcoholic. He was no match and the Chief knew it.

"The gloves were Bailey's. You know it, I know it and forensic know it. If we could identify a few more characters, we would go on the fingerprint evidence alone. But it's not to be. Because he managed to dump the gloves on the grass before you got to him, he's got a fighting chance of getting away with murder, Dave."

McCauley lifted a large S.O.C. photograph from his desk and solemnly handed it across the desk. It depicted Elsie May Townsend's frail lifeless body on her living room floor. Dave drank in the image.

The boss was silk. "All we need is a few lines changed in your arrest statement, and everyone is happy. Instead of finding the gloves on the ground, you found them in the little fucker's pocket. Get my drift? Are you with us, son?" He snatched back the picture from Dave hand, and his tone snapped the sentence shut. "Or are you against us?"

An expert interviewer knows when to stop talking. McCauley was an expert, and the silence tore the young man to pieces. Dave could feel the sweat on his palms and the dryness in his throat. He spoke very quietly.

"That would be perjury, sir."

The Chief's black eyes burned into Dave's. "No, not perjury. That would be justice, young man. Pure and simple; this country needs justice."

McCauley handed the second glass of Irish to Williams, who had been eyeing it greedily, and poured himself another.

"How's your old man, Dave? And your old mum? Not been too well for a while, I hear. Times are tough, Dave. They reckon they'll be three million on the dole by this Christmas." He took a drink and grimaced slightly.

"You need this job, David. Your folks need you to keep earning, don't they."

"Well, yes sir, but..."

"No fuckin' ifs or buts, Stewart. What will happen to them if you are out on your ear, lad? Do the right thing. This one small thing and all your troubles will be over, lad."

The detective had played the ace in his hand and with it, had defeated everything David Stewart had ever believed in. Dave felt completely helpless. The two senior officers looked directly at him. Silent; wanting;

McCauley slowly stood and handed Dave a pre-typed statement. "Sign it, lad. We'll take care of the rest."

Dave looked at Williams, who smiled kindly and spoke just two words.

"It's best," he said.

Dave took the document, unbuttoned his tunic pocket, removed a pen and signed away his integrity.

It was 8.30p.m. and Steve Jones was the cell duty copper till 10p.m. He'd had a long day and his stomach rumbled as he'd been without food since lunch. Steve liked his food and wasn't happy at missing his refreshment break. He was a red faced, rather overweight man with a dandruff problem, who suited his job in the depths of the nick. At forty-eight, he'd seen enough of life to be able to deal with most villains on their level. The regulars treated Steve more like an amiable hotelier than a copper. He knew them all, fed and watered them, arranged their visits and rang their solicitors for them.

Steve let William Bailey out of his cell to take exercise, which consisted of walking him a few steps to an underground enclosed yard. Bailey had been protesting about his long stay in the cells and the fact that he had not yet been taken to Court to answer his non payment of fines warrant.

Steve was a nice enough guy, but was in no mood for Bailey's complaints. He'd been having a bad day himself. His wife's homemade meat and potato pie was still sitting in the fridge in the canteen waiting for him, after all.

Steve knew that Bailey was a murder suspect and he knew his reputation. He didn't like the kid. He told Bailey to keep quiet and be patient. Billy lost control.

Regular cell duty officers tend to be towards the end of their career and Steve was no exception. He was far too slow to protect himself against an adversary so strong and much too quick. Billy's first punch caught the officer above his right eye splitting his eyebrow. It sent a splatter of crimson fluid up Bailey's forearm. The second blow broke his cheekbone. As the man fell, Billy finished the job by attempting to stamp on Steve Jones's head.

Instead he brought his considerable weight down on the back of the unconscious policeman's neck. The sickening sound could be heard thirty feet away at the charge desk.

He would never walk again.

Billy was in the process of being overpowered when McCauley entered the cellblock. He was screaming for his captors to release him.

Billy, prostrate on the floor and handcuffed, couldn't see where the calm voice of John McCauley was coming from.

"Let him up, gentlemen."

The several officers it had taken to subdue Billy hoisted him to his feet and faced him toward the senior detective.

An ambulance crew pushed by and started to work on the injured officer. The mood was sombre.

The Chief slowly paced toward the crew and looked down at Constable Jones. He'd seen enough assaults and injuries to know this was a bad one. He shook his head. Steve Jones may have been past his best, but he had been commended for bravery once. He'd rescued a child from the swollen waters of the river Ribble, almost drowning himself in the process. He'd never been a star of the show, but he was a good bloke and didn't deserve to be lying in his own piss on a cell floor.

McCauley could feel the flush of his anger as he turned back toward Billy.

He pointed over his shoulder with his thumb at the unfolding tragedy.

"You responsible for that?"

Billy sneered at the Chief, revealing a set of perfect white teeth. "What? The fat twat on the floor? Yeah, I did that an' I'll knock you out too if they take these cuffs off."

McCauley nodded slowly.

"OK."

The restraining officers looked at each other in disbelief.

The boss was deadpan.

"Go on, lads. Take them off the boy."

They did as they were ordered and the split second it was done, McCauley drew back his right arm and with thunderous force slapped Billy across the face. Billy had never been hit so hard in his life. His head spun, and small bright explosions lit his vision.

The Chief's face was so close to Billy's now that he could smell the whiskey. He had never heard a voice so intimidating. McCauley injected fear with every syllable. With the perfect delivery of a Shakespearean actor, he began a speech he had rehearsed a thousand times.

"William Henry Bailey, I am arresting you for the murder of Elsie May Townsend."

The detective stepped back and his voice became almost nonchalant, as if he had suddenly tired of his task. "You are not obliged to say anything unless you wish to do so, but what you say may be given in evidence."

Billy's jaw dropped open. The physical blow from McCauley was one thing. This was another. Billy's autopilot kicked in. Another shot of adrenaline burst into his body.

"This is fuckin' bollocks, you're makin' it up, I've done fuck all, I want a brief, I want a phone call."

Tears started to well in Billy's eyes. "Get me a solicitor...now!"

McCauley actually smiled at Billy. It was a genuine smile. There was never anything faked when he was winning. He had the confidence and power to achieve anything by any means. He turned to the desk sergeant. "Get this piece of shit his solicitor. I'll be doing the interview personally."

McCauley met Bailey's eyes. There was no contest in the stare. Billy was scared. The Chief wasn't.

"Won't that be cosy, sonny?" he said.

The art of interviewing any suspect lies first in the planning. To be able to walk in unprepared is a gift. The Chief believed in preparation.

He recalled his first major interview as a detective. His sergeant had been too pissed to do it himself, and he was the only duty Jack left standing after a divisional rugby dinner.

Who would have thought? 3a.m. Monday, and the uniforms had only brought in a kiddie fiddler.

You had to be sensitive to a child molester, even if your guts were churning at the thought of sitting in the same room as the pervert. It was the only way to get a confession from that type of criminal. McCauley knew it, spent seven hours with the creep, and got the cough.

It was the start of his CID career.

He found the technique difficult. His natural stance was far more brutal.

Now, all those years on, he sat in his office with his interview team; Clive Williams, Detective Sergeant Anne Wallace and Detective Constable Rod Casey.

All had their own expertise. Williams was so mild mannered he could befriend a rattlesnake. People mistook his shabby appearance and soft sing-song Cork accent for weakness. They were very wrong. He was the man who would determine when the suspect was ready to talk. When it was time to go for the kill, he would wield the verbal axe.

Anne Wallace was the only university graduate that Mackay had ever appointed to his team. Since her arrival at Preston division she had stamped her authority on the local CID. With her razor sharp brain came stunning beauty. Almost six feet tall, brunette, with sapphire blue eyes, she was as pretty a picture any man could draw. Her staggering figure was admired from a distance by most of the coppers in the nick, and viewed enviously by most of the female admin staff. Many of her male counterparts had tried to get close to Anne Wallace, but soon discovered her ice cold exterior was matched by an evil derogatory wit.

Anne's job was to advise the team on which points to prove, and in which order. She was an exceptional researcher and could mentally collate snippets of information most would neglect. If required, she would take part in the Bailey interview and would offer a soft and gentle female shoulder for him to cry on.

Rod Casey, at forty-four, was never going any further than constable. Which, considering his qualifications and experience, seemed unfair. He was a monster of a man. At six feet four and eighteen stone, his strength came from his natural physique, not a gymnasium. He had worked the streets of the division for twenty-five years. Not only had he arrested William Henry Bailey before, but also his brother, his father and grandfather.

It wouldn't have surprised the team if they were to discover that Rod had fucked Bailey's mother and two sisters either. Rod was the weakness man. He knew the family history. He knew their fears and the skeletons in their cupboard. McCauley had used Rod on every major interview he had conducted in the last ten years. Rod was 'the' bad cop interviewer.

Anne Wallace passed around folders containing the antecedence file of William Bailey. It was complete and up to date. A further list was stapled to it. This recorded Bailey's clothing worn when arrested, and items of property both in his possession at the time of arrest and recovered from a search of the family home on Callon estate.

A separate file contained detailed statements from the milkman who discovered Elsie May Townsend's body, offerings from the police surgeon, the Home Office pathologist, forensics officers, and of course P.C.239 David Stewart's newly altered effort. They were all typed and in chronological order.

The air in the office seemed almost blue with cigarette smoke. The Chief started with Casey. "What isn't in here, Rod?"

Casey avoided the use of notes. He didn't even consult the file Anne Wallace had handed to him. There was no need. Everything Rod required was in his head. His flat, northern drawl was deep baritone.

"Well, boss, I went out and revisited all the previous three burglaries on the Severn House complex. They all occurred over the last week. An antique engagement ring was stolen from one of the breaks. I'd bet next month's wages that the ring listed as found during the search of Bailey's bedroom, is one and the same."

McCauley grinned. "This little bastard is going nowhere. Get a team to take the ring to the victim and get an ID statement."

Rod immediately picked up the telephone and related his boss's orders to the CID evening team.

"OK." McCauley closed his copy of the file and turned to Wallace. His infamous smile had returned. "Anne, where do you think we stand?"

Anne crossed her legs, and every pair of male eyes in to room was temporarily distracted.

"From a legal standpoint," she began, "the forensic evidence may not be accepted by the judge. This business with the abrasion on the Marigold glove is far from foolproof. There are no stated cases on anything similar, so don't rely on it. The fibres they found on the doorframe are probably from a leather jacket. As we know there are thousands of them. We may end up with a trial within a trial, just on the Marigold evidence alone.

As for the other burglaries, even if we can charge him with those, the judge won't allow the jury to hear the evidence in the murder trial. The bottom line is, if we want a murder conviction, we need a confession that he intended to kill Mrs. Townsend or at least that his actions were likely to result in her death. Manslaughter..."

McCauley interrupted her and turned to his old friend. "What's your feeling, Clive?"

Clive had been so engrossed in Anne's legs he had lost the plot. He scratched his head, and embellished his Irish accent. "Err... yes boss. I agree with Anne now." He drew heavily on his cigarette. "It's all down to us, I reckon."

Rod piped up, "I've interviewed Bailey five times and he has never confessed anything. He's a hard little fucker."

"We'll show him hard." The Chief pointed a finger at Rod.

"Boss!" Anne regained control of the room for the moment. "I see little reason to beat a confession out of this kid." She pushed her hair from her face and secured it behind one ear. Anne felt herself reddening but did her best to conceal her discomfort at the situation. Her southern tone was businesslike.

"Let's put the pressure on from a different angle."

McCauley gave Anne a look that would have disturbed most male officers. Anne had seen it before.

"Go on, Anne, you have our attention," he said, with more than a hint of sarcasm, punctuated with a loud sniff. "Make it good, darlin'."

Again Mackay had managed to make Anne nervous. She was determined not to let it show. She had spent all her career fighting for the attention of men such as these. She was more qualified, worked harder and took more shit than any of them.

She concentrated her gaze on Clive. “William Henry Bailey needs a way out,” she began. “If you drive him into a corner you will end up with sweet fuck all. I say we offer him a deal.”

The Chief immediately exploded. “A fuckin’ deal! He’s a fuckin’ animal! There’s an old dear in the morgue and a damn good officer in the hospital, all inside twenty-four hours and you want to deal?”

Anne was calm. “Deal now or later.”

There was silence in the room. Nobody wanted to pre-empt the boss’s decision. McCauley held the bridge of his nose between thumb and forefinger, his eyes closed, all others on him.

He didn’t bother to open them to speak, and did little to hide the resentment in his voice. “What do you suggest, Anne?”

Anne opened the file on her lap. She cleared the nervousness from her throat. “A murder charge definitely won’t stick. The medical evidence shows that the old dear died as a result of shock, after suffering a broken pelvis, probably from a fall. The forensic guys suggest that she was thrown or pushed to the floor, in all probability, to enable our suspect to escape. Therefore, the alternative charge of manslaughter is our best option.”

She looked at McCauley, who had opened his eyes but appeared to be only interested in her breasts. She continued undaunted, “With good representation and a guilty plea, Bailey will be looking at nine years tops. With full remission he will be out in six.”

Rod shifted his massive frame awkwardly in his seat, his voice even deeper than before. "If it were my old mum lying in the morgue, he would be looking at a death sentence."

Anne continued, "We have, of course, other charges to bargain with. The injuries to the police officer sustained in the assault in the cellblock would make a charge of Section 18 wounding with intent a likely option. The chances of a conviction are high and that will carry a further five years."

Anne turned a page in the file and tapped a paragraph with a bright red nail. "We also have the four separate burglary charges to put to our man. With luck, a conviction would mean another three years."

She looked at her colleagues. "My advice, gents, is to offer to drop the Section 18 assault on PC Jones to a Section 47 ABH, and go for handling the ring rather than burglary, in return for a guilty plea on the manslaughter charge."

McCauley slowly rose from his seat and put on his jacket. Anne watched, amazed at his lack of respect for what she considered sound legal advice.

"Anne, you're a good copper," he tapped his own temple, "with a good mind. If our boy had beaten the shit out of his cellmate, I would go with what you say. But this little evil bastard has put one of our own in the hospital. Steve Jones will never go fuckin' dancing again, will he? Are you going to be the one to tell his missus that although we have a watertight case against Bailey, we're dropping the charge down to a 47! Like he'd just got a fuckin' shiner? No. Bailey's got to pay and it's up to us to make him."

Anne rose also. She made one last attempt. "But, boss..."

The Chief lifted his hand to signal he had heard enough. "Clive, get yourself down to the cells, have a word with Bailey's brief, I want to be ready to start the interview in half an hour. Oh, and organise some flowers for Steve's wife. You write the card from me, OK?"

Raymond Holmes was forty, looked thirty and had been a criminal solicitor for twelve years, full partner for four of those and was doing very nicely thank you. He loved clothes almost as much as he did himself, and followed the latest styles. He had represented the Bailey family throughout his career. Mum's prostitution and shoplifting charges, Billy's theft and burglary cases, and various other petty crimes relating to the father, brother and sisters.

The Bailey family were good clients. None were employed, so they always got Legal Aid. They invariably entered a plea of not guilty, no matter how severe the evidence to the contrary and best of all, one or more of the clan were in the shit every month.

The Bailey family, or rather the taxpayer, had bought Raymond Holmes a new BMW in the last year. Yes, the Bailey family were very good clients. This time though, Billy had got himself in a real heap of trouble. Holmes had that warm feeling he always got when it came to a really big pay day.

He sat opposite Bailey in a private interview room, and placed the start of what he hoped was to become a very messy murder trial file on the table. "Well, Billy, this is a mess."

The youth was in no mood to beat around the bush. He paced the room angrily, his muscles bulging from a dirty, white t-shirt tucked into Levis. "Listen, Ray, I'm not going down for the rest of my life for this load of shit. You gotta get me off."

Ray chucked a packet of Bensons on the table. "Have a cigarette for, God's sake, and calm the fuck down. It's me you are talking to, not some fucking plod.

You behaving like some twat out of a scene from McVicar does not impress your Uncle Raymond one bit." Raymond lowered his voice. "It all depends on what evidence the police have, and of course, what you have to say, but I don't think it's going to be so easy this time."

Billy ripped open the packet of cigarettes and tore one from it. The filter shook in his mouth until he clasped it tight and lit up.

He exhaled sharply; still extremely agitated, he pulled at his own hair and wiped imaginary drops from the end of his nose with the palm of his hand. His voice dropped to a whisper, although no one could hear.

"Look, Ray, I was clean as a whistle when I was lifted. I know they'll have no prints or nothin'."

Holmes was casual; he undid the clasp on his latest briefcase as he spoke. "You shouldn't be talking to me like this, Billy."

"Fuck that legal shit, Ray. You know me and what I am. You look after me and our kid, and you get well paid for it. Not to mention the little extras I've got you over the years," Billy paused and lowered his voice still further, "and the other stuff."

Holmes ignored the comments from the youth. "My advice, for the moment anyway," he postured, "is to say nothing. Give a full 'no comment' interview, until we know more of what they have. As for the other matter of the assault on the policeman, we'll look at a self-defence plea." Holmes took hold of Billy's chin, and turned his cheek to the light. "You seem to be developing a rather nasty bruise on your face."

Billy liked the sound of this. He knew Holmes wouldn't let him down. "You get me out of here, Ray, and they'll be a nice extra drink in it for you."

Raymond Holmes liked the sound of that.

Clive Williams arrived at the cells in time to see Ray Holmes leaving the interview room with Billy. "Ah! Mr. Holmes." Clive's lilting voice held the merest trace of sarcasm. "When will your boy be ready for interview?"

"My client," corrected Holmes, "requires a doctor before anyone speaks to him. He has been soundly beaten by one of your officers," a forced cough for punctuation, "whilst in these very cells, I believe."

The Detective Inspector had no choice but to give the solicitor his request and turned to the desk sergeant.

"Get the police surgeon out to Bailey, Sergeant, and tell the old quack from me not to take his fuckin' time about it!"

The sergeant jumped to the phone. Clive was not one to lose his temper, but if he did they'd be hell to pay.

Billy had witnessed the exchange between the two men. He had no way of realising his true plight. He was a socially dysfunctional outcast, believing every word from his greedy counsel.

"Hey! Dickhead!" Billy grinned like a Cheshire cat. "That tub of lard that attacked me. Is he out of casualty yet?"

How Clive Williams achieved the smile back at Billy and kept his composure, was beyond most.

"Not yet, Billy."

He turned again to the desk sergeant. "Call me the second the doctor has finished with him."

Six floors up, the night shift had started the first round of refreshment periods, and the canteen held a smattering of coppers.

"Cheer up, Dave." Andy Dunn carried two cups of evil-looking liquid that passed for coffee to the table.

Dave took a cup, and inspected a suspect brown lump floating in the centre of his brew.

"Sorry, mate, I can't seem to shake this one off."

Armless took the seat next to Dave and took a sip of the evil brew. "Jesus! It gets worse."

Dave hadn't confided in anyone about the second conversation with the Chief. After all, you didn't go around telling people in a police station that you were about to commit a criminal offence, did you?

"Look on the bright side," said Armless. "Our leave has been approved for the weekend. Two days leave and three rest days to recover from the ordeal."

Dave perked up at the news. "I didn't know that, when did you hear?"

"Just now, I found the note in my 'in' tray. Two of the boys are back from sick, so the weekend of wine, women and song is on!"

The door to the canteen opened, and Anne Wallace walked to the counter. Dunn lowered his voice, but Dave saw his chest expand and a big white smile appear on his face. "Now, give me just one night with that wee lassie and I would die a happy man."

To both the men's surprise, Anne walked slowly over to their table. Her heels made clicking noises on the tiled floor. Her skirt was short enough to make the men turn and look. A crisp white blouse covered some kind of lace camisole that Dave could only dream about. She had a reputation about the nick for being 'too good' for the troops. If you wanted to get into Anne Wallace, you had to dine in the officers' mess.

"Hi, guys," Anne flashed a smile, and Dave felt his face start to flush. "Mind if I join you?"

"Not at all," said 'Armless, standing and gallantly sweeping a chair under the perfectly rounded bottom of the Detective Sergeant, "always a pleasure to have a beautiful woman for company."

Dave cringed at his mate's unashamed flirting, but could not help admire the stunning creature sitting opposite. Dave noticed she smelled of Chanel No5.

Anne sat, and commenced peeling an orange. She looked up and revealed a mischievous grin. "You're Dave Stewart, aren't you?"

Dave was shocked she even knew his name. He tried to be casual, considered taking a sip of coffee and rejected the idea, as he would definitely spill it. “Yes, that’s right, Sergeant.”

“I thought so,” Anne purred, looking Dave straight in the eye. “I make a point of knowing all the handsome men I work with.”

Dave couldn’t help himself. For the first time in years, he knew he was blushing. Anne popped a piece of orange into her mouth and chewed slowly. She appeared to study the young copper intently, then stood, smoothed her skirt and brushed her hair from her face. “See you again then, David.”

Dave still hadn’t recovered from the fruit fantasy, and remained silent and open-mouthed.

Both men watched Anne walk from the room. She knew how to walk. Her hips swayed from side to side in the rhythm of a slow, sexual beat. It was practiced, of course, but neither man cared.

Andy Dunn was beside himself.

“You lucky wee shite. She’s fitter than that bird in Superman 2, and that’s sayin’ somethin’.”

Dave found himself smiling.

Anne Wallace was smiling too. She smiled all the way down in the lift until she reached the second floor. She felt a second little surge of devilment, just feet from her door. He is cute, she thought, bit young maybe, but cute nevertheless.

Once in her office, it was back to business. She sat at her desk with the Bailey file spread out in front of her. She felt uneasy at what she saw. Something just wasn’t quite right.

The night CID team had returned with the antique engagement ring found in Bailey's bedroom. Rod Casey had been right and would have kept his next month's salary. The ring sat on top of a statement identifying it as stolen from an earlier burglary on the Callon estate.

Bailey was their boy all right, but something was just not kosher. All police officers knew property was trouble. Never leave anything lying about where it could be 'misplaced.' Anne was about to return the ring to the property store, when she noticed that the ring bore the tag no D\1124\81.

'D' stood for Preston Division. The numbers related to the number of items of property entered in the store that year. The numbers ran consecutively, and were pre-printed.

When she checked the Bailey file, she saw that the Marigold gloves recovered by Dave Stewart bore the tag no D\1130\81. They should have been booked in hours before the ring had been discovered in the house search.

"Why?" Anne muttered to herself.

McCauley and Williams sat opposite Bailey and Holmes in a tiny interview room located on the second floor of the nick. Everything about the room screamed 1969, including a table that separated them. It had seen thousands of interviews since then. Many a tear had been shed in this room, many a deal struck. On one wall was a two-way mirror made of unbreakable glass. Behind the mirror sat Rod Casey in an even smaller room, a notepad on his knee, pencil in hand, waiting.

Raymond Holmes lounged alongside his client. He had removed his jacket to reveal a handmade silk shirt. He doodled on his own headed and embossed notepaper with a solid gold Cartier pen. Unlike his sap of a client, Holmes was confident of one thing. No matter what the outcome of this case, and that was by no means certain, he was on a good earner.

Clive Williams let out a plume of smoke, and started the preliminaries. "William Henry Bailey, I am Detective Inspector Williams and this is Detective Chief Superintendent McCauley. We are here to interview you regarding the murder of Elsie May Townsend. I must remind you that you are still under caution, and that you are not obliged to say anything unless you wish to do so, and that what you say may be given in evidence."

Raymond Holmes interjected, "Before we go any further, gentlemen, I must inform you that after consultation with my client, I have advised him not to answer any questions regarding this or any other allegation."

Holmes theatrically cleared his throat, leaning forward over the desk, ensuring both police officers caught a whiff of his latest Jordache cologne. "Further to that, my client wishes to make a formal complaint of assault against Police Constable David Stewart, Police Constable Stephen Jones and," he stared straight at McCauley, "the Chief Superintendent here."

He flicked through some notes, but no one in the room thought he needed them.

"A further complaint will be lodged that he has been unlawfully arrested on these matters and unlawfully imprisoned." Holmes rocked back in his seat and soaked up his client's wonderment. Bailey looked to him with youthful admiration and gave a ridiculous wink.

The Chief was unimpressed. His face said so. He wasn't about to be bullied by some over-dressed arsehole wearing too much aftershave. His body language was a picture.

He almost hissed, "Listen, Holmes, one more attempt to interfere with this interview and I will have you excluded. Understand?"

Holmes once again stared straight into McCauley's eyes. There was no love lost between the two men. Holmes had always made McCauley's teeth itch. To Holmes, the Chief was little more than an oaf. Holmes' voice was filled with acrimony. "Your comments have been noted for the record, Chief Superintendent."

Clive Williams opened his own notes. He appeared completely unaffected by the sparring heavyweights. His voice was even and calm, the soft Irish tone suggesting he could have been interviewing an innocent witness.

"Now, Billy, I want to start to ask you where you were between the hours of two a.m. and six a.m. on the morning of Friday March 9th 1981."

Billy leaned back in his chair, closed his eyes and made a snoring sound, followed by a nervous laugh. Ray's pep talk had given him true belief. 'Sit here and say nowt' is what Ray had said, and that's exactly what he was going to do.

He was unaware of the expertise around him. More importantly, he disregarded it at his peril.

Williams carried on undaunted, and repeated his first question.

Again Billy ignored the proceedings, and tried to focus on good stuff like going out and getting wrecked. *They'll get bored soon*, he thought. Billy was a clever boy, see, and Ray, well Ray was the best.

Williams' voice continued its soothing tonal message.

"Billy, I will ask you these questions over and over until I have an answer. We can keep you here until the morning, then put you before the court and request a further three days to question you. This is a very serious matter, and we will get that time from the court, Billy. You know we will; no problem. I personally don't want to do that, if you are an innocent lad and can explain this terrible mess."

Clive took out his packet of cigarettes and offered them. Holmes held up a derogatory palm. Billy ignored him, despite being desperate for a smoke. Clive left them on the desk, the packet open, facing the lad, sending their unspoken message.

The detective lit his own fag and pressed on, his voice subtly stronger. "Elsie May Townsend was eighty-three years old, Billy. She lived in bungalow, 11a, Severn House on the Callon. You know that area well, don't you, Billy?"

If Clive could get the kid to answer, he was about to prove his first point. "You ever visited that address, Billy?"

Bailey was feeling a tight ball developing in his stomach. He kept singing nonsense over and over in his head to drown out the demon. He had that terrifying, sickening feeling in his guts. He shot Holmes a glance, but the lawyer merely shook his head briefly, reminding Billy not to answer. Billy started to hum, this time out loud. Billy's favourite, The Tide is High, Blondie, now she was well fit. His eyes shot around the room. Each man in turn just stared back and gave him nothing. His stomach flipped again. *They'll get bored soon*. Ray would see to that. *Ray knows best. He'll make them stop*.

Clive tapped the packet of cigarettes on the tabletop, a gentle reminder of their presence.

"Elsie was a very delicate lady, Billy. She had brittle bones. She would only weigh about six stone, Billy. How would you feel if someone threw your old gran to the floor, smashed her hip to pieces and left her alone to die in the dark?"

Billy lifted his eyes from the floor and looked at Williams. In those wild, frightened eyes he immediately saw all he needed to see. Clive agreed with some that thought the eyes were the windows to the soul, even when the soul was as black as William Henry Bailey's.

Billy snatched up the cigarette packet from the table. It took him two attempts to remove one. Clive lit it, and noticed the tremor in Billy's hand. He smiled a much practiced smile at the youth. It was the kind of grin a kindly vet may give to a dog, when he's about to insert the final needle into the poor bugger. *Not much longer now, son*, thought Clive.

Clive's own mind dragged him back to Christmas 1974 and the very same interview room.

Back then, he and Rod Casey had been given the job of interviewing a major IRA suspect. Some job to give an Irishman.

Clive was indeed a patriot, but murder was murder and he was a copper.

There had been a high profile pub bombing down south, lots of dead kids on a night out; he was one of a group of five who had been arrested. He didn't speak a word for seventy-two hours. The guy never moved from his chair. He didn't eat, drink or smoke. He pissed himself where he sat. Rod had beaten the shit out of the guy to no avail. He was one tough son of a bitch. Clive had never seen anyone take a beating like it. He felt a shiver at the recollection, and forced himself to the present.

Billy was a different matter. Bailey just thought he was tough. Clive knew different. He opened a cardboard folder.

"An innocent old lady, Billy?"

Clive produced the same scenes of crime picture of Elsie May that McCauley had shown to Dave Stewart.

The old lady was lying dead on the floor of her lounge. Mouth gaping, lifeless eyes wide open. He placed it on the table and, very slowly, turned the image to face his suspect.

"What kind of man would do a thing like that, Billy?"

Someone who knew Clive Williams well would have noticed the tiniest edge to his voice, but it was expertly hidden for this performance. His deep-rooted anger at a needless death lay firmly hidden inside the man. To the many, Clive remained a casual, almost indifferent observer.

Billy was unable to take his eyes from the image. His stomach got worse, and he needed the bog.

His fear was running riot through his mind and body. This was worse than before a job. Much worse.

“Not me. It weren’t me,” he spluttered.

Holmes made to whisper a timely reminder of his legal advice not to speak.

This time McCauley gave him a look that froze him. He knew he could be, and would be, excluded by the detective, and it wouldn’t look good to the family if he was left sitting in the car park whilst their little jewel was fitted up with a murder or two.

Clive watched every move Bailey made. The youth rubbed the back of his neck to remove the imaginary stiffness. His eyes darted to and fro between his solicitor and the photograph. He was floundering.

Clive had seen enough.

“OK, Billy,” he snatched the photograph from the table. “Let’s just say I believe you, son.” The detective was the picture of understanding. “Say we’ve got it all wrong this time. There’s been a terrible misunderstanding and we have arrested you by mistake.”

Clive checked his file, although he’d written most of it himself. He moved slowly, deliberately. Billy watched his every move. As Clive theatrically turned each page, Bailey’s stomach was burning with acid. Every leaf was a mountain of proof against him. He shot the occasional glance to McCauley but the gentle monotone of Williams floated over the turning pages and held him transfixed.

“We do have certain evidence Billy,” Williams looked up sharply at the youth, making him jump, “and it points in your direction, son.”

Billy's heart moved closer to his throat. It was the almost casual way in which the detective spoke. He was so confident.

Clive's voice didn't alter. He let words fall from his mouth like gravy from a boat, their liquidity adding flavour to every syllable.

"I want to get this sorted out. If we are wrong, then tell me why. All I need is the answers to a couple of questions and all this will be over, Billy."

McCauley could see Bailey was responding to Clive Williams, and that his own presence only served to complicate matters. As he stood, Billy froze, expecting another slap.

The Chief sneered as he paced across the room.

"I've better things to do than look at you two choirboys." He held out a huge hand toward Clive, and he made a show of passing his boss a sheaf of completed witness statements.

Clive nodded. Of course, no independent witness existed, but neither Holmes nor Bailey had any way of knowing that.

Once the Chief had left the room, Billy visibly relaxed. Clive in turn moved closer to the young man, as if he were about to share a secret with an old friend. He drew two cigarettes from the packet, lit them both and handed one to Billy. Clive checked the eyes again. He had seen that look before. He'd worked with John McCauley for many years and seen hundreds of beaten men, maybe thousands, of grubby faces just like Billy's.

"Do you think there may have been some mistakes made here, Billy?"

Bailey drew hard on his fag and bit at mere stumps of fingernail.

"There 'ave, I haven't done 'owt."

"I've met you before, haven't I?"

Billy flicked ash onto the carpet, ignoring the ashtray. He gave a loud sniff before speaking. "You came t' our house once when me dad got lifted."

Clive was reeling in the fish, only 'yes' answers from now on. *Ask the right questions. Get the right answers.*

"I've always been fair haven't I, Billy?"

"Yeah. S'pose."

"Billy, I'm just doing my job."

"I know, boss."

"Clive, my name is Clive."

"Clive, yeah."

"You have to give me something, Billy. Give me an alibi, something I can take to my boss that is in your favour, something to help get you out of here."

Billy wiped his nose with his hand, and looked to Holmes for advice. The solicitor was busy inspecting his hair in the two-way glass. He was obviously aware of the proceedings, as he shrugged his shoulders and said blankly. "You know my advice, William, and it's simple, no comment." He continued to tease his locks, seemingly uninterested in anything Billy may say.

Billy eyed both men before resting on Clive.

"I was in watching the telly until late. We've got one of them videos. Then I went for a walk round the Callon, to see if anyone was hanging out. I was walking back home when I got lifted."

Clive rested his hands on his each side of his file.

"Did anyone see you while you were out, Billy?"

"Don't think so."

Clive abruptly snapped the file shut and rose. "That's all for now Billy, I'll see you later."

The break in the interview shocked Billy. It was intended to. It sent him back to his cell alone. A place where Billy could only sit and think. In Billy's case, it was the last thing he needed.

As for Clive Williams, he had proved his first point. William Henry Bailey had no alibi.

Billy was caught off balance. "How long will you be, boss?"

Clive smiled. That 'poor little dog' smile he had. "Don't worry, Billy. You have a think about what I said. People make mistakes, Billy. Sometimes it takes a big man to admit them."

Billy looked at Clive, and for a moment seemed much younger than his nineteen years. "I swear on my life, boss, I've done nothing."

Clive's hand was on the door. "Never swear on a life, Billy. Life is too precious. See you soon."

The three male members of the interview team were gathered in

McCauley's office, all were drinking coffee and smoking.

The Chief started, "Well, Clive, our boy seems to like you."

Rod Casey gave McCauley a nod that said he was on a wind up. "There was always this rumor about Bailey's old man," he said, rooting for sugar. "Billy's gran reckoned he was fiddling with them boys from an early age like, and reckoned it sent 'em both queer."

He pointed a plastic spoon in the direction of the Inspector.

"This little bastard is going to cry on your shoulder, Clive. I reckon the poof fancies you, like." Casey's massive shoulders shuddered as he released a comical guttural laugh that would have ensured the piss was taken out of it around the station, had it not emanated from one so feared.

Clive made no comment either. He took no joy from seeing anyone suffer, even the likes of Bailey. He'd seen enough violence to last him a lifetime.

McCauley continued, "I think Rod has a bit of a point there, Clive. We need to put the pressure on now, rather than later. I say let Rod have ten minutes with him and then, Clive, you enter and save the day."

It was the oldest trick in the book, but when Casey and Williams played it, it worked a treat. Both men nodded in agreement.

The door opened, and all heads turned to see Anne Wallace enter. "How's it going, chaps?"

"Just fine, Anne," the Chief offered a seat but Anne remained standing. Casey noticed something flash between the two of them, more than a look, more than just business.

I have some good news," Anne began. "The ring found in Bailey's bedroom has been positively identified as being stolen from 15b, Severn House, two days prior to the murder. The MO is identical, bodily pressure on the back door. A tidy search and the same Marigold glove prints everywhere."

Rod Casey examined every inch of Anne Wallace, and didn't like what he saw.

McCauley, though, was a different matter. He beamed from ear to ear and could see the headlines in The Evening Post, *'Murder solved within 24hrs.'*

"This is excellent stuff, Anne."

He turned to Casey.

"OK, Rod, I still think we go as planned. Use the ring. Drop it right in the bastard's hand. Go in hard, and Clive, you be ready to save the poor lad's skin."

Anne cocked her head to one side. "Anything for me now, boss?"

The Chief positively leered at the detective sergeant. "Yes, Anne. You can drive me to The Bull for last orders."

Anne smiled as best she could.

"Come on then, lads," said McCauley, rubbing his hands. "Get this thing boxed off before the clubs close, and the night team can have a piss up."

Rod Casey strolled between the boss's office and the interview room, with a sure knowledge of his abilities. He was more of a copper than any man in the building, and that included some with rank.

Was Rod Casey bitter?

Fuckin' right he was.

Once at the interview desk, he sat in the dark, removed his jacket, and rolled up the sleeves of his shirt. This was his bread and butter.

He made a formidable figure, and had an almost square head that appeared not to need a neck for support. It was a solid structure of meat and bone, seemingly strapped to a monstrous frame by an invisible force. His face bore the scars of many street brawls. Casey's nose, his most famous feature, was almost flat from so much punishment. But the greatest damage to his countenance had been caused in a fight at the Jalgos Club on Avenham Estate in 1977. An equally frightening Jamaican guy had bitten away most of its cartilage in one terrible scrap.

The story went that Casey never pressed charges, and the guy was let off with public order offences rather than a serious assault. He was out in six months.

On the day the guy was released from jail, he was found in an alley behind Clouds Nightclub, with both kneecaps smashed beyond repair. The hammer used was deliberately left at the scene. It had a brown cardboard label fastened to the shaft by a piece of string. It had the man's name typed on it.

On the day Winston Johnston lay critically ill in the Royal Preston Hospital, despite circumstantial evidence to the contrary, Rod Casey was said to be on holiday in Scotland. Three police officers, including John McCauley, testified to the fact.

The stolen engagement ring found in Bailey's bedroom sat in the middle of the table, the remarkably similar cardboard crime tag was still attached by string. Casey toyed with it. This time it displayed a simple property number rather than a name.

Bailey entered with Holmes at his side. Casey saw both men look toward the ring. Billy went pale.

"Sit." Casey's seemingly impregnable presence dominated the room.

Bailey sat warily. He knew Rod Casey. He'd suffered at his hands before, as had his family. Billy knew the oldest trick in the book, too. But he was powerless. It had already begun to work.

There was a tremor in Billy's voice. "Where's the other bloke? Where's Clive?"

"If you are referring to Detective Inspector Williams," scoffed Casey, "he's unavailable."

"Then I'm saying nothing," Billy countered.

Casey leaned across the desk, his face inches from the youth. "That's because you're scared. You're a frightened little shit, except when you are around little old ladies." Casey held Billy's chin between his massive thumb and forefinger. "Then you're a brave boy aren't you, Billy?"

Billy pushed the hand away. "You're full of shit, Casey."

Rod was warming to the task. "I'll tell you what you are, Bailey. You're scum. Just like your thieving father, your whore of a mother, your slag sisters and that unlucky half wit brother of yours currently taking it up the arse in Walton jail."

Billy exploded. He leapt over the desk to get at Casey. Holmes, who had sat quietly through the 'bad cop' routine, stood back and watched the show. His time would come, it just wasn't now.

Casey grabbed Bailey's ear in his left hand. With his right, he grabbed a handful of hair. Using all his weight, he slammed Billy's head into the table and held it there. Billy was a strapping lad, but no match for the bull strength of Casey.

The ring, still sitting in its original position, was now just inches from Billy's nose.

"You see that," Casey spat, "this is the last fuckin' nail in your coffin."

Exactly on cue, the interview room door burst open and Clive Williams entered. Clive grabbed Casey's hands and prised them from Billy's head. It may have been well planned, but it still took all of Clive's strength to get Rod to let go.

"Get off this boy, Constable!" Clive followed the age-old script.

"He's a fuckin' madman!" Billy howled, holding his ear.

Clive bellowed in almost pantomime tone, "Get out of here now, Casey! Go and calm down. I'll speak to you later."

Casey walked toward the door, but then turned to face Billy again. He was a truly sinister looking man. A broad smile appeared on his face. "See you later, Billy boy."

Clive Williams sat down and shook his head. "I'm sorry, Billy." The detective picked up the telephone on the desk and dialed. "Get us some tea in here, please."

Clive sat in silence for a few moments until the waiting tea, already made for the purpose, was dispensed. Billy shook as he sipped the hot liquid. Clive knew it was time. A young man in serious trouble needed all the help he could get. He took out a disgusting handkerchief, shook it out and polished his ancient reading glasses. Holmes grimaced at the sight.

"Billy, we need to talk, man to man. We have indisputable proof that you were in the house of Elsie May Townsend, in the early hours of this morning. Now I want to help you, you know I do. But you're facing the most serious charges, Billy. This is a terrible mess you are in, lad. Your answers to my questions now may determine where you spend the rest of your life, son."

Clive paused just long enough to pick up the engagement ring from the desk. He rolled it between his fingers, and stared straight into the face of the youth. "You're not a bad lad, Billy. You didn't mean it, did you? You didn't mean to kill her. Elsie May? Did you, Billy?"

Billy started to shake even more. Tears welled in his eyes. He felt sick. He'd done it this time, really fucked up. "It," Billy stammered, "it isn't her ring."

Clive's heart missed a beat. He couldn't believe that the old routine still worked so easily after all these years. The moment when a suspect breaks and starts to cough his crime still gave the seasoned detective a thrill. His voice remained as soft as silk. No one but the closest colleague would have detected his inner excitement. "I know that, Billy. I know."

Billy gestured to the ring with his chin. "That's from another job."

Clive reached forward and rested his hand on the youth's arm. It was probably the first show of affection Billy had known in quite some time. "Tell it all, Billy, and then I'll help you."

Holmes was redundant. He could no longer stop his client. He had to admit the show had been a slick one. Still, he could feel the plea bargain of his life coming on. All he had to do was think of the Legal Aid payments coming rolling in for this one.

"It was an accident, boss." Billy's voice was almost a whisper. "She woke up, and all I wanted t'do was to get out. Fuck off and do one, like."

Billy wiped his eyes. "The other jobs had been easy like, in and out, good pickings 'n everythin'. This one, well, she wouldn't get out't way. There were this alarm thing...."

Clive had him. Like a cat with a mouse, he had played with his quarry until the time was right.

"She were gonna pull it. Bring the coppers. I just pushed her. She fell. I didn't mean..."

Billy broke down. His muscular frame heaved. Tears poured from his eyes. Clive gently took the youth by the shoulders, like a father giving advice to his son. "We need to get this sorted officially, Billy, and I think we should do it now."

Clive took a blank statement form from his file. At the top he wrote:

*My name is William Henry Bailey. I want someone to write down what I say. I have been told that I need not say anything unless I wish to do so and that what I say may be given in evidence.*

Billy signed the introduction and then slowly, between sobs and Clive's cigarettes, dictated his fate.

Rod Casey looked at Clive through the two-way mirror. He was seething. His massive fists clenched. *Constable eh? Gonna take all the credit again, Clive? I'll give you fuckin' Constable.*

Jimmy Wilson owned the 'Top Hat.' It was a poxy little nightclub, frequented by coppers and villains alike. Jammed between a car sales pitch and a lawnmower shop, the club was definitely on the wrong side of town. Inside, the establishment relied on its subdued red lighting to mask the decaying décor and broken floorboards. In daylight you would look around and ask what Jimmy Wilson was doing with his profits, because it did very well.

It was a favourite haunt of local CID officers. Some of whom occasionally sought the favours of the various prostitutes who drank there. Always busy, any night of the week; full of big drinkers and big brawlers.

Jimmy looked at the time and wanted to close, but McCauley and his cronies were having a celebration about something or other, and Jimmy wasn't going to spoil it by shouting last orders. You never knew when you might need a man like John McCauley.

Besides, the bird in the short skirt that was with them was the best view he'd come across in a good while. He'd not seen her before and couldn't work out if she was a copper or not. She had a posh accent too, London, but not Cockney. She sounded like that Angela Rippon off the telly. Jimmy had told the DJ to keep playing until the team was ready to leave, and 'Stuck in the Middle with You' played at room-shaking levels.

Rod Casey was well oiled, and Jimmy was wary of him. A team of likely lads from Moor Nook estate were still in and just as pissed. There was a bit of friction in the air, and some finger pointing had begun.

Casey didn't give a fuck if the whole club wanted a ruck. He took a swig of his pint. "...And then Clive walks in and calls me...wait for it...fuckin' 'Constable!'"

McCauley and Williams were laughing out loud. The Chief slapped Rod on the shoulder.

"Don't take it personal, Rod, it's all part of the job. We had a good result there."

Anne Wallace on the other hand was as sober as a judge. To Anne, there was little point in celebrating. She didn't want to be in a slum like the Top Hat and she certainly was not in the mood to be in close proximity to John McCauley, some mistakes were best left buried.

She looked at her watch. It was 4.30 a.m. In the back of her mind was the little matter of the Marigold gloves. They bothered her, as did the handsome young officer who found them. She returned from her thoughts, as McCauley leaned against her and brushed his arm against her breasts for the third or fourth time in as many minutes. He breathed stale cigars and brandy in her direction.

He'd begun to slur. "You see, darlin'. I was fuckin' right. We don't make deals with these little bastards."

He pointed at Clive and Rod, who were now singing at the top of their voices, any rivalry seemingly forgotten.

"You're on a proper team now."

Anne removed McCauley's hand from her knee. She was too tired to point out that Bailey's confession would only result in a manslaughter charge in the end. When the barristers had finished with it, the whole mess would be carved up like a Sunday joint.

"It's time I was off, boss."

The Chief was now close to the point of incapable. He shuffled across his seat and moved even closer to Anne.

"Hey! Anne, darlin', how about it then eh? You an' me get a cab to my place an' carry on the party, like old times?"

"Not tonight, big boy," Anne was doing her best to keep it light. "I've got a file to finish before court sits in the morning. I'll ring you on Monday on my way in."

She stood, waved to Rod and Clive who had stopped their impressions of Stealers Wheel and were now in deep conversation. Rod didn't appear happy at all. Anne turned and left the bar.

McCauley watched every step. He could barely speak. "Stuck up fuckin' bitch."

The Chief strode to the bar the best he could, and grabbed Jimmy by the arm. He shouted above the music.

"Get us a double round in, Jim, put it on the slate, and get rid of those fuckers from Moor Nook, they're makin' my beer sour."

Anne stepped out into the cold morning air, and took large gulps of it. The smell of the club, so many sweating bodies and non-existent cleaning, were ingrained in her nostrils. She found the CID car, nicknamed 'the Danny,' and sat in it waiting for the windows to clear. It was a near new dark blue Mk11 Escort that the whole of Preston already knew belonged to the cops. She was familiar with the type of car, as her brother had the sporty 'Mexico' version back home. She shivered against the chill, and thought she'd noticed the atmosphere between the team grow uneasy since Bailey's confession. It was the least of her worries. The touch of John McCauley was a much bigger problem. She drove slowly back to the nick, ruing the day.

Anne rode the lift to her office. The pile of papers on her desk had continued to rise, despite the Townsend murder. It was Anne's weekend off and the paperwork had to be done before she left. So much for the glamour of being a detective.

Removing her jacket, Anne sat at her desk and felt dog-tired. She rummaged in her bag for a packet of cigarettes. Finding she had none, she swore under her breath and went on a hunt around the various detectives' desks. She found a pack, stole one and lit it.

Her father had been begging her to quit for years. She had made a decent attempt at New Year, and lasted ten days.

The first file she opened was William Henry Bailey's.

Anne skimmed through until she reached Dave Stewart's witness statement. It was typed and signed by the officer, but his original hand-written statement was missing.

Anne stared at the statement, and then looked at the pile of work to her left.

"Oh, leave it." Anne snapped the file closed. Whatever was bothering her could wait. Bailey had, after all, confessed and there were now other fish to fry. One thing she had learned since being promoted to sergeant was to get straight on with the next job. No point in basking in former glory, or dwelling on a missed opportunity.

Another busy officer sat in the parade room on the ground floor. Dave Stewart had four Drunk and Disorderly files to complete, and a rather nasty assault to box off before he could leave. He was also nursing an eye that was rapidly swelling and becoming black.

Friday night in Preston town centre was a rough gig for any copper, but the foot patrol lads were normally first on the scene and first to get thumped.

At 6.45 a.m. Dave collected his paperwork and went upstairs to the CID office to dump the assault file on the duty jack's desk. He was surprised to find the lights still on, and even more surprised to hear the voice of Anne Wallace.

"You forget to duck then, David?"

"What...?"

No one called him David, not even his mam. Anne's voice was velvet, and Dave stood a little open mouthed as he watched Anne stretch herself and yawn. As her clasped hands reached upward behind her head, her blouse lifted over the waistband of her skirt to reveal her flat pale belly. Dave was mesmerised and had lost all track of the conversation.

"The eye, David!"

Anne had finished her stretch and was pointing at his head. Dave remembered the gist of what she was talking about and touched his damaged eye absently. "Oh this ...err...it's nothing much."

Anne was replacing the tail of her blouse into her skirt. She stood and started to organise her desk as she spoke. "So, David Stewart, arrest any more murderers tonight?"

Dave allowed a smile and shook his head, feeling very tense.

"No, well not tonight, me 'n Armless have got the next five days off, so I thought I'd leave the poor murderers alone fer a while, like."

It was the first time Anne had seen Dave smile, and she was dumbfounded as to the reason it gave her butterflies. She picked up her briefcase. "Five days off, eh? You are a lucky boy. Anything or anyone special planned?"

Dave placed his report on the duty detective's desk. He could feel himself reddening. "Not really, Sarge, no, a few beers with the big fella, then maybe a run over to Blackpool for the night, y'know?"

Seeing his discomfort spurred Anne on, and she locked her gaze firmly onto Dave. It was a game she'd played many times before with men. Anne knew she was beautiful, she'd known for years, ever since Henry Olgaby had fought Clarence Hadley for the right to take her to the college dance. She'd let them fight, too. Both boys were strong and tough rugby players, and it was a vicious encounter that Anne watched until Olgaby was beaten and bloodied. Even though she'd felt a slight pang of guilt as the boy was helped away, the violence had excited her. She was aroused by it. Hadley had remained her 'squeeze' until university.

David Stewart was a powerful young man. Anne considered he was more than a match for many, and felt the familiar stirring as she admired his broad shoulders.

"It's my weekend off, too," she said, eyes set on him.

Dave was nervous. He knew exactly what was going on. It was just that this kind of thing just didn't happen to him. He knew what he wanted to say. In fact, he was rarely stuck for words when it came to women. But Anne was older and more experienced than he was, and he felt intimidated by her openness, confidence and beauty. This wasn't a girl from a council estate in Sheffield or Rotherham, after a couple of rum 'n blacks and a fumble in the back seat.

Anne had waited long enough for the young officer.

"Oh, David!" She flounced back into her seat sending her hair into her face, which made her look even more like Penthouse Pet of the Year. Her accent was posher than anything Dave had heard in real life, and it made every syllable seem sex-laden.

"Everything in this nick that sports a pair of testicles, and some that don't, try to get into my knickers on an hourly basis; simply everyone, David. Coppers, villains, solicitors; do I make myself clear? Here I am putting it on a plate for you, and you don't even notice!"

Dave had lost the plot, of course he'd noticed. "I'm sorry I..."

"Oh, forget it!" Anne was starting to feel like a silly schoolgirl whose game had gone wrong.

“No, Sarge, I mean, Anne. I’d love to get into, I mean, take you, aaagh!”

Dave held his head in his hands. Idiot! Idiot! Then he heard Anne laughing. It was a wonderful sound. She held her head to one side. Her hair fell past her elbow. It shone even in the dismal office light. Dave found himself holding his breath.

“OK, Mr. Romance, how’s your memory?”

“Pretty good.”

“Then remember this. 8.30, tonight, The Winchester. Dress nice. Bring wallet. Got that?”

Dave found himself drawn into Anne’s gaze, the eye contact telling both people the same story. Silent seconds went by that could have been minutes, yet neither had cause to break the spell. There was an atmosphere, electricity filled the air. At that moment all David Stewart’s worries were unimportant. Life was wonderful. With a beaming smile he said, “I won’t forget.”

Words spoken and the spell broken, Anne did her utmost to regain her own composure.

“Alright then.”

She stifled a giggle and put her hand on her hips. “Off you go then, Constable.”

Dave did a mock salute and strode from the office. He stepped into the lift, hit the ground button and fell against the wall of the descending elevator. He felt like a Pools winner. What a day he’d had.

Anne watched the lift doors close, walked back inside and stole another fag from the desk in the corner of the office. She sat at her desk and shook her head.

She needed a reality check. What the hell was she playing at? Stewart must be ten years younger than her, at least. The self-inflicted chastisement failed miserably, and she found that the smile was still on her face. It deserted her the second she picked up a pen and wrote:

*Boss,*

*I'm due a little time off, my desk is clear; I'm going to take three days. See you Thursday morning. You know where to reach me if anything goes pear shaped.*

*Anne.*

Billy paced his cell. His cold, bare feet made slapping sounds on the solid floor.

He had just awoken from a nightmare, a terrible vivid blast of colour, in which Elsie May Townsend and his long dead grandmother had been teaching him to read. A skill, incidentally, he still found almost impossible to master.

Both women were ghastly creatures, their flesh dropping from their faces in soggy puss-filled clumps.

His breath was short and a terrible weight was on his chest; as Billy attempted to read each word, another festering piece of flesh fell on the page obscuring his view. He had screamed so loud that the pig sitting outside his cell door had rushed inside, thinking Billy was topping himself.

For now though he paced, muttering to himself, eyes wild. With each turn he hunched his shoulders or gesticulated to imaginary demons. The already vulnerable young man was close to the edge of his sanity, total mental breakdown.

Billy had been formally charged with the murder of Elsie May Townsend, the malicious wounding of Police Constable Stephen Jones, and four counts of burglary in a dwelling. In all his young life, he had never been so scared. The fear baited him, dragged him down to the depths of despair. To Billy, the ultimate weakness, fear, was tearing at his soul. This time, he couldn't beat it.

Dave Stewart stood outside 'The Winchester', a Victorian manor house standing amid manicured grounds. It was once a family home for a wealthy Lancashire mill owner. It was now the premier country house restaurant in the county. To Dave, it just looked very posh.

He had been out that afternoon and bought himself a new jacket especially for the occasion.

To say he felt uncomfortable would have been a fair comment. When he drove into the car park, he found that his vehicle was the only one that was over five years old, unless you counted the classic red E-Type.

As he peered into the doorway of the restaurant, he felt like the proverbial fish out of water. You can take the boy out of Barnsley, and all that.

Taking a deep breath, he stepped inside. A very dour maitre d' in a tuxedo immediately met him. A small portly man, with a permanent look of rancour on his face, he was very bald, but did his best to disguise it with a comb-over that defied gravity. Unknown to him, a feature that was the source of great amusement to the young waitresses employed under him.

He spoke with a very large plum in his mouth. "Good evening, sir, have you a reservation?"

Did Dave have a reservation? He didn't know. He could walk into a bar-room brawl with all the confidence in the world but, at the end of the day, he was a boy from a council estate in Yorkshire. Had Anne made a booking in her name?

Dave must have taken too long to answer because the suit made a pathetic little coughing sound and said, "Sir, we are always full at The Winchester. If one has no reservation, I'm afraid that waiting is simply pointless."

The very rude little man then opened the door and, with a slightly camp flick of the wrist, gestured for Dave to leave.

This irritated him no end. He suddenly realised that he spent all his working days in a position of authority. Now was as good a time as any to demonstrate his skills. Dave towered over the headwaiter. His broad shoulders filling the new jacket he was sporting, his close-cropped hair slicked back especially for the night, he was a substantial figure.

Dave placed his hand on the shoulder of the maitre d' and

squeezed just hard enough to make his presence felt. He lowered his voice to a whisper. The guy knew he was in trouble, and was hoping he hadn't gone too far this time with the lower class clientele.

"Now listen to me, Mr. Waiter. I'm here to meet a young lady. Her name is Miss Wallace. My name, and you will remember this, is Mr. Stewart. Now off you go and check whatever you have to. When you've done that, come back and show me to a table. I'll be in the bar."

Dave thought that the man would faint. He'd turned a deathly grey colour and developed an instant stammer. "Y...Y...Yes, Mr....err..."

"Stewart," Dave prompted, smiled sweetly, and parked himself at the bar and ordered a scotch.

He sipped the malt. The liquid warmed his throat. It felt good. This was how the other half lived, eh?

Anne's voice snapped him back from his thoughts.

"David! I turn my back for five minutes and here you are frightening poor Maurice."

Dave turned to see Anne standing next to the maitre d', head tilted to one side, hand theatrically on hip. The pose was almost identical to that when he'd left her at the station. The big difference was how she looked.

Anne was stunning; a black satin dress hugged her figure like a second skin. It was worn just over her knees. Her bare shoulders shimmered in the subdued light. A small gold necklace nestled around her throat. Her hair was somehow held in place for once, like a crown on top of her head. Shimmering ringlets giggled either side of her beautiful face.

Dave was totally speechless.

The maitre d' had recovered his composure. "Your table is ready, Mr. Stewart."

Dave never took his eyes from Anne. "Thank you, Maurice."

They were seated in a corner of the plush dining room. The polished oak paneled walls and blood red Wilton carpets complemented just the right number of tables for romantic privacy. Maurice immediately presented the menu, and finally the pair were left alone for the first time.

Anne leaned forward and rested her chin on the back of her hands. The candlelight made her skin glow and her eyes flash.

"So," she began, "feeling firm and manly tonight, are we?"

"He's just, you know, he's a wind up merchant. I can't be doing with those types"

Dave lowered his voice and gestured with his thumb toward Maurice, "He's a snob and I hate snobs."

"So I see," Anne smiled, and checked the menu.

Dave did the same and blurted, "Do you come here often?"

Anne looked up at Dave and somehow managed to keep a straight face. As the very nervous young man realised what he had said, they both burst out laughing.

The ice broken, two strangers entered into the conversation of first dates. Anne banned the subject of police work, but announced any other subject as fair game. She talked of her family, university, her dreams of becoming a lawyer, and her love of anything that goes fast.

Dave listened and watched as Anne, animated and staggeringly beautiful, chattered away as if they were long lost friends. The first course arrived. Dave had never seen food presented like it. He hoped he had enough cash to pay the bill.

Eventually the wine started to have an effect and Dave's confidence level rose.

"I need to ask you something, Anne."

Anne drained her glass and lifted the bottle to refill it. "OK, shoot."

"Why did you come on to me at the station, you know what I mean, why me?"

It was a fair question. It could have thrown Anne but it didn't.

Instead, she reached across the table and stroked Dave's face with her fingers. The wickedest smile etched across her face. It was their first physical contact. A touch filled with the excitement of a new liaison.

New affection.

"You're cute," Anne pouted, "And I have a fetish for younger men."

"Really?"

"Yes, always been the case since John Stapleton, one year below me at high school. Well, that and you don't stare at my boobs all the time."

Dave laughed, "I do so. It's just that I'm sneaky about it."

Anne rested her chin on her hands. "Oh, David, I can't say why. I suppose you just seem a good guy, you're handsome, you have broad shoulders, and I'm sick and tired of lecherous fools. I need something different in my life, you know? Someone decent."

Dave considered the stark reality of his situation. He couldn't hide it. He was who he was. "Anne, where I come from, there aren't those choices you talk about. If you can find work it's the pit, or the steelwork. Most of the pits are going. Dad says they'll all be gone in five years, and God only knows what will happen then. My family had never even thought of having a child attend University. My mum isn't well, and me Dad, well he hasn't worked since...well, not in a long time."

Dave took a drink. He suddenly needed it, as much as he needed to get his cards on the table. It was the Yorkshire way, no point in painting false pictures.

"I know this is only dinner, Anne, and I know as well as anyone this may not lead anywhere, but I have to say you, not you personally, but what you are, frightens me. I mean, I'll bet no one in your family has ever been a bouncer in a bar, have they?"

Anne shook her head.

"And none of your family lives in a council house, do they?"

Anne jumped in, mildly irritated, "No and they don't work down a mine, wear flat caps or eat black pudding. So what does that mean to you, David? My family has money. So what? I'm not ashamed of that, or them, because they've done well and worked hard every day to make sure of it. I can tell you. I don't need to work at all, let alone fight every sexist boss in the force to try and make a career as a copper."

Anne took Dave's hand in hers. Her voice mellowed. "David, you have something that all the money in the world will not buy. People like you. They like you for what you are and not what you can give them. That's a precious commodity. It can't be bought."

It was Anne's turn to be serious. The eye contact made her giddy. She knew she should take this slowly, but something was pushing her on like a driverless rain.

"I like you, David. I like you a lot."

Dave tore himself from Anne's gaze, picked up the cheque for the food and wine that Maurice had slipped onto the table, and studied it. He allowed what had been said to sink in before he spoke, "I hope you like me enough to go halves on this bill!"

Anne was laughing again. She couldn't remember the last time she had laughed so much in one evening.

"I like you enough to take you dancing, too."

The pair stood in the car park of The Winchester and tried to work out who was sober and could drive. As neither could decide, they took a cab.

'The Square' was a nightclub that attracted the local constabulary in numbers. They had a strict dress code and door policy that kept the most of the local faces at bay, although those on the shady side of business were always welcome. It also attracted lots of single females.

Dave was halfway down the steps when he remembered Andy Dunn and their weekend plans. Dave knew he would be there, and when Andy saw him, he would give him shit. He and 'Armless' had planned the piss-up for ages. Dave hadn't even bothered to ring him to cancel. He had been too excited by his date.

Dave and Anne both pushed their ID cards in front of the doormen and were allowed straight into the bustling club, the entrance fee waived.

As they made their way toward the bar, Anne took Dave's hand and he held it tight.

Once the drinks were ordered, Anne left for the sanctuary of the ladies. Dave went in search of 'Armless'.

He didn't have to look far; he was lounging in a corner of the club, draped around the barmaid he was seeing on and off. Dave had seen her a few times when drinking in the Black Bull. She seemed a good sort.

Lucy was trying bravely to fight off the advances of the policeman. Andy Dunn was having a great time. It looked to Dave like Lucy would soon give in to her man, and seemed to be enjoying the game as much as 'Armless.

Dave stood in full view of Andy Dunn and waited for the avalanche.

"Oh! Ho!" bellowed 'Armless', over the booming music.

He temporarily released Lucy. "You wee jobbie of Yorkshire shite, you've finally shown up, eh?"

Dave raised his hands in surrender and smiled. "Sorry, 'Armless', but something important came up."

In a mock display of aggression, Andy Dunn rolled up his shirtsleeves, displaying the twenty-inch biceps that gave him his nickname.

"I think it's time to teach the sprog a lesson. What do you say, Lucy?"

Lucy was laughing so much that her more than ample assets seemed to be fighting to escape from her flimsy top. Right on time, Anne appeared at Dave's side. She slipped her hand in his and gave him a peck on the cheek.

Dave sported the stupidest grin Andy had ever seen.

Andy was shocked and impressed in equal amounts. He eyed Anne up and down. "F'God's sake, hen, you scrub up well fer a sergeant."

Anne turned her head to look at Dave. "I'm not the only one, Andy."

"So this is the important thing that came up then, Dave?" Andy gestured.

He patted the seats next to him. "Ok pal, I forgive you, come and join Lucy and me, and we'll have a right royal piss up."

Anne folded her arms in an act of defiance. "Andy, you are about to be drunk under the table by a woman."

The DJ played Heatwave and all around the club, the human mating ritual was taking place. Men trawling the circular dance floor hoping to catch the eye of an available female. The Square was not about true romance. This was casual sex on a plate territory. Everyone knew the score. There were more than a few wedding rings removed in the toilets, only to be replaced prior to the return home to the spouse.

For Anne, Dave, Lucy and Andy though, their stresses forgotten, it was time to party. The beer flowed and the truth came easier.

'Armless' leaned over to Anne. "Listen, Sarge, dinnae take me wrong like, but this big daft Yorkshireman is a grand lad. He'll make a good copper and someone a good husband. You'll be a hard act to follow for him. I'd hate to see him hurt."

Anne's eyes followed Dave, who was helping Lucy carry yet another round of drinks to the table.

She had to shout into the veteran cop's ear, "Andy, when it comes to picking men, I've had my moments;" she paused for thought for a second and decided attack was the best form of defence.

"Anyway, how old are you now, Mr.? I don't see you settled with the little woman of your dreams."

Andy shrugged. "Fair enough."

Anne made her point before Dave sat down.

"Listen, I think that David is a great lad too, but we've just met, first date, give us a chance."

The night turned to early morning, and the tempo of the music changed. Anne rested her head on Dave's shoulder. The alcohol had done its job. "You promised to dance with me."

They held each other for the first time in the melee of a crowded dance floor. She felt the solid strength of his body as he swayed to and fro in an ungainly attempt to move to the music.

“Take me home,” she whispered.

The taxi pulled into Royalty Lane, a tree-lined avenue in the semi rural area of New Longton.

Close to Lancashire Police headquarters, it boasted the grand accommodation Anne called home. It was a typical middle class development of 1930’s houses. Substantial dwellings with large airy rooms with high ceilings and higher prices; they were the kind of houses Dave could only ever dream of.

As the taxi slowed, Anne noticed a large dark saloon car parked directly outside her house. Her heart skipped a beat.

She tapped the driver on the shoulder. “Keep going, we’ve changed our minds.”

Dave’s head was full of wine, beer and some mad cocktail of spirits Andy had insisted on buying in the nightclub. “Where we going now, Anne?” he slurred.

“Your place,” she whispered; a feeling of disgust washing over her as she double-checked the registration plate of the car.

“OK by me,” murmured Dave, totally oblivious to Anne’s discomfort. “Driver!” he announced, “Lindle Court please.”

As the taxi left the affluent avenue and turned for the more modest dwellings situated in the grounds of Lancashire Police headquarters, Detective Chief Superintendent John McCauley snored noisily behind the wheel of his car. A bottle of wine and a bouquet of flowers lay on the seat beside him. It was not going to be the Chief's night.

Dave almost fell from the taxi as Anne held onto his elbow. She paid the driver, and the pair stumbled to the front door of Dave's police house. Lindle Court sat within 'The Colony,' the nick-name the coppers gave to the small estate of police-owned houses.

New coppers, those with less than five years service, couldn't buy their own houses, it was the rules. Dave found the keyhole and the couple stepped inside. Anne seemed to be doing her best not to fall over in the hallway.

"Oops!" she giggled, and again grabbed at Dave's arm for balance.

Anne pushed the lounge door open and it sobered her. It was immaculately clean and tidy. It was also comparatively empty. One worn armchair faced a prehistoric black and white television. An equally ancient indoor aerial with outrageous v-shaped extensions sat on the top, along with the only visible photograph. A monochrome couple smiled at the camera. Blackpool Tower rose behind them, and a new looking Triumph Bonneville motorcycle dated the shot around the late sixties. A book case was pushed against one woodchip covered wall. It was packed with dog-eared paperback novels, each neatly organised by author and genre. It appeared David liked to read rather than watch. There were no carpets or curtains, but he had managed to run to a small synthetic rug, placed in front of a pale green gas fire mounted inside a grey tiled fireplace.

Dave saw the look on her face, and he felt ashamed.

"Not much, is it?"

Anne looked up at him. She studied his face in the unkind light of an undressed lamp. He had three small scars, one below his left eye, another which dissected his top lip and traced half an inch upward toward his nose, and the last that parted his right eyebrow. Anne decided all had needed hospital treatment. Despite them, he was classically handsome. She had never seen such eyes on a man. They shimmered and danced with life and emotion when he spoke. They were the darkest, deepest chocolate and she wanted to drown in them.

She touched his cheek.

"Don't be embarrassed, David Stewart."

She felt herself smile, and nodded toward the hearth.

"Does that ridiculously ugly fire work?"

A flash of a grin spread across Dave's face.

"Yeah, yeah it does."

Anne dropped onto the rug, leaned forward on all fours and turned the dial on the fire until it made a tell-tale click. A small *oomph* sound indicated the gas had ignited, and she sat close, rubbing her bare arms to fight the chill of the room.

Dave found himself watching her. A wayward piece of her hair had found its way out of its clasp and kept falling into her face as she tucked her feet under her. She attempted to fix the problem, twice, gave up and released her mane so it fell in shiny ringlets over her shoulders and down her back. Dave was spellbound.

He turned out the naked lamp.

She patted the worn rug, and Dave sat. The fire was warming to its task, and he removed his new jacket and dropped it on the chair.

Dave looked into her eyes. The gas fire hissed, and bathed Anne in a crimson glow. He couldn't ever recall seeing someone so beautiful. He slid his hand around the back of Anne's neck and kissed her gently on the corner of her mouth.

Then, he released her. There was a long silence, then another, firmer, passionate kiss.

"Please stay," he said.

Three miles away, McCauley woke from his uncomfortable sleep. His back ached. Where the fuck was she? He checked the clock on the dash. It was 4.30a.m.

He looked over at the wine and flowers, and grimaced.

"Bitch!"

Billy was in a bad way. He smelled awful and looked haunted; the dark circles under his eyes gave his face a hollow, near jaundiced look. He hadn't washed, shaved or eaten since his arrest. It had been three full days of his own private hell.

It was time for Billy's court appearance, but Billy's concept of time had long since deserted him. He'd had the dreams though, the horrible rancid dreams.

Ray Holmes stood in the pungent cell next to his client, perfectly groomed. A clean set of underwear, a brand new shirt, suit, and shoes were stacked in his arms. They had cost him a few quid, but hey, this was going to be a big pay-day.

Holmes was repulsed by the stink, but he figured this case was a free holiday to Bangkok, one of his favorite locations, where he could indulge in his very private interests. "Get a shower and a shave, Billy, and then put these on." He held out the clothes. "Bought at considerable expense, I might say. Not your Preston market shit, this."

Billy rocked slightly on his bunk, mumbling to himself, seemingly unaware of his legal advisor.

"Billy!" The brief thrust the clothes under the nose of the young lad.

"Get your shit together!"

Bailey lifted the great weight of his head and stared blankly at Holmes. The dawning of a familiar face didn't quite reach his eyes. "Oh, it's you. What do you want, Ray?"

"It's time for your court appearance, Billy! You're in front of the beak this morning, mate."

Ray shook the suit under his nose in frustration. "You know? I'm here to help you get yourself sorted out?"

Holmes rested the clothes on Billy's lap.

"Look, get cleaned up and we'll see what we can do for you, eh?"

Billy pushed the clothes from his lap and stood. With an almost mechanical movement he pushed his head into the open hatch, and with great ferocity shouted to the cell officer to release him for his ablutions. Even Holmes jumped in fear. Billy was on the edge and his counsel knew it.

Holmes walked the floor of the stinking cell, re-reading the prosecution file. Something didn't smell too good in that little thriller, either.

As Holmes came to the end of the medical statements, Billy walked back into the cell. He was dripping from the shower, a prison towel around his middle.

"That's more like my boy," said Holmes.

Ray Holmes stared at the lad. Billy's broad shoulders and well-defined muscles sent shivers down his spine.

Ray dropped the court papers on the bunk and walked over to the troubled youth. His mouth was dry even though his face was beaded with sweat, and he licked his lips before he spoke. "I've always looked after you, haven't I, Billy?"

The solicitor stroked Billy's newly shaven face.

"Nice and smooth, William. I remember when you were called William, not Billy. The time you were just starting out, running away from that slag of a mother of yours, nicking sweets from Woolies. Remember, William? How old were you then? Ten maybe, just turned eleven?"

Billy knew what was coming next. He'd known from that very age, eleven years old. Holmes quickly checked the cell corridor through the hatch in the door. It was deserted. He turned and pulled the towel from Billy's waist, and held his breath as he drank in the view. He unzipped his own fly and released himself, then rested his hand on Billy's wet, blond hair. Billy dropped to his knees as he had so many times before. Holmes moaned at the first contact.

Within seconds, Holmes was ready. He motioned Billy to his feet and turned him to face the wall. Holmes spat on his fingers and pushed them into Billy. The solicitor then forced himself inside the youth in silent ecstasy. He imagined William, not Billy. The boy as he was when they first met, when he was the right age. That did the trick.

Satisfied, Holmes rearranged his clothes and gathered the papers he'd dropped so readily. A smug expression crossed his face.

"You know, Billy, you're going to be alright."

Billy stood, naked. He made no attempt at modesty. He stared at his feet, and snorted derision.

"Am I, Ray?"

Holmes stepped forward with his best 'client smile', and took Billy's chin in his hand. His lust had vanished, and William the innocent had become Billy the bonus.

"Yeah, you've got a lucky face, Billy. Know what I mean? A fucking lucky face."

Billy pushed Holmes' hand away with some strength.

"I don't feel too fuckin' lucky, Ray.

Holmes stepped back and stuffed the court file into his latest briefcase. He rapped on the cell door.

"Constable! Constable!"

Holmes was glad to hear the steady steps of the copper walking toward the cell. Billy was a live one at the best of times and he figured the least time spent in a confined room with damaged goods, the better. He could never have considered his own actions that of a deviant. Only the lower classes fell into that category. Neither had he considered he may have been central to Bailey's mental state. Pedophilia was an art-form to him. Something he had studied for many years. The grooming of young boys was no more erroneous to him, than ordering the wrong wine at dinner.

The lock turned, and Ray slipped out of the door to the relative safety of the corridor.

Billy's tears flowed freely as he dressed himself. The years of abuse at the hands of Holmes and his cronies massed on top of him, making it all too hard to draw a gulp of air to cry out loud. It had been that way for as long as he could remember. They had taken William Henry Bailey's life from him, without him knowing. Taken his very breath from his body, and now he just didn't care anymore.

He took to rocking to and fro again, for comfort. It felt right.

Minutes later, officers arrived at his cell door to escort him on the short journey to court. The guards were taking no chances after the injuries he'd inflicted on their colleague. Both coppers were young, fit, and muscular. They barely noticed his distress. Why should they care anyway? They handcuffed him briskly and marched him through the underground tunnel which led from the station to the magistrates court cells.

Bailey was kept separate from the other defendants. He was classed as 'vulnerable'. He had an officer with him at all times, except of course when with his legal advisor, which, unknown to them, was when he needed protection the most.

Within the hour Bailey stood in the dock of the magistrates court, flanked by the same two police officers.

It was a drab building of similar age to Lawson Street nick.

Ray Holmes sat in the allotted seat for the defence solicitor. The prosecuting inspector was talking to the magistrates, but Billy didn't hear a thing. The same tuneless song repeated in his head over and over.

Suddenly, someone was asking him to confirm his name. They asked once, then again and again. Inside his head he screamed at them to be quiet, to shut up and leave him alone. The bastard in the uniform was staring at him. Billy wanted to fuck him over. Billy wanted to fuck the world over.

Billy wanted out.

It took less than ten seconds for him to drop the guards who, on the misguided orders of the magistrate, had removed Billy's cuffs. He vaulted the dock like a gazelle, and raced for the exit. The public gallery erupted. A woman screamed at the sight of blood. A camera flashed. An elderly court usher attempted to block his path, but then had second and better thoughts.

Within thirty seconds, Billy was out in the rain and running for his life.

By the time the first radio transmission had alerted the police officers in the area of the court building of the escape, Billy had gone to ground.

Dave Stewart stretched himself. He lay with his head in Anne's lap.

Since the early hours of Sunday morning, they had never left his bedroom. He felt wonderful. They had made love so often and with such passion, that both were exhausted but happy. Something was developing between them that, although unspoken, was as powerful as any sonnet.

Anne checked her watch. "David?"

"Hmm?"

"I've got an idea, why don't we pack a few things and have a run up to the country?"

Dave sat up. "What, now?"

"Yes, now."

Anne leapt up and stood on top of the bed, naked and smiling. She jumped to the bare floor and started to pull on her only clothes, still scattered around the room where she'd left them.

"We'll go back to my place. I'll pick up some more suitable clothes, get my car from The Winchester and just...well...go!"

Dave looked at the beautiful woman fastening her dress that now looked somewhat out of place on a grey Monday afternoon.

"Anne?"

"Yes, honey?"

"I don't want this to end."

Anne looked at Dave. She appeared puzzled. "Did you just say end? This is just the start, darling. Don't be negative."

She jumped back onto the bed and held Dave tight, but as she closed her eyes and felt the strength of Dave's naked body, she felt suddenly scared. Scared of what? A genuine fear of falling in love? She shouldn't be reacting this way. For God's sake, she was thirty-one. She'd known this man for a few days and she couldn't drink in enough of him. This wasn't Mills and bloody Boon, it was reality. She had to get a grip; there were other more pressing problems. John McCauley, for a start.

She opened her eyes again and there he was. His powerful chest still glistened with sweat from their last encounter. She looked into his eyes and once again, none of it mattered. Her words came without second thoughts. All fear chased away by those deep brown pools. "You can't get rid of me that easily, David."

Dave held her to him again. The words slipped from his mouth without reservation. He knew he held someone and something very special in his arms.

"I have no intention of letting you go, Anne."

Anne's stomach did another flip at his casual honesty. Her head, though, was full of contradictions. She knew how powerful McCauley was, and how fickle the police service could be.

"Neither have I, but we might only have a short time, David. There are forces at work more powerful than either of us."

Dave didn't understand, but then again he had never understood any woman. All he knew was he wanted to stick hold of this one.

He smiled. "I'm sure that'll make sense to me in time, lass." He swung his legs from the bed and did his best to imitate the Queen's English. "Shall we, madam?"

Dave got himself together, and within twenty minutes the pair left for Anne's considerable home.

Dave stood and took in the view. In the middle of the room was a baby-grand piano. The décor reflected Anne's character. Feminine yet practical furnishings intermingled with the odd piece of art that would set you back a small fortune. The whole room, though, had one theme running right through it.

Class.

Anne was elsewhere packing her 'few essentials'. Dave looked around the room and noticed she had an answer-phone. Dave had only ever seen one in an office before, and studied it. A small red light blinked furiously on the top. Next to it a button that explained, *'message'*

Dave knew he shouldn't, but somehow he couldn't help himself. He pressed the button, and a tape somewhere inside the machine started to rewind. Eventually it stopped, and the message started.

"Hello, Anne, it's me. You there?" the message began. Dave recognised the voice instantly.

"No? OK. Well listen, I got your note this morning and I thought we could get together tonight. I'll be round about ten with a little something to get the mood going. I can't wait. Oh, and wear that little black number I got you."

The machine stopped and so did the blinking light.

Dave felt ashamed and sick all at the same time.

"What are you snooping around with, big boy?" Anne breezed into the room clutching an overnight bag.

Dave nearly had a heart attack. He leapt back from the answer-phone. He knew he must look guilty.

"Oh, just admiring your electrical appliances."

"Well, stop it and come and admire me!"

Anne put her arms around Dave's neck and kissed him heavily. Dave looked into her eyes. "I'm sorry, I promise to be more attentive in future."

Anne slid her hand down to his crotch and gave him a gentle squeeze. "I think I can keep you occupied, David."

Her mouth locked onto his and her perfume engulfed him. Dave was in heaven again and the message, for the time being, was forgotten.

Andy Dunn had a serious hangover. He'd taken some aspirin, swallowed gallons of water and even considered having another beer, he felt so bad. He and Lucy had been on a real bender. They had left the club just after Dave and Anne, taken a taxi to his house, and drank themselves into oblivion.

Eventually Lucy had to go back to work at The Bull, and 'Armless was left to his headache. He'd called Dave and got no reply. He presumed he was still engaged in carnal activity with the lovely Anne. Therefore, in a state of boredom, he rang the nick for a chat with his old mate Doug James.

Doug was the day desk sergeant at Preston nick. He didn't get involved in any proactive policing these days due to a back injury, but if you wanted to know what was going on, he was the man.

"You'll never believe this," croaked Doug, "but that lad Billy Bailey has done one from the magistrates court this morning. Kicked the shit out of two bobbies and done a Sebastian Coe across the ring road."

"Fuck me," Andy let out a low whistle, "so the shite has hit the fan then, pal?"

"You're telling me, 'Armless. This little fucker has got the whole nick in a right tizzy. It's been on the telly and everythin' today. Where the fuck you been?"

Andy rubbed his eyes and yawned. The drama was interesting, but he still could do with a serious kip.

"Well, Doug, what can I say? Me and young Dave Stewart had a few bevvies over the weekend and we both got lucky," he gave an evil laugh, "you know how it is, pal."

"Used to, Armless, used to, but I'm a bit long in the tooth now. I don't know where you get the energy from."

Andy lowered his voice for no reason other than effect; "Our young Dave has pulled for wee Anne Wallace."

Now it was Doug's turn to whistle, "Not McCauley's little

favourite?"

"One and the same, pal; as true as I'm standin' here"

Doug became grave. "You better tell your boy to watch his back. If the Chief finds out he's on the nest with that one he's likely to throw an epi."

Armless brushed off Doug's remarks. "Awe come on, Doug, you know a standing prick has no conscience. He's a young laddie and besides McCauley's too old for Anne Wallace. If I'd have had half a chance I'd have been there like a rat up a drainpipe. Fuck the Chief."

Doug's serious tone barely made it above the background noise of the nick, his voice now little more than a whisper. "I'm telling you, Andy, I've known John McCauley since we were cadets at sixteen. I've seen him do some real crazy stuff. He thinks he's above the law. He won't think twice about seriously hurting your young mate there, or his new found skirt either. You take care now and, if I were you, I'd keep that snippet of information to yourself."

"What do you mean, Doug, crazy stuff, like?"

Doug was having none of it. "Oh no! I want to keep my little number here thanks. My pension is only twelve months away. I'm saying fuck all."

Doug sounded very uncomfortable; Andy even thought he detected genuine fear. "I got to get back to work now, Andy."

Both men said their goodbyes, and Andy walked to the kitchen to make coffee. He pondered Doug's comments. He knew McCauley was a bit on the seedy side. He'd heard all the rumours. Nevertheless, Doug was always one for the station gossip. It was unlike him to clam up like that.

Andy opened a new jar of coffee, and realised he had one open already. He cursed under his breath. His head still throbbed unabated. Forget Doug, McCauley and all that shit. He just needed to feel better. He drank his brew and thanked the Lord that he had no work to go to.

For Doug James and the rest of the shift at Preston nick, it was bedlam. Teams of uniformed officers were being drafted in for the search for William Henry Bailey.

Dog handlers huddled in groups, waiting for their orders, while harassed sergeants tried to make sense of the search patterns their men were to execute.

Raymond Holmes stood in the CID office, dressed in the latest fashionable offering. His solid frame showed the suit off to a tee. He was unable to stop himself from admiring his own image in the reflective glass of the station windows. His latest client was waiting to be interviewed. In all the uproar, delays were inevitable.

He watched the proceedings with mild amusement.

Billy had caused a stir; even made the Granada news. Still, if what Holmes suspected to be going on really was the truth, then Billy's break for freedom would only assist the case.

Raymond knew if he got Billy off this one, well, every two-bit street kid in town would be clamouring for his services.

Fuck the 'Beamer'. He would have a Ferrari next year. Raymond walked over to the filing cabinet that contained the crime property ledgers. In all the confusion, nobody noticed the solicitor open the drawer and remove the book.

Raymond casually walked to the photocopier and copied the pages he required from the ledger. He then replaced the book and left the office, whistling his favourite song.

The Chief was having a real bad day. He sat in his favourite chair, a very large scotch in his hand.

Not only had that bitch Anne Wallace left him high and dry on Saturday night, but he had been unable to trace her or find out who she was with.

Then, to add insult to injury, the fuckin' woodentops had let his body walk out of the fuckin' magistrates court without a by your leave.

Now, to end a perfect day, that little queer Ray Holmes was on the phone.

McCauley was venomous. "What the fuck do you want, Holmes, and how did you get my home number?"

Holmes was calm and to the point. He was in the driving seat. He was convinced of it. "Keep your shirt on, Chief Superintendent, and listen for once. You and I need to meet somewhere discreet."

McCauley let out a false belly laugh. "You're not my type, Holmes, and, I have no desire to see your poof face outside office hours."

Holmes was too confident to be riled. "Listen, you bigoted arsehole, I know you've tampered with the evidence in the Bailey case and I can prove it. Therefore, if you want to collect your fat pension you'll meet me. "

McCauley took the phone from his ear and looked down at the mouthpiece with raised eyebrows. He found the whole idea of a queer bloke being demonstrative wildly amusing.

A few seconds later, he resumed the conversation. He let out a wearisome sigh. "When and where, Holmes?"

"That's better, McCauley," Holmes was smiling.

What Holmes couldn't see, was that the Chief was almost crying laughing.

Dave drove and Anne slept. They had been on the road for almost two hours and were now close to their destination, a small guesthouse off Coniston Lake, Cumbria.

The Sierra Cosworth car was a dream for Dave, fast and sporty.

He pushed the vehicle to its limits on the winding roads that led to the lake.

Anne awoke. "Hey, what's the hurry, Sterling?"

Dave was smiling. "Just enjoying myself, let me play with my new toy for a while."

Anne leaned over and rested her head on Dave's shoulder. He had changed into a T-shirt and jeans, and she admired his physique. She ran her hand down his bicep to his forearm. "I'm having a wonderful time, David. You really make a woman feel good."

Dave glanced across at Anne. She too was dressed casually. He couldn't help but notice how the tight ribbed sweater emphasised her fantastic figure. "You don't do too badly yourself, madam. You scrub up pretty good."

The two lapsed into silence as the car pushed on towards their final destination. Only people who are comfortable together can achieve happy silences. Anne and Dave managed just fine.

Dual carriageway turned to single track road. The fabulous Lake District countryside stretched out to either side of the couple, and they marvelled in its early spring beauty.

Dave finally pulled the car into a space outside an historic looking house, outside which, a sign boasted home cooked dishes and home grown produce.

No sooner had they stepped inside, when they were welcomed by a lady introduced simply as Doris, who by her shape, indulged in the home grown produce on a regular basis. She had the pallor of a farmer's wife, small red veins had emerged on her cheeks giving the impression that she was permanently cold. She was a jolly soul, and quickly settled them into their room. She warmed to her task as host, obviously enjoying the company of others. They showered, changed and made their way down the narrow stairs to the lobby.

"It's a beautiful room, Doris," Anne reported, as the pair sat down to dinner.

The landlady smiled at Dave and gave him a cheeky wink. "I don't think your young man here is too interested in the furnishings. He ain't taken his eyes off you since you arrived, ma'am."

Dave was ravenous, and ate heartily of venison and roast potatoes. All the recent exercise had given him an appetite, and the house's promise was more than true.

He noticed that Anne barely touched her meal and voiced his concern.

"Something wrong, Anne?"

Anne remained quiet for a few moments, obviously deep in thought.

"David," she spoke slowly, deliberately. "I think it's time for a little truth and consequences."

He tone took Dave by surprise. "Go on."

"Well, I've been sort of seeing someone for about a year or so," Anne grimaced and added, "if you can call it that."

Dave's stomach turned over. His mind reverted back to that blinking light and the voice on the answer-phone.

"How can you be 'sort of' seeing someone?"

Anne held up her hand, and Dave went silent. She spoke quietly, "It started when I was a DC over in Skelmesdale. Some colleagues from the nick were going over to the club at HQ for a retirement party.

I was driving, so I was watching my drinks. Anyway the guy in question joins our group and insists on buying a round. It was my own fault, I should have said no, but I accepted; just the one.

I remember it tasted really strong, but never thought more about it. When I said I was leaving, the same guy insists on buying me another. Again I accepted and we chatted at the bar for a while, talking shop and about my upcoming promotion board.

I felt fine to drive, but that's what they all say, isn't it?"

Dave nodded but remained silent.

"I got in my car, I only had a mile or so to drive, but as I pulled into my road, there was a Traffic car waiting for me with a uniform inspector and sergeant on board."

"That stinks," said Dave.

"Oh, there's more. I was breathalyzed and it was positive. I was arrested and taken to Preston nick. The police surgeon attended and took a blood sample, and I was suspended from duty awaiting the results."

Dave could think of little to say except, "Shit."

"Yes, it was. Everything I'd worked for was about to go down the toilet. Anyway a month went by and I was informed that the blood sample had returned over the limit. The court date was set a week later. My father arranged a defence lawyer for me and off I went, resigned to the fact that I was going to be prosecuted and subsequently sacked.

When we arrived at court, my lawyer told me there was a problem with the prosecution case. The original blood analysis forms had gone 'missing' and there would be no case to answer. The police would offer no evidence.

A few days later I was back at my desk, feeling like the luckiest girl in the world.

A month later I went on my promotion board and the same guy was one of the interviewers. After the board, he invited me for a drink. This time I made sure it was a soft one.

I wasn't attracted to him physically, but I did respect his work. We got along OK, and I suppose one thing led to another."

Anne took a large gulp of her drink. From the look on her face, Dave knew this wasn't an easy confession.

"Anyway the upshot of it was that I quickly got fed up and wanted to end it. The problem has been that he won't take no for an answer."

Dave was about to speak, but Anne continued.

"Before you say anything, there's more to it. You know how hard it can be for a woman in this job. Qualifications don't mean shit. He made it perfectly clear what the bottom line was. He'd pulled some strings for me with the drink-drive charge. He'd made the evidence 'go away.' and he ensured I made D.S."

Anne held up her hand to stop Dave from commenting.

"Don't say, *'well, just tell him it's off'* either. It's not that simple."

Anne lit a cigarette and exhaled. It was the first time Dave had seen her so agitated. She played with the stem of her glass. Her bottom lip trembled slightly.

She showed the merest hint of a tear.

"There has been a high price to pay for the rank. I've paid it."

The look on her face told Dave everything he needed to know about what the price entailed.

Anne nodded.

"Yes, David. I paid too long and too often. I can see the look in your eyes. I'm not a whore. I work bloody hard. I'm not the first woman to use her sex to get ahead, you know?"

She took another long pull on the cigarette. "He still doesn't think I deserve it, of course. The fact that my workload is higher than any other detective sergeant in the division counts for sweet bugger all. He just wants to keep me where he wants me."

Dave's thoughts turned to McCauley and that message, although he had no intention of coming clean about his indiscretion. He leaned back in his chair.

"You really are worried about this guy, aren't you? I mean he's obviously a copper. What the hell can he do to you?"

The moment the words came out, he thought back to his own run in with Detective Chief Superintendent McCauley. That man could do plenty. Anne gave a weak smile as if she'd just read Dave's mind. She stubbed out her cigarette.

"David, this guy is an evil bastard. He is a crazy man with no conscience. I don't want to put you in the position."

Dave took her hand. He was feeling things for Anne in these short days that he had never felt before. He couldn't tell her, of course. It was too soon.

"You don't know me that well, Anne. I'm not going to let anything or anyone come between us."

Now Anne smiled and, this time, the worry seemed to have left her face. She looked into the dark brown eyes of the man opposite her. It was true. She knew so little of him. After her recent experiences of men, she had seen David as a casual fling, someone to have a good time with and then part friends. She hadn't bargained on falling for him.

There was indeed more to him than met the eye. He was a very deep soul.

He was handsome, yet humble, so strong and powerful, but gentle and kind. At that moment, she truly believed that David Stewart would indeed do anything for her.

The pair sat in front of the roaring log fire in the tiny bar. Doris made hot toddies. Dave looked into the eyes of his lover. Nothing was said. Nothing was required. Their eyes said it all.

McCauley sat in his car. The radio played 'Hotel California' as he watched the BMW's headlights approach.

The meeting with Holmes had been arranged on wasteland that had once been a power station. The river Ribble that ran black and silent under the March night bordered it.

The only traffic that used it now consisted of lovers and dog walkers.

Tonight though, it was the scene of much seedier business. Holmes' car pulled alongside the Chief's, and both men alighted from their vehicles. Holmes was dressed casually, but sported a sheepskin coat and matching gloves against the night's chill. McCauley considered he looked like a second-hand car salesman.

Holmes removed a glove and spoke; "Well, Detective Chief Superintendent, how are you on this fine night?"

McCauley looked up at the clear sky and then down to Holmes. "Cut the crap and get on with it."

"OK. OK, no time for small talk." Holmes produced a thin file of photocopied documents. "I think you should take a look at these."

The Chief took the file but didn't examine the contents. Holmes looked hurt. "Aren't you even curious, John?"

The detective, much to Holmes' disgust, looked positively bored.

"I already know what's inside, Holmes. What I don't know is what you want."

Holmes sneered. This was going to be easier than he thought. McCauley wasn't such a tough guy after all. He was all bluster and no guts, just as he'd always thought.

"I want a letter, signed by you, stating that all charges against William Henry Bailey have been dropped due to insufficient evidence."

The Chief started to laugh.

Holmes went for the big sell. "Laugh all you like, John, but during my interviews with Bailey he was adamant that he was completely clean when arrested. I got suspicious when I first noticed that there was no hand-written statement from the arresting officer. A probationary constable, I believe? Then, certain information came into my possession in the form of crime property register entries.

The time the gloves were entered didn't tally with the time of arrest. Finally, I checked the record of Bailey's property entered by the charge office sergeant at the time of his arrest. Oh, the gloves appear on the record alright, but the handwriting is different to the rest of the sheet. Very sloppy work, McCauley, even for you."

Holmes was ready to close his sale. "I would lay odds, Superintendent, that should a barrister choose to give that young constable, what's his name, Stewart, a good grilling under oath or, better still, summons the charge office sergeant to court, that the rats would desert a rapidly sinking ship. That would put you and your precious little team of followers in the deep smelly liquid, wouldn't it?"

The Chief took a deep breath and stifled a yawn. His words were precise and measured; they came from a man still confident and assured.

"You're forgetting something, Holmes. The boy confessed all."

The lawyer was straight in there.

"Duress. I personally witnessed one of your officers bang my client's head on the table. I think that may be enough to convince a judge, don't you?"

McCauley turned and opened the door of his car. He lifted a brown envelope from the passenger seat and handed it to Holmes.

Holmes looked surprised. "What's this?"

The Chief remained silent, and simply gestured to Holmes to open the package.

Holmes pulled back the flap on the envelope and removed the contents. Holmes felt a sharp pain in his chest. He fell back against his car. His heart was about to burst, he was convinced of it. He felt himself start to sweat. His lips trembled.

"Oh my God!"

McCauley's laugh started as a low chuckle and grew to a thunderous roar. Holmes could still hear his laughter as the Chief Superintendent drove away.

Holmes had been supremely confident. He'd had McCauley exactly where he wanted him, but now, my God now, he was a gibbering wreck. He sobbed uncontrollably. The drive home was harrowing. He was unable to tear his eyes from the envelope on the passenger seat. Every few seconds he looked across and sobbed some more.

Within twenty minutes, Holmes sat in his living room, with the contents of the envelope on the coffee table.

He looked at each of the photographs in turn. Every shot was of him, committing sexual acts, with boys between the ages of eleven and thirteen.

Holmes' closest friend, Alan Clarke, had taken the pictures one summer in Brighton. The two men had gone on a spree of picking up rent boys and partying the night away.

Alan had never been in trouble with the police, so how had McCauley come by the pictures? Would Alan betray him? No, not ever, they went too far back. Alan craved the innocents as much as anyone. He was part of the circle.

When had he last checked the pictures were safe?

God, there were hundreds and not just of him and Alan either. Holmes poured himself a drink and threw it down his throat. In a sudden burst of temper, he pushed the photographs from the table and onto the floor.

Who else knew where the pictures were hidden? Some little shit had done for him eh? Well, if they thought that Raymond Holmes was going to lie down so easy, they were mistaken. Holmes slurred his words as the drink took hold, "This show isn't over yet, McCauley."

Billy looked at the house. Holmes was a rich bastard, all right, a BMW in the drive, a fancy house in a fancy street.

He still wore the suit that Ray had given him in the cell, although it was now crumpled and wet. He'd had a couple of hairy moments through the day. A Panda car had driven past him, and the pig inside took a long look as Billy was going for his stash. He always kept a few quid to one side for moments just like this. When he was running.

He'd had a haircut and now sported a skinhead. That would fool some of the coppers but not all of them. Right now, he needed somewhere to rest up, get his shit together and some more cash.

The problem for Billy was he couldn't think right now.

Every time he tried to think of a plan, Elsie May Townsend kept on interrupting him. Talking inside his head, wagging her finger like his old gran used to do, and telling him what a bad boy he was.

The little bitch that cut his hair kept on asking questions too.

"Where do you live? What do you do?"

Stupid.

Billy had considered fucking her, making her have it, but some old queen was snooping around in the back of the shop. Best not to. Billy had to go see his friend Ray. Ray always knew what to do.

Ray was pissed. He'd been plotting his revenge in the bottom of a brandy glass for two hours. So pissed in fact that he had picked up the photos and laid them out on the coffee table again, they began to arouse him. Ray's sap was rising as he remembered the little sluts from Brighton.

There was one in particular. What was his name? Carl? No, Cliff? Yes, that boy was sweet. Slim, young and willing, not too willing, mind. Ray liked a little resistance. Without realising, Ray had started to rub his crotch. Yes, it was time for a little self-indulgence. Then he remembered that the curtains were still open.

Ray nearly shit himself. Standing outside the bay window was Billy, and Billy didn't look too good.

In a flash Ray was sober. He ran to the door and almost dragged Billy into the house. He took a quick look outside to check for nosey neighbours, and closed the door.

Ray's voice was frantic, his normal work tone lost to his almost soprano camp. "Billy, what the fuck are you doing here?"

Billy was in a daze. His normally erect frame was hunched and tired.

Billy was distant, "You know what to do, Ray, you know what's best."

Ray's mind was now running at full pelt, he was scared, but at the same time excited. His mind was working again. *Say what you like about Ray Holmes, but he can think on his feet.*

"Yes, Billy, I always know what's best for you. We can work everything out. Me and you, Billy."

Ray knew he was on dangerous ground, but his sexual urges always did get the better of him. He started to take Billy's sodden jacket from his back. The shirt underneath was so wet Ray could see the youth's nipples. Ray felt another telltale twinge in his crotch.

"First though, you need to get warm, how about a nice hot bath? What do you say, Billy, eh?"

Billy looked past Ray. He was strangely vacant. It was a look Ray had never seen before and it disturbed him. Billy laughed as he spoke. It made him sound imbecilic.

"I know what you want. You want to play in the bath with me, don't you, Ray?"

"We could do that if you like, Billy."

Billy was a little old for Ray but their little meeting in the cell block had rejuvenated Ray's interest. Their 'arrangement' had begun years earlier when Billy had been placed in the care of the Local Authority.

Ray's friend Clarke ran the home. They both shared the same

tastes, and took great pleasure in showing the new boys the way to get on in their new environment.

No parent or co-worker had ever questioned the late night visits of a respected solicitor to the home. It had been, and still was, a very nice arrangement for Ray.

Ray stripped the young man and threw away the clothes. He made a mental note to get rid of them properly in the morning.

Billy lay back in the steaming bath, surrounded by fragrant bubbles. It felt nice. He felt safe and warm.

Else May Townsend had gone to sleep.

Ray walked into the bathroom with clean dry clothes. “Feel better, Billy?”

Billy dunked himself under the luxurious water. “Yes, Ray, thanks. I knew you would help me.” He gestured with his thumb in the general direction of the street. “I was getting a bit scared out there.”

Ray frowned. In all the time he had known him, he had never heard Billy admit that he was scared before. He was wary of the youth. Could he trust this boy? OK, he had known him for years, but the pictures had fallen into police hands somehow. After all, Billy had been under pressure in the nick. Had he sold him out for favours from McCauley? Maybe it was time for a test of character for the young lad.

“Does anyone know that you came here, Billy?”

Billy smiled at Ray. “Nope!”

“Good lad. Now get yourself dry and we can get comfortable.”

Ray went downstairs to the living room and had one last look at the photos on the table before putting them away. The negatives had been with the photographs. He had to find those negatives and any copies. Billy was just the man for the job.

Ray and Billy lay naked together on the sofa. A hardcore gay video played on the television. Billy was masturbating Ray furiously.

Ray stretched out his hand and rested it on Billy's. "Steady, boy, it's going to be a long night."

Outside in the avenue a car engine started and the vehicle slowly pulled away. The burly driver had seen enough for one night.

# CONSEQUENCES

Dave and Anne had spent the night exploring each other in the way that only new lovers do. After a massive breakfast, courtesy of the ever-jovial Doris, they took a walk to the lake. Spring was indeed on its way, and the Lake District pleased all the senses.

Dave spread a car blanket on the grass, and the couple sat. Anne pulled her knees up to her chest against the morning chill. The couple, who only days ago knew nothing of each other except a passing glance in a police station, were now firm friends and passionate lovers.

Dave leaned against Anne and put his arm around her shoulders. He viewed the lake and gorged on its beauty. "Would it be too much to ask to stay here forever?"

Anne picked up a stone and tossed it lazily into the calm water.

"My parents used to bring me here as a child," she said.

"They would drive through the night from London with me asleep in the car. We stayed in the same little guesthouse we're in. It was a very simple time in my life. Effortless and uncomplicated. Nothing to worry about."

She picked up another stone, throwing it further into the lake. "My father was dead against me joining the force. He thought it was no place for a woman."

Anne became suddenly morose. "Maybe he was right."

Dave held her a little tighter. She felt comforted as she listened to his deep voice in her ear. His hot breath warm on the nape of her neck.

"My father's politics are just left of Arthur Scargill. He didn't speak to me for weeks when I applied. He still hasn't told his mates at the Miners Welfare what I do. I have to pretend to be in the army when I go and visit."

Anne put her hand to her mouth to stifle a giggle. Dave shot her an icy glance.

"Sorry, David I wasn't making fun. It's just that we both seem to be in the same boat. My dad still tells his colleagues that I'm taking a break from my studies before going on to the bar."

Dave stood and walked the few feet to the water's edge. "Just recently," he began, "I've considered doing something else.

Anne looked puzzled, but Dave pressed on.

"You know when you were talking about this guy who wouldn't leave you alone?"

"Yes."

"And you said that you had paid the price for your promotion?"

"I did."

"Well, I think it could be some time before I pay for my mistake. Worse still, I think we both owe the same man."

Anne demeanour changed completely. She stood and walked briskly to Dave. She pulled at his arm so violently that he nearly fell in the lake.

"What the hell are you talking about?"

Dave looked her straight in the eye. "What I'm talking about is John McCauley."

Anne lowered her head. She felt shame well up inside her. OK, everyone makes mistakes, but this? How could you explain it? She had been callous. She felt dirty, like a common prostitute.

"So you knew?"

"Not at first, but it doesn't take a genius to work it out."

Again, Dave didn't mention his experience with the answer-phone. Anne let the information sink in and then her mind went into overdrive. She forgot her shame instantly.

"He's got you over a barrel with Bailey, hasn't he?"

It was Dave's turn to wonder how Anne had come by her information. He didn't have to wonder long.

There was an edge to Anne's voice.

"I was going over the file that morning when you came to the CID office. I couldn't understand why there was no hand-written witness statement from you. I checked on the crime property register and I noticed a discrepancy on the time the gloves were booked in. I was too knackered to think about it. Until now, that is."

Dave took hold of Anne's arms. "I had no choice, Anne."

"We all have a choice, David. It all depends on our morals."

Dave was immediately angry. "I don't think you have any room to talk about morals. John McCauley has played you along for a lot longer than me. If the truth be told, you have the financial backing to walk away."

Anne shrugged off Dave's grip. "Jesus, David! Is that all you think about? There's a lot more to life than money, you know."

"That's easy for a girl living on a Chief Superintendent's expense account to say. At least I'm not bending over for him."

Dave regretted the remark the second it was said. It was too late. Anne slapped Dave across the face with more force than he thought possible. He lost his balance and had to take a step backward to steady himself. Unfortunately, the ground behind the young man was soft, and he fell straight into the icy waters of Coniston Lake.

Anne screamed as Dave disappeared under the water, his heavy coat dragging him toward the bottom. The banks of Lake Coniston are sheer, and the water black.

Anne removed her own coat and jumped into the lake. It was impossible to see. She dived down once and then again. She was now in blind panic, thrashing around grasping at nothing but ice cold water. Her own limbs were numb with cold. She knew Dave wouldn't last much longer.

Then, in a fountain of spray, Dave breached the surface not ten feet away.

“David! Oh my God, David! I thought I’d lost you.”

The pair scrambled their way to the bank where Anne immediately threw her arms around the young man, briefly pulling the pair under the water once again.

“Fuck me, Anne,” Dave gasped.

“I’m so sorry, baby,” Anne was kissing him now, “so sorry. I love you. God, I love you.”

Dave couldn’t work out which was the biggest shock. Near death by drowning or Anne’s words. Using his considerable strength he lifted Anne from the icy lake. He recovered the blanket they had been sitting upon and wrapped it around Anne’s shivering shoulders.

He put his mouth to her ear. “You’re full of surprises, I’ll give you that.”

Anne looked toward him, covered in mud and slime, tears started. “It’s true, David. I know I should know better but…”

Dave put a finger to her lips. “Should we risk losing something special just because the calendar says it’s too soon to feel the way we feel?”

Anne kissed his fingers tenderly. She wiped her tears and looked to him. “We?”

Dave held her tight. “Yes, we.”

The lovers turned heads as they arrived back at the little guesthouse. Muddy, wet and shivering with cold, they shuffled inside, their shoes squelching with each step.

Having showered and warmed themselves by the open fire in their room, the pair sat in the small downstairs bar, discussing John McCauley.

A few other guests littered the bar area, but it was private enough for the business at hand. Dave took a sip of a wonderful malt whiskey.

"So, what can we do about this mess, Anne?"

Anne was scanning the local newspaper. She folded over a page and handed it to Dave. "I think you have another problem."

The article was headed *'Murder Suspect Flees Court'*, and a mug shot of William Henry Bailey stared back at Dave.

Dave studied the article for a few moments. His voice was calm and confident, "I don't think this is a problem, I think it buys us some time."

Anne raised a curious smile. Her lover was indeed a deep soul. "I'm all ears, Sherlock."

Dave became animated, "We need to get the Chief off our backs. Right?"

"Correct."

"Well, all we have to do is persuade him to go with the true evidence. The statement I signed hasn't been presented to the court yet, because Bailey did a runner. Until it is I haven't committed any offence...yes?"

Anne shook her head. "His solicitor will have a copy of the file."

Dave grimaced, thought for a moment and then countered, “Yes, but, what if we could offer the plea bargain to his brief that you originally put to McCauley?”

Anne sat up in her chair. She let her palms fall forward and hunched her shoulders.

“So, let me get this straight. We go tell the hard arse of the century that he has to plea bargain a case he already considers is in the bag. Then we happen to mention that his Detective Sergeant is in love with a probationary constable, who, incidentally, is so deep in his pocket already he eats lint for breakfast. What do you suggest we bargain with, David?”

Dave stared straight at Anne; there was fire in those eyes. “You know him better than me.”

“That’s not fair, David.”

He finished his malt and gestured the barman for a refill. “Nothing’s fair in this kind of game, Anne.”

Dave leaned back in the plush armchair. He took the new drink, waited for the barman to leave earshot, and spoke. It was so matter of fact Anne was open mouthed.

“When I was back in Barnsley, before I joined the job, I did some door work for a man who owned three nightclubs. He made John McCauley look like a choirboy.

Anyway, it seemed one of this guy’s business deals had gone wrong and he needed cash quickly. The next day I got a call to say there was some extra work for me. Was I interested?”

Dave sipped his drink. He oozed confidence. ”I’m on the bare bones of my arse, so I tell him yes. It's a little debt-collecting job. Nothing new, I'd done some before. The difference is the debtor is another mean son of a bitch. A guy called Tony Parkes."

Anne realised she was doing fish impressions, and closed her mouth.

"I thought you may have heard of him. Big prostitution man in the north, yeah?"

Anne nodded, intrigued with both the story and her man.

"Well, my employer had a deal with Parkes. His girls could use my boss's clubs and houses to do 'business', and Parkes paid him a monthly 'rent'. The trouble was that Parkes hadn't paid for some time and my employer wanted his cash."

Dave took another drink. "Now, you have to find a way to hurt a man like Parkes. It's no good going around to his house with a baseball bat. He'll just come back at you with a knife or a shotgun. You have to hurt him financially."
Anne listened, not completely sure she wanted to hear what came next.

"So the next night, my boss got all his doormen together and we toured our three clubs," Dave punctuated by finishing the second malt, "and kidnapped all Parkes' girls."

Anne was so shocked at Dave's candour she couldn't help herself. She let out a loud "fuck me", much to the consternation of the other bar customers.

Dave laughed. "Nice to see I'm in love with a lady."

Anne leaned forward and hissed, "I didn't realise I'd fallen for fuckin' Ronnie Kray either!"

Dave shrugged. "Anyway, the plan was a roaring success and Parkes paid up."

Anne held her head in her hands. "You don't want to kidnap McCauley, do you?"

Dave was excited and in control now.

"No, but the bastard will have a weakness and we have to find it; that's what I meant when I said you knew him best."

Anne flipped a beer mat between her fingers, deep in thought. "He keeps files," she began, "private files on all kinds of people. It's what keeps him safe. I've never seen them, but recently he would brag about them when he was pissed. He calls them his own personal Watergate. I reckon my blood analysis report and your witness statement are tucked in there, too."

It was Dave's turn to be intrigued. "Where does he keep them?"

Anne shrugged. "The house, I presume."

Ray Holmes lay in his bed. Billy had been having nightmares. Between the sex and the bad dreams, Ray hadn't had much sleep. He shook Billy awake.

"Come on, sleepy head."

Billy opened his eyes. He didn't know where he was.

"That you, Dad?"

Ray looked down at the sad young man. “No Billy. It’s me, Ray.”

Billy smiled, but his eyes remained flat and lifeless. “You all right, Ray?”

“I’m fine, Billy. Now, let’s get some breakfast, we need to talk about how we can get you out of this trouble.”

Billy was as compliant as a small child. “OK.”

Ray cooked breakfast for them both. He could hear Billy talking to someone in the next room and peered around the door to see. Billy was sitting on the sofa facing an empty chair. He spoke in sporadic bursts as if answering questions. He was very animated. He waved his arms and rubbed his head furiously. Ray didn’t like it one bit. If Billy wasn’t up to Ray’s little scheme, he had to go.

Ray stood, holding two plates of bacon and eggs.

“Who are you talking to, Billy?”

Billy spun around. “Ray. I’m glad you’re here. Tell her, will ya. Tell her to leave me alone.”

Rays voice was low, “Tell who, Billy?”

“Her!” Billy pointed furiously at the empty chair. “The old fart.”

Billy was pleading with all his features.

Ray was once again unnerved by Billy’s presence. The boy had lost it. Still if he could complete this one task he could be dealt with later. Ray had all the contacts for any kind of job.

Billy suddenly stood and took a plate from Ray’s hand. He sat, mumbled something about a television set, and started to devour the food.

Ray gingerly sat next to Billy and put his hand on the young man's arm. "OK now, Billy?"

Billy nodded, and with a mouthful of food said, "Can we watch another video, Ray?"

Ray Holmes' voice was quiet and even. Almost hypnotic, "You need to understand, Billy. I can't help you unless you help me first."

Billy was nodding but his attention was still drawn between Ray, the empty chair and the blank television screen.

"I need you to concentrate, Billy. You are the only one who can do this for me." Ray raised his voice slightly, "Billy!"

The young man jumped nervously, this was not the William Bailey who Ray knew so well. His own arrogance failed to see what he alone had done to the boy.

"I'm listening, Ray! For fuck's sake stop getting on my back."

Ray resumed his quiet tone, "OK, Billy, but we both need the same thing here. That copper, the one that slapped you in the cells, he's called John McCauley."

"He's a cunt," snapped Billy, now focused.

"He certainly is," Ray agreed. "Well I think, in fact I'm sure, that he fitted you up on this job, Billy."

Billy looked at Ray. His brow was furrowed, which gave him the appearance of a confused bulldog. Egg fell from his chin.

“I did kill her, though.”

“Are you sure, Billy?” Holmes was ready for this. “I don’t think you’re sure of anything at the moment; you‘re a bit confused. I don’t think that you’re too well.”

Billy became defensive, “I’m fine, me. I’m just tired, that’s all.”

Ray played his ace. “So why’d you get caught with the Marigolds?”

“I did fuckin’ not! I dumped them just before I was lifted.”

“Not according to the copper that nicked you. He says he found them in your pocket.”

Billy flew into a rage. He even frightened Ray a little. After all, he was a very strong individual. None too stable either.

“The lying fuckers! They’re tryin’ to stitch me, Ray.”

“They are too, Billy.” Ray took Billy’s hand and sat him back down. “And I know just what to do.”

The Chief stood at the bar with Clive Williams and Rod Casey. The Bull was quiet, except for a couple of off duty constables having a quick beer after the early turn.

Lucy had been serving the detectives for the last two hours. They had been putting it away as if Prohibition was around the corner. She stood within earshot. McCauley had been talking about the Bailey case and some problem with the solicitor who represented him. Lucy knew a little about it from Andy. She didn't catch all the speech, but McCauley had seemed very angry at one point. Williams had been trying to keep him quiet. The Chief didn't heed, and Casey looked very serious.

There was something about photographs and a special file. Williams had tried to quieten the conversation, without success.

McCauley had suddenly laughed at something that had happened in a night club called the Top Hat. He had slapped Casey on the back. Casey wasn't amused at all. Williams was most concerned and took the Chief away from the bar, but Lucy could still hear.

McCauley was brazen and half drunk, "Listen, Clive, I'm gonna sort this young prick Stewart." He took a drink, grimaced at its strength and continued; "He's after getting in Anne's knickers. She won't want anything to do with him when I'm through."

He gave a wink. "You know that, eh lads!"

He laughed and nudged Rod with his elbow. Rod had already heard enough but McCauley was unstoppable. "He's following her around like a lost fuckin' dog. Like some fuckin' love struck teenager. I'll tell you this," he poured more drink into his mouth, spilling some on his shirt, "If he don't leave her alone, I'll sort him good."

He tapped the side of his nose and shut one eye theatrically. "I'll be up her again before the week's out. See if the little bastard likes that, eh?"

The Chief returned to the bar to order. Lucy was no legal eagle, but she knew something wasn't right. She would have to speak to Andy about it.

Dave pushed the Cosworth down the motorway, his foot to the floor. Anne, who was a nervous passenger at the best of times, was slowly sliding down in her seat.

"Err, David?"

Dave was concentrating hard. "Yes, love?"

"Are you trying to kill us both before we go to jail for perjury, blackmail and burglary?"

Dave undertook a car, much to the disgust of its driver. "You know as well as I do, once Bailey is caught our plan isn't worth shit. It's now or never."

Anne rallied. "OK, but how do we know that McCauley will be out tonight?"

Dave remained silent. It took a moment and the realisation hit Anne like a train.

"Oh no! Not on your life, you can't possibly be serious."

"You don't have to sleep with the guy. Just take him for a drink for a couple of hours and, you know, make your excuses and leave."

"No."

Dave was indicating to pull off the motorway.

"You got a better idea, Sergeant?"

"No."

"Then we ring him as soon as we get to your place."

Anne reached across and touched Dave's cheek. "My God, I hope we know what we are letting ourselves in for."

It was no time for levity. Anne felt very uncomfortable with the plan. Fifteen minutes later, as Dave pulled into the driveway of her home; Anne felt the first steel fingers of fear. It was fine making these little plans whilst tucked away in the safety of the Lake District, but something about the sight of her own house brought her back to reality.

The pair walked into the living room. Dave immediately went to the telephone, lifted the receiver, and held it toward Anne.

"No time like the present," he nodded.

Anne was nervous and embarrassed. The last thing she wanted to do was speak to McCauley with Dave in the room. Her stomach was turning at the thought.

She checked her watch and dialed the Chief's direct line to his office.

"Speak," the voice was brisk and businesslike.

Anne did her best to sound cheerful, "Hi, John."

"One minute."

Anne was put on hold. She considered there was probably someone in the office. The telephone clicked in Anne's ear and he was back, his tone now different, "Anne, my dear, do you know I've been looking for you? Where in God's name have you been the last few days? You were very naughty the other night, left me high and dry."

Anne sat back on the sofa. Dave looked on, gesticulating with his hands for her to get on with it. She felt herself flush with embarrassment.

“I’m sorry, John, but an old girlfriend from university turned up unexpectedly,” she looked at Dave and bit her lip. Convinced her lies were obvious.

“And we went off on the rampage for a few days. You know how it is.”

Anne giggled nervously. McCauley seemed unimpressed; “Hmm.”

Anne quickly filled the silence, “Anyway, I’m ringing to see if you are doing anything special tonight?”

This news cheered him.

“Nothing as special as you, darlin’.”

Anne could virtually see the leer on his face, and shivered. She swallowed hard. “You fancy a beer somewhere, then?”

He chuckled down the line. “And the rest, Annie.”

Anne felt like she might falter, her confidence was on the wane, but she forced herself. “Steady on, boy. One thing at once, eh?”

The Chief was instantly businesslike once again. “I’ll pick you up at your place, eight o’clock.”

Before Anne could reply, the telephone went dead. She replaced the receiver and noticed her hands were shaking. She felt sick and looked towards Dave for support.

“I don’t know if I can do this, David.”

Dave sat next to her and held her tight. He felt the tell-tale signs of nerves, but he was also very determined. So much so that he now believed he could go through just about anything for Anne.

"You can, and you will, Anne. It's the only way."

She looked up into the face of her lover, tears starting to well in her eyes. "If he finds out," she wiped away a tear, "he's capable of killing us both."

Holmes had told Billy everything. He knew the truth now.

Those bastards down at Preston nick had tried to stitch him. They were in for a shock. Oh yes, you don't fuck with Billy Bailey. He had a good friend in Ray. Ray knew what to do. He always knew best.

Ray had given him some clothes too, smart clothes. Billy felt better than he had for a while.

The waking nightmares were still there. The old lady still bugged him, but when this was all over, maybe she would stay away.

Ray had taken Billy to a part of town he had never been before, with big houses, even bigger than Ray's house. Ray had shown him the one where the pig lived. Now it was up to him. He would do this for Ray, and Ray would look after Billy as he always had.

Billy knew about routine. It's what a burglar depended on. People do the same things every day. Go to work, walk the dog, shop, go to the pub.

This guy was a bit different, though. This guy didn't go to work at the same time every day. He was a pig. Pigs were different.

Ray wanted Billy to stay in the pub where he had been dropped off until it was time for the job. He'd told him exactly what he wanted, but Billy couldn't think in a pub. He always did his thinking in the old mill on the Callon, and that's where he was headed. Billy didn't even notice the car.

By the time Billy reached the broken mill gates, it was completely dark. Spring may have been on the way but for now, the winter nights refused to lose their grip.

At the rear of the mill, some of the boarding which covered a once glass window was loose. Billy always used the same way in. You see, burglars need routine one way or another.

The inside of the mill smelled musty. The only light came from the sodium street lamps on the main road, and that fell in narrow strips through the holed roof. The lack of light made any swift movement difficult.

Billy stepped through the layer of pigeon shit that almost covered the floor until he reached his spot. He liked this place. It was somewhere he could think, a haven where he could weigh everything up. Once he had his head together, a quick bus ride would have him close to the job. He always took the bus there and back on an out of town job. It was a rule.

Pigs don't pull buses, and there was nothing big to carry this time, just those dirty pictures that Ray wanted.

"When all this is over," Billy thought, "I'll be famous, be in the papers and everything."

The best thing was the pig would be in the nick for fitting him up, and everyone knows what happens to pigs in the nick.

Billy sat facing the gaping hole that once was a window. The breeze felt good on his face. Everything was quiet. He could see the rush hour traffic crawling slowly out of town; people, sitting in their cars, blissfully unaware of the seedy dealings of the world. They only knew what they read in the papers. They lived on nice, quiet estates. They had no fuckin' idea.

The first thing Billy felt was the coldness of the rubber glove, which gripped his forehead.

It was a very strong grip, and his head was snatched backwards with great force, his eyelids prised open by the movement. At first he thought to struggle, but Billy was suddenly aware of another cold object against his throat.

Then a voice whispered in his ear; a cold horrible voice, it came from the depths of hell.

"You're just one big let down, Billy."

The razor-sharp carpet knife sank into the soft flesh on the right side of Billy's neck. It severed the carotid artery, sending a crimson jet of hot blood several feet into the air. The knife travelled easily until it reached the thyroid cartilage, but then the assailant exerted further pressure.

There was a small popping sound as the cartilage gave way and then escaping air, as the windpipe was sliced. A split second later the job was complete. Billy's head hung backwards, stretching the hideous gaping hole in his throat like a second screaming mouth.

The assailant took a step back. He viewed the twitching body of the youth and took a plastic bin liner from the pocket of his bloodstained coveralls.

The man dropped the carpet knife inside and then calmly removed the coveralls, the paper shoe covers he wore on his feet and a pair of pink Marigold washing up gloves. A nice touch, he thought. He then placed the gruesome bundle into the bag and tied off the top.

He turned, straightened his tie, smoothed back his hair, and confidently walked away, swinging the bag as he went.

Anne's bedroom was warm, but she felt a chill deep inside her. She sat on her bed, a towel covering her after a shower. David had been gone for over two hours and she missed him already.

She kept going over the scenario of her date with McCauley in her head.

How on earth had she let David talk her into such a wild plan? She applied the barest of make-up and selected a pair of jeans to wear. It would be hard enough keeping John's hands off her without inflaming him further with revealing clothes.

She stood in front of the mirror and let the towel drop to the floor. She inspected her nakedness.

Yes, she had a great body. For once though, she wished she had not. She knew she had used her body, her looks and her wits, to get ahead. Never in a million years had she ever considered it would come back to haunt her like this. Anne pulled on a bra and pants, faded denims and a woollen sweater.

She scraped her hair back into a ponytail, stood back, and examined the results. It would have to do. Anne considered she looked as casual as she could get away with. Too little effort, and the Chief would smell a rat.

The telephone rang. Anne thought for a moment that the plan might be going to fail at the first hurdle until she heard Dave's voice.

"Hi, David, God, I thought you were him going to cancel."

"You wish."

"I certainly do, I'm shitting myself."

Dave was calm and collected. "Everything will be OK, Anne, just keep him busy until ten or so and leave the rest to me."

Anne wasn't happy at all. "You sure you know what you're doing, David?"

"Positive."

The tall man drove his car within all speed limits. Although it was unlikely that he would be stopped, he was taking no chances. The boss would be pleased with him.

He made his way toward the home of John McCauley. Everything was going just fine. Within a few hours, all these little problems would be sorted out. As usual, people came to him to sort out their mess. It would cost though. This was not cheap labour. The Chief Superintendent would be really pissed. It wasn't that the tall man had anything personal against McCauley. The guy had got careless. He'd upset the wrong people, and this was the result.

The bag of clothing, stained with the lifeblood of William Henry Bailey, was in the boot of his car ready for disposal. Once the next little matter was out of the way, the boss would be eating out of his hand and the tall man would be considerably better off. Everything was going to be just fine. Yes, just fine.

McCauley had taken off his suit, showered and changed into a pair of casual but expensive trousers, a cotton shirt, and his new Lancashire Cricket Club tie.

He could never bring himself to go out without a tie. He had worn a tie every day of his life since being a constable on the beat. His ex wife had always tried to get him to be more fashionable.

She would come back from a shopping trip with all kinds of trendy clothes, stuff that he could never wear. Shit, he even wore a tie in the house.

Diane, his ex, had left two years ago December gone. It had been just a week before Christmas. The silly, weak little woman had gone without a word, or for that matter, any of the Chief's cash.

But she had left.

He studied a photograph of Diane that still adorned the bedside cabinet. A pretty young woman looked back at him. Where did she go?

How could someone change so much over time? He hadn't

changed. He had still behaved the same way those eighteen years. How could she leave John McCauley?

He checked his watch. It was time to leave; time to collect his date. He picked up the car keys from the antique dresser that matched all the furniture in the bedroom, and walked down the stairs to the front door.

A creature of habit, he left the landing light on to deter the casual unwelcome visitor. He walked to the cubbyhole under the stairs and checked that his safe was locked. No bastard would get in there. Of that, he was certain.

Once outside he opened the door of his Rover car, the paintwork as clean and presentable as his home and indeed, John McCauley himself.

As he pulled slowly from the Avenue, he thought he noticed a car that seemed a little out of place. He put the thought from his mind, tuned the car stereo to his favourite station, and whistled along to Frank Sinatra doing it his way.

As McCauley drove, Anne paced the floor of the lounge. She had finished a second glass of brandy, considered a third and then decided a clear head was needed.

Her watch said eight fifteen p.m. He was late. Then she heard the car and saw the headlights in the driveway. Her stomach did a quick flip as she caught sight of McCauley behind the wheel. She collected her coat and bag, walked to the door, took a deep breath and stepped out into the night air.

The second she sat in the passenger seat of the car, the Chief leaned over to kiss her.

She offered her cheek but he roughly grabbed the back of her head with his left hand, and their mouths met. With his right, he pawed like an adolescent at her left breast.

Anne immediately pushed his hand away.

"John! Take it easy. I do have neighbours, you know."

He looked quizzically at Anne. "Never bothered you before sweetheart."

Anne remembered the script, but also knew McCauley liked a challenge. "I'm not some tart from the Cherry Tree Club, John. Keep this up and I can just as easy go back inside. Women can change their mind, you know."

Despite being a hard bastard, McCauley was still a sucker for a beautiful woman. Sometimes a man's brain is overridden by his groin. This was one of those times.

It had been two months since he and Anne had slept together, one excuse after another. She'd come around, though. He always knew she would. She knew which side her bread was buttered.

"OK, sweetheart, have it your way. Where are we going?"

Anne put on her best smile. "I thought a nice little pub in the country."

The Chief eyed the woman to his left, like a fox stalking its prey. Her dark hair was pulled away from her face. That perfect body, hidden by a thick wool sweater.

“OK,” he thought, “I’ll play your little game for now. It will soon be my turn, mark my words.”

He reversed the car from the driveway and pushed in a cassette. Some Radio Two-type smooch stuff. Anne was completely unimpressed. She thought of David. She could think of little else. She had to snap out of her muse. If she did this right, stuck to the plan, everything would be OK.

Dave packed his bag. Inside were the various tools he would need for the job; items he had acquired over the years prior to his much less dangerous role as a police officer.

Why he still kept them, he was unsure. He could only presume it was his Yorkshire upbringing. His father would always say, “Never throw owt away.”

He had a very useful set of kit. An array of keys and homemade implements that he had used in the past to recover cars, electrical equipment and people. He’d been required to make ‘collections’ from all kinds of weird and wonderful places during his employ in the shady clubland of South Yorkshire. Back then he had been the youngest of the staff. Quite often the debtors would underestimate him because of his youth. They quickly found out that to do so was a big mistake.

Dave dressed in neutral colours. The bag that contained the tools was an old brown briefcase. To the casual observer, he’d be a civil servant walking home late from his office. Nothing looked out of place. Even his gloves were the type worn on a cold evening by the average bloke.

One last check in the mirror, and Dave left the house.

He climbed into his Mini car, his large frame squeezed into the driver's seat. His plan was committed to memory. Nothing was to be written down, no addresses, times or dates. If everything went to rat shit, the less evidence he had on his person the better. If the worst was to happen, his briefcase would be dumped and he would be clean.

He drove the Mini cautiously. The old car was incapable of any great speed, but the last thing he needed was attention before he reached the plot. Some five minutes walk from McCauley's house was the pub where, unknown to Dave, Billy Bailey had been dropped by Raymond Holmes. The Anchor was situated in the heart of the suburban village of Hutton. It was a favourite place for senior policeman to reside, as the Lancashire Police headquarters was there.

The Anchor was busy on certain nights through the week, and attracted police officers who were on training courses at HQ. Dave parked the Mini in a space on the car park, took the briefcase from the back seat and locked his car.

He entered the pub by the front door and walked directly to the bar. He ordered a scotch and sat in a quiet corner of the room surveying the customers.

Dave stood out like a sore thumb. He was easily the youngest customer by ten years. At least five of the regulars surveyed him with suspicion. This was just as he had hoped. Dave was far enough away from the target house so people would not connect him to the upcoming job, and if a punter or a police officer recognised him, even better. They would be ready to confirm his whereabouts if he needed an alibi.

The next part was tricky. He had to leave the bar and return, without any of the patrons noticing his absence.

He had allowed himself just fifteen minutes to get to the house, gain entry, find the files and get back to his seat in the bar.

By the time he was halfway down his second drink, the bar was busy enough for him to make his exit.

Dave walked to the Gents, leaving his jacket on his seat and his scotch on the table.

Once inside the toilet, he looked for the window that led to the outside. If you are planning to do anything illegal, there are always some points that are risky and this was one of them. The sight of Dave's arse sticking out of the toilet window would be the beginning of the end.

The window was less than three feet square and sat about six feet from the ground. Dave tried the catch. It was stuck firm with several coats of paint.

He was about to give the offending article a second try when a customer joined him in the toilet.

Dave walked to the washbasin and turned on the tap. The first signs of nerves came over him. The man took an age to piss, but thankfully didn't stay to wash his hands. Once again, Dave took a firm grip of the window catch and applied pressure. There was a cracking sound, and the catch was free. The window, though, still remained firmly in place.

Dave cursed under his breath. He had done a drive past of the pub earlier that evening, which had confirmed the windows presence, but hadn't planned for this.

Despite his height, Dave couldn't get enough leverage on the frame to move it. He looked around for something to stand on. He felt a bead of sweat trickle down his back. The clock was ticking.

He noticed a metal waste bin in the corner of the room. He emptied its contents into the toilet basin, turned it upside down, and gingerly stood on it to see if it would take his weight. If someone came in now, the shit would hit the fan.

Balancing himself on the bin, Dave placed the balls of his thumbs on the window frame. He gave an almighty push and the window was open. Several pieces of paint had fallen from the frame. Dave scooped them up in his hand and threw them down the toilet with the other rubbish. He flushed the toilet and righted the waste bin in its original position.

His heart was beating fast and he was sweating now. He threw his briefcase through the opening.

Grabbing the frame with both hands, he pulled himself upward.

Dave wasn't the most graceful of men. He managed to get his right shoulder and head through the window, and then wiggle half his frame through.

He found himself dangling headfirst some three feet from the ground. There was no time to worry about the odd scratch. Dave let himself fall. He landed with a thump on the tarmac of the pub car park.

Dave stood and checked the area for spectators. There were

none.

Next he pushed the window back into place, leaving enough of the frame visible to re-open it again later. He collected his case, adjusted his clothing and strode purposefully toward the home of John McCauley.

In a quaint country pub, some five miles away in the village of Croston, the Chief was drinking heavily.

He had consumed at least three drinks to each one of Anne's, and was leaning over the table which separated them. He was in no mood to appreciate the brasses and antique furnishings that adorned the bar.

His speech was slurred, and Anne figured he'd obviously just topped up from dinner. Anne knew all abut the infamous liquid lunches with his good buddies Williams and Casey. She hated the macho bravado of those little gatherings.

"So, darlin', tell me. Where have you really been this past few days?"

Anne's stomach gave a lurch, but she stayed as calm as possible. She smiled, but played nervously with a coaster. "I told you, John, a friend came over and we...."

"Don't give me shit, babe. It's me you're talkin' to, not some young sprog. You can't kid me. You've got yourself another boyfriend, haven't you?"

Customers in the quiet bar were starting to notice McCauley's raised voice.

Anne again tried to calm things. "There's no one else, John. Christ I haven't time to see anyone at the moment, I'm swamped with work."

He stared into Anne's eyes, disbelief all over his face. How many times had he been lied to the last twenty odd years? He took a gulp of his drink and sneered. He stood and motioned to Anne.

"Let's get the fuck out of here."

His sudden movement and demanding tone took Anne by surprise. She stammered, "Err, where do you want to go next then, John?"

He took hold of Anne's hand and squeezed so hard it hurt. "My place, my little lying sweetheart, my place."

Anne used all her strength to pull away her hand. "No, John! I wanted us to have a nice quite drink and you are behaving like a complete arse!"

The Chief was in no mood to be reasonable. "What's the matter? Not up for a real man anymore? Got ourselves a toy boy, have we?"

The people around the bar had started to notice the argument, McCauley now inches from Anne's face.

"Listen to me," he stage-whispered. "Me and you are going to my place, or you," he pointed at her face, "will pay dear for it. Understand, lady?"

Anne was scared, but it wasn't time to show fear. Not to a man like him. That would be a big mistake. The spirit she had shown since childhood gushed from her like a torrent. OK, so she'd been a fool, but no more. She stared straight at him and hissed. "So if you don't get to fuck me, you want to bust me. Is that it, John?"

McCauley hardly noticed the challenge. The drink had defeated his logic. He swayed on his feet.

"I have information," he bragged much too loudly, "on you, on your new friend and on every other bastard that's against me these days."

Anne, now past the point of caring, took on her most patronizing tone, "Oh dear, are the big nasty boys all ganging up on you John? You're a drunken has-been. No one cares anymore, especially me. I don't want you in my life. You can't control me. I'll resign first. You can't even get the better of a two year probationer."

The Chief looked like he had been slapped. Suddenly the picture of sobriety, he turned pale with anger.

Anne wished she had kept her mouth firmly shut.

"Listen to me, girlie. You're just another slapper trying to do a man's job." He reached into his pocket and pulled out his car keys. "You'll be back with mummy and daddy by the end of the week. And your new boyfriend will be bouncing drunks from boozers for a living even sooner."

The Chief turned to the engrossed crowd in the bar, their faces a mixture of shock, disgust and embarrassed amusement. He pointed to Anne. "She's a good fuck, but too expensive for my taste."

He staggered to the door of the pub and almost tripped as he opened it. Seconds later, he was behind the wheel of his car and on the road to town.

It was a cold night, even for the time of year. Dave could feel the tips of his fingers tingle inside his gloved hands, as he walked the five hundred yards or so to the Chief's house. The telltale signs of one of the final frosts of the year were forming on the tarmac path.

The property stood alone, surrounded by mature trees and a high stone wall. Despite this, Dave could still see a light burning inside the hallway. In his stomach the earlier Scotch turned to bile in his throat. Had Anne not been able to keep him away?

Could it be McCauley had another visitor that they hadn't planned on? Dave's nerves jangled, and once again he felt the sweat drip cold in the small of his back.

This was not the first time he had 'collected' from a house. The difference was, of course, that previously he had nothing to lose. Now he had everything.

He knew there was only one course of action he could take. Take a deep breath, go and knock on the door, and see what happened.

Dave strode up the driveway holding the briefcase, looking like a salesman about to visit a customer. He scanned the frontage as he walked. His mind whirred, taking in every detail. No alarm boxes. Plastic frames, double-glazed and beaded externally. A clean way in if needed.

He stepped into the arched, open porch. The floor was a black and white tiled mosaic of the Lancashire crest. He had to hand it to the detective, he was patriotic to the last.

Checking out the front door, it looked brand new. Both Yale and mortise type locks adorned it.

Not impossible to defeat, but it would be time-consuming and time was of the essence.

Before ringing the bell he did what all good burglars do. He listened. Was the television or hi-fi on? Was there a dog in the house? Could you hear a washing machine?

There was silence.

Dave pressed the doorbell. To him, it had a chime like Big Ben. He stood perfectly still, trying to look as casual as possible and waited for the worst. If McCauley himself answered the door, he was in deep shit.

Nothing.

After a full minute of listening to his heartbeat thunder in his ears, it was time to move to the back of the house. People are notorious for fixing up their front doors and leaving the back until last, just because the neighbours don't see it.

This was no exception. The back door was probably as old as the property. It was in need of paint and was secured only by a single Yale lock.

Dave opened his briefcase and selected a bunch of skeleton keys. The idea was to cause as little damage as possible. Fewer traumas, fewer clues were the order of the day. Dave pushed the delicate instruments into the lock, and he could feel the notches of the tumbler moving under his touch.

His heart raced, but his hands were steady. Twenty more seconds of patience and the lock turned. He pushed the door slowly with a gloved hand, and it creaked open like a bad horror movie.

Dave waited until his breathing returned to normal and he was sure he hadn't caught any unwelcome attention from neighbours. It was a case of, so far so good. He stepped cautiously inside.

He found himself in the humid warmth of a laundry room. A stone floor, with a single square of frayed carpet in the centre, greeted him.

The first internal door was closed. Dave tried the handle. McCauley was not the type to lock his rooms separately, and the handle turned. Dave was now in the kitchen. It was a newly modernised room with pine cabinets. A large well-stocked wine rack had pride of place. The smell of disinfectant overpowered any residual cooking smells.

Dave now clicked on his torch and started his search.

People do hide things in the same places. Always look under beds, in the fridge, under carpets and under stairs.

Dave was convinced that what he was looking for would not be easy to get at. If the content of these files was able to hurt people, important people, maybe even jail them and, after all, that's what it meant to Dave, then they would be safely stowed.

Once in the hallway, he switched off the torch and immediately looked under the stairwell.

There it was. This guy was careful, but not careful enough. Sitting there was a safe that was probably made around the 1930's. This had to be what Dave was looking for.

In the movies, thieves blow up safes or use stethoscopes to pick the combination. In reality most thieves just steal the safe, take it somewhere quiet and open it in any way they can. It's normally a case of brute force and ignorance.

This baby was too big to be moved by four men, let alone one. It sported a large keyhole and a handle to turn the mechanism. Dave knew exactly what to do.

Searching his briefcase again, he selected a metal bar, similar in looks to a very long toothbrush.

At the business end, a slot had been cut into the metal and in the slot had been welded a section of wires from a wire brush. At the other end was a 'T' bar.

First Dave had to trim the wires to the length of the key slot. He did this using cutting pliers.

He then pushed the implement into the keyhole, removed a large pair of mole-grips from the case and clamped them onto the 'T'.

A standard mortise key works because the slots cut into the end of the key move the mobile splines in the lock. The gaps in the key simply sweep past the immobile parts, allowing the key to turn.

David's tool worked on the principal that the strong wires of the tool would move the mobile part of the lock whilst the immobile part would simply bend the rest of the wires out of the way. The process required some strength, as once the wire starts to bend the tool becomes very difficult to turn.

Dave checked his watch. He had been in the house for only five minutes or so. He was back on schedule.

He put his shoulder into turning the implement in the lock and as it tightened, the sound of metal on metal jangled Dave's teeth and his nerves. With a supreme effort, sweat pouring from him, Dave felt a telltale click. The heat in the confined space of the under-stairs cupboard was increasing by the minute. He held a small Maglight in his mouth. He turned the handle on the safe.

Bingo! It opened.

Inside, he found a neat stack of brown folders each containing differing amounts of documents on a shelf. Each of the folders bore a name. All were in alphabetical order. He flicked through the files until he came to 'Stewart D.'

"The sly bastard," he mumbled.

He lifted a few more files and came upon 'Wallace A'.

Dave was tempted to read there and then, but time was pressing now. He collected all the files and placed them in his case. He had no choice but to leave the tool in the keyhole, as it was now well and truly stuck.

No matter, how could McCauley report the theft of files that he himself should not be in possession of?

Dave eased himself out of the cupboard and into the hallway. He felt suddenly vulnerable with the light still on, but it was better than switching it off.

Some people are so nosey.

Within thirty seconds, Dave was back on the pavement outside the house. The back door was secured again. Only when the cupboard under the stairs was opened would the theft be discovered. Dave calmed himself and actually managed a smile as he walked back towards the pub.

What Dave failed to notice was the large saloon car, with its single male occupant, draw up at McCauley's house just seconds later.

Several miles away, Anne was beside herself.

The initial shock of her date walking out, and the embarrassment she felt under the gaze of the pub regulars, had now worn off. She needed a taxi, and quick.

She rummaged through her purse for change, found she had none and was forced back to the bar for assistance. After an even more embarrassing conversation with the landlord, who felt the need to advise her on her love life, she finally made it to the payphone with a handful of ten pence pieces. Anne quickly discovered that she was indeed out in the sticks. The taxi would be thirty minutes. Too late, McCauley would beat her to it.

The tall man watched the Chief detective's house. McCauley was an unpredictable bastard, so he wanted to make sure he would be out of the way. His evening had been a busy one so far. Sitting in the pub, watching that sorry little shit Bailey. His task was a simple one, wait for Bailey to steal the files, and then kill him. He'd been easy to follow.

Easy to kill.

The kid had bottled it and run home without the goods, so he had killed him anyway. He'd enjoyed it.

Why would anyone trust some toe-rag from Callon with an important job like that? You needed a professional, and he was just that.

The trouble was, the tall man's mind had wandered from the task in hand and as a result, he'd failed to notice Dave slip into the night wearing his smile.

He left his car and walked up the driveway to the house. He made his way calmly to the back door, adorned in a clean set of coveralls, raised one powerful leg, and kicked it open. There was no need for finesse in his line of work.

He stepped inside and began his search. He started upstairs. It was purposely neither tidy, nor professional. The man functioned on pure arrogant violence. He had never been caught. He never would. He pulled out drawers, emptied cupboards and left the contents strewn about the place. He knew what he was looking for, but where to look? Finally, sweating and breathing heavily, he found the under-stair cupboard. He opened the cupboard door and saw the safe, rifled.

The man let out an involuntary cry of anguish, which he then muffled with his own rubber-gloved hand.

This was not part of the plan.

His mind raced. He couldn't think straight. The vision of the jerking body of William Henry Bailey flashed before his eyes. Had the kid somehow beat him to the punch? No, impossible. He'd tailed him constantly.

He took in large gulps of air in an attempt to calm himself and clear his head. He had no doubt that many people would love to get their hands on the contents of the safe, but how many knew of the papers anyway?

Slowly but surely, his mind started to function. He viewed the tool that had been used to open the safe.

He nodded. This was a pro job all right and there was no sign of a forced entry. So, who would have a key?

McCauley's bit of stuff would have one, he'd bet his life, and she would know a face that could pull a job like this. She could be reading the stuff right this minute. Shit, with the cash that little lot was worth, she could be planning her early retirement.

The man sat in his car, his breathing now near normal. He knew that there would be many people with a lot to lose if the files were made public. Some were powerful people. Maybe his boss was not the only one to get wind of McCauley's recent use of the files. Maybe they'd got wind too. Maybe McCauley had stood on other well-shod toes. He had to sort this and it had to be now. He'd start with the girlfriend though. He had a feeling about her...

Less than half a mile away, Dave opened the door of his Mini car. He threw his briefcase onto the back seat and re-locked the vehicle.

A quick scan of the car park revealed nothing. There was no one around. It was time to make his entrance back into the bar. The customers would never even suspect he'd left.

This time the toilet window opened with ease. Dave just had to take a chance on the toilets being empty. He took a deep breath and hoisted himself through the opening. Again, his awkwardness did him no favours. He slithered into the men's room and fell heavily onto the offensively wet floor. As he picked himself up, inspecting his damp hands, the entrance door opened and an elderly man entered.

"You need to watch this floor, lad," said the old-timer. "You could break yer neck when it's wet like this."

Dave smiled meekly. "Thanks for the advice."

The old man walked to the urinal and began to pee. "Ahh! One of life's great pleasures, eh, son?"

He didn't get a reply, Dave was back in his seat sipping his scotch, feeling very pleased with himself. He nodded to two men at the bar. If he needed an alibi, he had one.

McCauley had driven like a madman. He was raging. What a tart. Dragging him out to that poxy little pub and trying to pull the wool over his eyes like that.

Miraculously, instead of going home, he had called into The Bull for another drink. He sat at the bar and brooded. He was going to make the bitch pay.

Did she really think she could get one over on the Chief? These women in the job were becoming too big for their boots. She was his, to do with what he liked and he would prove it.

He guzzled another scotch. He was calming down and started to rationalise what he 'knew.' Of course, she was playing a game with him. After all, she had contacted him to go out. She wanted it really, wanted him. He had played it all wrong. Well, if it was a game she desired, he would oblige.

He knocked back the remainder of his drink and waved his empty glass in the direction of Lucy. She took it disdainfully and filled it with a large Grouse. She had no liking for John McCauley.

He leered drunkenly in her direction and considered the prospect of asking her back to his place. She had big tits.

No, he had some unfinished business with Anne Wallace.

She may have a crush on this boy Stewart at the moment, but he could take care of him. What she needed was a real man.

He smiled to himself. He was just the man for the job.

Anne directed the taxi driver toward her house. Typical, she got the slowest driver in the world. She had shouted at him to hurry, even produced her warrant card, a thing she hated to do. It had merely resulted in the awkward bastard moaning about how the police were out to get all taxi drivers. *"It's a different story when they want something, etc. etc."*

Anne was in a mess. Tears pricked her eyes. This was all a massive mistake. How had she let herself get talked into such a hair-brained scheme? She ignored the driver's gripes. Her nerves were shot. Every possible scenario was flying through her mind. David could already be in jail.

David should meet her at her house after she had got rid of McCauley. Anne could only hope that David had got the job done prior to the Chief's early exit from the bar.

What if he had been caught? She could only wait and see. The waiting was the hard part. What on earth would McCauley do if he found out? Anne was nauseous at the prospect.

The taxi finally pulled up outside her home. She paid the still lecturing driver and opened her front door. The place was in darkness and there was no sign of David. At least the local nick weren't standing there with the handcuffs.

Anne reached for the light switch in the lounge. Once inside the plush room, Anne dropped her coat and bag onto the couch and walked to the kitchen. The strip light was bright and hurt her eyes. All the pristine work surfaces were white and reflected the light. She marveled briefly at her kitchen's cleanliness, and then realised that she hadn't cooked in her own kitchen for weeks. *That's being a copper for you*. She felt like a lodger in her own home.

Anne took a colourful mug from the kitchen cupboard. It had an amusing cartoon on it and a risqué joke about men and coffee. It made her smile momentarily as she remembered the day she bought it. Happier, simpler, times.

She switched on the kettle and prepared the drink. As she dropped the spoon in the mug, Anne felt a cool draught. The sort that makes you shiver as if you've left a window ajar.

The kitchen light went out.

A hand grabbed her hair, tearing some out at the roots. She was falling, off balance and shocked. The mug in her hand fell to the floor and smashed on the tiles. She let out a scream of pain and fear. She attempted to break her fall but was too disorientated.

The assailant did not speak. She was unable to see his face as she was physically dragged along the kitchen floor by the hair. She smelled him. Sweat and cigarette smoke.

As she was pulled into the lounge, she automatically held onto her attacker's hand to relieve the pressure on her hair. She felt the hand and realised it was encased in rubber. Anne's adrenaline had stopped the thought process, but now her common sense took over. It was as if her brain had suddenly started into gear. She began to struggle and cry out. The man ignored her.

There was a sound of breaking glass as her attacker kicked out at the lone lamp in the lounge, plunging the remainder of the house into darkness. Anne could hear the man breathing hard over her own screams as he dragged her through the house. Was he going to rape her? It had always been Anne's greatest fear. She bucked her body in an attempt to get a look at the man.

Her attacker realised her ploy, grew tired of the constant cries, and slammed a punch into her face with his free hand. The impact was so severe it pushed Anne's bottom teeth straight through her lip. Anne felt the sharp pain and her head swam on the verge on consciousness. She ran her tongue along the damaged area and, to her horror, found a second unnatural opening.

Her mouth filled with hot coppery tasting liquid, which she spat out onto her sweater, and immediately resumed her screams. She would be no pushover. She twisted her body using all her strength now, determined to be free from his grip. She ignored the tremendous pain of her scalp and mouth. She tried to grab at the man. It was a vain attempt. He had no conscience. He simply struck her twice more in the face, the first punch breaking her nose, and the second knocking her cold.

The man turned over the limp body of Anne Wallace. He ripped the telephone cord from the wall and tied her wrists behind her back. He then picked up her dead weight with ease and threw her onto the couch.

The only light in the room came from the open curtains. The man took a cursory look outside. No dramas.

He viewed the woman on the couch. Her face, no longer the picture of beauty it had been seconds earlier. Her body, though, was a different matter. He stared, transfixed for a full minute. It seemed forever. He licked his dry lips. His eyes darted over the shapely figure, bound beneath his gaze.

The man lifted Anne's sweater over her breasts, pushed his index and forefinger between her cleavage and lifted her bra. Her breasts released, he pulled off a Marigold glove and cupped her nakedness in his hand.

His breathing grew faster and he could feel his penis swelling in his trousers. He squeezed the breast harder and pulled on the nipple. Oh yes, he would love to fuck this one. He ran his hand down Anne's belly, stopping briefly at her navel. He pushed his hand beneath the waistband of her jeans and groped inside her panties beneath.

The man suddenly drew away, unzipped his fly and pulled out his erection. His penis immediately pulsed, and a jet of semen splashed onto the naked torso of the unconscious woman.

He let out an ecstatic moan, and he sank to his knees as he pumped the remains of his ejaculation onto Anne's body. The man slowly zipped himself. The instance of gratification was over. The woman was no longer of interest. He replaced the rubber glove. He hadn't had the time to finish searching the house yet. There was a good chance she had the files.

The job at McCauley's was done with a key. Someone knew where to look too. She had been having an affair with the detective.

There was plenty of evidence of that. Even so, the documents still eluded him.

He heard tyres on gravel, and peered suspiciously from the window. The last thing that he needed now was a visitor. He looked down at the pitiful figure on the couch. Her breathing, laboured and rasping through her damaged nose and mouth, still unaware of the sexual abuse she had endured.

The man quickly pulled her clothing to its original position. He felt a sudden twinge of guilt. It was short-lived.

All his feelings were paralysed the moment he heard the noise at the front door.

"Anne! Anne!" McCauley made several attempts to get the key to turn in the lock. Eventually he succeeded. He was so drunk he nearly fell into the hallway.

"Anne, baby, are you home?" he slurred. He got no reply as he fumbled for the hallway light. His hand brushed the wall in vain. It was there somewhere, he knew it.

Finally he found it and the passageway was bathed in a welcome glow. "Uuh, that's better," he murmured, almost to himself. He looked at the keys in his hand, raised his eyebrows in a surprised expression and stuffed them into his pocket. Then he seemed to recall why he was there in the first place.

"Anne!" A cough. "Anne!"

The Chief pushed open the door to the lounge and peered into the darkness. He was sure that he could see Anne lying on the couch. His voice softened, and an unseen smile came to his face.

"Anne?"

He was struck with such venom he fell back into the hallway, hit the wall and slid to the floor. He didn't know who or what had hit him, but he knew he was in trouble. Had he been younger, or a little less drunk, he may have had a chance.

The man came at him with appalling force. McCauley was so slow he had the time to pick his spot. The figure slammed his right foot into the Chief's throat, cutting off his air.

McCauley knew he had to get away. The law of the street hadn't left him. He'd been in more pub brawls than he could remember, drunk too. He brought his own fist upward with all the strength he could muster, and connected with the back of the man's knee. As the knee bent he shifted his body weight, and scrambled to his right.

For a brief moment, he was free. It would be his only chance. The man had fallen to his hands and knees but was already getting to his feet.

Blood was pouring from a cut over the Chief's eye where the first punch had connected. He wiped it with his sleeve and launched himself at his attacker. This bloke was a big fucker, but he had never been frightened of anyone in his life. You wanted to play rough? John McCauley was your man.

The man turned, and there was a flash of steel. The shock stopped McCauley in his tracks. It was his final error.

The man plunged the carving knife into the Chief's body. It was the largest and sharpest he could find in the kitchen.

He brought the knife downward in an arc, the whole weight of his huge upper body behind it. In his frenzy, this first lunge was wayward and sank into his victim's chest just above the collarbone.

McCauley felt tremendous pain, but grabbed the blade with his hand. It was an automatic but fruitless reaction.

The man pulled the weapon backwards, cutting McCauley's fingers to the bone and rendering his hand useless.

The man's second thrust was lower and more effective. The knife entered the chest cavity between the third and fourth ribs, puncturing his lung, deflating it instantly.

Each time the man withdrew the weapon, blood flew from the tip, splattering the walls of the hallway. McCauley didn't even have enough breath to scream as the knife entered his stomach.

The man was now in total control, and he knew it. He had time to set himself. He forced the knife further into his adversary.

Bending his knees, he slammed the knife upward. It entered under McCauley's breastbone and tore into his heart.

The Chief seemed to be suspended in a grotesque pose of surprise and agony. His lips began to mouth a single word, blood now filling his mouth with each failing heartbeat.

The man withdrew the knife and his victim sank to the floor, first to his knees, his damaged hand flailing about, grabbing his attacker's clothing and spreading his own lifeblood down the man's overalls.

The assailant took a step backward and let McCauley fall on his face. The last air was escaping from his body, blood bubbles were forming at his nose and mouth. A pool of thick crimson seeped into the luxury carpet beneath him.

The man stared at his handiwork for the second time that night. He placed a paper-covered toe under the head of his victim and used it to look into the face.

He smiled; his voice could have been the devil's own.

"You drunken old fool."

*Now*, he thought, *the papers*.

As he walked back into the lounge to continue his search, Anne was moaning quietly where he had left her. She was still unconscious and unaware of the drama.

"No point in loose ends."

He breezed toward the sofa, casually lifted her head with her hair, and cut Anne Wallace's throat.

# STICHED

Dave drove steadily to Anne's house. He was desperate to see the contents of the files, and even more desperate to see the look on McCauley's face when he stuck it to him. Anyway, the job was done now. The hard part over, he wanted to put up his feet and make love to the woman of his dreams. The more he thought about her, the lovelier she seemed.

He'd had enough of worrying about the Chief for one night.

As Dave pulled up at the house, he saw a large saloon car in the drive. The number was familiar. Very familiar. It was John McCauley's.

He looked to the house. The only light came from the bedroom. His heart sank, and he felt sick to his stomach. He couldn't believe it. How could she? It was just a drink, a way of getting McCauley away from the house. Was she so weak? Was he such a fool?

He stopped the car engine and stared at the imposing home. He had fallen in love too soon with a woman he knew nothing of. Starting the motor again, Dave turned the Mini around and drove to his home.

This time the drive was not so careful. Dave screeched into his drive. His anger had overtaken his feelings of hurt. He took his briefcase from the car, which contained the tools and documents. What would happen now? Anne could sell him out without a second thought. She was way out of his league. What had he been thinking of?

The only thing he could do now was to cover his back until he knew more. He couldn't bring himself to even look at the files now. Dave walked in the darkness to a shed at the bottom of the small garden. Standing among the clutter of shovels, rakes and hoses, he removed a floorboard and pushed the case inside the gap. Once the board was back in place, he pulled a sack of garden fertilizer over the spot, secured the door and slowly walked the path to his house.

He lay on his bed, the radio playing quietly in the corner of the room, his head, so full of differing emotions. Pictures of the previous days flashed before him. Anne had told him she was in love with him. That must have been a lie. She was so scared of McCauley. It didn't make any sense.

He took a glass from the bedside cabinet and filled it with straight Scotch. Two gulps later, it was empty again.

He stared at the telephone. Should he call? God, he wanted to. It could just be a mistake. He wanted it to be a mistake. He wanted everything to be right again.

He looked at his bed, still unmade, left that way since he and Anne had risen from it. He felt sick to his stomach again. He refilled the whisky glass and repeated the process until sleep eventually came to him.

"Wake up, sonny."

Dave heard the voice but couldn't make out if it was real or not. His head felt like something was attempting to get out using a hammer and chisel.

"Come on, get up!"

This time, whoever was the owner of the voice accompanied it with a firm shake of Dave's shoulder. Yes, it was reality. Dave felt his brain rattle inside his skull. The whisky had done its job in aiding sleep and was now reluctant to loose its grip.

Dave slowly opened two very red eyes.

"I am Detective Superintendent Marshall," said the voice somewhere to Dave's left. "Can you hear me, Stewart?"

Dave raised himself onto one elbow and surveyed the scene in his bedroom. He hadn't heard the doorbell. The entourage had let themselves in somehow.

The voice came from a tall and slender man in an expensive looking overcoat.

Dave rubbed his eyes and ran his hand through his hair. The dawning of his predicament slowly penetrated his dulled senses. Anne had really done it. She'd set him up. Dave cleared his throat and noticed that three other men in smart suits accompanied the superintendent. He failed to recognise any of them.

"What do you want?" he croaked.

The superintendent brushed his coat to one side and slipped his hand into his trouser pocket. Dave noticed they, too, seemed equally expensive. The man was almost casual in his manner, but spoke with all the authority in the world.

“We want you, sonny.”

Dave needed time. He had to think. He sat up, fully displaying his muscular physique. He stretched and tried to look relaxed. He was thinking on his feet. Stall, all he could do right now was stall.

“Before you do anything, you’d better show me some ID and tell me what this is all about.”

“Cheeky fuck,” chirped one of the suits.

The superintendent shot the suit an icy glance. He slipped a hand into his inside jacket pocket and produced a warrant card. He held it close to Dave’s face for a second and then resumed his pose, hand in pocket.

“Happy?”

Dave nodded, deflated.

Marshall placed his hand on one of Dave’s well-defined shoulders. “David Stewart, I am arresting you for the murder of John McCauley and Anne Wallace. You are not obliged to say anything unless you wish to do so...”

Marshall continued the caution, but Dave didn’t hear. His heart pounded. He felt it would burst from his chest. Every sinew in his body tensed. His fists clenched involuntarily. Anne! My God, Anne! He lost all control and let out a terrible anguished cry.

The men in his room, presuming the worst, leapt upon him. Dave was in panic. The first hand upon him was Marshall's. It was quickly followed by several more, all of them experts at restraint.

Dave's physical strength and determination was amazing. He caught hold of a wrist and twisted. A head came into view and he punched, a forearm, and he bit.

Then pain. He started to feel pain. He was being struck with something hard. He presumed it was a truncheon.

He saw blood. Blood on his body, on his hands, on the bed sheets; it was his. Finally, he saw nothing.

The limp body of Dave Stewart was bundled into an awaiting police van by his Serious Crime Squad arrest team.

The uniformed van driver took a long look at Dave. He had that, '*so this was the kid who'd killed two coppers*', look about him. He made a deep guttural sound and spat a large, green, phlegm-ridden mess into Dave's face. It ran down his damaged nose and mouth.

The constable slammed the door of the van and turned the key in the lock. He turned to Marshall, who was wiping blood from his coat with a handkerchief. "Do you want him taken straight to the nick, boss?"

Marshall nodded. "Yes," he paused and pointed a knowing finger, "... and, Constable..."

"Yes, boss?"

"Let's get him there in one piece, eh?"

The uniformed man frowned, and then nodded in agreement.

As the van drove away, Marshall started to bark orders to the rest of the team. He wanted the Scenes of Crime Unit, a search team and an interview team to start their work.

Paper-suited men were already preparing their kit in the front garden of the house. Neighbours were peering through curtains at the early morning activity.

Marshall took a small notepad from his pocket and wrote,

*'The accused, Stewart, made no reply when arrested.'*

Marshall gave his men some further instructions and then beckoned his driver.

He sat in the front passenger seat. Marshall could never get used to riding in the back, no matter what his rank.

Two colleagues were dead, horribly murdered.

He'd never liked McCauley, or his methods. He didn't know Anne Wallace, but from what he'd learned, she'd been a good copper. The boy Stewart was just a probationer. What the fuck had he been thinking of? Apparently even he was highly thought of on the Section. The whole thing was a mess. The fuckin' press would have a field day.

He turned to his driver. "Preston nick, Barry."

The mood in the station was black. The murder of a police officer in any civilized country is a major event. The murder of two officers belonging to this north England county force doubled the number of deaths in the force history.

The whole of the station was in a state of shock. Officers arriving for work, unaware of the night's events, were quickly informed of the murders.

There is a common bond between all officers. It comes as a result of the knowledge that one day you may need a colleague to save your life. It was common practice for events such as these to be investigated by officers from another division, or even another force, and the presence of Detective Superintendent Marshall and his men was met with suspicion and anger by the local CID.

In the confines of his second floor office, Rod Casey was blazing. "Who the fuck do they think they are?"

Clive Williams sat smoking at his desk, he didn't answer. He was deep in thought. Attempting to piece together the events leading to the death of his closest friend, and find a way of covering his own and McCauley's backs.

Rod was still sounding off, "I mean, we give them Stewart on a plate and they swan around the nick in their posh suits playing the 'great I am'."

Williams raised his head slightly, and stubbed out his latest cigarette. The normally calm and affable man spat at Casey. He was desperately trying to finish his report through a haze of scotch. Once Stewart was in interview, he could spill everything. He couldn't allow him to discredit the Chief.

"Shut the fuck up, Rod! I don't give a monkeys if we do the job, 'Serious' do it or any other fuckin' department in this force. A good copper, the likes of who you or I will ever come across again, is dead. He also happened to be my best friend. Therefore, if you don't mind, Constable, I would like some time to myself. Do you understand?"

Rod flew at Clive. He took hold of the man's already crumpled jacket and pulled Clive's face inches from his own.

"Now you listen to me, you fat lazy fuck. I've watched your back for years, you and John fuckin' McCauley's. I've done your dirty work and watched you all climb the ladder except me. It suited you and him to keep me where I was, but things have changed. McCauley got stupid. He leaned on the wrong boy for once. Remember what I said about Stewart in the pub the other day? You wouldn't have it. No one would have thought that the silly bastard would have had the bottle. But he did, didn't he? If he hadn't been so fucked up over Wallace, he would have ditched the gear and we may never have caught him. He made sure that Bailey was never going to court, didn't he?"

William's eyes widened. Rod had to laugh. The man was pathetic.

"You haven't a clue what day it is, have you? Bailey's been found on The Callon with his head half hanging off."

Williams had been so distraught at the second murder scene he hadn't even heard the radio transmissions from the first. He'd hit the bottle hard since.

Rod sneered, "All you and McCauley had against Stewart was just a bunch of useless paper, but he was cleverer than you thought, weren't he? It could have all been swept under the carpet and forgotten. He knew the alterations in the register wouldn't stand up to scrutiny. But with Bailey gone, if you'd tried anything, he'd have taken you all with him. But no, big macho man McCauley had to have his tart back.

This is what happens when you get too big for your boots. I for one am glad this happened. We could all have gone down the tube. You were both conducting investigations from the inside of a scotch bottle."

Williams was nodding at Rod. He had no idea what day it was. Rod gestured to the paper on Clive's desk. "So now you write the end of the script to protect your little friend from the vultures. Keep his good name. It's fuckin' over for you, Clive. A jealous boyfriend, some kid, has finished your whole comfortable career. I advise you to get this report just right. Tidy the loose ends good and proper, or you'll be history. "

Casey released Clive, who dropped back into his seat like a rag doll. Rod gently took hold of the Inspector's tie, straightened it and with a bizarre smile he concluded, "Now you drunken shit, don't fuckin' ever call me 'Constable' again."

Williams put his head in his hands and started to weep. Casey went for lunch.

Detective Superintendent Trevor Marshall was a high flyer. He had started his police career in the London Metropolitan force, at age twenty.

He was a detective sergeant by twenty-four and after a spell at Bramshill Police College, became the youngest ever inspector in the force history.

Despite his youth and academic background, Marshall was not averse to getting his hands dirty.

He boxed, played rugby for his force and relished the opportunity of the practical street work in the capital.

At twenty-seven, he married a girl whose family lived in the east Lancashire town of Clitheroe. They had two children in two years and seemed blissfully happy.

When he was offered a chief inspector's post with the Lancashire Force, his wife begged him to accept.

She wanted to be nearer her ailing father, and was concerned at the high crime rate in their London suburb. Marshall did accept, and he and his family loved the country home they could now afford. He found the northern people hard to grasp at first, but by the time he made superintendent, he had a firm circle of friends from various ranks and at thirty-seven still played rugby for his division.

Marshall headed the force's serious crime squad, a team of twenty-four detective constables, six detective sergeants and two detective inspectors. The squad's main tasks related to the investigation of organised crime, armed robbery and serial killings. His team had been seconded to a very messy murder inquiry in the Yorkshire area, and he had spent too much time away from his wife and his girls recently.

The job had been a complete mess, and the clear up had taken nearly two years.

Now he was home again and he had the biggest test of his career in front of him. He studied the reports on his desk. This was indeed a nasty business.

He had met John McCauley on several occasions. He was a brash, old school type. His last encounter with him had resulted in an argument. Marshall had not been the only person to notice the smell of booze on the Chief Superintendent.

He had never met Anne Wallace. From her picture and her personal file, she had been a good officer and a very beautiful woman. She had been a detective sergeant for over a year. Her clear-up rate was impressive. Rumours had surrounded her promotion, but she had more than proved herself. The name, though, rang alarm bells in Marshall's head. He just couldn't place it right now.

A postman had discovered the bodies of McCauley and Wallace. The front door of the house was left open, presumably by the killer. Bailey had been found less than an hour later by a vagrant who used the old mill as a doss.

Local CID officers, Williams and Casey, had attended Wallace's home and got the ball rolling. Both officers were members of McCauley's team. They had behaved very professionally in terrible circumstances. Both men were aware of a personal relationship between the two victims.

Williams had submitted a comprehensive report regarding the suspect Stewart's alleged involvement in evidence tampering. It appeared that Stewart had altered a statement and property ledgers in the Bailey case. He had been the arresting officer, made a stupid error regarding a property find, and attempted to cover his mistake. McCauley had got wind of these discrepancies and was about to spill the beans.

Williams had also produced a half-finished report typed on McCauley's stationery. The Chief Superintendent was to recommend the dismissal of Stewart for the offences he believed had been committed. Marshall presumed Williams had recovered the document from the Chief's office. It wasn't signed.

Williams' report also covered the year-long relationship between McCauley and Wallace. The Chief had recently confided in Williams regarding Stewart's obsession with Anne Wallace. McCauley wanted him out of the picture.

Williams reported that Stewart had stalked Wallace constantly after she innocently agreed to have a drink with him. No one realised the extent of his obsession.

Williams and Casey were still at the murder scene when the news of the Bailey slaying broke. They put two and two together and came up with he oldest motives in the book. They made a very quick and correct decision.

They went to Stewart's house and had found what appeared to be the murder weapons, together with two pairs of blood-stained overall and overshoes in Stewart's Mini car. They would have made the arrest too, if Marshall and his men hadn't arrived minutes later.

Marshall stared at Dave Stewart's file. Twenty-five years old, born and raised in South Yorkshire. He was a tough lad from a tough area. Still a probationary constable, his reports from training and supervisors were all glowing. No reports of excessive force; well liked by his colleagues, he was described as quiet and conscientious.

Marshall could have been looking at his own history, not the file of a triple killer. Could jealousy really be the motive? He'd seen it before. The calmest, affable men turned lethal by the green-eyed monster. Or could the Force have been harbouring a psychopath?

Before he spoke to Stewart though, he would need more information. Preparation is everything.

Marshall picked up the telephone and dialed the section sergeant. He hadn't lost his north London accent, and was immediately recognised. "Hello, Sergeant, I wonder if you could tell me who tutored Constable Stewart when he arrived here?"

Marshall listened and wrote down Andy Dunn's name on a pad, together with his telephone number and address. He thanked the sergeant and replaced the receiver.

Marshall knew Andy, as they played rugby together every week. Andy was as straight as they came. Marshall called his driver and pulled on his coat. It was time to pay 'Armless a visit.

Dave felt like a train had hit him. His left eye wouldn't open. Every time he tried, the pain was intense. Handcuffs cut into both wrists. He couldn't feel his right hand. He tried to touch it with his left but felt nothing but stone cold flesh. The cuffs had stopped the blood flow.

Where the fuck was he?

Dave attempted to sit up. He found it difficult as he was cuffed behind his back and the pain in his wrists was tremendous.

On the third attempt, he managed it. Memories were slipping

back into his head. The sight of the cell door snapped him into reality.

Anne was dead. McCauley was dead. At that moment, Dave Stewart wished for the same. How had he got into this mess? He had been doing his job, done his best, met a beautiful woman and fallen in love.

OK, the burglary was a crazy idea. McCauley was a bastard, that was true, but he didn't deserve to die.

So how had it happened? Who was responsible?

Anne, his darling Anne. Had she suffered?

Dave forgot his own pain. His head spun with images of Anne. His tears began slowly with a silent single droplet, falling like a solitary raindrop. Then they flowed freely, his huge shoulders bucked with each quiet sob. There were no tears of self-pity. He no longer cared what happened to him. Overwhelming desperate sadness blocked everything from his heart and mind. He was incapable of feeling worry, fear, pain or pity.

All David Stewart had left inside him was the need for revenge.

No matter what happened to him now. One thing Dave was certain of, he would find out who had killed Anne.

As his tears dried on the cold cell floor he whispered to himself.

*I promise you, Anne, I will find them.*

Marshall found Andy Dunn in the middle of his daily weight training routine. One bedroom of his small home had been converted into a gym for that very purpose.

A bubbly female with a gravity defying figure who he presumed was Andy's latest conquest, had let Marshall in.

'Armless was wearing only shorts and training shoes. His upper torso was bathed in sweat as he bench-pressed a monstrous weight. Marshall could only look on in awe at the physique of the man. Andy Dunn was over forty years old, but was fitter and stronger than most men Marshall knew.

Music blasted from a stereo in the corner of the room. Marshall cut 'The Kids in America,' short. It got the attention of the straining man.

Andy spotted the bar, sat up and started to wipe his body with a towel. He beamed at Marshall and extended one huge hand towards his colleague.

He spoke with his distinctive Scottish twang, "Well, well, well. What have I done to warrant a visit from the highest ranking winger on the force?"

Marshall took Andy's hand and shook it. Marshall could see from Andy's manner that he was still unaware of the night's tragedies.

"It's good to see you, Andy," Marshall began, "but I'm here with some bad news, I'm afraid."

Andy lifted a glass of water from the floor and took a long drink. He had no family left alive so he knew the bad news couldn't be anything to do with them, so he concluded it had to be a mate.

He looked Marshall in the eye. “Shoot, pal.”

The detective could be nothing but businesslike, there was no easy way to impart the news. “About six thirty a.m. today, the bodies of John McCauley and Anne Wallace were discovered by a postman at Wallace’s home. McCauley had been stabbed repeatedly, a frenzied attack. Wallace had been beaten and her throat had been cut.

Marshall looked sickened. “It was a fucking bloodbath, Andy.”

Andy was open-mouthed.

Marshall continued, “We arrested a suspect about three hours later. In fact, that’s the reason I’m here, Andy, I need some background before I interview him. I believe you know him quite well.”

Andy pulled on a T- shirt and stood. He spoke almost to himself, “Jesus…Anne Wallace…Dave will be… err…yeah…anything… Trev…”

His brain refused to work for a few seconds. Eventually he began, “I’ve worked in Preston for near eighteen years. I should know most of the villains in town, but to be honest, Rod Casey probably knows more than I’ve forgotten. Who is it, Trevor?”

Marshall pulled out a packet of cigarettes and offered one to Andy, who took it and waited for the senior officer to light it.

“He’s a copper, Andy, a young lad by the name of Stewart.”

Andy nearly choked on the smoke. “Dave Stewart? Oh fuck me! No, Trev, you’ve made a big mistake there.”

Marshall held up his hands. “Not so fast, Andy, there is some serious evidence to back it up."

Andy was silent for a few moments; the latest jolt slowly sank in.

"Trev, this is crazy. I took this kid out when he arrived at Preston. He's the salt of the earth. Steady as a rock, no wild temper. I would bet my next year's pay cheque that he has nothing to do with this business."

Marshall was doubtful. "Steady on, Andy, just think for a minute. As I understand it, Stewart was in the shit. McCauley was about to pot him because he cocked up some evidence in a murder investigation."

Marshall looked for a place to drop his ash and continued, "The Chief and Anne Wallace were lovers. As I understand it, our boy had got himself so obsessed with Wallace, he was following her. The words 'Crime of Passion' are already being used. You've seen what jealousy can do, Andy."

It was Andy's turn to raise his hands and his voice. "Stop right there, Trev! I know where you're heading here, but it doesn't make any sense."

Andy nodded towards the door. "Lucy is the barmaid at the Black Bull in town. She told me McCauley was there 'till late last night."

Andy took a long pull on the cigarette, "She told me he was very pissed off about something and she got the impression that something was Anne Wallace. She also told me that it wasn't the first time McCauley had been mouthing off about Anne of late, even making threats."

Andy lowered his voice, "I know you can't use this information in a legal situation, but Lucy has overheard conversations between

McCauley and Williams. They were as thick as thieves. She's convinced that Mackay and Williams were blackmailing somebody."

Marshall was straight in, "Whoa! That's a bit strong, Andy."

"I'm only telling you what she said."

Andy took a further pull on his cigarette and exhaled a large plume. "As for Dave Stewart, I was there in the canteen a few days back when Anne Wallace came on to him like a train. I know I was there! They had a bit of a fling and from what I could see they were quite sweet on each other. I mean, I was actually with Dave and Anne on Saturday night in The Square. It doesn't fit with him being obsessed and following her around, does it?"

Marshall stubbed his own cigarette out and shrugged. "Who knows? She may have been the prick teaser of the century. Maybe she wanted to make McCauley jealous. You know as well as I do, Andy, no one knows what goes on when that front door closes."

Marshall moved closer. "This must go no further, Andy, but we found the murder weapon in Stewart's car."

Andy considered this latest information. He sat and motioned Marshall to do the same.

"Trev, it's my turn to ask for some secrecy."

Marshall nodded. "OK, Andy."

"This business with the Chief finding Dave Stewart cocking up evidence... Well, I have a different story. Dave did arrest a lad called William Henry Bailey. It was just on a non-payment warrant. Obviously it turned out to be a lot more than that so it was a good lock up for the young lad. He came to me the next day to ask my advice. He'd made a mistake with a property find. Something we've all done in our time. He told me McCauley was putting pressure on him to make changes to his witness statement. As you could imagine, he was between a rock and a hard place.

McCauley's team could all have been involved in that decision. Williams would definitely know about it. He was that far up McCauley's arse he knew what the Chief had for breakfast. Thick as fucking thieves the lot of them, Casey included. Don't think you'll get no help from them though, Trev. They'll clam up tighter than a duck's arse in a sandstorm, Williams would do anything to stop his best buddy looking dirty.

As for Wallace and McCauley being lovers, Ha! You must know the rumours about how Anne Wallace made DS. How much dirt the Chief had on her is nobody's business. I'd be more inclined to think that she wanted away from the old man. You can't go off anything McCauley's team tells you. They were old school, jobs for the boys. Jesus, they must have been working together for twenty years."

Andy thought for a moment. "Besides, to cover everything, Dave would have to knock off Bailey and lose the paperwork too wouldn't he?"

Marshall was dour. "Bailey is dead. Same M.O."

Andy put his head in his hands.

"Dead? Oh, pal, this whole thing stinks worse than a Fleetwood prozzie. It's just not right, not fucking right at all."

At Preston station, the press had arrived en masse. Marshall considered there was a copper a few quid better off courtesy of the Daily Mirror or other red top. Indeed, reporters from all the main papers were jammed into a nearby waiting room. Television crews were busy setting up their equipment in a makeshift conference room, hastily put together by the Crime Squad.

Marshall barked at his secretary. He didn't know her. She had been appointed that day to work with the Serious Crime Squad officers.

"What is your name, love?"

The woman, a plump, mid thirties, flowery dress type, was slowly losing it.

"Sharon, sir," she flustered.

"Well, Sharon," snapped Marshall. "Can you explain to me, how the hell this circus got in here?"

"I arranged it."

Marshall spun around to see the figure attached to the voice, a very smart looking woman in her forties holding out a perfectly manicured hand.

"Jennifer Rawlinson, press officer."

Marshall ignored the gesture. "Well, Ms. Rawlinson. It may have escaped your notice, but I am in charge of this investigation and I should have been consulted before your single handed attempt to turn my office into this freak show."

Rawlinson was unperturbed by the officer's temper. "Don't tell me my job, Superintendent. I am not a police officer. I answer directly to the Chief Constable. It was he who made the decision to call this press conference."

Rawlinson lifted a receiver from a nearby phone and held it toward the detective.

"Now, if you would care to take the matter up with the Chief Con?"

Marshall glowered at the press officer.

"I'll do just that, one of my officers will show you out now, Ms. Rawlinson."

Marshall closed his door and sat behind a desk piled high with paper. The pressure was well and truly on.

Sharon knocked, and put her head inside the door. "The Chief Constable is on the line, sir."

Marshall picked up the receiver. "Superintendent Marshall."

The Chief sounded strangely jovial. "Hello, Trevor, how are you?"

"I'm well, sir. But I need to speak to you about this press situation."

"This is my idea, Trevor. I understand that we have our man in the cells." The Chief lowered his voice. "This is a real mess. I want the lid put on this business as soon as possible. Get this boy charged with the three jobs and give the press what they want. This goes all the way to the Home Secretary, Trevor. I want it boxed off and our boy in the dock ASAP."

"But, sir, there are some lines of enquiry that I..."

Marshall was abruptly cut short. "Trevor, I think I have made myself perfectly clear. As far as I am concerned, we have a young officer gone mad. Maybe he has always been mad. I expect the whole business to end there."

His tone verged on the brink of patronising, "John McCauley and Anne Wallace will be buried with full honours. Ms Rawlinson has a prepared statement for the press. You have enough experience to fend off any awkward questions. I'll be watching from the office."

The telephone went dead.

Marshall was in shock. This whole job was going to be laid at the feet of one young officer, no questions asked, to keep the good name of the force. Christ, he hadn't even been interviewed. Marshall could understand why the boss wanted a quick result. However, this was outright madness.

Marshall called for Sharon. "Get Rawlinson back in here."

The woman had obviously not left the building, and swept into Marshall's office. She sat without being asked.

"Now, Superintendent," she began, "I trust we have that little matter of authority straightened out?

She didn't wait for a reply.

"Good. I have a press release for you to read."

Marshall took it and smiled cynically. "Thank you."

The document read:

*Ladies and gentleman of the press; This morning the bodies of Detective Chief Superintendent John McCauley, Detective Sergeant Anne Wallace and the escaped murder suspect, William Henry Bailey, were discovered in the Preston area.*

*All three had been attacked with a sharp instrument.*

*Bailey's arresting officer, Probationary Constable David Stewart, is currently in custody.*

*Chief Superintendent McCauley had been the senior investigating officer in the Bailey case. Anne Wallace, the antecedence officer.*

*It is anticipated that Stewart will be charged with all three murders in due course.*

Marshall couldn't believe his eyes. He knew that these decisions had been made in order to protect the name of the force and, of course, its senior officers. Nevertheless, this was beyond all usual protocol.

After his conversation with Andy Dunn, Marshall knew that Stewart's motive was suspect.

He had yet to be interviewed. He may even have an alibi.

This was a bold statement to the world and Andy was right; the job stank. Marshall was to be drawn into the fray and become part of it.

He waved Rawlinson away without comment. She flounced from the office, leaving him with his thoughts. There was little time. Paper had been arriving on his desk all morning. He picked through the witness statements.

First, he read the statements of Stewart's neighbours.

They put Stewart out of the house long enough to have committed the crimes. Nothing there of any help to the boy.

Marshall respected the information from Andy Dunn. His revelations about Williams' and McCauley's relationship swam around in Marshall's head. The detective lit yet another cigarette and picked up the telephone. "Sharon, get me Detective Inspector Williams."

He dropped the phone onto the hook and re-started his examination of the documents on his desk. Moments later, Williams entered the office. He looked like shit.

Marshall was curt. "Sit down Clive."

"How come the press is here, boss?" The Inspector was distant, and smelled of booze.

"That's the reason you're here, Clive. I need some answers and quick."

Clive shrugged and seemed uninterested. "The job seems cut and dried to me. What's to add? The little fucker deserves all he gets."

The telephone rang. Marshall didn't even check to see who was calling. He just barked, "Not now," into the receiver and slammed it back down. He then unhooked it and lowered his voice. The change in volume did little to hide his impatience.

"Well, I happen to think that this thing is not so 'cut and dried.' And I want you to pull yourself together and answer my questions."

Marshall was intense; "First, who decided to change Stewart's statement on the Bailey arrest?"

Clive remained silent.

"Come on, Clive, a boy's life is at stake here."

The dishevelled detective leaned forward onto the desk in front of Marshall. His voice was a whisper. He was obviously drunk.

"John McCauley was a good officer," he slurred. "He suspected Stewart of falsifying evidence regarding a property find in the Bailey case. The cock-up could have cost us the case. The boss wanted him sacked. That's all I know."

He leaned back and folded his arms in finality. "That's all I have to say."

Marshall was fuming. He positively hissed at Williams, "Well then Inspector, do you think you may indulge me a little further and tell me of Anne Wallace's involvement in this mess?"

Clive was unimpressed. "John McCauley's private life was his own business. Anyway, the death of William Bailey tells everyone, everyone with sense that is, that Stewart killed to cover his tracks and that jealousy was not the only motive. Now if you'll excuse me, I have lost a close friend today and intend to mourn him as I see fit. I'm taking some sick leave."

Clive stood to leave. He was very unsteady, but managed to make his point.

"Starting right now."

Marshall didn't care for the obvious rank-closing. He reached across his desk with the speed of a striking snake, and grabbed Williams firmly by the wrist.

"If I find out you are lying to me, Williams, your leave will be permanent."

Williams looked down at Marshall's hand clamped on his wrist, then into the eyes of the officer. His voice was strangely steady and laced with sarcasm.

"With all due respect, sir, I suggest that you concentrate on the boy you have in the cells, courtesy of my officers' good work, and leave the good name of John McCauley to rest in peace. That way, you will do the whole Force a favour."

Marshall released his grip.

Williams left the office in silence, walked to the nearest toilet and vomited. He sat in the cubical, head spinning. He'd done his best for his friend. He hoped it was enough. Clive Williams was very, very tired.

Marshall stood in front of the melee of press. Flashguns exploded the second he entered the room. They continued for several minutes, coupled with a barrage of shouted questions. He waited for quiet, and began.

"Ladies and gentlemen. My name is Trevor Marshall. I am the Detective Superintendent in charge of the Serious Crime Squad."

Marshall looked down at the prepared press release. "It is my task to investigate the murders of Chief Superintendent John McCauley, Detective Sergeant Anne Wallace and William Henry Bailey."

Marshall couldn't bring himself to roll over. Not even for a Chief Constable. "Their bodies were all discovered earlier today. All had been attacked with a sharp instrument. We currently have a suspect in custody, who has yet to be interviewed. That is all the comment I am prepared to make at this time."

The room was in uproar. Press people shouting more questions and complaints. Marshall had even prevented Rawlinson from issuing copies of the statement, although he suspected that some of the information had leaked from that source.

Marshall left the room, followed by two of his team.

By the time he made his office, his telephone was already ringing.

He lifted the receiver to hear the Chief Constable's voice. The joviality had left him. "What the hell is going on, Marshall?"

"Sir, I understand the urgency in this matter, but in all fairness, I don't think you are aware of the full circumstances of...."

"I don't give a shit about minor details, Marshall. I told you exactly what I wanted and you deliberately disobeyed my orders. As far as I can see, we have a solid case. Now, I want this boy charged tonight. Do you understand?"

"Yes, sir."

"And, Marshall..."

"Yes?"

"Don't forget your report comes straight to me."

"Yes, sir."

Marshall took a deep breath and sat back in his chair. Something wasn't right and he didn't like it one bit.

---

He walked two flights to the office provided for the visiting crime squad officers, and sat in front of his investigative team.

He had selected five men and one woman for the case, all with their own brand of expertise.

The requirements for selection to the Serious Crime Squad were rigorous. All must have had CID, Drug Squad or Special Branch experience. All must be qualified firearms officers and be trained in close protection.

Marshall's right hand was Detective Inspector Ian Jemson. Jemson looked more like a male model than a police officer, and had gained the nickname 'Slick'.

With the Chief's comments still ringing in his ears, Marshall looked toward his inspector for some good news.

Slick spoke with the voice of a trained politician, "Boss, we have all the preliminary post mortem results, the initial scenes of crime reports, plus all statements from witnesses. We've also done some work on the movements of McCauley and Wallace prior to death. We have some background on Stewart and his movements. The whole package makes interesting reading, but it's still sketchy."

Slick paused for effect. "There is one more thing, boss. First impressions of the gear found in Stewart's car, the coveralls are police issue and the rubber gloves are the same type and colour as the ones he alleged Bailey had on him."

Marshall grimaced at that titbit.

He was scanning the wad of reports in front of him. "Prints inside the gloves?"

Slick shook his head. "Full of talc, boss. Our boy's no fool on that count."

Marshall frowned. “Fool enough to let us find them.”

“This information,” Marshall pointed to his team, “stays in these four walls. We are going to interview Stewart at nine p.m. He has refused any legal representation, so we have a straight run at him. I can tell you that this case has attracted interest at the highest level. We are under pressure to finish it quickly. Has anyone anything else?”

Detective Sergeant Marie Baker raised her hand. She was an athletic looking woman who never wore make-up during work hours. Her striking looks always attracted lots of interest from the male members of the squad. She was bright, brave and a first class firearms expert.

Marshall nodded. “Yes, Marie?”

“Boss, I can’t get my head around this guy. Why should someone go to the trouble of protecting his clothes, shoes and hands, so as to leave no forensic traces and then be so sloppy as to just drop two bin bags of weapons and clothing into our lap? I mean, this guy is no fool. I’ve been doing the background on him.”

Marshall cast his eyes around his team. He and Marie, as usual, were on the same wavelength.

“Anyone else think this is all too easy?”

Slick broke the silence, “Maybe he only meant there to be one killing. Maybe he lost the plot after he found Wallace and McCauley together.”

He looked at his notes.

“But just to throw a further spanner in the works, McCauley’s house was screwed either before or after his murder. The back door was kicked in and the safe done, a pro job using a wire brush key. What was in the safe we can't say; there's nothing in Stewart's place that looks favourite. We have to presume that whatever was in that safe is related to the case and could be a motive. "

Marshall stood and paced the room. He thought about Andy's story of dirt and blackmail. It was all starting to fit.

"OK, people, let's cast around what we have. If we believe all we are told, the motive for these killings is two-fold. First, that McCauley was about to pot Stewart. He had doctored a witness statement and some other documents to cover his arse in the Bailey case.

Bailey had to go. He couldn't risk him getting to trial and the alterations being discovered.

"We all happy with that one?"

Marie shook her head.

"Bailey alive or dead, trial or no trial, Stewart would still have been found out."

Marshall nodded.

"OK, let's look at the jealousy angle. The loss of his job, maybe prison, would mean no more contact with his beloved Anne Wallace. Second, he was so infatuated with Wallace to the extent he was tailing her. He finds her and McCauley together and boom! He snaps."

"Messy," chipped Jemson.

Marie looked troubled.

"It doesn't make sense. I think whatever was in Mackay's safe had more to do with it."

Marshall thought about his conversation with Andy Dunn, and felt as worried as Marie looked.

Slick tapped his temple with his forefinger. "Let's just assume that Stewart has been infatuated with Wallace for some time. She was a very striking woman. Her relationship with McCauley was starting to get to the lad. McCauley catches Stewart bending the rules, which angers Stewart even more. As he sees it, his rival has got one up on him yet again. He can't do anything; he's powerless against a chief superintendent.

He can't believe his luck when Bailey escapes. All he needs is Bailey out of the way and to destroy any original paperwork, and he's in the clear to try and win the lady's hand from the boss. He finds Bailey on his own patch and does the business. For some reason, he screws McCauley's house. Who knows, maybe the Chief had the original copy of Stewart's statement at home?"

"Dirt," thought Marshall. He lifted the phone as Slick continued.

"He believes he's in the clear and goes to see Anne Wallace. He gets to the house, has a look through the window and sees the terrible truth. The boy snaps, goes in through the back, lifts a knife from the kitchen and bang! Whatever the supposition, we can't overlook the fact that we have enough evidence to charge him right now."

Marshall dropped the phone on its cradle and looked straight at Jemson. "You bought a crystal ball recently, Slick? The original

Bailey file has gone. Either stolen from here, or as you suggest, McCauley's safe. It's all looking ominous for our boy."

The door to the incident room opened and a young constable walked in. He looked very embarrassed.

"Yes?" barked Marshall, adding to the young man's fluster.

The officer held out a statement form. "I... I've been on the house to house team sir, in Sergeant Wallace's street. I err, think this is important."

Marshall took the document and scanned it. He looked up at the young officer. "Yes, son. It is important. Well done. Off you go."

Marshall waited for the constable to leave. "Well, it seems our boy is getting deeper in the shit as each minute goes by."

He checked the text again. "The lady that lives opposite Anne Wallace is a right nosy old bird. She says Anne left with McCauley, in his car, about eight thirty p.m. and came back in a taxi about an hour or so later. She heard the Chief's car return not long after. She says maybe a quarter after ten."

Marshall sifted through papers on his desk until he found what he wanted. "She also says, that about ten forty-five p.m. she saw another car pull up outside. She thinks it was yellow or cream coloured. She's positive it was a Mini."

He held up the paper he had just found. "Dave Stewart owns a yellow Mini."

Marshall had heard and seen enough.

"OK, folks, Slick and I will do the interview. Marie and Bill, I want you to go to Barnsley and speak to the Stewart family. The rest of you I want on hand to check on anything we get during interview or from the outside."

The team all stood and set about their allotted tasks. Many of them were already tired. They had been on duty for twelve hours. Jemson and Marshall remained in the briefing room.

Jemson lit a cigarette. "What do you think, boss?"

Marshall took the cigarette from the inspector's hand and took a long draw on it. "I think our boy is going down for a long time, Slick. I also think that we may never be allowed to get right to the bottom of this job. The politicians are screaming for blood. I think you have it almost right. But there's one thing you don't know. Rumour has it McCauley had some dirt on Anne Wallace too. Maybe, before he visited her, Stewart did Mackay's safe to protect his girl."

Jemson recovered his cigarette. "You could fill an ocean with the blood spilt for God and true love, boss."

Marshall rubbed his face with both palms. He needed a shave.

"Maybe so, Slick, but killing Bailey just doesn't fit and I can't get past it."

Dave was in agony. His hands, still cuffed, were now so swollen they had started to discolour. The charge office staff had visited him on two occasions.

Both calls had involved abuse and a beating. Dave realised he had no friends left in this place.

He didn’t care about the pain. He didn’t need friends.

He needed Anne.

He needed answers.

His cell door swung open and Dave braced himself for another few kicks and punches. Instead, he saw Marshall standing in the doorframe.

The detective bellowed at the charge office sergeant. “Who the hell is responsible for this?”

The sergeant looked uneasy. “Err, he has been a bit, err, difficult, sir.”

Marshall was unimpressed.

“I want this man’s cuffs removed, and get him cleaned up now! Then I want him brought to the interview suite. If I see one more mark on this man, Sergeant, I will personally ensure that you occupy the next cell to him. Understand?”

“Yes, sir.”

Dave looked at Marshall. “Thank you, sir.”

Marshall appeared to ignore the comment.

“Twenty minutes, Sergeant.”

Marshall and Jemson sat opposite Dave Stewart.

The murder file and crime scene photographs lay on the table that separated them. Dave could see the image of William Bailey lying on a floor somewhere with his throat gaping open.

Dave knew that it was common interview practice, but he didn't think that he could stand to see pictures of Anne.

Jemson began, "Dave, do you know why you are here?"

"Yes."

"Do you want to tell us what happened yesterday?"

"I didn't kill them."

"We find that hard to believe, Dave."

"I didn't kill them."

"When did you last see John McCauley?"

He cleared his throat; "Last Friday."

"Where?"

"Here, the police station."

"What about William Bailey."

"When I arrested him."

"Anne Wallace?"

Dave swallowed hard, Marshall and Jemson noticed.

"I last saw her yesterday afternoon."

"Where?"

"Her house, we had been on a trip."

"A trip?"

Dave could feel himself losing control. Tears were close. "We went to the Lakes for a couple of days."

Jemson countered.

"You mean you followed her to the Lakes, Dave?"

Dave's head was spinning with this stupid line of questioning.

"Followed her? I don't understand. Please, I need to know something."

Marshall's tone was gentle enough.

"I think it's up to us to ask the questions at this stage, Dave. Don't you?"

Dave ignored the comment.

"I need to know, err, I need to know..."

Tears were now falling from Dave's face, his voice a trembling whisper. "Please, I need to know what happened to her... to Anne."

Jemson looked at Marshall who nodded an unspoken agreement. The Inspector lifted a photograph from the file and handed it to Dave. Dave's hands were too swollen to hold it and it dropped to the floor.

Marshall was like lightening and scooped the picture from the floor. He held it inches from Dave's eyes.

The grotesque figure of Anne Wallace, her beautiful face beaten, her clothing disheveled and her throat cut wide open was too much for Dave to bear.

Dave fell forward onto the desk and sobbed. Jemson was straight in. He lifted Dave's head by the hair and pushed the photograph under his nose.

"This is your handiwork, David. There's no point crying over spilt milk. You couldn't persuade the lady to leave McCauley, so you topped her. Anne Wallace knew which side her bread was buttered. She was John McCauley's girl. She was just playing with you. She wanted to make John jealous, that's all. You did for them all, son. McCauley, Wallace and Bailey; You're going down for life."

Dave shook off Jemson's hand with great force. His face contorted in grief and pain. Marshall was about to go in, when Dave held up his damaged hands.

He tucked his chin to his chest, expecting a further beating. Marshall felt a sudden pang of guilt.

Dave's voice still shook, but not with pain and sorrow. Marshall couldn't recall ever hearing a man speak with such venom.

"I," Dave swallowed hard, "did not do this. I loved her. She was wonderful. You had better find the people who did this, or as God is my witness, I will."

Dave fought for control. He looked at his interviewers with one good eye. "Then you can call me a killer."

Marshall stood. His demeanor and stature immediately dominated the interview.

“David, we found two sets of bloodstained clothing and two knives in your car. How can you explain that?”

Dave looked at the officer in total shock. Who was setting him up? He certainly couldn’t trust any police officer. The pain in his face and hands told him that.

He had to have time to think. “I have only one thing to say,” Dave’s voice faltered, “I didn’t do this.” He pointed at the photograph. He shook his head violently from side to side. He looked like he may vomit. Dave straightened his back and spoke as clearly as he could.

”Now I want to go back to my cell. I have nothing more to say to anyone.”

Jemson was unmoved. He had witnessed too many theatrics.

“You can go back to your cell, alright. For about thirty fuckin’ years.”

Dave lowered his head and remained silent. Despite all Marshall and Jemson’s further efforts, David Stewart didn’t speak another word.

Marshall and Jemson sat opposite each other in the quiet of the darkened office, both smoking, both deep in thought. Jemson, who had removed his shoes, was massaging his own aching feet. He broke the silence.

"You going to charge him, boss?"

Marshall nodded. "No choice."

Marie had called from South Yorkshire, where she had been digging into Stewart's past. It seemed that he was a far darker horse than they thought. He had worked for some serious faces in Sheffield, Doncaster and Barnsley. He'd been a lot more than a club bouncer. He'd collected some serious debts in his young life and he would definitely have had the know-how to open McCauley's safe.

Marshall was starting to doubt Andy Dunn's character assessment. Stewart had even refused to offer any alibi. His silence gave Marshall little option.

The Chief Constable had been on the telephone again. He wanted a police psychologist to interview Stewart. Dave refused to see him. No, Marshall really had no choice.

Two floors down in the cellblock, Dave Stewart sobbed quietly to himself. The terrible images of Anne haunted him. How he loved her.

He needed help, but whom could he trust? He couldn't do anything from a cell. He had to get out.

His morose musings were interrupted by noise in the corridor outside. There was the telltale rattle of keys, and his cell door opened to reveal Marshall standing in the opening. Dave knew what would happen. He collected himself as best he could and followed.

He counted his steps to the charge desk. With just thirty-four paces he was standing in front of the charge office sergeant. Marshall stood to his left side.

Marshall formally cautioned and charged David Stewart with three counts of murder.

Dave was unable to write a reply or sign the forms, his hands still too swollen to hold a pen.

Marshall offered to write for him.

Dave looked him straight in the eye and spoke just three words.

"I am innocent."

## FRIENDS IN HIGH PLACES

Sharon, Marshall's temporary secretary, walked into his office.

"Don't you ever knock?" Marshall had slept badly. The bruised face of David Stewart had been a recurring theme of his restless night. He felt like he had been prematurely pushed into charging him. All the evidence was there, but something wasn't sitting right in Marshall's gut.

"Sorry, sir," Sharon couldn't get used to Marshall's temper, "but there is someone to see you."

The visitor stood, shoulders back, like a military sentry, framed in the doorway. The man looked tired. His totally white but full hair swept backwards to reveal what had once been a handsome face. He wore half-moon glasses which he peered over. His eyes, despite their obvious exhaustion, still burned bright blue and intelligent. He stepped forward, his hand extended toward the superintendent, slim shoulders draped in Saville Row.

Marshall stood and took the hand. "Superintendent Marshall." The handshake was firm, the man's skin soft.

When he spoke, the man's voice came straight from the boards of a Shakespeare tragedy. “We’ve met. Robert Wallace, I’m Anne’s father.”

Marshall suddenly remembered why he knew Anne’s name. Of course, she was the daughter of the most revered barrister in London. Marshall himself had felt the wrath of Robert Wallace’s tongue under cross-examination, during his time in the Metropolitan Force.

Wallace’s sadness was all consuming, only his British ‘stiff upper lip’ preventing breakdown.

Marshall felt he had no words, “I’m very sorry for your loss, sir.”

Wallace remained businesslike although it was impossible to hide the trauma of his loss from his voice, which wavered slightly.

“Thank you, Superintendent, it was a great shock. One expects one’s children to outlive one.”

Marshall felt strangely nervous in the man’s presence. “Indeed, sir.”

Wallace sat and crossed his immaculately clothed legs.

“I’m sure you are curious about my presence, Superintendent.”

Marshall had to admit he was, but remained silent.

“What interests me right now,” he began, “is the state of the investigation and the young man you have charged with my daughter’s murder.”

“Of course,” Marshall started, “Stewart will be appearing in court this morning. We expect a remand in custody, prior to a committal to the Crown Court. As you will be aware, I am not at liberty to discuss the details of the investigation."

Wallace produced a business card and placed it on Marshall's desk. It had the appearance of pale linen, etched with gold.

Wallace gently tapped it with his manicured finger as he spoke. "That is where you are wrong, Superintendent. You see I have retained a barrister to defend Stewart and a good friend and colleague, Sir Peter Davits, will act as defence pathologist."

Wallace stared into space for a second, as if lost in thought.

"I wish I could defend the boy myself. That, of course, would involve a conflict of interest."

Wallace sharpened again. "He will be defended by the gentleman on that card. I would be grateful if you would afford him every convenience. A copy of the prosecution file should be in his possession today, so he can commence an interview with his client. I trust that will not be an issue?"

Marshall was stupefied. It was the most bizarre scenario he had ever encountered.

"Of course, sir, I'll get a copy for you by this afternoon. But, sir, I..."

Wallace didn't give Marshall the opportunity to finish.

"I spoke to my daughter on the very day she was killed, Mr. Marshall."

There was the merest hint of emotion, the slightest chink in the deep baritone voice.

"She told me she was in love. In love with David Stewart, the man you have marked as her murderer. She had never been so happy."

Wallace's eyes pierced Marshall, searching for a reaction, his rich, impeccable English tone was stirring,

"She told me other things, too. She was worried about her job, her rank, and the fact that John McCauley had a very unhealthy grip on her life. She wanted to be away from his influence. Do you not think it strange then, Superintendent, that she should be in his company last night?"

Marshall didn't want this conversation. He certainly couldn't voice his own doubts, and definitely not to Wallace.

"I think, Mr. Wallace, that it is best we don't discuss this further. As I say, I will have a copy of the file to you by this afternoon."

Wallace stood. There would be no nonsense.

"I want that file within the hour. Should you wish to contact me, I will be at the hospital. The Royal Preston, I believe. I want to see my daughter."

For a second Marshall thought Wallace's sadness would overcome him and he would falter, but the feeling quickly disappeared. Somehow the man composed himself.

"There will be a second post mortem for the defence," explained Wallace. "I wish to be there."

Marshall couldn't believe his ears. How could a father witness his own daughter being sliced to pieces? The Superintendent thought back to the many operations of this kind he had been forced to witness due to his job. Then he thought of his own girls, and his stomach turned over. This was one hard bastard.

Wallace saw the look on the face of the policeman.

"I know what you're thinking, Superintendent. I can see it in your eyes. Sir Peter Davits has travelled from London for the procedure. I intend to get to the bottom of this crime. I also intend to see the right person or persons in the dock. Then, and only then, will I be able to rest and grieve."

Marshall pinched the bridge of his nose, eyes closed. "You will have every co-operation from me and my men, sir."

Marshall considered his next words and actions carefully. He thought of his own two girls, tucked up in their beds, safe and loved.

"You may wish to speak to this officer."

Marshall wrote Andy Dunn's details on a slip of paper and handed it to Wallace.

"I am relying on your discretion, Mr. Wallace."

"You have it, Superintendent, thank you."

Wallace stood, shook the hand of the officer and left.

Marshall sat back in his chair and started to read the Stewart file, but within seconds dropped it to the desk.

Stewart was an anomaly, gangster's muscle turned copper. You had to be smart not to get caught in that game; smarter still to get past the vetting to become a copper.

Marie was right, he didn't need to kill Bailey to achieve his goal and finding the murder weapons like that was all too easy.

Now it seemed that Anne Wallace was in love with him. Had they known each other long enough for that?

He had fallen for his own wife within days, so why not?

Anne's own father seemed supremely confident that the police had it wrong. This was not legal posturing, and Wallace and his team would make formidable opponents at any trial.

The tiniest hole in the evidence would result in a Not Guilty verdict, and Marshall could see gaping wounds in the file on his desk.

He had to inform the Chief Constable of the new developments. The boss would not be happy.

The Royal Preston Hospital was ten minutes drive from the station. Robert Wallace and Sir Peter Davits sat in the rear of a chauffeur-driven Rolls Royce. The two men had been friends for over thirty years. They had met at Oxford when both were young students, and although they had always worked in different fields, both were fiercely competitive.

Davits had been Anne's godfather and was in sombre mood. He was most concerned for his friend.

"Are you sure you want to do this, Robert?"

Wallace turned. "Firstly, I am here to see Anne. Once I have completed that task, Peter, I will make a decision regarding the post mortem exam."

"You are one tough customer, Robert. I know that as much as anyone. However, you know what is involved in this procedure. The task is going to be difficult enough for me. Anne and I were close, you know that. My God, Robert, this could tear you apart. Please reconsider."

Wallace seemed briefly distant, as he had in Marshall's office, but then snapped back into his businesslike mood.

"Who's the best forensic scientist you know?"

Davits thought for a moment. "John Staples is the resident at Manchester University. He's the best in the crime field and he's only about an hour away from here."

Wallace nodded slowly. "OK, we will get him all the samples he could need by this afternoon."

Sir Peter shook his head. Wallace hadn't even considered that Staples might not have the time or inclination to do the job. Wallace wanted it, so it would be done. No question.

Wallace tapped on the glass divider inside the Rolls. "Step on it, Harry."

As the car sped through the early traffic, Dave Stewart was meeting his defence counsel. The man sitting opposite Dave wore a suit that cost more money than Dave earned in a month. If you took in the shirt, the shoes and the watch, Dave would have to work a year to pay for them.

George Thomas introduced himself to Dave. He explained the reason for his presence and the situation regarding costs. Dave had no need to worry. The company, 'Thomas Associates of London', would handle everything. Dave could trust him. He was on his side. He had to tell him everything. Thomas would have a copy of the file very soon. Dave would go to court today. He would be remanded in custody, but he would be out, and soon.

Stewart took an instant dislike to Thomas. He didn't trust him. Jesus, he didn't trust anyone, especially a barrister from London wearing a fancy suit.

Dave also found it hard to believe that Anne's father had agreed to pay all the costs of his case.

George Thomas, on the other hand, had seen it all before. Police corruption was a common practice as far as he was concerned. He had defended the most heinous criminals anyone could wish to meet.

Thomas had been briefed by Robert Wallace, and from the outline this case stank. The boy may be innocent. This was a minor detail to Thomas, of course. George was the brightest young barrister in the country, or so he would have you believe. Unfortunately, he had already made the mistake of underestimating David Stewart.

To Thomas, Dave was a young, inexperienced copper. A low class boy from coal mining stock who had got himself involved with a woman who was far too good for him.

Thomas himself had always felt that he and Anne could have made a good couple. He'd met her several times at the family home. Robert Wallace and Thomas's father had started the law firm back in the sixties. They had later gone their own ways. Both were extremely successful.

Thomas's father had retired, and George Thomas the second was now a full partner in one of London's busiest law firms. He was already a very wealthy young man.

Robert Wallace believed that Stewart had nothing to do with his daughter's death. Thomas didn't care what anyone thought. He just wanted out of this one horse town and back to London a.s.a.p.

Dave thought Thomas was a condescending twat.

"So, David," preached Thomas. "I need to know everything. I don't care how bad you think it sounds, but unless I know, I can't help you."

Dave sat, massaging his damaged hands. They were of more concern to him at that moment than Thomas. He had not shaved or showered since his arrest. His face was still swollen and bloodstained. He looked like shit.

Dave looked straight into the eyes of the barrister.

"Anne and I had only been together for a few days. In that short time, we, well let's just say, we became close. I learned that McCauley was putting pressure on her. He wanted her. She wanted out.

Anne and I went away for a short break to the Lake District; just to take a break; her father knows the place, they will confirm we shared a room. We took Anne's car. Check for yourself. For some reason the police think I followed her there. I left her at her home late in the afternoon on the day she was killed. We had agreed that she should meet McCauley so she could finish it for good."

Thomas was making notes. He spoke with a detached voice that needled Dave, "Was that the last time you saw her alive, then?"

"Yes. I went home. I went for a drink, to the Anchor at Hutton. I was there from about nine thirty 'till near closing. Again, you can check. Lots of people saw me.

I drove to Anne's place and when I got there, McCauley's car was in the drive. So, I turned straight around and went home. I got home about eleven fifteen."

Thomas was still scribbling. Dave's temper was about to flare. The irritation, evident in his voice, "Now by my calculations, that would be a fair alibi, don't you think, Mr. Thomas?"

Thomas didn't like the attitude. He paused and almost mocked, "Why on earth didn't you explain this to the police in interview?"

Dave was curt; "Because, Mr. Thomas, someone involved in this case has dumped two sets of bloodstained clothes in my car. Until I have a better idea of who that is, I'm reluctant to say anything at all. Even to you."

Thomas had dealt with criminals with bad attitudes his entire career, but he was losing his patience. Had this working class bonehead any idea of the cost of his services? Did he not realise how lucky he was?

"Well, Stewart, you had better start trusting me. I am the only friend you have right now."

Thomas looked at his notes. "Your alibi is decent, but far from watertight. I can't say for sure until the police release the file to me later today. In the meantime, get a shower and a shave. You look terrible. I'll get you some clean clothes to wear for court. There is a great deal of press interest in this case. Let me do all the talking. OK?"

Dave was weary. "You talk all you like, mate. Just get me out."

The hospital morgue was in the basement. A large area split into three main rooms. The first contained the recently deceased bodies. They were held in what looked like giant filing cabinets. The bodies themselves were identified by a label on the drawer of the cabinet, a band on the wrist, and a third tag on the toe.

This was the backstage; definitely a no frills type of place.

A hospital trolley stood in the middle of the room.

Two uniformed police officers and an undertaker's assistant were stripping the body of an elderly lady and tagging it. The three men all shared a joke. Life was going on in the midst of so much death.

The lady they worked on had died peacefully in her sleep but had not been visited by a doctor in recent weeks. Therefore, a post mortem was necessary. It was known as a 'Coroner's death.'

The second room of the three was accessed through a pair of heavy plastic swing doors.

A bright, white, sterile place, this was the room in which the post mortems took place.

Three specially grooved porcelain tables ran along the centre. They were little more than draining boards that disposed of the bodily fluids of the corpse.

Despite being spotlessly clean, this room had a smell unlike any other. Anyone who has ever experienced the smell, never forgets it.

Death has its own bouquet.

The remainder of the room had the appearance of any other laboratory.

Lab technicians and a pathologist worked methodically. One hummed a jolly chart tune as she weighed the internal organs of a corpse on the table.

The final room was the public face of the hospital morgue. No one cracked jokes or hummed tunes here. Known as 'The Chapel', this was the place where a body was taken for identification by a relative or friend of the deceased.

This room, much smaller than the other two, was dimly lit. The concrete walls shrouded in purple velvet cloth. Piped music played softly, soothing the dead.

The morgue staff would place a body on the table in the chapel. After attempting to cover any disfigurements with cloth, the police officer in charge of the coroner's death would lead the relative in, and the identification would formally take place. Anne Wallace had been formally identified at the murder scene.

The chief hospital administrator met Robert Wallace and Sir Peter Davits in the hospital reception. They were expected. She was sorry for their loss.

The standard words of comfort were lost on Wallace and Davits. A walk along a maze of polished corridors, a short journey in a lift, and the two men stood in the morgue area. Sir Peter could sense Wallace's discomfort in his surroundings.

Anne's body had been removed from its cabinet and laid out in the chapel. The staff had done their best with the facial damage, and had wrapped a shroud high around her neck to hide the death wound.

The two men stood in the doorway of the chapel. Davits rested his hand on the shoulder of his oldest and dearest friend.

"I'll leave you two alone for a while, Robert."

Wallace looked pale. He nodded to his pathologist friend. "Thank you, Peter."

Wallace took one stride inside the room and stopped. His emotions were about to overtake him. "Not yet." He breathed deeply. Invisible needles pricked his eyes.

He walked slowly to the table where his only child lay. His leather soles sounded each slow pace on the tiled floor. Then, slowly, he knelt and stared. For several minutes he was unable to avert his eyes. He recalled the first time he had held her; a bundle of pure joyous life. She was so beautiful. She hadn't cried as he had expected when he took her from her mother. She simply looked at him with those deep, expressive eyes. He had loved her from that moment. The bond was forged. She had made their lives complete. His mind flicked through the pages of its own personal family album. Her first day at school; the red dress she insisted on wearing to every party. Her embarrassed smiles when her second teeth were late. It seemed only yesterday. He relived it all again, filled with the pride only a father can feel.

Robert took Anne's lifeless hand, and although he'd expected it, the chill of her flesh shocked him. He spoke quietly. "Rest now, my little one. Daddy's here."

For a second the famous voice failed him. He cleared the torment from his throat. "You were our greatest love. Some people could live their whole lives and never show the same strength and courage as you. If you can hear me now, honey, and your mother and I believe that you can; remember we always loved you. Soon we will take you from this awful place. You know what must be done. I know you understand. Then we will take you home, baby."

Wallace stood and looked down at his daughter's damaged features. With shaking hands, he stroked her hair. Finally the immensely proud man's composure broke.

The tears began.

He knew he shouldn't. He knew the pain it would bring, but he was helpless. He took hold of the shroud and gently pulled it away from Anne's throat.

His revulsion was absolute. His whole body began to shake. His voice rose with each word until it was a bellow.

"Whoever did this to you, will rot in hell."

Davits heard his friend's sobs. His heart was being torn from his chest. He looked around the door and saw Wallace gently replace the shroud and take out a handkerchief.

He watched as Wallace wiped his eyes, cleared his throat and stepped into the hallway.

"She's all yours now, Peter. I'll be in the car when it's over."

Davits watched his friend walk from the morgue. He was grateful that Wallace had decided not to witness the post mortem operation. It would be almost impossible for Davits himself to remain detached. Things would be easier with his friend out of the way. He had to tell himself that it was what Anne would have wanted.

The morgue porter approached him, unaware of the pathologist's personal involvement. To the porter, it was back to tune humming. He was a stocky man in his forties; his unusually long white hair in a ponytail. He chewed as he spoke.

"Shall I move her, Doctor?"

Davits nodded, and the porter pushed his trolley into the chapel. He rolled Anne onto it; just another corpse.

"She was a bonny little thing, weren't she?"

Davits was unable to stop himself. "Just be a little more careful with her, and we'll have less of your comments too."

The porter looked mildly hurt. Why be careful with something that you are going to slice to pieces?

"Sorry, Doctor."

He moved Anne's body into the pathology lab and placed her onto the centre table with more care than usual. He didn't want the 'Doc' kicking off again.

Sir Peter looked down at the naked, empty vessel that had once been his goddaughter. He clenched his teeth in grief and anger. He turned to the hospital pathologist who was to assist him. He removed a Walkman from his pocket and set it to record.

“I want to start with tissue samples from the throat wound. There is some blood in her hair. I want a separate sample of that. When I have completed the P.M, all forensic samples will go with me so I will need carrying equipment.”

Sir Peter selected a scalpel and the two men then started their ghastly task.

David Stewart looked a little better. He had showered and shaved, a painful experience, but needed.

Thomas had brought some changes of clothing from Dave’s wardrobe at home. When Dave saw the jacket he had bought especially for his first date with Anne, the tears came again. He was still unable to fasten his own shoes or tie. Thomas reluctantly obliged.

Thomas was unmoved by Dave’s pain. “OK, David, we have about an hour before we get into court. As you know, we are only allowed one bail application. If I attempt it now, we can kiss it goodbye. Once in the court, all you have to do is confirm your identity. I don’t want you to make any other comment.”

Dave’s voice was flat, “So I’m going to jail?”

Thomas was nonplussed. “Yes.”

“You do realise what will happen to me in there, don’t you?”

Thomas put his hand on Dave’s arm, the gesture as genuine as a Hong Kong taxi meter. “You will be well protected, David. They don’t put police officers in general population. You will be classed as rule 43.”

"Great, so I'll be in solitary at best. At worst, I'll be sharing with some fucking child molester."

Thomas stood. "It won't be for long, David. The committal will be in six weeks. You will be brought back to court every week until then. If at any point we feel we have a good chance of bail, we can apply on one of those appearances."

"What's the worst case scenario?"

Thomas snapped the catches on his briefcase. "Well, I suppose, if it goes all the way to trial, it could be six months."

Dave put his head in his hands. Could it get any worse? Watching Thomas leave, he decided that his initial character assessment had been correct. Thomas was indeed a condescending twat.

Dave was to be transferred to the court cells, and Marshall and Jemson flanked him in the back seat of an unmarked police vehicle. It was a short trip and the three men travelled in silence. The only sound being the occasional squawk of the police radio. Despite the clear day, Marshall held a raincoat in his hand.

As the car approached the Courts, Marshall placed the raincoat over Dave's head. It shocked the young man, and at first he objected.

Marshall gripped Dave's forearm. "Steady on, son. Do you want every piece of shit in Risley to see your face on the front page of the Daily Mirror tomorrow?"

Dave murmured thanks from under the coat, and the car pulled to a halt.

The area was a mêlée.

Newspaper and television teams surged towards the car. The usual crowd of baying public-spirited citizens closely followed them, hoping to get a glimpse of the triple killer. Dave was big news.

Shouted threats and press questions mingled together in Dave's ears. The cacophony engulfed him. He had never been so scared. He was bundled over a pavement and through a doorway. The noise began to subside, and he realised he was inside a corridor.

The coat came off and he stood looking straight into the face of Marshall. Dave found it strangely reassuring.

"Well, we got you here in one piece, Dave," said the Superintendent, who to Dave's surprise, was smiling.

"Thanks."

Dave looked into Marshall's eye and saw something strange. He lowered his voice, "You believe me, don't you? You think I'm innocent."

Marshall's smile disappeared. He remained silent, turned on his heels and walked away.

Two burly prison officers, who had already been briefed regarding the special nature of their charge, immediately flanked Dave.

The taller of the two spoke, "Right, lad, we will take you to your cell under the court. When it's your turn, we will escort you to the dock and stand with you. I don't want any funny stuff in the courtroom. After your appearance, we will escort you to the remand centre. Any property that you take with you will have to be cleared by us. We realise your problem, as does the Governor. You will be classed as 'Rule 43', but I'll tell you now, you'll still have to watch your back."

Dave nodded, although he wasn't taking much of the information in. His head was still spinning. Everything was happening so quickly. The two officers led him further along the corridor and past a row of occupied cells. They each contained several other prisoners who were appearing at court that day. A spotty faced youth of about seventeen had managed to get his whole head out of the hatch of his cell door, and was watching Dave approach.

"Hey! Piggy! Piggy! Come to see how the other half live?"

The youth screwed his face up into an evil sneer. "When they bend you over, pig, I'm gonna be first."

Dave was close enough to the youth now that he could see he had the word "Banger" tattooed on his forehead.

Bright.

As Dave got in line with the hatch he faked a trip, stuck his elbow out at a right angle and connected sharply with Banger's nose.

Dave's sarcasm oozed, "Oops! Sorry, mate, floor's really slippery."

The youth was howling like a stuck pig and nursing his damaged nose. Dave's escorts didn't flinch. The taller man of the two simply turned to his partner and smiled.

"When Banger feels better, we'd better get him to mop that section of floor."

Dave was placed alone in a cell at the end of the row. As the tall prison officer closed the door, he spoke absently, “Oh, by the way, I nearly forgot, Stewart. You have a visitor waiting. I’ll organise it now.”

Dave’s spirit rose in leaps. A visitor!

After what seemed like an age, Dave’s cell door was opened and he was led to an interview room where his company was waiting. Dave thought he was having an attack of déjà vu. Sitting at the graffiti-ridden table was none other than his old employer, Steve Ross.

Ross had started out as a bouncer, working the doors of the roughest clubs in and around Sheffield. He’d dabbled in petty crime and some ‘contract’ muscle work for moneylenders. It was during this period he had been suspected of killing a night club doorman with a single punch. The man had refused him entry to his favourite drinking establishment. Ross was arrested but never charged.

A year after that drama, he opened his first club. Within five years, he was the most feared man in Yorkshire.

Now he was the proud owner of three nightclubs, which in truth were only fronts for his main sources of income. Ross was now the picture of respectability. His massive shoulders encased in the finest silk suit. He rested shovel-sized hands on the table. The minute he saw Dave, he stood and a broad smile revealed a gleaming gold tooth.

Once the two were alone, Ross’s smile disappeared and his fine, well-dressed, image was shattered by a voice that sent shivers down the spine.

"You seem to have got yourself in a mess, son."

Dave held both hands out for Ross to see. "Don't be offended if I don't shake hands, Mr. Ross."

Ross took Dave's hands gently in his own and inspected them. "Cuffs?"

Dave nodded.

Ross shook his head. "Bastards, I could never understand why you didn't stay with me, Dave. I had big plans for you."

Dave just smiled meekly.

Despite Ross's reputation, which was well deserved, Dave couldn't help but like him. He was intelligent and had a great sense of humour. He, like most Yorkshiremen, never forgot a good turn.

Ross returned to his seat and produced a box of cigarettes from a very expensive looking briefcase. The box appeared perfectly sealed. Dave was about to remind his old boss that he didn't smoke, when he spoke.

"Don't open it. There are some items in there that you might need."

Ross lowered his voice.

"Your old dad came to me yesterday. He told me as much as he knew. The coppers have been round to your house asking questions. I used some favours to find out what they really have on you. It ain't much. I know you, Dave. You always worked well. This isn't your style."

Ross lowered his voice further, "Tell me who you need sorting. The boys will look after it. Just say the word and it's done. Then, when you're out, come back and work for me, eh?"

Dave had finally found someone he could trust. Of all the people he could have chosen, he found it strangely comforting that honour and reliability surfaced in the form of a reputed gangster.

"Mr. Ross. Things are moving pretty quick for me right now. I've got a few ideas, but I need some more information. I can't do anything in here."

Dave paused, "You know I wouldn't ask if it weren't important. I do need a favour and it won't be easy. I need something collecting from my house, and I need it kept safe."

Ross's smile returned at the mention of the favour. His dental jewellery gleamed. "Collection is my business, Dave."

Wallace and Davits were on the move again. It had taken a while to recover Anne's effects from the police. Wallace had to threaten the officer with a personal telephone call to the Chief Constable.

Wallace looked even more tired. He spoke to his driver, "How much further to the University, George?"

"About ten minutes, sir."

Wallace then turned to his friend. They had not spoken about the post mortem since leaving the hospital.

"So, Peter, what were your first impressions?"

Sir Peter held a copy of the police pathologist's preliminary report. "From what I saw today, Robert, my conclusions are very similar to this." He tapped the file and continued, "I think he missed some things, though. There is nothing in here about testing a blood sample from Anne's hair. It could be her own of course, but I have a feeling that it isn't. A knife with a serrated blade caused the throat wound. Probably the one from the second bag found in Stewart's garden, which was very convenient. She had some scalp damage, presumably from being dragged by the hair. Her nose was fractured and she suffered some dental damage, punches likely; someone very strong. Then of course there is the bruising to her wrists."

Sir Peter looked across at his friend to see how he was dealing with the hard information. Wallace sat rigidly in his seat and looked straight ahead.

He nodded occasionally. Finally he spoke, "Thank you, Peter. It must have been a difficult task for you." He paused, the information settling in his mind, "Did you say bruising to her wrists?"

"Yes, she was bound."

"If Stewart were responsible for this, why would he tie her up?"

Both men lapsed into thoughtful silence until they arrived at Manchester University.

Professor John Staples met Wallace and Davits at the door of his office, the pathologist holding a large cardboard box. It contained the samples he had taken earlier and Anne's personal effects.

Staples looked more like a reject from Woodstock than an

esteemed professor of forensic science and criminology.

His long greying hair brushed his shoulders and small round, 'John Lennon' style glasses, gave him the look of a middle aged rock star.

If Davits hadn't recommended Staples, Wallace would have turned around there and then. Staples saw the look on Wallace's face. He smiled and offered his hand. "You must be Mr. Wallace. Please allow me to introduce myself. You obviously don't care for my taste in clothes, Wallace, but I'm the best forensic man in the country."

His smile broadened. "I play a mean harmonica too."

Wallace took the hand, and softened slightly.

"I'm sorry, Professor; my daughter always said I was too old fashioned. I'm grateful to you for your prompt attention."

Staples nodded. "And I am sorry for your loss, sir."

The three men walked into the organised clutter of Staples' office.

Davits found a small space not covered by files or exhibits, and placed the box onto a table. "John, these are the P.M. samples and Anne's clothing. How soon can you start?"

Staples began emptying the contents of the box and turned to Wallace.

"Can I see the police file?"

Staples sat and started to read. He immersed himself in it. Wallace and Davits watched in silence as the man read and re-read the paperwork. He took a magnifying glass and studied the scenes of crime photographs.

Finally, Staples leaned back in his chair and removed his glasses.

“This case, gentleman, doesn’t make sense. Unless of course, the defendant, err...Stewart, is mentally ill.”

Wallace was quick to react. “I can say, sir, with a great deal of certainty, that my daughter would not have involved herself with a lunatic. Also, if you are concerned, you can rest assured that you will be well compensated for your time.”

Staples nodded. “In that case, Wallace, I will take it as my duty to assist you, in any way possible. I will be honest; this case has attracted a great deal of publicity already. It will do my department and me a great deal of good, should of course we come up with the goods to free the young chap. Therefore, whatever fee you pay me, this is a double edged sword. I need this kind of work. The high profile stuff does no harm when it comes time to renew our government grants.”

Staples patted the file. “Give me a day or two, and I will get back to you.”

The men stood, shook hands and parted.

The two esteemed men walked slowly to the Rolls. Wallace turned to his friend. “Peter, you haven’t said too much about this whole mess. Am I putting too much faith in Anne’s judgement?”

Davits had marveled at the man’s faith and indeed, did have doubts. Stewart’s motive was thin, but people had killed for less. Despite some odd discrepancies, the evidence against Stewart was pretty convincing, he had to admit.

If Wallace was right, then this case must involve corruption within the police on a large scale. Notwithstanding his fears, Davits decided that this was not the time to vent them. He halted, and observed a very tired Robert Wallace.

"I'm with you all the way on this one, Robert. Anne was the daughter I never had. I want justice done too."

He took Wallace's arm. "We can do no more today. Let's go to the hotel and rest. You look like you need it."

Wallace suddenly stiffened. "Nonsense! If we hurry, we will catch Stewart before he is taken to the remand centre. I need to speak to him personally. I have some questions."

Davits shook his head. "OK Robert, whatever you say, let's go."

Dave Stewart climbed the stairs that led to the courtroom. He found himself counting again. Twenty-six. The two prison officers flanked him.

As he appeared in the dock there was a flurry of excitement around the packed court. Dozens of pens and pencils scribbled away behind him.

The magistrates had yet to appear.

Thomas leaned over the dock to whisper a last minute reminder to Dave. He had not to make any comment.

Dave didn't like Thomas at all. However, he had to admit he dominated the courtroom with his presence.

Dave looked around the court and saw Lucy sitting in the public gallery. He caught her eye. She smiled and gave a discreet 'thumbs up' sign.

It made him feel slightly better. He scanned the room for Ross, but couldn't see him. He wasn't that surprised. Ross was probably arranging Dave's 'favour'.

Suddenly the court usher stood and announced the commencement of business. All were to rise. Three magistrates filed into their seats. One woman and two men; all looked very sombre. They would have known of the seriousness of their task.

The sound of pen on paper started again. Dave started to sweat.

The magistrates had no legal training, and it was the responsibility of the magistrates' clerk to lead the proceedings. Dave felt lost. The clerk had warned the press regarding restrictions. Dave had been asked to confirm his details. He tried to be as confident as possible.

The charges were read.

More scribbling sounds deafened Dave.

Thomas was speaking. He was eloquent and precise. The speech aimed at the press more than the magistrates. Within minutes, it was over. Dave was being led back down the stairs. He looked over towards Lucy. She was crying.

He walked the steps again and was inside his cell within seconds.

Thomas joined him. "Quite painless, David."

The smell of the barrister's aftershave was overpowering.

Dave was attempting to remove his tie. “For who?”

Thomas sat. He was far from comfortable in the stench of the cell. “Look, Stewart, I’m here to defend you, innocent or guilty. I’m not here to wet-nurse you, so let’s get things straight right now.”

Dave was angry but controlled.

“Well, let’s get this straight, shall we. I didn’t ask you to defend me. You may well be a good lawyer, but as a man, you make my teeth itch. I have lost someone very dear to me. I’ve lost my job; my family will be under siege from the press and,” Dave lost the battle with his tie, “I don’t think I’ll ever play the fuckin’ piano again!”

Thomas was about to retort when the cell door opened to reveal Robert Wallace. Dave had never met or spoken to the man, but the family resemblance was obvious.

Thomas was creeping, “Robert, ah, I’m just briefing David here. Err, how are you, sir? You look tired.”

Wallace brushed the comments aside. “I would like to speak with Mr. Stewart alone, George.”

It was evident to Dave that Wallace shared his opinion of Thomas, who looked uncomfortable as he stood.

“Of course, sir.”

Wallace closed the cell door and sat next to Dave. He extended his hand. Dave painfully took it.

“I’m Anne’s father, Robert Wallace.”

“Pleased to meet you, sir.”

Wallace inspected the damage to Dave's hands.

"You must be pretty confused right now, David, so let me explain a few things first. Anne and I were close. Despite the miles between us, we kept in touch regularly. I spoke with her on the day she died. She told me about you. She told me she was in love."

Wallace actually smiled as he recalled, "She hadn't told me that since she was fifteen and some schoolboy had taken her fancy. It wasn't something she would say lightly. That conversation is the sole reason I set all this in motion, the reason why I am fighting to prove your innocence."

The smile left his face. "Heaven help me if I'm wrong."

Dave looked Wallace in the eye. "You're not wrong. I was very much in love with Anne. I would never have harmed her. She was the best thing that ever happened to me. I just can't believe she's gone." Dave realised he was talking to someone equally bereaved. "I'm sorry, Mr. Wallace. It's just that no one seems to want to get at the truth."

Wallace became animated. "We need to know why that is, David. You must be able to help us. We need to work together."

Dave needed to trust this man. He seemed genuine. Why would he do this for him? Dave was confused. He wanted to talk, but now was not the time. He had to do this his own way.

"I don't know, sir. Anne was under pressure from McCauley. She was meeting him to end their relationship. I have told Thomas all I know."

Wallace stared at Dave for what seemed like an age. His eyes burned for the truth. He got no indication from the young man that he was lying.

"I have to believe I am doing the right thing for my daughter. I'm sure you are a fine young man. I promise I will do all I can to get you free as soon as possible."

Dave looked upon Robert Wallace. He sat perfectly straight like some retired military general, his pride obvious for all to see. He saw Anne in him, her persistence and determination.

Dave stood, and it was Wallace's turn to see. He saw something in the young man that surprised him. It convinced him more than ever that Dave was innocent. Dave's eyes burned with hatred.

"I need to be free, Mr. Wallace."

Wallace turned and opened the cell door. "You will be free, David, I will see to that."

Two men sat on the park bench. Ducks wandered around the edge of the pond they faced. The park was nearly deserted. At this time of year few ventured into the cold. Neither of the two wanted to be seen together.

One was a large and powerfully built man, the other, smaller but more affluent, being dressed in the latest designer clothes. The shorter of the men spoke first.

"I told you what I wanted done. When the situation with Bailey arose, you had to dispose of him. No one was going to miss the little shit. However, two serving police Officers, that's a different matter. It's on every front page. This will mean close scrutiny of all concerned. I can't have that. I didn't want this situation."

The tall man sneered, "If those files get out it won't make a difference. Jail is jail. I went with what I had on the night. Bailey had bottled out. I followed him and sorted it. When I got to McCauley's, someone had got there before me, someone who knew; someone with a key. With the information I had, Wallace was the obvious choice. When McCauley turned up, I had to take him. He'd have recognised me and connected me to you. Is that what you wanted?"

The man threw a pebble at a passing duck.

"I thought you, of all people, would have been glad to see the back of him. Anyway, the whole job was clean. No forensics. I dumped the gear just where you said."

"So where are the files?"

The tall man shrugged his shoulders. "Someone else obviously knew that McCauley had finally used one of his aces. Whoever opened that safe was a pro."

The shorter man looked tired. The strain was starting to show. He thought out loud, "If the press gets that material, I'm ruined. I may as well be dead alongside McCauley."

The taller man snapped, "You really are a baby, aren't you? Look, the files have gone. McCauley is dead. Whoever has the files wanted them for one of two reasons. Either McCauley had dirt on them, or two, they're in the blackmail business. So, they'll either bury them forever, or they will be in touch. If they like living, they'll bury them."

"I don't like it. I have a lot to lose."

The tall man stood. He picked a speck from the smaller man's overcoat. "I never lose. Just don't forget what you owe me."

The shorter man walked away, his voice more reassured. "Get me what I want and you'll get your money."

Dave sat in a tiny space inside the prison vehicle. It was the size of a removal van. Royal blue coachwork gleamed on the exterior. The Lancashire Constabulary crest, emblazoned in gold and red, told any casual onlooker exactly what the vehicle was for. The interior was a different matter. That was split into cells, each about the size of a toilet. A corridor ran along the centre and two very harassed prison officers sat at either end. The stench of the van made Dave gag.

The ride to the remand centre was noisy. Prisoners were shouting abuse at the prison officers from their claustrophobic cubicles. They hurled expletives to their unseen captors, banging their handcuffs on the walls, demanding various rights. The officers had heard it all before. Scores would be settled in the privacy of the centre.

There was a knock on the wooden partition to Dave's right. It jolted him from his thoughts. A voice spoke to him in a hoarse whisper, "Copper! Hey! Copper!"

Dave ignored the voice, but it was persistent.

"You'll be in the same block as me, so you'd better be friendly.

Know what I mean? I can help you. Show you the ropes."

Dave let his head fall back against the panel behind him and closed his eyes. As the van rattled along relentlessly to its destination, his thoughts once again turned to Anne. Justice? Where was the justice? He placed his damaged palms together and prayed for the first time in years.

The prison van finally came to a halt in a large square. It could have been public gardens. Men in overalls were tending large, open areas of lawn and flowerbeds. Benches without customers were set around the displays of early spring colour. Unfortunately, the three storey buildings with barred windows and the eighteen-foot concrete wall, which surrounded the foliage, spoiled the look.

The van had been stationery at the security gate for a long time. The wait had made Dave even tenser.

The prisoners were released one by one. Dave could hear the process. He was also aware that he and the talkative man in the cell to his right were to be the last off.

Finally, his door opened.

The same officers who took him into court led him into the daylight. Instantly a cacophony of abuse was hurled in his direction from a prison block some thirty yards away.

They didn't know who Dave was, only that the Rule 43's came off the van last. The men tending the flowers were given the task of getting a good look. Nonces needed to be identified. Criminals had a strange code. All considered their crimes to be more socially acceptable than their peers. The nonces were at the bottom of the pile.

Dave was quickly herded toward a separate block and into a reception area. Another man was being searched and processed. He looked a real hard case. Dave presumed he was the voice in the van. A young officer spoke to Dave over a high counter, whilst other officers searched his clothing and a bag of belongings. No one questioned the 'unopened' box of cigarettes from Ross.

He confirmed his name, date of birth, address and religion. He could wear his own clothes whilst on remand.

He was informed of his rights, visits, telephone calls, meal times and exercise. He carried a blanket and linen sheets, and was led along long corridors with dark green linoleum floors. The occasional trustee was mopping sections of the floor. Each had a long look at the new boy.

Dave had forgotten nearly everything he had been told by the time he got to his cell.

To his horror, he was not alone.

The cell was no more than eight feet by six feet. One metal framed bed at each side. A stainless steel toilet and washbasin sat dead centre.

A man about Dave's age lay on the left-hand bed dressed only in running shorts. He was small but muscular. He obviously worked at his physique.

The cell was spotlessly clean and tidy. The man's possessions lay neatly around his half of the tiny space. Dave stood in the doorway, prison bedding under one arm, his meagre possessions in the other. He was rooted to the spot and speechless. Suddenly, he felt claustrophobic.

His escort barked in his ear, bringing him from the brink of panic, "Right, Stewart, get your bed made and settle in."

The officer gave Dave a sharp nudge in the back and the cell door slammed behind him. To Dave it sounded like the death toll.

The man inside the cell sat up. A small, sharp-featured face with crew cut blonde hair. He spoke in quick bursts with a strong Manchester accent. His obvious joviality was an immediate irritation.

"This has gotta be your first time?"

Dave ignored him. The man shrugged and lay back down. "Suit yourself."

Dave began the task of making his bed. His sore hands made the process slow. Once this was complete, he unpacked his possessions and lay them inside the confines of his half of the cell, copying his cellmate.

The man opposite watched his every move with mild amusement. "Can I make a suggestion, like?"

Dave looked over, his eyes cold and dangerous. "Suggest away."

The man sat up again and rested himself on one elbow. He pointed to the unopened box of cigarettes. "You need to hide them or they'll walk."

Dave pointed at the locked cell door with his chin. He stared straight at his cellmate. "Who's going to nick 'em, except you?"

The man shook his head like a father would to a stumbling child.

"We're not locked down all the time, y' know. The screws open us up at seven each night, 'till ten. We get visitors. Some welcome, some not."

The man continued, "Cigarettes are hard currency in here and you seem to be rich, like."

Dave became defensive, "Look, don't even think about it."

The man held up his hands.

"Whoa, boy! You're too big for me, mate. Just givin' you some helpful advice, take it or leave it. Know what I mean?"

"Everybody wants to help me today."

The man smiled and nodded. "Listen, mate, I know exactly how you feel, but the fact is you are here on '43'. Which means either you're a nonce, a grass or a pig. Every man jack on this block wouldn't last two minutes outside in general population. The cons on '43' don't give a monkey's why you're on this block. But remember, there are some seriously sick fucks in here and there's still a pecking order, like. You have to find your place and stick to it. That, or fight for your fuckin' life."

Dave stared straight at the man. "...and where are you in this order? Top nonce, top grass or just a sick fuck?"

The man pretended to look hurt. "That's not nice, mate. I'm just trying to be friendly, like."

Dave sat on his bed. "Just don't try and get too friendly."

The man lay back once again, his voice casual. He had no fear of Dave.

"You're not my type, mate. Besides, why should I want to get close to someone who slits throats for a living?"

Dave exploded, the shock at the man's knowledge catching him off guard. "I'm innocent, you fuckin' piece of shit! Innocent, you hear! I don't belong in here with you, or any of this other scum!"

The man remained in position, seemingly unimpressed by Dave's show of aggression. His voice remained level.

"Ain't we all, pal."

Dave flung himself back onto his bunk. He was frustrated and scared. He wished the man had taken the bait. He wanted to punch him, hurt him. He closed his eyes and tried to calm himself. "My God," he thought, "what is happening to me?"

The cell remained quiet. The Manchester face was silent, opting to read a book. Dave listened to the activity going on outside. He was amazed at the level of noise. It seemed everyone with a radio or tape player only had one volume level. Full up. People shouted to each other between cells. He had no watch, time had stood still.

Then a different set of noises came to the block. Dave sensed something was happening. Eventually the cell door was opened. It was time for food and recreation.

He didn't move. He wasn't hungry and he didn't want to socialise with the others.

His cellmate stood and pulled on a football shirt. "You comin' for some grub or not?"

Dave didn't answer. The face shrugged, resigned to the fact his new cellmate was a moody fucker, and left to eat.

Dave was alone again. He sat on the end of his bunk and handled the carton of cigarettes Ross had given him. He thought about inspecting the contents but decided to wait until he knew more about the regime in the jail. Instead, he took off the cotton cover from his pillow, removed sufficient stuffing, and inserted the carton in the space; not the best hiding place, but it would do for now.

Dave put the stuffing he had removed down the toilet and relieved his bowels on top of it. He replaced the pillowcase and rested his head on his prize possession, whatever it was.

An age passed. The smell of boiled food permeated the air inside the block. The strange rattle of plastic cutlery and a blaring television echoed around the bare hard surfaces of his cell. Eventually the sounds of the men returning from recreation made Dave sit up.

Dave's cellmate walked in with another older male. Dave ignored them both. The older man stood and stared at Dave. He waited for the face to leave, but the staring continued, silent and menacing.

The visitor was grossly overweight. Large rolls of fat rippled under a very dirty T-shirt. It was difficult to be precise but Dave put him at middle-aged. His balding head glistened with sweat, and what hair remained was greasy and unkempt. He was also causing a very unpleasant smell.

Dave could feel his temper rising again. He was about to fuck the fat bastard off, when a guard appeared to announce 'lock down.'

The fat man shuffled out of the cell without speaking. The cell door was closed, and Dave's cellmate spoke.

"What did you think of Henry, then?"

Dave's eyes remained fixed on the ceiling. "He stinks. Why did you bring him here?"

The man smiled. "I didn't. Henry wanted a look at you. He's not a full shilling, if you know what I mean like? Plus, if Henry thinks you don't like him, well, he's the type to put a few holes in you with his toothbrush. Like I said, there are some really sick fucks in here."

Dave eyed his cellmate. "I didn't realise I was such a celebrity."

The man seemed thoughtful. Eventually, he spoke, "Listen, mate, we got off on the wrong foot before, me and you. We both have to share this box for a while, so," the man extended his hand, "I'm Jimmy."

Dave was reluctant, but took the hand. There was no chance of a firm handshake just yet. "Dave."

Jimmy took a small pile of books from under his bunk and handed them over the small space. "Here's some reading material. You'll go mad without it."

Dave took the tatty paperbacks and flicked through the first. It had a picture of a woman in a bikini on the front. The title told the story. Dave was unimpressed. "I don't think I'm in the mood for 'Beach Babes'." He turned to the next book, "Or 'Randy Riders'." He noted the rest of the books were on a similar theme. "Where did you get these then, Jimmy?"

"The library trolley; it comes around once a week, like."

Dave sighed and added sarcastically, "The fuckin' highlight of the week eh?"

Jimmy grew serious, "Look Dave, I don't care if you were a copper, and before you say, yeah, everyone knows. The bush telegraph, like. I got nothing against coppers. To me, people don't have anyone to blame for being in here but themselves. Take it from me; the whole block knows why you're here. Most will give you a wide berth, like, you having been in the filth. Some though, will still come after you. So you watch your back."

Dave let the words sink in for a moment. "I've been watching my back for a long time, Jimmy. I'm getting pretty good at it."

Jimmy stood. He couldn't help but notice Dave's physique. "I can see that."

The wiry man walked the few paces to the toilet. He dropped his shorts and sat. He read Dave's face. "You'll get used to this. There's no privacy in here. Some wank in front of each other, too."

"I don't, I do it in the shower. Trouble is, every time I go out in the rain now, I get a hard on."

Dave smiled at Jimmy's attempt at humour, but it was short lived.

The two men lay on their beds in the semi darkness, the central heating over doing its job. The incessant noise still came from outside, jangling Dave's nerves. Both had been silent for a while, when Dave spoke, "Why are you here, Jimmy?"

"Me? I'm a pimp. Rent boys, like."

Jimmy's voice was flat, as if the information was the most natural thing in the world. In the half-light, Jimmy could see the look of disgust on Dave's face.

"Like I said, there are some really sick fucks in this place."

Andy Dunn had just finished his evening tour. He walked from the nick to the 'Black Bull' feeling very sorry for himself; he had been unable to concentrate all day.

The place was packed and filled with smoke. He had to walk sideways to get to the bar. He must have excused himself ten times on the way.

Lucy smiled when she saw her man. She, of course, was busy and was pouring pints for England. She shouted over the din of inebriated fellows. "Hi Andy! Just give me a minute, love, and I'll be with you."

Moments later, Lucy placed a pint of Andy's favourite bitter in front of him. She leaned over the bar, displaying mountainous cleavage. "How you doin', Andy love?"

The burly officer drained almost half of his beer in one go. He wiped the foam from his mouth and shook his head. He couldn't get his mind around what Marshall had told him.

"I'm OK, I suppose. Just been thinking about poor Dave locked up with all that scum."

Lucy straightened, and pulled a second beer in readiness. "I was in the court today. It was so sad. Dave looked like a little boy. Can't you do anything, Andy? I'm sure they've made a mistake. He's such a nice lad, always so polite."

Andy drained the remainder of his first drink. “I’m going to try, love. But you know there are some real high flyers involved in this job and they don’t take much notice of an old beat copper like me.”

Lucy beckoned Andy closer and whispered, “There’s a few of them in the taproom now. They’ve been talking about the case but I couldn’t hear much.”

Andy nodded, collected his new beer and walked into the small, even smokier snug. This room had once been the domain of men only, and Andy was old enough to remember.

Marshall, Slick Jemson and a woman Andy didn’t know were seated at a table in the corner. Marshall saw Andy first. The senior officer looked a little pissed.

“’Armless, come and have a beer with us.”

Marshall’s words were the worse for the drink, confirming Andy’s first impressions. He joined the team, and Marshall put his arm around Andy’s massive shoulders.

“Andy, I think you know Slick here, and this is Marie.”

Andy shook hands all round.

Marshall spoke a little too loudly into Andy’s ear, his cockney accent more pronounced than usual. “Well, me and the team here are having a celebration. We just wrapped up a triple murder in record time.”

Marshall picked up his glass and raised it toward his colleagues. “Here’s to fucking justice, eh?”

Andy had never seen Marshall so out of control. Even on their rugby drinking sessions, Marshall was always on the ball. Slick stepped into the breach. He put his hand on the shoulder of his senior. "Come on, boss, I think it's time we were off."

Marshall ignored Slick and shrugged off the hand. The alcohol had loosened his tongue. He didn't care who heard. "Listen, Andy, you were right. This job, it stinks. It really stinks."

'Slick' had a second go. "Come on, boss."

This time Marshall stood. He seemed very unsteady on his feet. He tapped the bridge of his nose. "You'll be getting a visit, Andy. Just you be careful. This whole business could take a few people down with it. Mark my words."

Andy wanted to know who would be visiting, but it wasn't the time or place to be asking questions. Andy let the remark pass, and the three Serious Crime Squad officers left the bar. He pushed his way back through to the main bar and resumed his previous position, watching Lucy pull pints. He mulled over what he had witnessed. If Marshall was so uncertain, the job must be dodgy. Andy knew Marshall well. He was a good bloke. Straight as they come.

Andy had to do something. It couldn't wait any longer. He beckoned Lucy, "I'm off, love. Are you coming back to my place tonight?"

She giggled trying to be light hearted, but she could see her man was in a serious mood. "Ooh, always the romantic aren't you. Yeah, I suppose so. I've got my key."

Andy drained the remnants of his drink. Someone was out there free, and his mate Dave was stuck in jail. Well, whoever was responsible now had another serious problem. Andy Dunn.

His head was full of pieces of information as he walked from the pub to the nick. He entered through the garage door and used the lift near the charge office. The nightshift had already left for duty, and the place was deserted.

He reached the second floor unnoticed, and saw that the incident room was in darkness, all the detectives having left for the night. He knew of course, he shouldn't be there.

He definitely shouldn't be poking around in the files but it was the only place he could think to start.

After a few minutes of searching, he had found what he was looking for and set about copying the huge file that now represented Dave Stewart's fate.

The Xerox whooshed and clicked away. Andy felt less and less comfortable. He was on the final page of the file when he heard the footsteps.

He moved quickly for a big man. He scooped up his photocopies and pushed the originals back into the cardboard sleeve. By the time the figure stood back lit in the doorway, Andy was concealed in the darkness, crouched behind a nearby desk.

The man walked cautiously in the half-light to the copier that still buzzed from its recent use. He studied it and lifted the lid.

In his hurry to conceal himself, Andy had left the last sheet of the Stewart file in the copier. Curious, the man lifted it closer to his face in order to see the written text.

To Andy's relief, the man then simply slotted the sheet into the remainder of the file, which lay on the nearest desk, fumbled for the switch and turned off the copier.

To Andy's discomfort, the man didn't leave. He walked to a desk and sat. He produced a packet of cigarettes and lit one. The light from the flame revealed the man's face. It was Clive Williams.

Clive didn't look too good. He always looked a little rough, but today he looked like a vagrant. His clothes looked wet, as if he had been walking in the rain for some considerable time. He rooted in the desk cupboard and found a bottle of scotch.

Clive simply sat in the darkness, smoked one cigarette after another and guzzled the contents of the bottle.

Andy's legs were numb with the wait, but he couldn't move. He had to stay, and hope Williams didn't investigate further.

After the fourth cigarette, Andy's wish came true. Williams stood to leave. Clive could barely walk, and Andy presumed that the scotch had not been the first of the day. It seemed everyone involved in this job had been either celebrating, or drowning his sorrows this night.

Andy waited until Clive's footsteps faded into the distance before leaving his hiding place. He had to get home and study the file. It was a small step, but where else could he start? He had to do it for Dave.

The walk to the rooftop car park revived Andy. He started to think more clearly. By the time he made it home he was in determined mood.

Lucy was making tea. She had only recently got used to making the brew the way Andy liked it, very strong, with only the slightest hint of milk.

He sat on the sofa with the mountainous file scattered on the coffee table in front of him as Lucy produced his brew.

"How's it going, sweetheart?"

Andy placed the cup away from the papers, took hold of Lucy by the waist and sat her on his knee. He gave her an affectionate squeeze and then looked down at the file.

"Well, Lucy, I'm no legal expert, but the whole of Dave's so-called motive is in these papers. He is supposed to have changed his statement in the Bailey job, but there's no copy of his original here. That means, no one can say for certain. Dave told me that McCauley wanted it changed; was that the truth or was Dave covering himself with me? Did Dave change it, or did someone else?"

Andy picked up two sheets of paper and held them up for Lucy to see.

"This is a copy of Bailey's property sheet. This is filled in as soon as a prisoner arrives at the nick, by the charge office sergeant. It lists everything a prisoner has on him at the time. As you can see, there is a record of a pair of rubber gloves being in Bailey's possession. Now, Dave told me himself, he left them in his coat by mistake. Again, did Dave add it to the sheet to keep McCauley happy, or did someone else involved in the case do it?"

Andy turned to the second sheet. "And this is a copy of the Crime Property Ledger. This shows the gloves against Bailey's name, but the times are uncoordinated. The entry is late. The whole job revolved around these gloves. Did someone else change these documents, as well as his statement, in order to please McCauley, or do we believe the police evidence that he did it all off his own bat?

If you believe the police, Dave then killed Bailey to keep this information from coming out. But why would he need to do that? Bailey was just a street thug, a small time burglar and brawler. All Dave needed to do was steal and destroy the original Bailey documents.

Finally, he supposedly went to visit Anne, found her with McCauley and we are meant to believe that he was in such a jealous rage, he killed them both.

It all seems very unlikely to me. Basically, the police believe that Dave acted alone in this job. OK, he did cock up. I know that, but did he change all these documents? Did he lie to me in the pub that day about McCauley?"

Lucy seemed puzzled, looked at the papers, and pointed to the final entry on Bailey's property sheet. "This handwriting is the same as the writing in the property thingy."

Andy nodded, "Yes, but did Dave write it? I haven't got anything to compare it to."

Lucy jumped up. "I have."

Lucy was gone for a few moments and returned to the room holding a greeting card. "Remember this?" she bubbled. "You and a few of the regular lads got it for my birthday. Dave wrote a message in it and signed it."

Andy took the card, and for once was pleased that Lucy did clutter his bedroom with what he referred to as junk.

He studied all three samples of handwriting for a few moments and shook his head. "Well, someone has been very sloppy here. This handwriting on the card is nothing like the writing on the documents."

Lucy positively squeaked with pleasure, "So I solved the case?" Andy was forced to smile. "It's a step in the right direction, sweetheart." Lucy leapt to her feet and let out a joyous cry. Andy sat back and looked at his girlfriend with growing affection. "OK, baby, but it's far from over yet. So we know Dave didn't alter the papers. If it was McCauley though, why is he dead?"

Andy rubbed his eyes. He was fading fast.

Lucy gave him a look that he had come to recognise. She lifted her T-shirt over her head, revealing her ample charms in all their glory. Her voice became babyish, "Now you can put those papers away and come and play with Lucy."

As Andy lay on his bed, still sweating from the exertion of his encounter with Lucy, his mind wandered to Dave.

How was he coping with life inside jail? Was he OK, and who should he go to with his new found information?

There were too many questions without answers. Hopefully, he would have some of them tomorrow.

Dave had slept fitfully and was already awake when the guard opened the cell hatch to announce breakfast.

Dave wearily slid from his bunk and took the plastic plate from the man. It contained bacon and beans swimming in grease.

The guard asked for Dave's cup and filled it with tea from a large pot. Dave tasted it. It came with milk and lots of sugar whether you wanted it or not.

Jimmy didn't move and the guard didn't offer food to him. Dave sat on his bunk and sipped the sweet, lukewarm liquid. He decided against the food. He didn't think his stomach could take it anyway.

One plus, his hands seemed to be recovering. He could now feel all of his fingers and grip his mug with a certain amount of comfort. He picked up one of the trashy paperbacks that Jimmy had given him. He flicked through the pages but couldn't get interested. His mind kept wandering to Anne.

Dave had been out with a number of women. He had a steady girlfriend for over a year, back in his days in Yorkshire. He had dated a few since his move to Lancashire too.

None compared to Anne.

She had been different. She was a mature and beautiful, intelligent woman with a great sense of fun. Dave lay back on his bunk and closed his eyes.

He could almost see her beautiful face, smiling, happy and full of life. Her lovely hair fell around as she cocked her head to one side.

Without warning, her features changed to the grotesque image Dave had seen on the crime photographs. Her battered and bloodied features screamed silently for help.

Dave forced his eyes open and sat bolt upright on his bunk. He looked down at his hands and noticed he had torn the paperback book in half.

He heard Jimmy's voice.

"You OK?"

Dave murmured he was.

Jimmy yawned and rubbed his eyes. "You're a noisy fucker, I'll say that."

The Manchester face saw the book. "And you'll have to pay for that as well."

Dave shrugged, "Take me to court."

Jimmy swung his legs out of bed and stretched. "Can I make a suggestion, like?"

Dave wiped perspiration from his face. "Suggest away."

"We're stuck in this rat hole all day, like. So, we tend to sleep late rather than get bored shitless until recreation. You get the drift?"

"I don't intend to be here that long, Jimmy."

Jimmy took on a pained expression. "Do you really think you have a choice, buddy?"

Dave shook his head, "I have to think that way, or I'll go crazy in here. I can't eat the food. I can't sleep. Right now, I'm wondering if I can take a shit in front of you."

Jimmy laughed. It was a strange high-pitched nasal sound. "I've seen more things than I would care to mention, mate. The sight of you parking your breakfast is no problem at all."

Dave knew he would have to do it. He couldn't wait until seven in the evening. Even if he did, the cell door was then open and anyone could walk in. That could be even worse, knowing the quality of clientele in the wing.

Dave rose from his bed and approached the toilet. It was situated no more than two feet from the end of Jimmy's bunk. The semi-clothed man had his eyes firmly fixed on him. Dave had no choice. He undid his trousers and pulled them down together with his underwear. He sat as quickly as he could but his penis had still been in full view of Jimmy, albeit fleetingly. Dave suspected that Jimmy was enjoying the show.

To his surprise, this was not the worst part. He had been in all male showers and baths before. He wasn't homophobic, but the problem now was he had to evacuate his bowels and wipe his arse in front of this creep.

The shame was overwhelming to him. Jimmy's eyes never moved. In fact, a wide smile had now developed on his face.

Once again, Dave wanted to punch Jimmy. At least verbally abuse the pervert; but for the first time in his memory, he felt too vulnerable to speak. He finished his movement and raised his body to wipe himself.

He felt tears start to well in his eyes. He barely managed to prevent them. This place had already stripped him of his freedom, and now he was stripped of his dignity.

Once he was fully dressed, Dave felt his confidence rise.

He sprung with the speed of a big cat and grabbed Jimmy by the throat. Dave's thumb and forefinger slotted neatly behind the trachea, a trick he had learned from his old profession in Yorkshire. He felt no pain in his hand.

Jimmy couldn't breathe.

Dave spoke quietly, "The next time I need to use the toilet. You!" Dave squeezed a little harder, "will turn your head and be a gentleman."

Dave increased the pressure once again.

"Understand?"

Jimmy nodded frantically. Dave released him, and he coughed repeatedly gasping for air.

"You mad bastard! Can't you take a fuckin' joke?"

Dave lay back on his bed, his hands rested behind his head.

"No."

To Dave's surprise, Jimmy didn't let it go.

"OK, big man, you think you're a hard case. But it don't matter in here. You gotta sleep, take showers and turn your back. You understand? I've taken more kickings than you've had hot dinners. Been stabbed twice, and yeah, I take it up the arse when I have to. So if I find it a bit amusing, like, when a new boy don't like the facilities, that's tough. You can live with it. You have to live with it. If you want to spend the rest of your time here looking over your shoulder, that's your problem. One word from me and my good mate, fat Henry, will scoop out your eyeball with a teaspoon. Geddit?"

Jimmy calmed slightly. "I don't fancy straight men. I don't want you to fuck me. I don't want to fuck you. I want a quiet time. Just do my bird and get out in one piece."

Dave was confused. He had only thought of himself. Of course, no one had any dignity in this place, guilty or innocent.

Moments of silence passed, until Dave relented.

"Ok, I'm sorry, Jimmy. Just give me a bit of time, OK?"

Jimmy looked thoughtful for a moment, picked up the torn paperback and lay on his bunk rubbing his throat.

"OK."

Andy Dunn could hear his doorbell. It was Robert Wallace and Sir Peter Davits. He answered the door in his boxer shorts, his face still creased from his own fitful sleep. Even so, he made a formidable sight.

If Andy looked formidable physically, then Wallace and Davits were equally imposing characters in stature and dress.

Andy squinted against the morning sunlight. This was obviously the visit Marshall had meant.

He cleared his throat, "Yes, gents, what can I do for you?"

Wallace started, "Mr. Dunn, I am Robert Wallace, Anne's father. This," he turned to his friend, "is Sir Peter Davits."

The title suddenly seemed to make Andy realise his lack of

clothing and he felt a degree of embarrassment. Wallace recognised the situation and offered apologies for the early hour.

Andy would have none of it. “No problem, gents, err, come on in now, I’ll get some clothes on.”

The three men stood in the tiny hallway, and Lucy made her entrance at the top of the stairs. She wore only a blue police issue shirt and a pair of huge carpet slippers shaped like bloodhounds. The moment she saw the visitors she emitted a squeak and ran to the bedroom.

Wallace let out an embarrassed cough into his hand. “We could call back a little later, Mr. Dunn. I must say, however, it is a matter of some urgency.”

Andy ushered the men into the sitting room.

“Not at all, gents;”

He offered them a seat. “I’m sorry, that’s just Lucy, my girlfriend.”

Davits showed some mild amusement. “Never apologise for that delightful creature, Mr. Dunn.”

Andy was slowly coming around. “Right, I’ll just be a minute and I’ll get Lucy to put the kettle on.”

Wallace looked around the sparsely furnished living room. There were few trappings to suggest a female presence at the house. Lucy was either a casual visitor, or new to co-habitation with Dunn. Pictures of Andy in various rugby strips adorned the walls. A large colour poster of a semi-nude model, which some card had scribbled a beard and glasses onto, had pride of place over the fire.

Wallace also noticed the Stewart file on the coffee table.

Andy entered, tucking a T-shirt into faded jeans.

He looked over the two men and felt like a beggar in the company of kings.

Wallace still held the Stewart file in his hand. It made Andy feel uncomfortable. He may not be a 'Sir,' but he knew when to keep his mouth shut. He shouldn't even have the file.

Wallace stood. "Mr. Dunn, it may seem strange to you, but I am currently investigating the death of my daughter. I have reason to believe that David Stewart is innocent. Therefore, I have engaged the services of an excellent trial lawyer to defend him. Superintendent Marshall, to his credit, suggested I speak with you."

Andy relaxed a little at the mention of Marshall's name. He sat and motioned to the file.

"The whole job stinks, sir. I took Dave out when he first arrived at Preston. The lad is the salt of the earth, a hard bugger, if you'll pardon my French, but a good sort."

Andy paused, "Anyway, what I think of Dave doesn't matter. More importantly, I think I have some interesting news for you about the case."

Andy took the file from Wallace and spread the documents on the table. He selected the copies that he and Lucy had been examining the previous night. He then produced the greeting card for comparison.

The three men were engrossed in the papers when Lucy teetered into the room with a tray.

“Now then, fellas! I’ve done you some tea and a shed load of bacon sarnies. There’s more if you want ‘em.”

Andy was aghast, “Lucy, we’re busy here, love!”

Her face dropped. “Oh, I’m sorry, Andy.”

Davits came to Lucy’s rescue. “Madam, I haven’t had a bacon sandwich in years.” He patted his stomach. ”My wife is constantly watching my weight.”

Lucy shot Andy an icy look. “See, at least someone is grateful!” She smiled sweetly at Davits. “It’s nice to have some gentlemen in the house, unlike some I could mention, ...oh, and it’s Miss.”

Davits, despite his position, had never been guilty of snobbery. He also had a liking for blonde, buxom women. Lucy fitted the bill perfectly. He charmed, “Then it seems our Mr. Dunn here needs to rectify that situation, and make you a Mrs.”

Andy had to see the simple but lovely nature of his girl. He looked over at Davits and smiled. “You never know, sir, I might just do that one of these days.”

Lucy seemed delighted, and positively bounced out of the room.

The mood quickly became one of concentration on the evidence at hand. Davits spoke first; “Why didn’t Thomas see this?”

Wallace considered the remark and then spoke, “Because David hasn’t written anything since his arrest.”

Now Andy was perplexed. “Why?”

Davits was quick to react, the disdain in his voice was poorly hidden.

"Because of your colleagues, Andrew; they left a pair of tight handcuffs on his wrists for over twelve hours. The blood flow was restricted and he was unable to hold a pen."

Andy shook his head, "I still can't believe Dave is inside. I was there the first time that Dave and Anne first spoke. It was the day he came to me to ask my advice. He'd cocked up, and not booked in a pair of gloves he found near to Bailey when he arrested him. He told me he'd been put under pressure from McCauley to change his statement. He thought he was for the chop. I think that McCauley's inspector, Clive Williams, was involved in that part too. He was sniffing around Dave at that time. The same evening we were in the canteen and Anne approached Dave. It was obvious that she was attracted to him. The next thing I knew, they were together in a nightclub, all dressed up and all over each other. It's the last time I saw Dave free, and the last time I saw Anne alive."

For the first time, Wallace seemed pained at the mention of Anne's name. He quickly recovered his composure.

"We need to piece together Anne's and David's movements after you last saw them. We know they went to the Lake District, to a hotel, but after leaving there we know very little."

Andy thought for a moment. "I'm sorry, but I can't help you there. All I know is, Dave came to me for advice. I told him to keep his mouth shut. We had enough on Bailey, anyway he confessed, didn't he?"

Lucy walked in. Without any apology for her obvious

eavesdropping she spoke, "I know I'm only a barmaid and I'm not as clever as you blokes, but I know that Dave and Anne were crazy about each other. When you do my job, you get to know all kinds of men. Dave is a lovely man. I know he wouldn't hurt a woman. Not ever."

Wallace smiled at Lucy. "Thank you, Miss, I believe you are correct. Anne thought so too."

Wallace spoke quickly into a miniature tape recorder. Andy had never seen anything so small. He needed to obtain a sample of Dave's handwriting that was usable in court. He had to contact a graphologist. He mentioned two names. Andy presumed they were expert witnesses.

Wallace turned to Andy again. "I don't know if you are aware, but Anne's house was ransacked by her killer. In addition, John McCauley had a safe at his house; that too, was broken into.

The police are assuming that it was Dave looking for the original Bailey file, which has been stolen. Presuming we are correct and Dave is innocent, do you have any idea what the person could have been looking for?"

Andy was shocked. "No, I didn't know about the break-in, or the ransacking. I have no idea what they could be looking for, sorry."

Lucy looked as if she would burst. Davits once again came to the rescue. "Do you know, Lucy?"

Andy shot Lucy another icy glance, but she spoke anyway.

"Well, I hear lots of things behind a bar. John McCauley and Clive Williams were in the pub the night before the murders. They were pretty pissed, I mean, drunk, sorry."

Wallace was hanging on every word. He waved away the apology. "Go on, Lucy, please."

Lucy swallowed and seemed nervous, now the centre of attention, "Well, they were talking at the bar. McCauley was bragging about getting one over on some bloke, I didn't hear who. He said he had some dirty pictures of him having sex or something. They were laughing. Then McCauley said he had plenty of dirt on Anne and Dave. He was planning something. He said he would get Anne back, and get rid of Dave."

Andy was angry. "Why the hell didn't you tell me about this?"

Tears suddenly came to Lucy's eyes. "I'm sorry, but with everything that has happened, I forgot."

Wallace suddenly stood and beckoned his colleague. "Don't blame yourself, Miss. It may be of help though, if you remember any more, to tell Andy here. I must thank you for your efforts, Mr. Dunn. This evidence, with a little more, could be enough to get David bail. Let us hope we can find that evidence."

Andy shook hands with the two men. "You can depend on Superintendent Marshall, gents. He's a good bloke. He won't be swayed by politics."

Davits smiled, "Thank you, Mr. Dunn, and please, look after this lady."

Lucy was wiping her eyes but shook hands too. "I know you'll get Davie out."

Wallace stood erect. "We will get to the truth too, Miss."

The two distinguished gentlemen left the tiny terraced house and walked to the car, which in truth, was worth more than the home they had just visited.

Once inside the plush leather interior of the Rolls, Davits spoke; "A very profitable visit, I thought?"

Wallace was deep in thought. After a few moments, he replied, "If McCauley was blackmailing someone. We need to find out whom. I think the answer will lie with Inspector Williams. I also think we will need more than a pleasant manner to persuade him to talk."

Davits was ready; "Then let's pay him a visit."

Wallace was working at a different level. "No, let's speak to Thomas and get our man out of that hell hole first."

Dave had refused lunch. Jimmy had slept most of the day. As the evening recreation approached, Dave was hungry and ready to get out of the cell and clean up. He was already finding the confines of his meagre accommodation mind-numbing.

Finally his door was opened and he ventured out into the corridor. The men emerging from other cells looked bemused and half-asleep. Dave realised he was probably one of the few inmates who had been awake all day.

A small weasel of a man, who wore the thickest glasses Dave had ever seen, approached him. Fat Henry wasn't the only one to take interest in the new boy.

"Hello! You're new, aren't you?" the weasel squeaked. He even lifted his nose like a rodent. Something about the man reminded

Dave that he hadn't showered.

"Come on, I'll show you around. I knows everyone."

Dave was about to refuse, when Jimmy piped up from behind him, "Fuck off, Smithy! He don't need a guide."

Dave looked at Jimmy with some surprise.

"He's a grass," Jimmy pointed out, "and nobody needs a grass, not even us lowlifes."

The weasel looked hurt, and shuffled along the corridor in a pair of old training shoes without laces. In fact, everyone shuffled. No one was allowed laces.

The two men followed the rest toward the end of the corridor. It opened up into what, to all intents and purposes, was a games room. A pool table sat in the centre and a television blared, unsurprisingly, on full volume in one corner.

A pair of swing doors led to a canteen, which smelled very similar to a school dining room. Several prison officers stood around the room watching the scene.

Jimmy led Dave to the end of the queue for dinner.

The men were given plastic cutlery, which Jimmy pointed out, was counted and had to be returned. Two dog-eared plastic plates and a tray completed the set. The clanking metal Dave had heard the previous day belonged to the servers; inmates, who apparently volunteered for the job.

Dave noticed the food quality hadn't improved since breakfast.

He collected what vaguely passed for cottage pie, vegetables and a slab of apple tart. They sat at a Formica table that was firmly secured to the floor. Several others shuffled to join them. Including, much to Dave's disgust, Fat Henry, who ate the way he looked.

The man sitting directly opposite Dave looked him up and down between mouthfuls of food. He was well-built, with a shaven head. Dave recognised him. He was the hard case from the prison van.

"You like to work out?" he said.

Dave nodded.

"I'll show you the gym after, if you like."

Once again, Jimmy seemed possessive of his cellmate. "We'll all go together then, eh Dave?"

Dave looked at both men in turn, shrugged, and continued to eat.

The hard case tried again, "You don't talk much." He stared directly into Dave's eyes.

Dave stared straight back. "I haven't got anything to say."

"Is that 'cos you don't want us to know you're a fuckin copper?"

The explosives were punctuated with splatters of food.

The rest of the table went silent, as did all others within earshot. The prison officers didn't react.

It was Jimmy again who spoke, "Fuckin' leave it, Stevie. None of us have room to talk."

Stevie was having none of it, "I hate fuckin' coppers," he pointed his knife at Dave, “and I hate you.”

Dave sat quietly and waited for the next move. He didn’t have long to wait. Stevie lurched over the table and thrust his plastic knife toward Dave’s face.

Dave was ready. He parried the thug’s lunge and grabbed him by the wrist. Using Stevie’s own weight against him, Dave simply pulled him across the table. When Stevie’s elbow joint came level with the table edge, Dave thrust all his own weight downward on the wrist.

There was a horrible pop, as Stevie’s elbow joint gave way. He screamed so loud that the whole of the canteen reverberated. Stevie fell to the floor, clutching his damaged arm. Dave stood. He took a step back and penalty kicked the arsehole in the jaw. Stevie’s head flew backward until it smacked the linoleum floor. He laid unconscious, blood forming a pool around his shaven crown.

The next Dave knew, two prison officers grabbed him. He gave no resistance. He simply held up his hands and repeated the words, “self defence,” over and over.

Stevie was coming around and howling like a banshee. Two other officers tended to him on the floor, attempting to stem the flow of blood from his head wound.

Dave was led away by the officers. He was frog marched along several long corridors and became completely disorientated.

Finally, he arrived at an office door. The officer to his left knocked, and a voice from within beckoned.

Dave was made to stand directly in front of a large desk. Behind it sat a very pompous looking officer. He was still receiving details of the incident by phone.

His northern accent didn't match his look. "Well, Mr. Stewart, you seem to be making a name for yourself already. Are we going to have to put you into solitary?"

Dave didn't give a shit. "Well, at least I wouldn't be attacked in there. I was given assurances that I would be protected."

The senior officer didn't care for Dave's attitude. "Maybe a set of extra charges, to go with the ones you already face, will focus your attention, Stewart."

Dave felt his anger rise again but remained outwardly calm.

"I was acting in self defence, sir. The man was trying to stab me. I don't want any trouble."

The officer seemed placated by Dave's submissive tone. He turned his attention to the guards. "How is the other party?"

One did his best to hide a smile as he spoke. Stevie was obviously unpopular with the guards. "He's off to the infirmary now, sir. I think his elbow's busted. He'll need a couple of stitches too."

The officer nodded, considered the information and then came to a decision. "OK, take Stewart back to the block and lock him down. He will have no privileges for one week." He looked directly at Dave but addressed the officers. "And keep an eye on him. I don't want a repeat of this."

Dave was led back to his cell in silence. He didn't know what his privileges were, so he wasn't too bothered. Besides, he had other things on his mind.

Jimmy was waiting when Dave got back to the cell. Apparently, everyone had been locked down because of the incident with Stevie.

"They do it all the time," explained Jimmy.

"Everyone gets a bit excited at the sight of a rumpus, so they lock us down. It's a fuckin' pain."

Dave lay on his bunk in silence, but Jimmy was talkative.

"Where did you learn that move, like? It was pretty nifty. Not in the coppers book of moves, that."

"I wasn't always a copper.'

Jimmy smiled. "Well, I think Stevie will stay away from you for a while. After that display, so will most. You'll still need to watch yourself, like. It won't just go away. It never goes away."

"I'm locked down for a week anyway, no privileges."

Jimmy laughed, "What fuckin' privileges?"

The two men lay in silence for a long time. Finally Dave spoke, "Jimmy, how does someone end up as a pimp for rent boys?"

"You mean, how does someone stoop so low, like?"

"No, well, I mean, you seem OK to me. It just seems strange."

Jimmy smiled, "It don't happen overnight, mate, I can tell you that. I've been around it for a long time. It started with being in care as a kid. Fuckin' joke really, using the word care, for what we got."

Jimmy turned on his side. He didn't seem to mind the subject matter.

“I was in this kid’s home like, up your way. I would be about twelve. Me mam was from Salford like, that’s where I’m from, but she was on the knock herself and I got took off her and sent there. I got nicked for shopliftin’ and ended up in the local nick at Preston. The boss of the children’s home came down with this brief, Holmes, his name was. That was the start.”

Alarm bells rang in Dave’s head. “Raymond Holmes?”

Jimmy nodded, “That’s the twat.

Wallace and Davits had taken a suite at the Tickled Trout, a beautiful hotel situated on the outskirts of Preston.

Davits marvelled at his friend’s tenacity. With the minimum of rest, he had worked constantly since the dreadful news of Anne’s death.

Wallace now sat at a desk in the suite, slowly disappearing under a mound of paperwork.

He had been on the telephone constantly.

He had harassed Thomas about the handwriting discrepancies the barrister had failed to notice. He insisted the barrister’s early return to London was unwise, and told him in no uncertain terms that his attitude toward the case had better change. Wallace wanted results, and Thomas had better produce.

Like a man possessed, he bulldozed his way through unhelpful secretaries to get to graphologists. He only wanted the best. He barked at prison officials, finally berating the governor himself, to arrange a visit for Dave.

In between this deluge, he set about the heart-rending task of arranging the funeral of his only daughter. The task of consoling his grieving wife sapped his strength.

Finally, he sat back in his chair, removed his glasses, and rubbed his eyes.

"It's so damn frustrating, Peter. This young man shouldn't even be charged with these murders, let alone be languishing in a remand centre."

Davits nodded, "I agree."

Wallace shuffled some papers until he found what he was looking for.

"Look, Anne was tied up. You have mentioned the marks on her wrists in your report. It's here in the officer's statements. David would have no reason to tie her up. He had the run of the house. They were lovers, for Christ sake. I mean, according to the witness, David's car arrived at the house after Anne and McCauley. So when did he tie her? Whilst McCauley looked on? Is he supposed to have repeatedly stabbed the detective whilst Anne just made tea? It just doesn't work, does it?"

Just then, the telephone interrupted Wallace's flow. It was John Staples, the forensic expert, and he was in fine fettle.

"Wallace, how are you, sir?"

Wallace had no time for small talk; he was tired. "I'm well,

Professor. Do you have something for me?"

"I most certainly do. It would seem our friends at Preston have missed a vital piece in the jigsaw. But first, can you tell me, do I have all the paperwork available in this case?"

"You do, please go on."

"Well, there is no mention of any sexual activity in the notes. Sir Peter makes no comment regarding any recent intercourse in the post mortem. Yet there are semen stains on the inside of Anne's sweater and brassier." There was a brief pause and he continued, "This is pretty tough, Mr. Wallace. Maybe I should speak to Sir Peter?"

Staples waited for a reply.

The news hit Wallace like a steamroller. He sat back even further into his seat and moved the receiver away from his ear. He took the deepest of breaths. How much more had his only child endured? How much more could he himself take?

Finally he could speak, "Just give it to me as it comes, Staples."

"Well, I can understand how the evidence could have been missed. But even so, sloppy at best;"

Staples paused, whilst he checked his notes.

"From studying the scenes of crime photographs and the location of the stains, I would conclude that the offender lifted Anne's sweater and brassiere, without removing it completely. He probably then masturbated over her upper torso and then returned her clothing to its original position. They missed the stain, as it was on the inside the clothing."

Wallace could hear further shuffling paper as Staples searched his notes.

"We have tested the semen, which gives us the offender's blood type. It's 'O' Rhesus Negative, quite rare really. Only three percent of the population has it. I just got off the telephone to an old friend of mine who is a registrar at The Royal Preston Hospital. David Stewart was treated there several times for minor injuries. His blood type is 'A'. I also checked McCauley's post mortem report. He is type 'B'."

Wallace was still recovering from this last demeaning act his daughter had been forced to endure. He forced himself to sound positive.

"Excellent work, Mr. Staples. We seem to be getting somewhere."

Staples hadn't finished.

"There is one more thing; Anne was tied with electrical flex. Although I can't be certain until I examine the actual cord, from the photographs, I would say that whoever tied those knots, is left-handed.

The throat wounds on Anne and Bailey are also cut right to left, suggesting a left hander.

What about our boy Stewart?"

Wallace was quick to react, "We haven't that information at hand. But it won't take long."

Staples was obviously pleased with his own work.

"Well, Mr. Wallace, I think that will put the cat amongst the pigeons at Preston station. If you have any more for me, don't hesitate. Goodbye."

Wallace bid Staples a good night's rest and related the details of the conversation to Sir Peter.

"With this information, plus the handwriting anomalies, Thomas will have sufficient to make a bail application to the magistrates on Monday."

Davits was deep in thought. He flicked through the files and made the occasional note. Wallace waited for his friend to speak.

The man spoke quietly; "Robert, the more I look at this file, the more I'm confused. In the space of forty-eight hours, we have uncovered several major gaffes in the prosecution evidence. One, the handwriting; I mean it is so obvious, even a child could see that it's different.

Next is the sloppy forensic work. To miss a major find like that on Anne's clothing is a poor or very rushed performance.

Finally the cord; it's normal police practice to photograph the knots on evidence of this nature, they would normally cut the rope, or whatever, leaving the knots intact. There are very strict rules regarding the protection of ligatures, as they can tell us so much. Now, I would be very surprised to find that any investigating officer hadn't had this kind of evidence checked."

Wallace poured two glasses of brandy from the mini bar and placed one in front of Davits.

"So, what are your conclusions, Peter?"

Davits took a sip of the drink. "Well, I think we have two lines of inquiry. The handwriting is separate to the rest.

The paperwork was never meant to be looked at closely. Bailey had confessed his crimes. I can only presume that McCauley or a member of his team altered the documents just to tidy up the mistake by Stewart, and that is just what I believe it was, tidying the loose ends. This was nothing to get killed over! They knew he would play the game, or lose his job.

Now, the defence would easily plead their way out of a murder conviction. They could point out Bailey's confession and how helpful and remorseful he had been etc. They too would probably overlook the changes to the documents.

The defence would look good. Bailey's other charges would have been dropped in the process of the plea bargain.

Everyone is happy. McCauley gets his man. Dave keeps his job and Bailey gets a reduced sentence."

Wallace was listening intently to his esteemed colleague.

"If everyone is so happy, why have we got three people, including my daughter, lying in the morgue?"

"The answer to that will lie with the people still alive. All of whom have the same information."

Wallace ran through the possibilities. "That means David Stewart, Inspector Clive Williams, and the Constable, Rodney Casey."

Davits corrected his friend, "And the solicitor, Holmes."

Dave waited quietly for Jimmy to continue his story. At the mention of Ray Holmes, Jimmy had fallen silent. He stared into the distance, exploring his own personal thoughts.

Finally Dave spoke; "Me and you have some common ground, Jimmy."

"Yeah? Have we, Dave?"

"We do, pal. Holmes was Bailey's brief, one of my so-called victims. He has a reputation as a nasty piece of work.

"That's him, like, bastard that he is. Him and Clarke, that's the boss of the home like. They got it all started for me." Jimmy looked saddened for a moment, "and a few others who are no longer with us."

Dave suddenly felt a twinge of sorrow for Jimmy. He wouldn't normally want to pry any further into what he knew was Jimmy's sleazy life. Despite that, the mention of Holmes' name was too much of a coincidence. He needed the information.

Dave pressed, "Sorry, Jimmy, I shouldn't have asked but I've had some dealings with Holmes. He's real bad news."

Jimmy returned to his troubled, personal place. He looked puerile and vulnerable.

He slowly moved his head from side to side. He looked pained. "Someone like you couldn't understand what it's like to be alone in a place like that. A home where people, the ones who are supposed to be in charge, take advantage. You know, really take. "

An edge of bitterness came to his voice and he added, "They take everythin', everythin' you got."

Dave was as gentle as he could with his questions. "You're right, Jimmy. I mean, I grew up in a shithole place, but my mum and dad looked after me as best they could."

Jimmy smiled briefly, "Yeah? Your old man and mum still tickin' on are they?"

Dave felt suddenly homesick. "Hmm, yes they are mate, thanks."

Jimmy's smile faded. "Never met my dad. My mum weren't too interested. She were on the game; got hooked on the drugs, y'know. So me and me sister get chucked into care. I end up with those bastards, Clarke and Holmes. Those two had a thing going, you see?"

Jimmy stopped and looked straight at Dave. He waited for a reaction, a judgement.

When he didn't get one, he cleared his throat and continued, "Both Clarke and Holmes had a liking for young boys see. A physical liking, if you know what I mean? What a pair! Like I said, I'd been at the home for about a month, when I got lifted for robbin' in the shops in town. Holmes turned up, did some clever talking at the station, and I got away with a bollocking from the inspector."

Jimmy fidgeted with his fingers, a small child confessing the theft of the last sweet in the jar.

"I paid for it though; in other ways, like. You can imagine the rest. You were a copper. You've heard it all before. I don't want to talk about it no more."

Dave somehow knew that this story was important. He kept trying.

"You don't have to talk, Jimmy. I understand, but try to remember, whatever happened then, wasn't your fault."

The cell was quiet again. As the minutes ticked by, Dave considered the conversation over.

In the silence, disorder raged through Jimmy's head. His story left untold for so long, swelling like an untreated cancer in his gut. Why should he tell now? Why should he explain himself to this stranger? He'd managed to bury the whole business deep inside. It was his self-preservation, his in-built defence mechanism. Eventually he sat up and looked directly at Dave. It wasn't so much a confession, more a discovery. The first sentence was almost blurted.

"Clarke picked me up from the nick, exactly as he should, but Holmes followed us. It was late, after bedtime. The other kids were all tucked in for the night. They took me to Clarke's room. They gave me pop and a cake."

Jimmy stared at an invisible point and laughed sarcastically to himself. "Then, after a bit, Clarke left me alone with Holmes. He started asking me questions about sex. I was twelve for fuck's sake, just started taking an interest. Anyway, Holmes gets this porno magazine out of a drawer and shows me some pictures. He asks me if I'd like to borrow it. 'Our little secret'."

Dave could see what was coming.

Jimmy shook his head. "Of course I wanted it. I was a curious boy. Any boy would have wanted it. Then he made his play. He asked me if I liked wanking.

I was getting scared. I wanted to go to bed, get away from him, y'know. He was havin' none of it. He told me to show him how I did it. I didn't want to, but I was scared like. So I did. I got my dick out, looked at a dirty picture and started pulling myself off. Fuckin' clever eh?"

Jimmy looked to Dave and read his eyes for the slightest reaction. Anything would have stopped the tale; pity, loathing, amusement, anything at all. He got nothing. The man just lay there in the gloom, listening, impassive.

Satisfied, Jimmy continued, "I was embarrassed to fuck, but I did it. Then Holmes says I'm doing it wrong and he'll show me how. He grabs my dick and starts to wank me. I was fuckin' petrified.

I was starting to cry. Just as I was coming all over the carpet, in walks Clarke, right on cue. How many times they'd worked that one is anyone's guess, eh?"

Jimmy fast staccato diction became heated, "Clarke pretended to be angry. I know now, like, it was all an act, but not then, I didn't know then. I didn't know anything. I didn't have time to think.

He rants and raves about what a bad boy I am and how I will rot in hell for what I'd done. He's pointing at a statue of 'Our Lady' in the corner. How she has seen the whole thing. Then it was how he will tell the social workers, the cops, the lot. Told me I would have to be sent to a different home where 'my kind' were locked away.

Then of course, they had me where they wanted me. I was broke. Flooding like a tap I was. They didn't give a fuck. I begged him not to tell. I'd do anything, just don't tell, like."

Jimmy had changed from the hardened, streetwise criminal, to a pathetic childlike creature, re-telling a catastrophic event in his life. Dave guessed this was the first telling. The kind of scenario every parent prays never to hear from their own child.

Jimmy took a deep breath. It was all going to come out now. The floodgate was open and nothing was going to stop it.

“When Clarke pulled my trousers down, I honestly thought he was going to tan my hide. Instead, they took it in turns to fuck me.”

This time, Dave was unable to hide his horror, “Jesus, Jimmy.”

Now Jimmy actually seemed pleased to get the reaction from his cellmate. “Yeah, fuckin’ hell it hurt. Clarke kept telling me what a naughty boy I was. He was doin’ it, yet he spoke to me as if he was giving a lecture or having his fuckin’ tea. It was as if nothing was happening. Every time I cried out, Holmes stuck his dick in my mouth. One thing though, neither of them came in me. They were careful not to want to leave any evidence. It weren’t pure lust like. No, they were completely in control. It was all planned. Every last detail was planned.”

Jimmy paused for breath. He was actually sweating. Dave could see he had pushed his fingernails into his palm during the story.

The blood on his hand seemed to jog his memory and his voice dropped again, his eyes watering, close to tears.

“I was bleeding quite bad; Clarke stuffed a load of tissues down my undies, told me to keep my mouth shut and sent me to bed.”

Jimmy fell silent for a while. He looked deflated. “That was the start of it all. Not a pretty story eh?”

Dave was shocked. He’d never heard anyone recount such a harrowing tale. He could think of nothing, else to say but, “Jimmy,

I'm sorry."

Jimmy seemed to regain his composure. The cheeky street face returned to mask what Dave knew was beneath.

"Hey, fuck it. It was a long time ago."

Dave still needed more information, he pressed his luck. "Do you still see Holmes?"

"Oh yeah. He's the fuckin' reason I'm on remand, isn't it."

Jimmy settled into his story again. All trace of emotional sadness alarmingly gone.

"Look, after that night, there were lots more nights. Sometimes it would be Clarke, sometimes Holmes. I was introduced to other boys in the home, all doing the same, then to other friends of Holmes. I'm not saying that what Clarke and Holmes did turned me the way I am, but I started going with the other boys.

I admit I enjoyed it, even then. We were sort of friends. Comrades in arms like, a boys club. I felt like I belonged to somethin' for once."

"Then one day," Jimmy laughed, "Holmes tells me I can make some money. Lots of it."

Jimmy rubbed his thumb and forefinger together to make his point.

"He gets me and another boy, to put on a little, 'private show' for one of his mates. We do the business, while this fat old fart watches and tosses himself off in the corner. We made twenty-five quid each. It was a fortune. So, we start doing it regular. Holmes and his friends were a good source of punters. I somehow forgot how they got me in and started to think more about the ca..."

Jimmy stopped dead. There was silence again, then quietly, each syllable painful, "...the cash."

Dave thought the man might falter, but somewhere inside him he found the words.

"Some boys though, they never got used to it. Some weren't strong enough. I know of two who topped themselves. One was only fuckin' nine when they started on him."

Jimmy shivered, as if to shrug off the image only he could see. "Anyway time ticks on and I get too old for the tastes of Holmes and his mates. By now, of course, I have lots of contacts for boys and clients. So, I started putting two and two together and went into business for myself. I provide some freebies to Holmes, you know, boys of the age he likes and in return, he looks after my legal problems. That is, he used to. When I got lifted this time, Holmes had done a runner and I was left high and dry."

Dave was intrigued. "Why'd he do a runner?"

Jimmy shrugged and blew air from his mouth. "I dunno, couple of days ago he just disappeared. The coppers just tell me he's not available. I was left with some arsehole of a duty solicitor who doesn't know a thumb from a pair of tits, and I get remanded."

Dave sat on the end of his bunk and brushed his fingers through his hair.

"Very strange, Jimmy, very strange indeed."

Jimmy looked straight into Dave's eyes. There was one more tale to tell.

"I'll tell you this though, Dave, I look after my boys and before you say it, no, I don't get them into it. I just look after the ones who are already in. Take them off the street, like."

Dave didn't go a bundle on Jimmy's version of social conscience. His was a sad story, but he was sure every con on the wing had one. It wasn't that Dave didn't have feelings, but he wasn't Marjory Proops either. He just wanted to know about Holmes. It was the only link to his case in this place. It just may be the link he needed.

"Did you know William Bailey?"

Jimmy shrugged. "Not really, met him a couple of times. He was a bad boy, from all accounts."

Dave lay back on his bed and contemplated the information. So, Holmes was bent. What difference did that make? Could McCauley have had something on Holmes? Did Holmes know about the files?

Dave needed out more than ever.

Jimmy snored loudly in the darkness. Dave toyed with the unopened box of cigarettes. Finally, he decided to open the package. He flipped open the top. Everything still looked normal. He removed the top layer of packets. The bottom layer had been cut out in the centre and a sealed plastic bag sat where cigarettes should be. Dave quietly tore open the package and spread the contents on his bed.

Two keys, one obviously for a vehicle, another for a house; a bank card, in the name of J. Jackson, and a note.

It read,

*Dave,*

*For when you get bail.*

*Red Volvo in garage.*

*10 Walker Place,*

*Blackpool.*

*PIN no 8876*

*Use as much as you need.*

*Ross.*

# IT'S IN THE BLOOD

The morning sun had yet to grace Lancashire with its presence. The only light in the bedroom came from the hall. Trevor Marshall had been awake for over an hour. He waited for his alarm clock to sound.

For the first time he could remember, Marshall was dreading going to work. He had always loved his job, even the danger it sometimes posed.

His wife slept soundly next to him, taking advantage of the fact that the kids were away at their grandparents for a few days. Marshall gave in and switched off the alarm a full hour prior to its setting.

He showered and dressed, being careful not to wake his wife. He made coffee and toast for himself and sat at the breakfast bar.

During his first mouthful, the telephone disturbed him. It was Marie Baker.

She had been allocated as exhibits officer on the murders. Marshall had told Marie to release certain items of Anne's clothing for examination by the defence. Now she had a further problem.

"I've had Mr. Wallace on the phone twice already this morning, boss. I've asked him to wait until you get in at ten, but he's a very persistent gentleman."

Marshall could hear the sarcasm in Marie's tone. "Marie, I've already told you to release anything they require. Let's not make an enemy of this man. He's a very influential gentleman, not to mention the father of a dead colleague."

Marie seemed mildly irritated, unusual for her, "I know what you said, boss, but this is a big problem."

"Go on."

"Wallace wants his forensic guy to inspect the cord that tied Anne's hands. I told him I would have it for him later today."

"And?"

"It's gone."

"Gone where?'

"Missing."

Marshall couldn't believe his ears. "Who has had access, other than our team?"

Marie thought for a moment. "All the hard evidence is kept in the CID property store. There is a constable in there during the day. But at night, any officer can get the key from the charge office."

Marshall's head spun. This was all he needed. "I want the property store P.C. and the charge office sergeant in my office within the hour. I don't care if you have to wake them. No excuses."

Marshall slammed the telephone onto its cradle.

He spoke to the empty kitchen. “I’ve had enough of this.”

Marshall stormed from the house and took his own car. He had no time to call his regular driver. He wanted answers, before he had to deal with Wallace.

He drove swiftly through the early morning traffic. There were so many question marks against this case now. Someone on the inside, or someone with enough money to buy them inside, was taking the piss.

Finally, after much cursing and swearing, he arrived at Preston police station.

He burst into the incident room. Marie Baker and Slick Jemson were already there.

“What the fuck is going on here?” Marshall threw his coat onto the nearest table.

Slick tried to calm him. “We’re already on with it, boss, the guys you wanted are on the way.”

It didn’t have any effect on Marshall. “I don’t give a fuck. What I want to know is, what have you lot done?”

The two officers looked blank.

Marshall flared, “Fuck all, I see. Well, we will start with a search of the store. I want every item in the store checked against records. Not just our job, but every single fuckin’ piece of property in the place. With luck it will turn up.”

Marie started, “But boss, I have already…”

Marshall was unstoppable. “Then do it again!”

The final syllable was followed by the slam of his office door. The two officers looked at each other. Marie shrugged. “We’d better get on with it.”

Marshall stormed around his desk, his head full of questions. He knew this job was just too easy. Why the fuck didn’t he stand up to the Chief? This was the final straw.

Unfortunately, his day was about to get worse.

“Superintendent Marshall!”

Marshall spun toward his door to see Robert Wallace standing in the doorway. Marshall stopped himself from asking how the fuck Wallace got there. This was one resourceful bastard.

Wallace, by comparison, was the picture of serenity. “Having a bad day, Superintendent?”

Marshall flopped into his seat and beckoned Wallace to sit. “I’ve had better, sir. Now, what can I do for you?”

“You can release the item of evidence I requested two hours ago. May I remind you of the law regarding such matters?”

Marshall didn’t wait for the act and section. He held up his hands to stop Wallace. “We are currently doing everything in our power to provide the item you requested sir. The problem is, our own forensic specialists are currently examining it.

Wallace raised his eyebrows at the lie. He had spent the best part of his adult life questioning people. He could smell an untruth at twenty paces. Wallace stood, his serene manner replaced with one of irritation.

"Your case, Superintendent, is in tatters. In the space of two days my colleagues and I have torn it to shreds. We will be making a bail application for Stewart on Monday morning. Rest assured, it will be granted, with or without the exhibit I request. Now, I realise that you assisted me by putting me in touch with Constable Dunn, so, I in turn, will give you this advice. I strongly recommend that you put as much distance between yourself and this prosecution as possible; for your own sake and the sake of your career. Do I make myself clear?" Wallace turned to the door, then added, "Be very aware that the longer this young man spends in jail, the stronger the case for unlawful imprisonment becomes."

Wallace was gone before he could reply.

Marshall opened his desk drawer and removed the Stewart file. What had Wallace and team found that made them so sure of themselves? Was Wallace just playing games? A light suddenly came on in Marshall's head.

Marshall picked up his telephone. "Get me Constable Andy Dunn."

This was a race now and Marshall did not intend to be second.

Wallace walked to the Rolls. Davits could see that he was empty-handed.

"They didn't hand over the cord, then?"

Wallace was still angry. “I have a feeling that we are never going to see that particular item, Peter.” He tapped on the divider, and beckoned his driver to move on.

“Whoever is responsible for this latest error, if indeed that is all it is, has made a grave mistake.”

The car sped off into the traffic. Wallace was on a roll. “Thomas will be here within the hour. The graphologist, Simmons, will arrive around the same time. Staples is already on his way. We will hold a conference this afternoon. Once the bail hearing is out of the way and David Stewart has his liberty, the real work will start.”

The witch-hunt at the police station had started.

Marshall had grilled the property room constable and the night charge sergeant. They knew, or were saying, nothing. The search of the property store revealed the same.

Now it was Andy Dunn’s turn.

Marshall was in no mood for pleasantries. “What the fuck did you tell Wallace, Andy?”

Andy, too, was pissed off at Marshall. “Now wait a minute, Trevor. If I recall, it was you who put Wallace in touch with me. I didn’t go looking for this.”

It didn’t wash with Marshall. “Don’t fuck me around here, Andy. If you only told him what you told me, then why is he so fuckin’ confident?”

Andy wasn't about to tell anyone that he had been poking about in the Stewart file.

"You'll need to ask Wallace that. All I told Wallace was what I knew about Dave. How he met Anne, that kind of thing."

Marshall calmed slightly. "OK, Andy. I'm sorry for landing you with this, but it's getting to the point where I don't know who to trust anymore."

Andy felt bad about misleading his friend, but should he jeopardise Dave's bail by tipping off the prosecution? As far as Andy was concerned, Dave was innocent, simple as that.

"Listen, Trevor, you know that Dave's motive for this job stinks. Don't you think the whole job seems too easy? I mean, come on, leaving all that evidence for all to see. It's not right."

Marshall needed help. "Please, Andy, there's more. I know it."

Andy squirmed in his seat. "OK, check the handwriting on the property register against Dave's."

Marshall's stomach turned. How could he have missed it? All the pressure from above had made him sloppy.

"It's different?"

"Nothing like, boss."

Marshall rubbed his temples with his fingers. "Jesus Christ, Andy, we're in trouble here."

Andy sighed, "There's more. I got another call from Wallace this morning. He wanted to know if Dave was left or right handed."

"Did he say why?"

"No. I just told him he was right handed."

It was of no consequence. Marshall already knew why.

"Thanks, Andy."

The second the door closed, Marshall picked up the telephone to gather his troops. Now his own integrity was on the line, this was no time to sit and wait.

Within minutes, Jemson and Marie Baker were sitting in front of their harassed boss, who was surrounded by piles of paper and exhibits.

"OK," Marshall was tense, but he was never the kind of man to roll over easily. "This party is well and truly over. What I am about to tell you is strictly confidential. It stays in this room. Nothing is to be written down until we know more. No one, and I mean not even your mother, gets another scrap of information unless I clear it. Understood?"

Marie was concerned for her boss; she had never seen him in such a mood. "What's going on, sir?"

Marshall held up his hand. "I'll tell you what I know, and then what I believe is happening. After that we bounce it around and plan just like always.

He cleared his throat and took a deep breath.

"I believe that someone on the inside wants this inquiry to be swept under the carpet. They, whoever they are, want it bad enough they are prepared to steal evidence to achieve it."

Marshall held up two sheets of paper.

"First, I'm no expert, but even I can see David Stewart did not write the entries in the property register, or Bailey's arrest sheet. That information alone blows most of his motive to kingdom come."

He handed copies of the documents to his team, together with a handwriting sample of Dave Stewart's. The two officers studied them for a moment.

Jemson let out a low whistle. "How did we miss this?"

Marshall shook his head. "That's not important now, Slick. What is very pressing is, who did write it?"

Marshall handed a further handwriting sample to the two officers. "Look familiar?"

Marie was first. "The writing looks the same to me. Whose is it?"

Marshall was grave. He virtually spat each word, "Detective fucking Inspector Clive Williams."

"Fuck me."

It was unusual to hear Marie swear, but it seemed like the opportune moment.

"Exactly," added Marshall.

Slick continued to examine the documents and finally spoke. "Who else knows this?"

Marshall sat up straight. "The defence knows about the discrepancy and they've known for at least a day."

He paused, "Now." Marshall produced photographs of the electrical flex that tied Anne's wrists. He asked two questions he already knew the answers to. "Why is the defence so interested in this cord, and why has it gone astray?"

Marie studied the picture and shook her head. Slick did the same.

Marshall prompted his team, waiting for the light to come on.

"OK then, why does the defence want to know if Stewart is left handed?"

"Because of the handwriting discrepancies," said Jemson.

"No!" Marie Baker was open-mouthed. "It's not that at all. It's the cord. I'd lay odds that their forensic guy believes the knot was tied left handed."

Jemson seemed doubtful. "Can you tell from a knot?"

All three people in the room had no answer, but all suspected you could.

Marshall broke the silence. "We're just coppers, at the end of the day, that's why we have experts. I know that there has been a lot of work done in the States recently on ligatures and bindings. I agree with Marie though, I think it's the cord."

Jemson stared at the photograph once more. "Then who's got the cord now?"

Marshall ignored that particular dilemma and removed three graphic crime scene photographs from the file.

"I want our forensic pathologist to give me an expert opinion on whether these wounds were made by a right or left handed person, and I want it today. Now, let's plan our day."

Wallace and his team had far more answers. The hourly wage bill of the five men, gathered in the hotel suite would keep an average family for a month.

Arthur Simmons, graphologist, Professor John Staples, forensics, Sir Peter Davits, pathologist, George Thomas Q.C., barrister at law, and of course, Wallace himself.

The men were a formidable force and had Dave Stewart known of the might of his team, he may have felt a little better.

Wallace had gone through the preliminaries, what they knew, what they needed to discover.

Simmons spoke first, "Well, gentlemen, I can say with certainty, that Stewart did not write the entries on any of the documents. All I can say about the man who did is that he is right handed and between thirty and forty-five years of age. I would like a sample of handwriting from all the officers involved in the case for comparison."

"Will a signature do?" asked Wallace.

"No, sir."

Wallace nodded and made a note. "Mr. Staples?"

Staples looked completely out of place in the room of expensive tailored suits. He wore faded denims and a checked cotton lumberjack shirt. He had obviously not shaved for a couple of days. His appearance though, was of little importance; he was not to be underestimated.

"As far as the forensic side goes, gents, we are well and truly cookin'."

His casual remarks brought a look of disdain from George Thomas. Staples noticed the look, gave Thomas a cheeky wink and continued, "The handwriting side will be backed up by fingerprint evidence, once we get hold of the relevant original documentation."

Thomas was cutting; "That would be fine if the originals hadn't been stolen."

Staples shot the lawyer a look. "More importantly, we can now say positively that a male person, with a different blood type to Stewart, McCauley, or Bailey was present at Anne's house on the night of the murders. Furthermore, I have been talking to a colleague, Alec Jeffreys at Leicester University, who is researching a method of testing and typing DNA from semen or blood. They say, this will be as good as a fingerprint, although how admissible it will be is your department, Thomas."

Thomas had never even heard of DNA testing. Therefore, he kept quiet.

His point to Thomas made, Staples continued, "As for the cord, well without the actual item, I'm afraid I can only say that I am about seventy per cent certain that it was tied left handed."

Sir Peter interrupted, "I can assist there. I can now say with certainty that the throat wounds, on both Bailey and Anne, were made by a left handed person."

Wallace leaned forward across the table, around which all the men were gathered. "Then we are looking for two men, a right handed forger and a left handed killer."

Thomas could contain himself no longer. "Surely we are only interested in getting our client free, not solving the case," he added in condescending tone, "let the police do their job for once."

Wallace struck like a snake. "Whilst I retain your services, George, I will decide what lines of inquiry we follow and how far we take them. Is that clear?"

Thomas remained silent. He knew better

"So gentlemen, David Stewart will be in court, Monday ten a.m." He glared at Thomas again. "I expect everything to go smoothly."

"In the meantime, we need to speak to the man who forged the documents. If I were a betting man, I'd say we need to pay McCauley's good friend Inspector Williams a visit."

Davits looked uneasy, Wallace noticed. "Problem, Peter?"

"Well we all seem to be overlooking something."

"Go on."

"The motive, gentlemen; the motive we were all led to believe at first is now shot to pieces. We know Stewart didn't forge the documents. We know he was in love with Anne and that that love was mutual."

Thomas snorted quietly. Davits ignored it. "The real motive must have something to do with the burglary at McCauley's house."

Davits leaned his elbows onto the table.

“Let’s just imagine that whoever was responsible for the burglary is also responsible for all three murders. Reasonable?”

Thomas gazed out of the window. The tedium was killing him, and showed in his tone.

“Obviously.”

Sir Peter was again undaunted. “Well if it’s so obvious, why are we not looking more closely at what could be so valuable to the killer? He didn’t find it at McCauley’s house. So, he thought that it would be at Anne’s house.

What could Anne have that would be worth killing for? Moreover, is the murder of Bailey connected to the fact that he was loose at that time?”

Wallace turned to Thomas. “What do we know about William Bailey?”

Thomas shrugged. “Not a great deal, the best person to speak to would be his solicitor,” Thomas looked at a file and found the name, “Holmes. But he’s not in his office.”

John Staples raised an eye. “Raymond Holmes?”

Thomas gave the forensic man a tired look. “Yes, Raymond Holmes.”

Staples returned the look. The two men were not going to be comrades in arms.

“I’ve heard some very nasty rumours about that man. He’s reported to be, how shall I say, of dubious character.

I recall a senior detective from the Greater Manchester force being very interested in Holmes. The investigation surrounded pedophilia, if my memory serves me correctly. I understand nothing was ever proved, but my man was convinced of his involvement."

Wallace shook his head. "Blackmail, gentleman."

He pointed toward his friend. "Remember, Peter, that barmaid friend of Andy Dunn's. She said she overheard McCauley saying something about having information on people. She heard them mention dirty pictures. What if McCauley had information on Holmes? Say Anne was party to it and Bailey knew of it. Maybe Bailey even offered the information to McCauley as a plea bargain. I agree with Sir Peter. Let's take a look at the motive."

Sir Peter was first, "Well, the way I see it, there must be some physical evidence that McCauley or Anne had access to. As you say, pictures or similar. Alternatively, maybe something that McCauley had and the others simply knew of. We know that Stewart doesn't know."

"No we don't."

Again, Staples was on the ball. "Just because our man wasn't responsible for the crime, doesn't mean that he has no knowledge of anything else. He was well and truly set up. He may as well have been the fourth victim. If I were he, I wouldn't trust a living soul right now, and if I knew the real reason behind it all, I would be keeping it to myself."

"All this would explain something," said Wallace. "As you said, Thomas, Holmes is not in his office. I have been attempting to contact him for several days. He appears to have gone to ground.

He could be our man."

"On the other hand," said Staples, "and I'm playing devil's advocate here. If you were the only one left alive or free, and you weren't responsible, what would you do?"

Wallace took the floor again. "So we have two lines of inquiry, Holmes and Williams. Sir Peter and I will take that on board. The rest of you, ensure we get our man free on Monday."

Dave and Jimmy were playing cards for cigarettes. Jimmy had been winning, but it had not been due to expertise. Dave wanted him happy. He wanted information on Holmes.

"You say you knew Billy Bailey then, Jimmy?"

"Umm."

"Was he at the kid's home with you?"

"After me, I'm a bit older than him."

"Was he used by Holmes and his friends too?"

Jimmy became a little defensive. "Seems to me, that's somethin' you don't need to know, Dave."

"It is," Dave pressed, "because the reason I'm here at all, is all down to me arresting William Bailey. Plus, your man Holmes is the only surviving link in the chain. Just think, Jim, I lock up Bailey for murder. Days later, he and two of the investigating team are dead, I'm in jail and his pervert brief has done a runner."

A light suddenly came on in Dave's head. Had he just answered his own question? He closed his eyes and tried to remember. He had flicked through the files briefly on that fateful night. Was there one on Holmes?

Dave was desperate. "Please, Jimmy, just tell me; would Bailey know about Holmes's little scam at the children's home?"

"Of course he knew."

Dave's head spun. Maybe Bailey had given McCauley something on Holmes to gain some kind of favour. A plea bargain? The Chief would have loved that.

Could McCauley have tried to use the information against Holmes? Could Holmes have been after the same files?

What if McCauley already knew about Holmes's perversion before the Bailey job? Had Holmes tried to pressure the Chief?

Dave pleaded with Jimmy. "Jim, I need to know all you know about Holmes."

Jimmy gave up on the card game, he knew it was pointless.

He pinched the bridge of his nose, closed his eyes.

"Alright, alright. Holmes is a bastard. You know that. What you don't know is how much of a bastard. He's been on the take for years. OK, he gets his fee from the legal aid, we all know that. The fee isn't enough for him. He isn't happy unless he gets a drink out of the poor bastard in the dock as well. That means, either cash or sex."

Jimmy looked straight at Dave. "If you're under sixteen and male, it's always sex he wants."

Dave nodded. “What if he was cornered, what is he capable of?”

“Oh, he’s a hard case alright, but he wouldn’t do the dirty work himself. No, he’s got plenty of little helpers. You know the type. You busted the arm of one in the canteen.”

Dave knew the type. He had been one himself. Hired muscle was a lucrative career for the poor of any city.

Dave pressed on; “I think Holmes may have had Bailey killed.”

Jimmy shrugged. “Don’t surprise me,” he lowered his voice to a whisper, “Listen, there was this kid at the home, Holmes and Clarke had been workin’ on him for a while, if you know what I mean. He’d be about twelve or thirteen. Problem was, he was a real little tough nut and havin’ none of it, like. Anyway, one night, Holmes comes over and takes the kid downstairs. Tells him it’s to do with his case or somethin’.”

Jimmy swallowed. Dave thought he looked close to tears again. He had to pause, and the words came hard.

“I heard him screaming, pleading with them. I wasn’t the only one who heard, either.”

Now Dave did see tears.

“He was just a fuckin’ kid, Dave, real small. They didn’t give a fuck, I should have done somethin’, stopped it, somehow….”

Jimmy broke down. His wiry shoulders heaved, and he covered his face with his hands, his embarrassment and shame too much, even for him.

“You were young too, Jim,” Dave soothed.

Jimmy wiped his eyes and regained his composure. "Yeah, we were all young. No one would have believed it, would they? Not from us; we were just little shits from the gutter."

Jimmy's eyes turned cold. "He called for me! For me, Dave! I didn't do a fuckin' thing!

Dave could feel Jimmy's agony. "You were a frightened child."

Jimmy nodded furiously, tears streaming. "I'll tell you somethin' though, we never saw that kid again after that night.

Clarke reported him missin' the next day. Kids are always goin' missin' see? Fuckin' coppers don't care. His mam and dad didn't care. He never turned up again. Know what I mean?"

Dave knew exactly what Jimmy meant.

"I'm sorry I had to ask, Jim, but I needed to know."

Jimmy lay motionless on his bed and stared into space. Faces only he could see flashed in front of him.

The conversation was over.

Dave knew now that Holmes was his top suspect.

Marshall surveyed the modern detached house. It sat in a line of other identical detached houses, ugly box-like structures, devoid of any character or thought.

This one belonged to Clive Williams. His garden, in comparison to the others, was a mess. Marshall thought it reminded him of the way Williams dressed.

Marie Baker stood at his side. She carried a briefcase and was dressed in a smart pinstripe suit, which showed her figure off to good effect.

Marshall was in no mood to pussyfoot around with Williams. He knew the officer was in the shit. A criminal conviction loomed for him. His only possible escape would be to confess all and hope that the Chief Constable would let him retire gracefully when the dust settled. He pressed the doorbell and heard it ring in the distance. No reply;

Marie was at the garage. “Car’s here, boss.”

Marshall nodded. “I’ll go around the back.”

He pushed open a high gate that led to the rear of the property. The rear garden was even worse than the front. He noticed that the area had never been grassed. It had been left the way the builders had seen fit, even though the property was three years old. The lack of care coincided with Williams’ second divorce.

Marshall peered through the rear window. It appeared to be the dining room. The gas fire blazed away. Williams was at home, he knew it. He positively hammered on the back door and called out to Williams. Then he tried the handle. It was unlocked. It opened into the kitchen. Pots and pans, interspersed with dirty plates and cups, littered every surface.

Marshall turned to Marie, who had joined him. “A right little home-maker, eh?”

Marie lifted an empty scotch bottle from the waste-bin. It was one of several. “Maybe this is the reason, boss.”

The pair walked from the kitchen and into a narrow hall. Various police awards adorned the walls. Marshall noticed three commendations for bravery, and suddenly felt very sorry for Clive Williams. He opened the door to the lounge. It was unusually heavy, and Marshall needed a shoulder to complete the task.

Once inside the extra weight was obvious. Clive Williams was hanging on a coat hook on the inside of the door and was very dead.

"Jesus Christ!" Marshall gasped.

Marie reached toward the dead man's throat and checked for a pulse. It was a gut reaction, and a pointless exercise. Williams had been dead for some hours.

Marshall took hold of Marie's arm and motioned her away from the body. He surveyed the scene. A small footstool was lying just inside the doorway. No doubt Clive had used it to stand on, in order to connect the ligature around his throat to the coat hook.

The cord looked like plastic coated washing line, or electrical flex.

It had cut so deeply into Williams's throat, that it could barely be seen. His face was the colour of a well-ripened plum. His eyes bulged grotesquely in their sockets.

Marshall inserted his hands into his pockets, as did Marie. Old fashioned police practice, but very effective.

If your hands are there, you can't touch anything you shouldn't.

The Superintendent leaned as close as he could towards the face of the dead man. Nasty looking bile had dribbled from his mouth onto his shirt, and had formed a yellowish patch below the chin.

Marshall also saw some deep scratches on Clive's throat. Maybe he changed his mind at the last minute?

He checked the fingernails. Yes, there was blood under them.

Classic.

The officers walked slowly into the living room. It was as cluttered as the rest of the house.

Half-eaten takeaway lay on the coffee table, together with cardboard cups of soft drinks. Numerous ashtrays overflowed everywhere, and yet another bottle of scotch sat next to an easy chair.

In one corner of the room was a desk, covered in documents. A typewriter had pride of place in the centre.

Placed on top of the machine was one A4 sheet. It bore one word and no signature.

It read,

*'Sorry.'*

Marshall turned to Marie, "Call out the circus."

The two men stood on the promenade of the seaside town. They stared out into the Irish Sea, its rolling greyness hypnotic. Drizzle mixed with spray on their faces.

The shorter of the two turned up the collar on his expensive overcoat.

"Was it clean?"

"As a whistle, no worries."

"Shame about Clive, I liked him, but loose cannons and all that."

The taller man sneered, "He was a pussy; he shit himself."

"And the files?"

"No."

"You sure he didn't have them?"

"You ever been hung?"

"I need those files."

"He didn't have them."

"I don't like this business with Wallace's father. He's a powerful man. He already knows too much."

"No one can connect you. Without those files, none of this means shit. You are home and dry. Just don't forget my money."

The smaller man walked away without looking back.

"Stay in touch, you know where I am.

The prison officer shocked Dave. His constant lock down had given him time to think. He had grown used to the lone company of his cellmate.

"Come on, Stewart, you have a visitor."

Dave was curious. “Who?”

The officer was curt, “You’ll find out when you get your arse over there, won’t you, chum.”

Dave pulled himself up from the bunk, pushed his feet into his training shoes, and followed the officer in silence.

It was a long walk to the visiting area. The noise and smell of the remand centre filled the air. Dave wanted out more than ever now. He had a place to start. If indeed Holmes was responsible for Anne’s death, both he and whoever the muscle was would pay dearly.

The visiting room was bedlam. Twenty or so desks firmly fixed to the floor. Prisoners already occupied most of them. Women and children of all shapes and sizes made up the rest of the picture. The room filled with the odour of unwashed feet and cheap perfume; Dave saw Thomas sitting stiffly at a desk in the corner.

Dave sat. “Mr. Thomas, come to see how the other half live?”

Thomas was unimpressed with Dave’s sarcasm, and not at all happy to be visiting the shithole he found himself in.

“Let’s get on, Stewart. I have no intention of spending one minute more here than is absolutely necessary.”

Dave forced a smile. “The feeling’s mutual, Thomas.”

The brief opened a file. “Then let’s get on, shall we? Your bail hearing is set for tomorrow morning at ten. You will leave here about eight and be transported to the court. Once you are there, I will provide you with clothes for the hearing.

When you get bail, Mr. Wallace has booked you a room at his

hotel. He will brief you on the information we have collected so far."

Dave's heart was pounding. "How can you be so sure I will be released?"

"That's something I have neither the time nor inclination to explain to you right now. Mr. Wallace will tell you what he wants you to know. So, for now, just be a good boy and listen."

Dave could have gleefully punched the patronising ass there and then.

"I'm all ears, hot shot," Dave said, with more than a hint of derision.

"As before, I don't want any comment from you other than to confirm your details. The press will be there. Your release will cause even more of a stir than your arrest. Mr. Wallace would be very upset if you talked to them. He has already spent a great deal of his valuable time, not to mention money, on this investigation. You should be very grateful."

Dave was starting to lose patience with Thomas. "I'm sure Mr. Wallace can afford it."

Thomas seethed, "Personally," Thomas waved his hand around the visiting hall. "I think you and your type would be more at home in a place like this."

He snapped his briefcase closed. "Just remember your instructions."

Thomas started to leave. "Oh, by the way, it was fortunate that the killer had sexual urges, or you would still be here for the summer holidays."

Dave felt like he had been punched. "Wha..."

Thomas rose quickly and walked to the exit.

Dave flew into a rage. "Come back here, you fucker! What do you mean?"

A prison officer took hold of Dave's arm. "Steady, son, after what I heard, don't spoil it now."

Thomas walked to his Jaguar, smiling.

Marshall sat in the mobile police station which had been set up outside the home of Clive Williams.

Marie Baker and Slick Jemson sat opposite. Marie was sipping from a can of sugar-free drink. She stared absently out of the window, as the local undertakers were removing the body of Williams.

"What d'ya think, boss? Tragedy, isn't it."

Marshall was reading a diary recovered from Williams's desk. He stopped and looked at Marie. "I don't like it. The electrical flex could be a coincidence. The scratches on the neck are normal in a suicide, but the note? No signature. No, I don't like it at all."

Jemson spoke, "He did have good reason though, boss. He was heavy into the bottle. Second wife left him. Best mate murdered, and looking at the sack at best."

Marie didn't take her eyes from the hearse. "Is that what they want us to think?"

Marshall stood and stretched. "Look, I don't know about you guys, but I'm beat. We won't know anything until the forensic boys are done. Let's get some rest. We need to be sharp in the morning. I'll be at Stewart's bail hearing at ten. After that we'll meet and see what we have."

The three officers wearily found vehicles and went their separate ways.

Marshall, to put his children to bed, Jemson to see his girlfriend for the first time in a week, and Marie to the station; she had no one to see her lover was in Blackpool for the weekend.

Andy Dunn was contemplating going for a pint at The Bull, when the phone rang.

It was Wallace. "Good evening, Andy. Sorry for disturbing you so late, but I need another favour."

Andy was wary, after his bollocking from Marshall. "What is it, Mr. Wallace?"

"I need the address of Clive Williams. I need to speak to him."

"You can't."

"I'm sorry, why?"

Andy took a breath. He figured the man would find out soon

enough. His tone was flat, devoid of emotion. It was too much for him now.

"He committed suicide this morning."

Wallace sounded sympathetic. "I'm sorry, Andy."

"So am I." Andy cradled the telephone and decided the pint was indeed a good idea.

Wallace stared at the buzzing receiver and then looked at his friend Davits. "Well, Peter, the plot thickens."

Jimmy hadn't tried to speak to Dave since his visit from Thomas. He'd been pacing his cell like a man possessed. His fists clenched tight, the muscles in his shoulders and neck taut and ready; even Jimmy was scared of his cellmate right now.

Dave finally sat on his bunk. He looked directly into Jimmy's eyes. Hate burned in his expression. "Where might Holmes be?"

Jimmy felt nervous. If he'd known where Holmes was, he would have told. "I dunno, Dave; he's got the cash to be anywhere."

"Clarke will know, won't he?"

"Maybe."

"Then where is the children's home?"

Jimmy picked up a pencil and a scrap of paper. He scribbled down an address. His hand shook in his haste.

"Whatever happens, it didn't come from me," he said, his voice wavering, "and I don't want to know what the fuck you're up to."

Dave took the paper and put it in his pocket. Thomas had better do his job tomorrow. He had to be free, and soon.

The courtroom was packed.

Dave stood in the dock flanked by two prison officers. They were a different pair from Dave's last appearance. Both men had travelled in silence in the prison vehicle and had watched him constantly. Orders from above insisted that this boy didn't do anything rash.

Dave wore a brand new suit, shirt, tie and shoes, all courtesy of Wallace.

Thomas had avoided him. This was their first meeting since his comments in the remand centre.

Had Dave not been handcuffed, he would have been tempted to strangle the objectionable bastard there and then in court.

He looked around. He saw Lucy sitting a few rows back. The monstrous frame of Andy Dunn was squeezed next to her. They both gave a smile. Marshall, and two of his team Dave didn't know, were to his right. Wallace and several other men, one of whom looked like an ageing rock star, were to his left.

The magistrates entered, the atmosphere electric; Dave was so nervous he was unable to stop his legs shaking.

It took the magistrates' clerk several attempts to obtain silence. Finally he opened the proceedings. Once again, he read Dave's personal details and the charges to the enthralled public gallery. Dave confirmed his details, and was allowed to sit.

A specially trained police inspector spoke for the prosecution. He stood and addressed the court.

"Your Worships, the prosecution is here this morning to apply for a further remand in custody for the defendant.

The seriousness of the charge and the likelihood that he may, if free, interfere with witnesses, are our grounds for opposing bail."

It should have been cut and dried for the prosecution.

Thomas stood. He swung his body briefly so that all could see his countenance. He oozed confidence from every pore. He was impeccably dressed.

"Your Worships, I represent the defence. It is our intention this morning to make an application for bail for David Stewart."

The courtroom went into uproar. The press had not expected this. Neither had most of the gallery.

Thomas paused, first for quiet, then for effect. The magistrates and magistrates' clerk consulted each other.

The senior magistrate finally spoke, "Continue, Mr. Thomas."

Thomas puffed out his chest, took hold of the lapels of his suit and spoke in his best courtroom voice.

He outlined the evidence the prosecution had offered. Then, with all the confidence in the world, tore it to pieces. Within seconds he had the public hanging on every word. Within twenty minutes, he had the court eating from his hand.

He had quoted peerless lawmakers and offered expert opinion from the best medical and scientific minds in the country, and with fine theatrics, introduced each in turn to the court.

The handwriting evidence brought gasps from the court.

The revelation of the semen stain and subsequent blood-typing even made Marshall heave.

It tore into Dave Stewart's heart. Now he knew what Thomas had meant in the remand centre.

By the time Thomas re-took his seat, Marshall was already in deep whispered conversation with the prosecuting inspector. It was all they could do to limit the damage.

The inspector stood. "Your Worships, this is the first the prosecution knew of these findings. We would ask that we be given time to study the information."

The inspector had the look of a beaten man. "Despite this, we have no desire to restrict the freedom of the defendant more than is necessary. Therefore, we would have no objection to bail on the condition that he resides at his home address and reports to the police station on a daily basis."

A cheer erupted from Lucy and 'Armless. The remainder of the courtroom was a buzz of activity. Dave couldn't believe it. He could feel the handcuffs being removed from his wrists. The magistrate was speaking, but he didn't hear. He was walking forward now, onto the carpeted area of the court. Lucy was hugging him. 'Armless pumped his hand.

David Stewart was crying.

There was a lot of hand-shaking and backslapping going on. Dave didn't have a clue who the people were. He didn't care. He was free.

Finally Wallace came to him. "Congratulations, David, I have a car waiting outside to take us to the hotel."

He extended a hand to the young man. For the first time in days, Wallace's face revealed his great sadness. "I'm sure Anne is very pleased this morning."

The drive to the Tickled Trout was a comfortable one. Dave had never ridden in a Rolls Royce before. The smell of hide, walnut and Wilton filled his nostrils. Sir Peter was beside himself with cheer.

"I'm so glad to see you amongst the free, David. The pressure has been mounting on the police evidence for days now. It was only a matter of time."

"And a great deal of expertise, Sir Peter," Dave corrected.

Thomas had made an early exit for London. That pleased Dave; he had no wish to cause a scene in front of Anne's father. After all, Robert Wallace had got Dave out of jail, even if his choice of barrister was a little misinformed.

The car pulled into the hotel grounds. A porter was eagerly awaiting the arrival of the party. No doubt a large tip was anticipated.

The men were expertly shown to Wallace's suite. Dave sat on a chesterfield, sporting his new clothes. He held a flute of champagne he couldn't stand to drink.

"This is a little different to my cell at Risley."

Staples noticed Dave's discomfort and made light. "Long may it continue, Dave. After what you've been through this last week or so, you deserve a little luxury."

Dave slowly nodded his agreement and turned to Wallace, who was standing with Davits. "What's your next move, Mr. Wallace?"

Wallace joined Dave on the plush leather sofa. He placed his hand on his shoulder. "Well, I would imagine that your charges will be formally dropped within the week. We have turned over all the information we possess to the police. Our job was to get the police to start looking in the right direction. That is about finished, Dave. I know you are pretty desperate to get to the bottom of this. So are we, but..."

He paused. His features seemed to fall. He suddenly looked every year of his age. "I'm tired, and I must make the final arrangements for Anne."

Dave felt a lump come to his throat. "I would like to be there, Mr. Wallace. Will that be possible?"

"Of course, I'm sure Anne would want you there. The service will be on Wednesday. You may travel to London with Sir Peter and me if you wish?"

Davits changed the mood, he was still curious. "Is there anything you can tell us about a possible motive, Dave? Obviously the police evidence has been shot down in flames. We have been discussing the possibility of blackmail."

The second Dave heard the word, his stomach turned over. How much had the team discovered? He played his hand close to his chest. "Blackmail? No, sir, I couldn't even start to help. All I know is that John McCauley used his position to get me to alter the evidence in the Bailey case. The next thing I knew, I was in jail."

Sir Peter looked into Dave's eyes. "Did Anne confide in you about him?"

"I knew they'd had a relationship."

Staples saved Dave. "Hey, let's just chill out for a while, gents. This is a celebration. I'm sure Dave has had enough questions to last a lifetime."

Sir Peter was apologetic, "Of course, I'm terribly sorry, David."

Dave waved away the apology. He looked around the room. Anne had the power to gather this team of men, even after her death. Why did she not sort McCauley earlier?

Marshall could hardly believe his eyes. The events of the morning were even worse than he could possibly imagine. Reading the reports prepared by the defence expert witnesses was professional agony.

He had sent copies to the Chief Constable, together with a transcript of the morning's court proceedings.

He was expecting a very abrupt call back. Heads would roll.

Some of the legal errors, of course, were down to the forensic boys and out of his hands.

He had mastered the art of absorbing blame for others. He often turned it to his advantage. Never be seen to turn your back on a colleague for his errors. Correct them, and learn from his mistakes.

This was different. He had known all along that something had been wrong. He shouldn't have allowed himself to be rushed. As he read each salient point of John Staples' report, Marshall vowed never to be rushed again.

He was reading for the second time when Marie Baker blew into the office. "Sorry to burst in, boss, but this is important."

"Go on, it can't get much worse." Marshall mumbled, knowing from Marie's face that it damn well could.

Marie sat and opened a thin file. "Well, boss, you were right. It was blood under Clive Williams' fingernails."

Marie traced the page with her finger and found the place she wanted. "Problem is, there are two types."

Marshall sat up and brushed his hair from his eyes. "Go on."

"Type 'A', which is Williams' own, and type 'O' Rhesus Negative, which obviously is not."

Marshall scrambled through the Stewart defence papers, his mind thumbing through its own interior logs as he searched. Finally he found John Staples' statement and read. "The semen stain on Anne Wallace's clothing was 'O' Rhesus Negative."

Marie had already suspected as much. "And that's rare, right?"

Marshall was grabbing his coat. “Three people in a hundred rare enough?”

Marie followed. “Where are we going, boss?”

Marshall was almost running. “The Tickled Trout Hotel and I hope you’re dressed for it.”

Marie found herself visually checking her clothing. She looked up at Marshall and found him smiling. It was good to see him smile, even if the joke was at her expense.

A ten-minute drive found Marshall and Marie standing in the plush suite, feeling rather like fish out of water. Wallace and Davits, on the other hand, were relaxed in the surroundings. Marshall hated to ask Wallace for help, but desperate times and all that.

Wallace broke the ice; “I was about to come and see you, Marshall. I’m leaving for London tonight. Anne is to be buried Wednesday morning and I wanted to update you on our conclusions. After the shoddy way in which this enquiry has been run so far, frankly you need it.”

Marshall was to the point. “I’m not here to trade insults, Mr. Wallace. I need all the help I can get and I’m fully aware of the shortcomings of this investigation. What you don’t know is, there has been another development.”

Wallace interrupted, “Yes, the suicide of Inspector Williams.”

“No, sir, the murder of Inspector Williams.” Marshall didn’t wait for a reaction. “We have just received the forensic reports from our lab. We found two types of blood under Williams’ fingernails. His own, type ‘A’ and another, type ‘O’ Rhesus Negative.”

Davits came to life. “That’s the same as...”

“The semen stain on Anne’s clothing.” Marshall completed the sentence for him, and added, “So, gents, I would be very grateful for your conclusions.”

The four sat and discussed the case from the beginning. All agreed that the burglary at McCauley’s home was linked with the murders of Anne, the Chief and Bailey. Williams was definitely aware of the dirt McCauley kept sealed away. Had Clive Williams been silenced for what he knew? The name constantly being mentioned was that of Raymond Holmes.

Where was he?

He hadn’t been seen since the murders. His office had been told no more than he had taken leave. Was he responsible? Which of his dismal secrets could McCauley have uncovered? Were they worth killing for?

The four started to go over old ground, and Marshall had little time. “What about our boy Stewart? What does he really know?”

Wallace came to Dave’s defence, “I think David has been through enough. He doesn’t know anything.”

Marshall was dubious. He knew that McCauley had Anne over a barrel. Stewart could know why.

“Then you won’t mind if I have a quick chat with him?”

Wallace shrugged. “He’s in the next suite.”

Marshall and Wallace stepped into the richly carpeted corridor and gave a courteous knock on the suite door, which swung open with ease. Dave Stewart had gone.

He had his own plans for Raymond Holmes.

# BEST SERVED COLD

Dave walked from the hotel to a cash point on New Hall Lane. It was a rather run down area of town, and his smart dress drew passing attention from the local youths. A street prostitute smiled at him, her young face pale, with dark circles under her eyes signaling her drug abuse. Dave ignored her, quickly drew five hundred pounds from a cash point using the card Ross had provided, and took a taxi to the railway station. The driver had a good look at him. That was fine. He had probably seen Dave's picture in the evening paper. Once at the station, he bought a ticket to Blackpool and sat drinking foul coffee from a Styrofoam cup.

He knew that the conditions of his bail required him to sign on at the police station each night; he also knew that wasn't going to happen. This was business.

The train to Blackpool was dirty, noisy and late. Once again, several surly characters eyed him. Dave stared back and they quickly lost interest.

After a short walk from the station, Dave stood in Talbot Square,

Blackpool. He shivered as the cold wind blew off the Irish Sea.

The seaside town was deserted by holidaymakers. The annual illuminations over, Blackpool looked every inch a sad and dismal place. Dave found a late store and purchased a map of the town from a bored spotty youth.

Walker Place, the address Ross had found for him, was on the south side of the resort. Dave decided to walk, a good way of orientating himself.

Blackpool South appeared to be made up of streets of small bed and breakfast houses and holiday flats. Many of the flats had been let to lower income families and unemployed. This was the council's answer to its housing problem. It offered only temporary accommodation and was a major irritation to long-term residents. Dave would just be one of many short-term inhabitants who had no wish to be found.

10, Walker Place sat next door to a small sex shop. It boasted 'Hard Core Vids' in orange Day-Glo letters across its frontage; an under inflated blow-up doll dressed in tacky red underwear lolled in the front window. She was surrounded by a collection of marital aids and pornographic magazines. The shop and the house both belonged to Ross. Another string to his bow; Dave allowed himself a few seconds to gaze into the window of the shop whilst waiting for the short street to clear of pedestrians.

Once alone on the footpath, he quickly opened the door to the house and stepped inside. Warmth washed over Dave's chilled features. The central heating had been switched on prior to his arrival. Ross had looked after him again.

The house was a small 'two up two down' affair, sparsely

furnished, but clean and tidy. It had a large back yard with a garage that Dave presumed would contain the Volvo.

On entering the kitchen, he opened the fridge to find basic groceries. Tea and coffee sat on the work surface, ready for use.

He unlocked the back door and walked into the yard. On opening the door to the garage, a very clean red Volvo 340 awaited his use.

The model may be boring, but it was also inconspicuous.

The inside of the vehicle had been valeted. Dave checked the glove compartment. It contained a driving licence, registration document and insurance certificate, in the name of James Jackson, together with a current MOT certificate for the car. Dave popped the boot. The hydraulic supports hissed as it opened to reveal two suitcases.

He lifted them both from the car and walked back inside the house. Warm again, Dave made himself some tea and sandwiches. He hadn't realised how hungry he was. The heat of the house made him drowsy.

He sat staring at the two cases for a while, and then set about opening them. The first contained clothes.

Coveralls, boots, gloves and a balaclava; Dave allowed himself a smile, this was standard Ross employee equipment.

The second case was Aladdin's Cave. It was split into two layers. The first held an array of tools, not dissimilar to his own collection back home. The sight of them brought back memories of the fateful night at McCauley's. His mind wandered to Anne, and he was overcome with black memories, suddenly transported to her death scene by his tortured mind. He pinched the bridge of his nose and fought to regain his concentration. *Check the tools*, he told himself. Yes. All basic entry stuff, a small Maglight torch completed the set.

Dave lifted out a foam template to reveal the second layer. It contained a Remington pump action shotgun. The barrel and stock had been shortened for ease of concealment, and the magazine extended to hold five cartridges.

Dave donned the gloves from the first case and picked up the weapon. First, he racked the mechanism to check the weapon was clear. It made a satisfying, yet terrifying sound. All identifying marks had been removed with what appeared to be acid.

Two types of cartridge sat in the case; 00-buck, which contained nine pellets, all about the size of a 9mm pistol round and rifled slug, which holds one single ball of lead weighing about an ounce.

Dave raised an eyebrow at this. It was standard police issue kit. The 00-buck was a real man-stopper cartridge, but the rifled slug was normally used to kill large animals. It would drop a one-ton bull at fifty yards.

What did Ross think Dave was up against, a herd of elephants?

Dave replaced all the items into their cases and carried them to the landing. There he found the loft access. Tall enough to open the hatch by standing on tiptoe, he pushed the cases through the opening and secured the hatch. From there, it was directly to bed. Tomorrow the real work would begin.

Marshall sat with Marie Baker in The Bull. He drained the last of his beer with a grimace and waved his empty glass at Lucy. Marie nursed a gin and tonic. She put her hand over the top of her glass and shook her head at the barmaid.

"Not in the mood, Marie?" Marshall asked.

"I'm driving over to Blackpool tonight. A friend of mine has been there for the weekend and has decided to stay a few more days," she sipped her drink thoughtfully, "so I thought I'd pay the seaside a visit."

Marshall smiled at the young woman. "Who's the lucky man? Anyone I know?"

Marie looked up at her boss. Her dark eyes sparkled and a broad grin revealed a perfect set of teeth. Marshall had always thought Marie attractive, but tonight she'd made herself up a little. The effect was quite stunning.

"No," she said. "No one you know."

"Well," said Marshall, raising his second pint, "as long as you're back by the morning. It's none of my business."

Marie changed the subject, "Where do you think Dave Stewart will go?"

Marshall swallowed and wiped fresh froth from his lip. "I think our boy has his own agenda. I just hope he doesn't do anything stupid. Personally, I think that wherever Holmes is, Dave Stewart won't be far behind."

Wallace and Davits sped along the motorway toward London. The comfort of the Rolls gave little solace to the occupants. The atmosphere was anything but comfortable.

“I can’t believe the David would just take off like that, Peter.” Wallace was disappointed.

“I can,” replied the doctor, attempting to read ‘The Times’, outwardly irritated by the whole business. “Just think back to when you were his age. Imagine having lost everything you hold dear. Then being wrongly accused and imprisoned. What would you do if you knew who was responsible?”

“Yes, but does he know? He’s still a police officer.”

Sir Peter mellowed at Wallace’s’ remark. He put his hand on the arm of his friend. “So was Anne. What would she have done?”

Wallace nodded. “My God, heaven and earth won’t stop her.”

Wallace realised he had used the present tense regarding his daughter and felt a strong pang of sorrow. “Let’s get the funeral over with. I need to put Anne at rest before I can think clearly now.”

Harry dutifully steered the car on its journey to the capital, its saddened and tired occupants silent.

A far smaller and less luxurious car made its way along the M55, headed for the seaside town of Blackpool.

Marie Baker did her best to concentrate on her driving, but her mind was in turmoil. It wasn't the murder case. It was her private life.

Marie's problem was her sexuality. She'd had a few boyfriends. Two of them had lasted. Had she been unhappy?

No, she had been very happy, especially with Steve. That had been a good time in her life. She was still attracted to men. In fact, she thought Dave Stewart was a real hunk. So what was she doing, driving to Blackpool to see Zoë?

They had met when Marie's cat was sick. Zoë was Marie's local vet, a tall, very pretty blonde, with large expressive hazel eyes and long legs.

She and Marie had always got on well. They had shared a few laughs. Then, on one visit, Zoë suggested they went for a drink. Marie had thought nothing of it, but it turned her life upside down.

On their night out, they had both had far too much to drink. The 'quick one' in the pub, turned into several and a visit to a night club. Whilst they shared a taxi, Zoë invited Marie in for a nightcap.

Marie was still unaware of any other motive than friendship. They had sat on the sofa in Zoë's lounge, drinking far too many gin and tonics. Marie talked of just having split from Steve. The conversation became a little bawdy and the two women laughed over some early sexual secrets.

There was a lull in the conversation. Zoë stared into Marie's eyes and it happened.

Zoë kissed her. Not a friendly peck, but full on the mouth. If you had put the scenario to Marie prior to that night, Marie would have said she would have run a mile.

She didn't. They had slept together and it had been good. Marie, far from being a shrinking violet, had found herself taking a very active part in their lovemaking. Marie had felt a warmth and tenderness she had never experienced before.

The 'morning after' was a different matter, and the days that followed were hell for Marie. She couldn't understand her actions. One moment she felt excitement, the next she felt sick. Was she gay?

The motorway became 'A' road and brought Marie back to the present. She now had to find 'Lucy's', a gay bar in the centre of Blackpool. Marie had told Zoë that she wanted to meet in her hotel, but Zoë was having none of it. Marie felt like she was being pushed too far too soon.

So, why in the hell was she going?

Marie had no way of answering, and within minutes she was parking.

'Lucy's' was a renowned haunt for gay men and women. A basement club, it nestled under another bar, where a live rock band blasted out their music to a young appreciative audience. Marie pushed her way through the crowd until she found her way to the stairs leading to Lucy's.

The lighting was very subdued, forcing her to stand at the bottom of the well for a few moments until her eyes became accustomed to the darkness.

She scanned the bar for Zoë and found her sitting in a corner of the room with three other women. All looked very butch, with crew-cut hair and nose jewellery. The sight of the other girls made Marie even more uncomfortable in her strange surroundings. The bar was bad enough. She needed anonymity right now.

If the job were to find out, it would all be over for her.

Zoë stood and walked over to Marie. Her hair fell over one shoulder. She looked beautiful. As she reached Marie, she smiled and kissed her on the mouth. "Hi, baby, I thought you weren't going to make it."

Marie could feel herself blush. "I nearly didn't."

Zoë smiled and recognised the look in Marie's eyes. "If you feel that uncomfortable, we can go straight to the hotel."

Marie glanced over to the others and then back to Zoë. "I think that would be best."

Zoë didn't look disappointed. She stroked Marie's cheek gently and smiled. "I'll say goodbye, just a sec."

Marie was left standing in the centre of the room. She played with the clasp on her handbag whilst Zoë kissed cheeks in the corner. Then she saw a young man standing at the bar, far too young for Lucy's over 21 policy. He could have been no more than sixteen.

The boy was having his long blonde hair stroked by a middle-aged man who wore a smart business suit.

The suit was Raymond Holmes.

Marie was mortified. All her morals told her to walk over to Holmes and arrest him.

"Do it," she told herself, "lock the sleazebag up."

How could she? How would she explain her presence in a gay bar?

"I could have simply followed him here," she thought. Just then, Holmes turned and looked straight at Marie. She froze. Would he recognise her? His face failed to reveal his thoughts.

Zoë ended the dilemma.

In full view of Holmes, she took hold of Marie from behind, squeezed both her breasts and whispered, "Let's go."

Marie was horrified. She broke free of Zoë's embrace and fled the bar. Rain lashed her as she exited onto the street. A near gale blew in from the promenade. She ran to her car, head down, thinking of nothing but her anonymity. She felt the criminal, the pervert, pursued. With each splashing step she felt tears closer. How did she get here?

Once in the vehicle, she sat breathing hard, started the engine and punched the heater on. Marie started to organise her mind. She had to remind herself who she was. The promises she had made; she had to do something.

She owed it to herself and the team. She had made a mistake. Maybe she could put it right.

From her position she saw Zoë leaving the bar. The woman was looking up and down the street. Marie sank down in her seat. Zoë walked right by the car. No, she couldn't do it. Coming out was not an option. She could lose everything. Everything she had ever worked for. As soon as Zoë was out of sight, Marie headed home.

Dave rose at six am. He showered but didn't shave. The beard would help change his general appearance.

Dressed casually in jeans and a sweater, he ate a breakfast of cereal and toast. Once the cases had been removed from the loft, Dave selected the items he required for his trip to see Clarke. He knew where the school was, and Mr. Clarke was in for a very rude awakening.

Next he needed to contact Ross. The telephone rang only once. "Ross."

"Sorry about the early hour, Mr. Ross."

Ross was wide awake and had been since five am. He was obviously delighted with the court result.

"Davey boy! Welcome to the land of the free. How's the pad?"

"Fine, thanks, Mr. Ross."

"Good, good. Now what else can I do for you, son?"

"Well, I need you to look at that package you collected for me."

"Just a minute."

Dave heard some activity in the background. He presumed it was the sound of a safe being opened. Footsteps came closer.

"OK, it's here in front of me."

"Is there a file there on a Raymond Holmes?"

There was a shuffling of paper whilst Dave said a little prayer to himself.

"Bingo," said Ross with the thickest of Yorkshire dialect.

Dave's heart skipped a little at the news. "Great, what about a man called Clarke?"

"Alan Clarke?"

"Could be."

"There's one here on him, n'all."

There was a pause from Ross. "You don't want to see what's in here though, mate."

Dave had every idea, after Jimmy's tale. "I need those two files, Mr. Ross, and I need them today. The rest can stay there for now."

Dave heard Ross speaking on another line. He barked a few orders at whoever it was. When he resumed his conversation with Dave, his tone changed completely.

"OK, Davey. Drive to the motorway services at Charnock Richard. They're on the M6. Drive on the south side. Look for a blue Merc with a private plate. My man will be there in two hours."

"Thanks for everything, Mr. Ross."

"If you get in shit, give me a call."

The phone went dead.

Dave was amazed. Ross didn't ask any questions. He presumed that Ross felt that the less knowledge he had, the better. Considering the kit Ross had left him, he probably knew exactly what Dave had in mind.

The back yard of the small terrace was still cobbled, and the stones glistened with rain in the early dark. Dave stood with his kitbag and took several deep breaths of morning sea air. He loaded the kit and sat behind the wheel of the Volvo. His mind once again flashed to the night of his last job at McCauley's house. This was an altogether different scenario. Just the thought of his task raised his adrenaline level, and he felt the muscles in his shoulders twitch in preparation. His body was readying for fight or flight.

He shrugged to loosen the offending muscles, and hit the accelerator. He was on his way to the meeting point.

The Mercedes bubbled away on the car park of the services. Dave pulled up alongside. A very large man sat in the driver's seat. He looked over at Dave, pressed the electric window and threw the package through the open window of the Volvo. Within seconds, the car had joined the motorway and was out of sight.

Dave opened the package. He checked the contents of the files. Yes! These were the men Dave wanted to speak to.

Clarke would lead him to Holmes, and Holmes would lead him to the muscle.

*Steppingstone Home for Boys has quite a pleasant ring to it,* thought Dave. *How can a school hold such terrible secrets for so long? How can men like Holmes and Clarke sleep at night?*

Dave drove the Volvo like a pensioner with a pacemaker. He was careful to obey all the traffic regulations. The last thing that he wanted now was a pull.

The care facility was situated in substantial grounds. Typical of most Lancashire County Council establishments, the eighteen-bedded unit housed boys from eleven to eighteen years old. Most, if not all the residents would have had long histories of domestic difficulties. Some would already have suffered sexual and physical abuse by their own kin.

To the boys in care, Steppingstone should have been just that, a stepping-stone to adulthood, a safe place to call home; at least for a while.

Large grassed areas with mature trees shielded the red brick built building. The morning sun had yet to make an appearance. The half-light allowed Dave to negotiate the walk from the Volvo to the rear of Steppingstone with ease.

He had changed into black coveralls, boots and the balaclava. He carried a black canvas holdall, which contained the tools he required, and more menacingly the Remington shotgun. He looked the part, now for the real job.

Once in position, Dave tried the rear doors. They were firmly secured by a mortise lock. He had neither the time nor the inclination to defeat it.

There was no need. A downstairs transom window had been

conveniently left open; probably an easy exit for some of the boys' late night escapades. With the minimum of trouble, Dave found himself in a kitchen.

Large stainless steel work surfaces had been scrubbed clean, either by staff, or the boys. The room smelled and looked like a school canteen.

He was completely focused and moved with unusual grace, making no sound. The Remington was racked open, safety on, nestled in his gloved hands. From the kitchen, he needed to cross a small hallway. He flashed his head outside the frame. Clear. Two further heart-pounding paces and he found the place he wanted.

The staff office was a small oblong room with a cluttered desk and two chairs. Children's drawings adorned the walls. To the casual observer, it was no different than any other school staff room. Dave felt sick with rage.

Steppingstone's dark secret was about to be blown wide open.

After maneuvering one of the chairs into the position he wanted, Dave took the other for himself. The moment he sat he felt suddenly calm. It was if he possessed no nerves at all. He placed Alan Clarke's file on his knee. McCauley had thought of everything, and a picture of Dave's prey was stapled to the front.

Dave's right hand dangled at the side of the chair, the shotgun rested absently on the cord carpet.

Dave could hear his own breath. It had started to form condensation on the inside of his balaclava and felt wet against his mouth. He heard movement from outside the room and for a brief moment his serenity left him. Dave started to worry.

What if Clarke wasn't on duty?

What if one of the boys was to come into the office first? Dave knew that the staff had bedrooms in the school. What if there was more than one member on this morning?

The noise became definite footsteps. Adult footsteps;

Clarke stumbled sleepily into the office holding his newspaper and coffee. He was right on schedule, and he was alone.

His hair was a little longer than his photograph and there were more streaks of grey, but there was no mistaking him.

He was overweight, very tall, maybe 6' 5". A full beard had turned salt and pepper, and his lined face was further creased from his recent sleep.

Clarke was so enthralled in his tabloid he didn't notice the intruder until far too late.

Dave slipped the garrote over Clark's head with frightening speed.

The weapon was made from heavy-duty fishing line. A section of wooden doweling secured to each end gave the firmest grip.

Clarke didn't even have time to take a breath.

He clawed frantically at the ligature on his throat, but the line had sunk too deep into his flesh.

Dave had to use considerable strength to hold onto the man. He had started a mental count. Twelve seconds should be enough to render a man unconscious. Any longer, you may kill him. That would be a mistake at this stage. Dave needed to speak to Clarke. He needed answers.

Clarke was now in his final throws. His bladder gave way and the smell of morning urine filled Dave's nostrils.

Dave eased the pressure, and sat the barely conscious Clarke onto the chair he had prepared. Dave had to hold onto the back of the man's shirt to prevent him from sliding to the floor.

He took four plastic cable ties from his pocket and secured Clarke to the chair by his wrists and ankles.

Total control.

Dave surveyed the man. His head lolled forward, his breathing laboured from his ordeal, the wetness still growing in his trousers. Clarke started to come around.

It had been a near silent operation so far. Dave had no wish to change that.

Dave collected the Remington from its resting place and pointed it directly at Clarke's head. The sight of the burly young man, dressed head to foot in black, face hidden by a balaclava, gloved hands gripping the sawn off shotgun, would have scared anyone.

Clarke was terrified.

"Good morning, Mr. Clarke." Dave's voce was a monotone, accent-less whisper under the balaclava.

Clarke didn't speak; his eyes glued to the weapon in Dave's hands. Eventually Clark's lips began to move. His voice still didn't want to work. The area around his airway was still swelling.

"D...D...Don't kill me," Clarke stammered.

Dave put a gloved finger to his lips in a silent command. Clarke obeyed instantly, but his mind was starting to work. “The other staff,” he whispered, “will be here in a minute, and the boys are starting to get up.”

Dave’s voice was calm but chilling. “If we’re disturbed, I’ll kill you.”

Clarke was starting to lose it. His hands pulled violently at his restraints, making a vain attempt at escape.

“What? What do you want?”

“You, Clarke,” Dave brought the closer, just an inch from his captive’s face. “I’ve come for you.”

“Me?” Clarke was close to tears, making his voice even worse. “But, I’m just a schoolteacher. Why should anyone want to hurt me?”

Dave’s hands were gloved, but dexterous. He took a pace to his left and picked up the brown cardboard file. He flicked the cover open with one hand and selected a photograph. He held the image up so Clarke could see it in all its disgusting glory.

It showed Clarke, sitting on the very chair he sat on now, his trousers around his ankles, a young boy, no more than fourteen, was performing oral sex on him.

“Your pupil, Clarke?”

Clarke was horrified. “That’s not me! I know it looks like me, but hey! It’s not, I’m a teacher, that’s all, you have this all wrong, you’ve made a mistake.”

Dave was unimpressed. “Save it, I’m not interested in your pathetic excuses.”

Clarke continued his denial, although it was fruitless. “That isn’t me!”

Dave struck with the strength of an ox. The butt of the Remington connected just above Clarke’s jaw line. The blow catapulted Clarke’s head to the right. Blood poured from his damaged mouth.

He was barely conscious again. Clarke started to sob. “Please, stop, what do you want?”

Dave was breathing hard, the adrenaline fuelling his violence.

He gritted his teeth and hissed, “I want Raymond Holmes.”

Clarke was spitting blood. “He...he’s... gone away. I...I don’t know where.”

Dave plunged the muzzle of the shotgun into the partially open mouth of Clarke.

The force of the action snapped Clarke’s two front teeth clean off at the root. The barrel sank into the roof of Clarke’s already damaged mouth. It tore into his soft palate and finally came to rest. Clarke nearly passed out with the pain.

Dave regained Clarke’s attention by racking the action forward, sending a cartridge into the firing position.

Dave’s voice was positively venomous, “Last chance, Clarke.”

The petrified man’s eyes bulged, tears poured down his face and mixed with the bright red fresh blood that was rapidly turning the front of his shirt crimson.

He nodded furiously at Dave.

Dave slowly withdrew the gun from Clarke's mouth. Clarke gagged and spat out his teeth together with a nasty looking lump of flesh that had been torn from the roof of his mouth by the weapon.

Dave wiped the muzzle on Clarke's shoulder. "I'm waiting, pervert."

Clarke was trying to speak, but his tongue was swollen to twice its size. "Black...pool...Imp...heer...ial...Ho...thel.

Dave felt a surge of satisfaction. So, Holmes was in Blackpool too. How very convenient. His mind turned to his old boss.

Coincidence?

He quickly dismissed his thoughts. There would be time for conspiracy theories later.

Then, he looked at the photograph lying on the floor next to Clarke. Small splatters of blood had fallen onto it.

He remembered Jimmy, his story of the young boy, screaming for mercy at the hands of Clarke and Holmes.

Dave sat. He knew he shouldn't. He'd got what he came for, but something drew him to the file on the floor. He knew he didn't want to see. He knew he had to.

Dave slowly emptied the file of its contents. It revealed several more photographs of Clarke in compromising positions with children.

Other pictures were of even younger children. Clarke, or one of his circle, had scribbled names or information on the back of each.

There were letters from other men around the world; Amsterdam, Thailand and the U.S.A.

Pedophilia was big business.

Then he saw the last picture. A boy, no older than seven, sat naked on the end of a grubby bed. He looked Thai or maybe Korean. His left leg was manacled to the frame. His beautiful brown eyes stared straight into the lens. He was crying.

Dave turned the picture over in his fingers. On the back was written in biro, "Remember Bangkok, Al?" The initial 'S' followed.

Dave's revulsion grew.

He leapt from the chair and plunged the Remington into Clarke's groin. Dave took a deep breath and flicked off the safety with his thumb. Clarke groaned in pain.

His eyes pleaded with Dave. "Pl...eath...don...t."

Dave shook, his mind swimming between revenge and justice, unable to distinguish between the two.

His index finger curled around the trigger of the gun for the first time. Just a little pressure and the weapon would simultaneously send nine lumps of lead into the crotch of the pervert.

"Give me one good reason why I shouldn't, you piece of shit?"

Clarke sobbed. It was a pathetic high-pitched sound.

Dave looked at the excuse for a man. He withdrew the weapon, collected all the documents from the file, and methodically pinned them on the wall of the office for all to see.

Dave lifted the receiver on the office telephone, dialed 999 and rested it on the desktop.

The operator would try to get a response, fail, trace the call and contact the police.

By the time the local police officer was drawing up outside Steppingstones, Dave Stewart was on his way back to Blackpool.

Alan Clarke, however, was stuck firmly to his chair. The evidence of his sordid past, pasted to the walls of his office.

Marshall and his team were having a working breakfast in Preston nick canteen.

It was a busy morning. The uniform section patrols, traffic and dog handlers all filled one long row of tables; section CID and plain clothes, another.

Various civilians were having their tea and toast wherever they could fit.

Marie was deep in thought as she toyed with her cereal and low fat milk. She had yet to reveal her secret.

Marshall, in truth, shouldn't have even been in the room. An officer's mess was situated in the next room, where inspector ranks and above ate their meals. He was in no mood to discuss anything with his fellow officers this morning.

Marshall had slept fitfully. The strain of the last few days was starting to tell on his face.

The team was discussing jobs for the day. The priority was to locate Holmes. They would start with searches of his home and office.

Warrants for both premises were already signed by a very tired magistrate. Jemson had visited her around seven am. He wasn't popular.

Marie was in turmoil.

Bob Belmont, a seasoned dog handler, approached the table chewing a slice of toast. He sported a full set, and crumbs had settled in the ginger mass. A large man in every way, his voice resonated within his copious chest.

He nodded at Marshall, surprised at his presence.

"Superintendent!"

Marshall acknowledged the constable. He knew him from the force rugby team. Bob no longer played, but took full advantage of the post match libation.

"Morning, Bob."

Belmont pushed the remainder of his toast into his mouth and wiped his beard with his hand. The station had spoken of little else than the murders. Marshall hoped that Bob wasn't expecting some juicy morsel of information. He was in no mood for gossip.

Bob swallowed his toast. "You hear about the job at Steppingstone school today, boss?"

The team had not. Bob had the floor and enjoyed the feeling. He took hold of his tunic lapels and started the monologue.

“Seems some bloke broke in, we don’t know how. Lay in wait for the head, tied him to a chair and beat the living shit out of him.”

“Apparently,” Bob postured, “stuck a sawn-off in his gob too. The bloke says he looked like some sort of SAS man. All dressed in black, hood and the works; made him out to be some kind of James Bond type. The funny thing is, whoever it was, thinks he’s some kind of vigilante.”

Bob paused for effect. He had everyone’s attention now.

“He’d taken this file with him, all official-looking like, with a picture of this bloke on the front. It seems our teacher was a very naughty boy, and our man had gone to a great deal of trouble to set him up.

Stuck all the evidence on the wall, and fucked off without leaving a trace.”

Marshall was curious but didn’t see the relevance to his case. All that was about to change, as Detective Sergeant Pierce, the divisional Scenes of Crime officer virtually sprinted into the canteen.

He made straight for Marshall.

“Boss, this pedophile job.”

Marshall was more confused. “Hang on, lads, what pedophile job?”

Bob was first; “Oh yeah, I forgot. The file was full of dirty pictures.”

Pierce gave Bob a dark look and he went quiet. The sergeant lowered his voice to a whisper.

“We just lifted a set of prints from the pictures.” Pierce leaned even closer to Marshall. “They’re John McCauley’s.”

Marshall stood. “Who’s with the teacher now?”

Bob shrugged. “Fulwood CID were up at the Royal with him, I gather he ain’t saying too much.”

The whole team rose as one. Breakfast was over early and they followed their boss out of the canteen.

Bob waited for them all to leave, and picked up a slice of bacon from Jemson’s plate.

“Take it you don’t want this then?”

Marshall and his team crammed into the lift and headed for the basement garage. The Detective Superintendent’s head was overflowing with information.

“Slick, you take two and go to the scene, get some uniforms and do house to house. I want any sightings, vehicles or bodies.”

Slick nodded.

“Marie, you come with me to the hospital. I have a sneaking suspicion who is responsible for this little incursion.”

The lift opened and the officers found respective vehicles. Marie had never seen Marshall so intense.

“This fucker is connected to Holmes. I know it. I can feel it in my bones, Marie.”

Marshall drove like a lunatic. On several occasions they had to swerve violently to avoid traffic. Finally, much to Marie’s relief, they parked outside the hospital.

Marshall marched down a seemingly endless maze of corridors, Marie, almost running to keep up. He barked at nurses for directions until they came upon the bed of Alan Clarke.

A lone detective sat by him reading a newspaper.

Marshall flashed his warrant card at the detective. "Leave us."

The detective checked the rank on the card, took on a slightly pained expression and sloped off to the hospital canteen.

Clarke was a mess. His throat was swollen and a dark blue ring had formed around his neck where the ligature had cut into him. The left-hand side of his face was so distorted his own mother would have had trouble recognising him. A shotgun butt was a formidable club.

His lips would have put Mick Jagger to shame, and were sliced top and bottom. He lay, eyes closed, a drip poking from his arm, his breathing laboured.

Marshall took hold of Clarke's wrists and noticed they too were blackened, no doubt from his attempts to free himself.

"Clarke, I am Detective Superintendent Marshall. I want to speak to you. Can you talk?"

Clarke opened his eyes and looked at the two detectives by his bedside. He shook his head slowly. Clark had no intention of talking to anyone just yet.

Marshall leaned over and whispered into Clarke's ear. He was in a public ward, and the officer had no wish for anyone else to overhear. "Listen, you perverted piece of shit, if you think you feel bad now, just think what will happen when you're on remand in general population. You're looking at twenty fuckin' years. I think you should help me with my enquiries."

Marshall gave Clarke's damaged wrist a firm squeeze.

"Right now."

Clarke slowly turned his head towards the detective.

His voice like sandpaper, he struggled to sound his words without his teeth. He was obviously in great pain.

"I don't know...who it wath."

Marshall was losing patience. "Never mind that. What did he want? Was it one of his kids in the photos, or what?"

Again, Clarke slowly shook his head, a movement that didn't come easy.

"Holmths...it wath Holmths."

"Raymond Holmes, the solicitor?"

Clarke nodded.

Marshall looked at Marie in triumph. "Do you know where he is? Did you tell him where he was?"

Clarke was grimacing in pain now. "I want... thome protection."

Marshall squeezed the wrist some more. "Don't fuck me aroun,d Clarke. Believe me; things can get a lot worse."

Tears started to fall down the bearded face.

"Blackpool, The Imperial."

Marshall stood and almost knocked a very irate-looking doctor off his feet. "What the hell are you doing with my patient, officer?"

Marshall had no time to argue. He pushed the intern to one side.

"Reading him his horoscope.

Dave was working on his appearance.

The suit Wallace had bought for him was ideal. He had purchased a black leather briefcase that would hold the Remington and tools he required. He'd visited an optician and bought a pair of horn-rimmed glasses with clear lenses. He wouldn't need Holmes' file for this job.

Dave stood in front of the full-length mirror in the bedroom of the tiny house and surveyed his handiwork.

He had brushed his hair into a side parting and gelled it firmly in place. Something he had never done before. It wasn't quite long enough to be convincing, but it would do. He added the spectacles and there it was, David Stewart, solicitor;

Darkness was two hours away. Dave would wait. He didn't want to spoil his plan now. He had already telephoned Ross for his final favour.

Marshall and Marie were back in the station. Jemson and the rest of the team had been recalled. It was time to formulate a plan of action. The mood was pensive.

Marshall was wearing the previous three days on his face. His voice, though, was steady.

"OK, the only people involved in this investigation are sitting in this room. The Chief Constable is now being peeled off his office ceiling and is taking a personal interest in our efforts. Let's get it right from now on, or all our backsides are on the line. Let's look at what we know now."

Marshall had the floor, he had already written notes onto a dry wipe board. Names, dates and places, all joined together with connecting lines. Photographs of crime scenes and suspects were pinned everywhere in date order. Every sliver of information, including Wallace's findings, was at his fingertips.

Marshall started at the beginning, "This whole mess, begins on 9th March 1981, with the manslaughter of Elsie May Townsend on Callon estate.

Our boy David Stewart was responsible for the arrest of her suspected killer, William Henry Bailey. I am now certain that Detective Chief Superintendent McCauley and Detective Inspector Williams put pressure on Stewart to change his statement, in order to beef up the evidence against Bailey. Williams was guilty of altering the other documents necessary to complete the picture.

We now believe that McCauley, with the knowledge of Williams, liked to keep private files on various people. We presume these people were unaware of the existence of these files until recently.

These documents were probably kept in the safe at his home; the same safe that was emptied on the night of his murder."

I have been in contact with officers from the Greater Manchester force. They believe that Raymond Holmes, Bailey's brief, is involved in pedophile activities. Whoever put Alan Clarke from Steppingstone School in the hospital knows the connection, and wanted us to know too."

Marshall produced a photograph recovered from Clarke's office wall. He passed it around the team.

"The boy in this picture is none other than a very young William Henry Bailey. Most of you will recognise the other party."

Raymond Holmes' face stared back at the team.

"Our first presumption was that Bailey gave McCauley this information to use against Holmes and Clarke so he could obtain favours; very doubtful in my opinion.

As we now know, Holmes has groomed Bailey from a young age, but it has never stopped the lad using his services as a solicitor for the last eight years or so. In fact he was Bailey's best option; he'd defended him successfully several times before. If anyone was going to play dirty and get his client off a murder charge, it was Raymond Holmes.

Let's presume Holmes had got wind of the changes made to Stewart's statement and the property register?

What if he had gone to McCauley and threatened to blow the whistle?"

Marshall pointed his finger at the tens of incriminating pictures on the board.

"McCauley's prints are all over these photographs, not Bailey's, and the Chief was overheard bragging about having 'dirty pictures' of someone, just a couple of days before he died.

If I were a betting man, I'd say John McCauley has possessed these pictures for some time;

When Holmes threatened to blow his case and his career out of the water, McCauley played his ace card.

Anne Wallace, McCauley, Williams and Bailey are all dead as a result of the contents of those files.

Raymond Holmes is currently our number one suspect."

All the team was enthralled, except Marie Baker.

Marie spoke quietly, "So who was it that plastered those pictures all over a staff room wall for us to find?"

Marshall smiled at his sergeant. At least one of his team was on the ball. He motioned Marie to continue.

"You tell me."

Marie rubbed the back of her neck as she spoke. She was feeling the pressure too. "OK, Let's say Holmes wanted the files, badly enough to employ some real heavyweight muscle. He dispatches them to recover the files and take out the main players.

At first, Holmes presumes, like us, Bailey has dropped him in it, so his man shuts him up. He then lies in wait for McCauley and Wallace. Anne arrives at the house. He ties her up and starts to beat her to obtain information about the files. The Chief arrives unexpectedly. He kills him, and returns to the job in hand.

Before she's killed, she tells him of the safe in McCauley's house.

He tries there, but someone has beaten him to it."

Slick was getting restless. "Aw, come on, this is getting ridiculous."

Marie gave her senior a sharp look, but carried on.

"The killer then dumps the incriminating clothing and weapons at Stewart's house to put us off the scent. Our own poor investigation didn't help.

Still empty handed, Holmes can only think of one other player close enough to McCauley, who might know who stole the files that night; Clive Williams.

So now we have four people dead, and Holmes still doesn't have the pictures.

The person who does, had the know-how to do a pro job on McCauley's house and secrete them until today. He wants Holmes because he believes he is responsible for the murder of Anne Wallace, yet has enough moral fibre to box off this other pervert Clarke. He's fit, fearless yet careful. This man is now on a one man revenge mission, and I reckon he's the man with the biggest gripe in the world right now."

Marie pointed to the name in the centre of the board.

"Police Constable David Stewart."

Marshall, Marie, and Jemson were kitting up.

They weren't alone. Twelve other specialist firearms officers were in the same room. This was the arrest team for Holmes.

Of course, Holmes wasn't considered a threat, but Dave Stewart was. Marshall had convinced the Assistant Chief Constable that the chances of running into Stewart were high. Marshall was as certain as Marie that it was Stewart who had paid Clarke a visit that morning.

The firearms team dressed in dark blue coveralls, Kevlar bulletproof vests and NATO style helmets. Each was issued with a Smith and Wesson .38 revolver and twelve rounds of semi jacketed, semi wad-cutter ammunition. Six loaded into the weapon, six in a speed-loader.

Marie was loading her revolver.

She, Marshall and Jemson, all wore civilian clothes with covert body armour. All of them, though, wore blue baseball caps with a chequered band and chequered wristbands, indicating that they were armed. All officers on the operation needed to know instantly if a plain-clothes colleague had the capability of defending themselves.

The kitting up period was the worst for Marie.

Once she got on the plot she was fine, but right now, she could quite happily throw.

A final check on the kit and radios, and it was time to move.

The drive from Blackpool Central police station to the Imperial Hotel was a short one. Intelligence from the hotel via covert officers told that Holmes was in room 907, and he was alone.

Descriptions of Dave Stewart had been issued to all patrols in the Blackpool area. He was now circulated as wanted for a serious assault on Alan Clarke and firearms offences; although the whole team knew that they would have one hell of a job proving it. Dave's description was of no help to the officers on the ground either. He was relaxing, unnoticed in the foyer of the Imperial hotel, sipping coffee.

Dave had no idea of the plans of Marshall and his team. He was simply observing the routine of the hotel before making his move.

The firearms team were climbing the rear fire escape. All kit tucked neatly away; to the casual observer, it would have seemed impossible for so many people, carrying so much equipment, to climb a metal fire escape and make virtually no noise, but a slow, quiet approach and swift, accurate entry was what they trained so hard for.

Once the team were in their containment positions, an armed officer dressed as a bellboy would simply knock on the door and await an answer.

The door open, Marshall, Marie and Jemson would make the arrest. The team would clear the rest of the suite in case the unwelcome Dave Stewart had somehow managed to beat them to it.

"The best laid plans," thought Dave. He had been sitting in the lobby now for over an hour. He had delivered a note for Holmes and had hoped that the receptionist would place it in the pigeonhole allocated to Holmes' room, giving away his location.

So far, Dave's note remained firmly on the receptionist's desk.

What he couldn't know, of course, was that the whole of the hotel staff were under strict instructions not to contact Holmes during the operation.

As Dave relaxed, the team had completed its silent trek and was in position. All radio transmissions were on a separate channel to the rest of the officers on duty in the division. Each team member wore covert earpieces to ensure silent transmissions.

Marie listened as each officer confirmed his position by a coded call sign. Her heart was starting to race. The body armour she wore under her blouse was sticking to her skin. She felt a bead of sweat trickle down her back. Her hands, though, were dry.

From her position she could see the officer dressed in the hotel uniform approach the door. Just ahead of her, she saw Marshall push his jacket to one side. A weight deliberately placed in the jacket pocket aided the movement. He rested his hand on the grip of his revolver.

The atmosphere could be cut with a knife.

She felt for her own weapon and clicked off the fastening on the holster.

The fake bellboy knocked.

No answer.

He turned to Marshall for silent advice. Marshall motioned him to knock again. The man obeyed.

As the closest to the door, the 'bellboy' was the first to hear the activity. He gave a quick 'thumbs up' to the rest of the team.

On seeing the signal, all the team members made ready.

The door handle turned, and the 'bellboy' made his exit.

Marshall, Marie and Jemson moved as one to the opening door. Marie was the first to see that it was the youth with long blonde hair she had seen in 'Lucy's', and not Holmes himself at the door. So much for the intelligence that Holmes was alone.

He was naked, except for a towel wrapped around his middle. His face was frozen in a look of horror.

The sight of the three officers, brandishing handguns in his direction, was just too much for the youth to assimilate. Marshall moved quickly and took hold of him by the forearm, pulled him out of the doorway and towards the hall.

A member of the team commanded, "Armed police! Get down on the floor!"

The youth dropped to his knees, terrified.

He was immediately covered by two of the uniformed team, who barked further orders at him, "Look at me. Put your hands behind your head. Do exactly as I say and you will not be harmed."

The path into the hotel room cleared, the three serious crime squad officers entered.

Jemson went left and low. Marie took two steps to her right and trained her weapon in an arc.

Marshall went straight ahead, his revolver gripped firmly with both hands.

Holmes was standing by the large double bed. By its appearance, both he and the youth now handcuffed in the hallway had just got out of it. Holmes wore only boxer shorts. He stood rooted to the spot, his mind racing.

As Holmes was obviously unarmed, Marshall holstered his revolver and walked over to him.

“Raymond Holmes, I am arresting you on suspicion of murder, I must tell you...”

Holmes lost it. He stepped back, away from Marshall and pointed his finger randomly at the three.

As he spoke, he visibly shook and tears were welling in his eyes.

“No! No! No! You have this all wrong. I haven’t killed anyone. It’s me they want to kill. Don’t you understand? That’s why I’m here.” He started to laugh hysterically.

“I sent Bailey after the pictures, see. He never made it. That’s all I wanted. I can’t go to jail! You know what they will do to me there. We can make a deal.”

Marie now approached him from the right. Holmes’ eyes were wild. He didn’t even notice that armed men had completed the clearance of the suite and were now watching the show.

“Stay away from me, you...you...dyke.”

The words stopped Marie in her tracks. He had recognised her after all. Anger welled up inside the young woman, anger at Holmes and herself. She, too, holstered her weapon. Her voice came out, and to her surprise it was strangely level.

"You are going to jail, Holmes. And you're going to get what you deserve."

Holmes bit his bottom lip, tears flooding down his face now. He shook his head furiously, his face reddening by the second.

Marshall and Marie lunged at him, but for once they were too slow. Holmes spun around on the ball of his foot and launched himself at the window behind him.

The window exploded into thousands of fragments.

Marie was the closest, and dozens of shards of razor sharp glass flew in her direction. She covered her face with her hands too late.

Holmes seemed suspended in mid air.

The interior lights of the room illuminated his near naked torso. A large pointed section of glass was embedded deep in his back.

Holmes couldn't feel it. He was falling now. He felt the cold night air on his face. He could clearly see the promenade. It had a tram sliding effortlessly, silently along it. His stomach turned over, just like it does in a dream when you step off the end of a cliff. Except this wasn't a dream.

He didn't even have time to ask for God's forgiveness.

The nine-storey fall took less than five seconds. Holmes landed on his right foot. The severity of the impact destroyed the ankle joint completely, cartilage, bone and tendons separating simultaneously.

Holmes' tibia and fibula punched a pair of neat holes in the tarmac of the car park.

His leg folded like a concertina. His femur snapped clean in two. The sound reverberated off the brickwork. The shattered bone tore a hole in his thigh and severed the femoral artery. Black blood instantly drenched the floor.

The greater weight of his upper body bent him double. There was a sickening snap as his spine gave way and a rather nasty slapping sound as his face finally found its final resting place.

He lay in a steaming pool, the final throes of his life draining away.

Dave was in the lobby when the commotion began. He heard a scream. Not from Holmes, who had met his end in horrified silence. But from a woman, who had innocently parked her car just feet from where his ravaged body now lay.

Suddenly the place was awash with uniformed police officers. Dave's nerves were on edge. He quickly calmed as he realised that they knew nothing of his presence.

He moved outside to where a small crowd of onlookers had gathered. Several police officers in firearms kit were trying to preserve the scene. Dave knew of the danger, but he was unable to help himself.

He pushed his way to the front of the increasing crowd, stretched necks hoping to glimpse the shattered remains of a human being.

Fuel for future nightmares.

His heart was in his mouth. He saw the crumpled and bloody form lying on the car park. He moved closer. Standing directly in front of a police officer, his stomach turned over, realising his plan had been ruined.

All hope of revenge was lost.

The fact that Holmes had met with a violent and painful death meant nothing. He felt cheated.

It was over.

Suddenly he felt nothing, a massive void, he had last felt this way lying in the police cells on the day he learned of Anne's death. The commotion going on around him meant nothing. Then he heard Marshall's voice. He was clearing a path for himself, pushing onlookers out of the way. Dave saw that his face was damaged. Blood trickled from small cuts on his forehead and cheeks.

Dave stepped back into the crowd, further and further away from the scene. Then he was walking, the sea air in his face, his guts churning over. He hailed a cab and jumped inside. The driver pointed to the commotion on the hotel car park.

"See that," chirped the cabbie, "one way of getting away with your bill, eh?"

# AT WHAT COST?

The rain was incessant.

It pounded on the array of black umbrellas, drowning out the voice of the vicar for all except the closest mourners.

Wallace stood at the graveside, his proud frame rigid, and his arm firmly around the shoulders of a tall and still beautiful dark-haired woman.

Sir Peter Davits stood to the right of Wallace, head bowed, eyes closed.

The vicar read the Lord's Prayer. It was Anne's favourite.

The television cameras, although a discreet distance from the mourners, used their powerful lenses to obtain a close up of the coffin draped in the Union Jack. A policewoman's hat had pride of place close to the head of the casket. Dozens of bouquets of flowers surrounded the grave. Six police officers from the City of London force had the task of lowering the coffin into the grave, their impeccable uniforms drenched by the rain.

One removed the hat from the coffin and folded the flag. He marched slowly over to Wallace and his wife, and presented the items to the grieving couple. Wallace solemnly accepted the items, handed them to Davits and immediately replaced his arm around his wife's shoulders.

The beautiful woman was weeping.

The officers strained on the tapes as the casket was lowered further into the grave. Rain poured from their noses.

"... and yea, though I walk through the valley of the shadow of death, I shall fear no evil..."

The coffin scraped the sides of the grave but the officers stood firm.

"...thy rod and thy staff they comfort me..."

The coffin came to rest.

"... and I shall dwell in the house of the Lord forever."

The camera panned back from the grave, revealing a large crowd of mourners. It panned further and further, the commentator somberly describing the scene and the recent developments of the case.

Dave was hunched over the small television set.

There were no tears, just an aching emptiness. The thought of revenge had spurred him on the last days, but now, he was deflated and beaten.

He rubbed his face with both hands, stood and turned off the set.

There was only one thing left for him now.

Yorkshire.

Blackpool Victoria hospital casualty department was overrun. This was not unusual. The staff were always overworked, but tonight there had been a large disturbance in a local club, and four separate road accidents.

Sod's law, they all came at once.

Along a spotless corridor sat Marshall. He had been cleaned up, and two small slivers of glass had been removed from his face.

None of his wounds needed stitching. He was lucky.
Jemson stood next to him. The Inspector looked tired. He had just returned from the other side of the hospital. Marie Baker was still in surgery.

"How is she, Slick?" Marshall was monotone.

"Not good, boss," Jemson stared at a poster warning of the rabies threat without really seeing it. "The doctors say she'll probably lose her sight in one eye."

Marshall shook his head. "Jesus, Slick, how much more shit can this job throw up?"

Jemson looked down at his senior. "Dunno, boss. At least we're at the end."

Marshall wasn't convinced. "Are we? Do you think Holmes was lying before he jumped? I don't know. It doesn't make sense; any of it."

A very harassed looking nurse strode down the corridor towards the two men. She held a clipboard in one hand. Her uniform made swishing noises above the clip clop of her shoes.

“Either of you two Superintendent Marshall?” she asked curtly.

Marshall rose slowly. “That’s me.”

She handed Marshall a piece of paper. “You need to ring the guy on there,” she gestured at the slip with her chin, “he’s pretty keen to get in touch.”

The nurse turned on her heels and then added, “Oh, and when you speak to him, remind him of his manners, will you? He’s an ignorant bastard.”

Marshall looked at the details on the scrap of paper.

Slick was curious. “Who is it, boss?”

Marshall managed a wry smile. “Vinnie Morrison.”

He pushed the paper into his jacket and got ready to leave. “You stay here with Marie. Call me at Fulwood nick as soon as you know more.”

Jemson nodded. “You want me to contact her mum, boss?”

Marshall thought for a moment and then shook his head. “No. I’ll do it.”

It came with the rank.

Vinnie Morrison was short for a copper. He had joined as a cadet at sixteen. Although you needed to be at least 5′ 9″ to be considered for the Lancashire force, if you were 5′ 8″ at sixteen, they wagered that you would grow the extra inch by the time you made P.C. at nineteen.

Vinnie didn't grow.

Everyone took the piss and he had been given the nickname 'the poison dwarf'. No one used it to his face these days though, as he had now risen to the rank of detective inspector. His bright red hair was cropped close to his head and he sported piercing green eyes. He spoke with a strong Northern Irish accent that refused to leave him and if red headed people are noted for their bad temper, Vinnie was the mould from which they all came.

Vinnie hated everyone and everything with equal ferocity.

Marshall's swift drive from the hospital had taken twenty minutes. He entered Vinnie's office. The Irishman was in the middle of abusing some poor bastard on the telephone.

He slammed down the receiver. "Fuckin' wanker!"

He looked up and saw the Superintendent. He didn't give a toss about rank. To Vinnie, you were all in the same job. If you did it well, he tolerated you. If you didn't, you were a wanker.

"Hello, boss," Vinnie stuffed a cigarette into his mouth. "Fuckin' hell! You can't get any bastard to do the job right these days."

Marshall couldn't help but like the man. He smiled. "Hello, Vinnie."

The Inspector didn't return the smile. He was investigating the

Steppingstone School job and had just completed a lengthy interview with Alan Clarke. Vinnie was married with two boys of his own. The subject matter of this investigation was too close for comfort.

He hated speaking to Clarke. The man made his flesh crawl, but it was part of the job and Vinnie was very good at his job.

"I'll not beat about the fuckin' bush here," began Vinnie, "but I think you boys at 'Serious' have been barkin' up the wrong fuckin' tree with this pervert Holmes."

Marshall felt the hair on his neck move. "Go on, Vinnie. I'm all ears."

The Irishman threw his feet onto his own desk. "Well, this dirty bastard Clarke is absolutely shitting himself. I've just had over four hours with him. He knows he's in the shit and is being very fuckin' co-operative.

Him and your flyin' solicitor friend have had a nice little arrangement goin' for years. How we never got wind of it, I'll never know."

Vinnie exhaled.

"Anyway, it seems that John McCauley did know.

At some point, persons unknown screwed Holmes' office and a very comprehensive set of photographic evidence was nicked. McCauley somehow got his hands on it."

Marshall's mind was ticking over. Did Bailey screw the office?

Vinnie pointed a finger. "When Holmes found out that the evidence in the Bailey job had been fucked with, he had a meet with the Chief. Holmes demanded the case be dropped. It would have been a big feather in his cap. McCauley, of course, was havin' none of it and stuck Holmes with some of the pictures."

Vinnie stubbed out his cigarette and immediately lit another. "So, when Bailey does one from the court, he runs straight to Holmes, who puts him up for the night, or should I say, puts one up him. Anyway, Holmes plans a little revenge mission for McCauley and a test of faith for Billy. He ain't too sure who nicked the photos in the first place, see?

He sets Billy up to do McCauley's house, shows him the plot and drops him at the local pub. Trouble is, Billy ends up on a slab in the morgue and Holmes is left high and dry.

Holmes thinks that the Chief has done the deed, until he hears that he too, has joined Billy in the land of nod.

Holmes runs to Clarke and warns him that everything has gone to rat shit. Holmes goes off to hide in Blackpool in the hope that everything will just go away. Clarke doesn't know what to do. Then Captain Marvel shows up, sticks a shooter in Clarke's gob and lets the cat right out the fuckin' bag."

Marshall was taking it all in. "How much faith are you putting in Clarke, Vinnie? He could be lying."

Vinnie finished the second fag, took his feet from the desk and leaned towards Marshall.

"About an hour ago, we recovered the remains of a twelve year old boy from a pond just outside Chorley. Clarke wasn't fuckin' lyin' 'bout that, was he?"

Slick sat beside Marie's bed. She had been given a private room away from the ward.

Of the numerous cuts to her face, some had been stitched, some had tape over them. Her left eye was heavily bandaged. The surgeon had been unable to repair the damage caused by the glass.

Holmes' final act had resulted in another tragedy.

She was groggy from the anesthetic but still managed a smile for Jemson. Slick had always thought a lot of Marie, but she never showed any interest in him. They had kissed once at a Christmas party and Jemson had thought that the event might have been a catalyst for more.

It never had.

"How you doin', Marie?"

Her throat was dry. She swallowed hard and licked her lips. "Been better."

"You look great," Jemson lied unconvincingly.

"I'll bet."

"The boss is going to see your old mum and tell her what a brave girl you are."

"Cut the small talk, Inspector, and tell it as it is."

Jemson had been dreading this moment. Marie would never be able to carry a firearm again, so her position on the Serious Crime

Squad was unworkable. The fact of the matter was it looked like her career was over. A sick pension loomed.

All the financial compensation in the world wouldn't repair that. Or her pretty face.

"It's not good, sweetheart."

"I didn't think it was."

Marie swallowed hard again. "The eye, I'm blind, aren't I?"

Jemson took hold of her hand and squeezed it affectionately. A tear traced its way down her face.

"Yes."

Marie bit her lip, but managed to stay in control. "Holmes?"

"Dead."

She nodded. "I… I think I'd like to be alone now."

Jemson rose. "I'll come back later."

Marie turned her head towards the handsome inspector, tears now pouring. "You still got the hots for me, Inspector?"

Jemson was near to tears himself, his voice close to breaking, "I certainly do."

As he left the room he could hear the quiet sobs from inside. He walked quickly to the male toilet at the end of the ward. Once inside, he broke his heart.

Marshall and Vinnie sat in the corner of the snug at 'The Bull'.

Both men were dog-tired. Vinnie was, as usual, pissed off. "Where the fuck d'ya go from here then, with all this bollocks?"

Marshall shook his head and stared into his beer. He and Vinnie had just returned from Marie's house. Her mother, recently widowed, seemed grateful her only child was still alive. Marshall knew the shock would wear off and the realisation would hit soon.

To add insult to injury, he had taken a very nasty phone call from the Chief Constable. He was even more pissed off than Vinnie. They both needed the drink. It had been a fucking hard day. Marshall just couldn't think clearly. He was trying to remember what his wife and kids looked like.

Was this job worth it?

Who actually gave a shit, anyway?

All the politicians and do-gooders were constantly on your back. More for less, was their motto.

Fuck, his little girl came home from school crying the other day. Some kid had called her daddy a 'Pig.' The violence and depravity was starting to take its toll on him. He was human, after all.

Marshall finally spoke. "How do you cope with all this shit, Vinnie? I mean you've been doing this job for twenty fuckin' years. It seems to get worse. Whilst we sit here drinking, we know that some poor bastard is weighing the liver of that little kid you fished out of the pond today. A fuckin' good copper is lying in the hospital half blind, and all the Chief can think about, is boxing the whole job off nice and neat."

Vinnie frowned. “Wha’? The Chief don’t put any weight behind what Clarke says?”

“Nope, he thinks the shooting match is over. He wants the team stood down by the end of the week.”

The two men lapsed into the silence of the unbelieving. Vinnie ordered another beer and spoke, “I know people think I’m a hard bastard and I know I’m a bad tempered arse at times, but I still have feelings. This twat Clarke should be strung up by the bollocks.”

Marshall absently nodded his agreement. “Yeah, it’s funny, isn’t it. Some coppers seem to just breeze along. Nothing ever affects them; they sit on the outside and just get on with the job.”

Marshall stretched. He stood, threw some cash onto the table, and pulled on his coat. Vinnie was following.

“Where you goin’, boss?”

“To the nick; I need to look through it all again.”

“Mind if I tag along?”

Marshall was glad of the company. “Two heads are better than one Vinnie.”

The pair walked in silence to the nick. The first splatters of rain were in the night air. Having ridden the lift, Marshall and Vinnie sat in the dimly lit incident room. Piles of paper, actions and statements surrounded them. A telephone rang in a corner of the room. Marshall stood wearily, and walked to the noise.

“Incident room, Marshall speaking.”

It was a harassed female voice. “Hello, I’m sorry to bother you, but it’s very urgent.”

Marshall took out his pen and found a scrap of paper. “Go on, madam, I’m listening.”

“Well I’m trying to get in touch with Detective Constable Casey and he’s not at his desk...”

Marshall was curt, “This is the murder incident room, madam.”

The woman was insistent. “Well, I was informed he may be helping on your enquiry. Look, Officer Marshall...”

“Superintendent.”

“Whatever. I need to speak to Mr. Casey...”

“Well, madam....”

“It’s Doctor, actually. I’m calling from The Royal Preston ICU and this is very urgent. You see Rodney Casey has a rare blood group, ‘O’ Rhesus Negative. We need a donor immediately. He has helped us before. I’m desperate to get in touch with him.”

Marshall’s head felt like it would explode. He spoke slowly into the telephone.

“I will do all in my power to find him, Doctor, but I think he may be unavailable for some time.”

He dropped the receiver into its cradle. “Vinnie, there is a God after all.”

Marshall stormed into the CID office.

A lone detective sat at his desk. He visibly jumped when the two men entered.

Marshall was frantic. "Where's Rod Casey?"

The detective shrugged. "He was in this evening. He said he had to go out of town on a job though, I've not..."

Marshall had no patience, "OK, OK, which is his desk?"

The detective was a little scared by the senior officer. He simply pointed nervously at a desk by the window. Marshall worked like a man possessed. He searched through the piles of paper on the desk and then in the drawers. He came upon a locked drawer and, to the surprise of the young detective, simply forced it open with a screwdriver. He found what he was looking for. Most officers keep one.

A small blue-coloured book.

Nearly all policemen give blood and keep their registration card handy, especially if they have a rare type. Rod Casey was no exception.

Marshall's hands shook as he opened the small document. There it was, in black and white. Rod Casey's blood group was 'O' Rhesus Negative.

Marshall pushed the record into his pocket and rummaged through the rest of the papers. He found a telephone address book and took that too. Finally, he found Casey's duty diary. He flicked through the dates he was interested in and made a few notes. "Right, Vinnie, do you want to go home, or are you going to get your hands dirty with the rest of us?"

Vinnie smiled at the Superintendent. "The fuckin' wife won't be speakin' to me by now anyway."

"Right then, let's go out to play then."

Marshall turned to the still scared detective. "I want you to get onto control room and check every officer on duty in the force area for this blood group." Marshall scribbled on a scrap of paper and handed it to the man. "Then contact ICU at Preston if you have any joy."

The detective nodded at the men as they disappeared from the office.

# GOD'S COUNTRY

Dave left the train and put his collar up against the chill of the Yorkshire night. It had been almost a year since the last visit to his home. Now, on this return, he was unemployed again. He could never go back to the police service. Not after what had happened.

He still had Ross.

The man may be a villain, thought Dave, but he stood by him when the police didn't.

His parents' house was a mile or so from the station. The walk would do him good.

The streets were deserted except for the odd lowlife. Dave hardly noticed, his mind awash with different emotions. As he neared his road, his senses tingled. He had played on these streets as a child. His school was just yards from his house. He had courted his early girlfriends on the recreation ground that he now walked by. It was a strange mix of feelings. It felt familiar, but did he belong here? He used to, but since his move to Lancashire, he had hoped to forget the dismal poverty of his youth.

As he approached his parents' house, he stopped. All the curtains were closed, but a telltale light glowed in the living room window. The television, as ever, flashed shapes either side of the drapes. Dave could imagine his parents sitting in their respective chairs. His mother would be sipping her 'medicine,' a mixture of vodka and orange juice; his father, engrossed in the programme, chain smoking. Not the prettiest of sights, but to Dave, a very warm and reassuring one right now.

He may not have had the most opulent childhood, but his parents never showed him anything but love; simple people, making the best of a bad lot.

Dave opened the gate that led to the small front garden of the house. Weeds were everywhere. It wasn't that his father was lazy, he just hated the garden. If it had been his own home, rather than a council house, Dave's father would have had the whole lot paved.

Dave lifted a large plant pot that was minus its plant, and recovered the front door key. How many times had he warned his parents about this? Some things never changed.

He slotted the key into the lock and stepped inside. All his senses told him he was finally home.

Several miles away, one lone Yorkshire mobile beat constable drove his Metro car slowly through the derelict buildings that had once been a carpet mill.

The new dark blue Escort car stood out like a sore thumb. It was parked well enough and when the officer got out to check, it was all locked up.

He sat back in his car and contacted his control room. He went through the standard procedure of checking the car on the Police National Computer. The reply was swift, but puzzling. The vehicle registration check came back 'blocked'. It was a security device built into the computer. It prevented 'ordinary' police officers from checking certain vehicles used by other police forces or government departments.

There was nothing more the officer could or wanted to do. He simply presumed it was the R.C.S. or Serious Crime Squad sitting on a job. It was none of his business. In fact, he got the hell out of the area. He didn't want to queer the pitch.

Besides, it was time to end his duty and go meet his girl.

Dave walked along his parents' hallway. The sound of some late night show blared away in the lounge.

He opened the door to the small sitting room and popped his head around the door. Something he had done hundreds of times before.

Dave reeled with the shock.

The television was on its back in the corner of the room. The normally untidy room was devastated. Drawers were ripped from wall units and their contents strewn about. The lounge suite had been up-ended and the base coverings torn away. Dave ran to the small dining room, his breathing laboured from the shock. The same scene met him.

"Mum! Dad!"

Dave was frantic. He bounded up the stairs, taking three at a time.

"Mum! Dad!"

The three bedrooms were all ransacked. Even the bathroom was torn to pieces. Dave returned to the lounge, tried to calm himself and had a closer look. There was a note stuck to the mantel. He snatched it up and read its contents. The message chilled him to the bone.

Marshall and Vinnie had made it as far as the basement garage, when they ran into Jemson.

He was collecting his gear from the back of the crime squad car. He looked pale and very tired. Marshall was still flying from his revelation. "Come on, Slick, we're going on a trip."

Jemson's face fell. "Oh, come on, boss! I'm beat. To tell the truth, with Marie and everything, I wouldn't be any good to you right now."

Marshall heard Vinnie mutter a few "lazy wanker" expletives, but ignored them.

He looked at his watch. It was one a.m. The whole team had started duty at seven a.m. the previous day. "OK, Slick. You get yourself some sleep. We can manage."

Marshall got on the garage telephone. They would need someone fresh to drive them. As he was dialing, the huge folding garage doors started to open. Andy 'Armless Dunn drove the section van inside.

Vinnie gave Marshall a nudge in the ribs. "Now, here's a bloke that won't be too fuckin' tired."

Andy jumped from the vehicle. "Hello, boss!"

Andy was considerably more cheerful since Dave's release from Risley.

Marshall smiled at his old chum. There was so much to tell, but time was of the essence. "Andy, get some plain clothes on and tell the night inspector you're coming with the Detective Inspector and me."

Andy raised his arms. "I only got jeans and T-shirt, boss."

Vinnie was lighting another cigarette. "We're not goin' fuckin' dancing, 'Armless, just be sharp about it."

Andy was indeed sharp. Within minutes, the three men had commandeered the fastest car in the garage and were speeding into the night. They made a formidable team. They held nearly sixty years of police experience between them. No one would have the desire to meet any of the three down a dark alley.

'Armless drove, whilst Marshall filled Vinnie in on the details. Andy was enthralled by the tale.

Could a serving police officer really be responsible for all this carnage? All three had the same question.

What could possibly be in the mysterious 'files' that was of such importance?

'Armless was listening intently. A lull in the conversation was his cue. "I think Dave Stewart screwed McCauley's house that night."

Marshall's jaw dropped. "Go on, Andy. I'm all ears."

Andy floored the accelerator of the car as they hit the slip road to the M55. "Well, think about it. He was in the shit with the Chief. Therefore, McCauley would hold a file on Dave. He was madly in love with Anne Wallace. From what I've heard, he had a file on her too, remember that drink drive charge that was blown out at court some time back?

Marshall and Vinnie exchanged a look.

"They had been away for the weekend. I think they made a plan. Dave persuaded Anne to take McCauley for a drink, get him clear of the house, so he could do the safe. If they could get the files, he would be off both their backs."

Marshall was dubious. "I think it sounds far fetched, Andy."

The car revved steadily under Andy's control. "I know that Dave had the expertise to do it. He worked as some kind of debt collector, or something, over in Yorkshire." Andy was gaining confidence in his story. "Look, the Chief was going off the rails. We all knew it. He was hitting the bottle hard. He probably started to brag too much. Even Lucy heard some of the gossip. I think there was something heavy in those files; police business too. Maybe Casey is protecting his own back. It must involve him..."

"...and Williams." Vinnie was with Andy.

"That's why Williams was topped. He knew what was in there. Casey was scared. Williams was close to spilling the beans. We know Bailey was gonna do the burglary for Holmes. What we didn't know, was that three different sets of people wanted those files. Everyone has underestimated Dave Stewart. He'd beaten them all to the punch. Well, they say things come in threes."

The police vehicle sped from the motorway and onto the A583. Within minutes, the men were back at Blackpool Victoria Hospital. Marshall needed another slant on the evidence.

Despite her pain and exhaustion, Marie was delighted to see the men. Coffee and sandwiches were ordered and consumed. Again, the story was recounted. Notes made, arguments raised. At last, the small team of dedicated officers had just about all the pieces of the jigsaw.

All that was left was to put them together.

Marshall spoke through his tiredness, "Casey's duty diary says he's here in Blackpool. He has been one step ahead of us all along the way. I have no reason to suppose that has changed. He'll know about Holmes. He'll know about the information that Clarke has given. I think he'll be after Dave Stewart."

Marshall looked at his colleagues and got nods of agreement from all of them.

"So," said Marie, "go find Dave Stewart."

Marshall rubbed his eyes. "Easier said than done, Marie; he could be anywhere."

Marie tried to lift herself from her bed. Vinnie helped her. She was not about to give in. "Look," she started, "where would you go to nurse your wounds? The lad has been through bereavement; he's been locked up, beaten and then left to his own devices. He's been on a revenge mission. Like everyone else, he thought Holmes was responsible for, or would lead him to, Anne's killer. He'll know the outcome by now, be sure of that. He'll feel cheated."

She pushed herself further up on one elbow. "There's one thing he won't be expecting."

Vinnie didn't give her chance to finish. He removed his head from the open window where he'd been smoking.

"Yeah, Rod fuckin' Casey."

Marie nodded slowly. "Which car is Casey using?"

Marshall shrugged. "Dunno. I presume the section CID car."

Now Marie was getting impatient. "Well, boss, I suggest you find out and see if it's been checked."

Marshall was very tired, and not quite on the ball. Marie could see it, and helped her senior. "If you ring PNC at HQ, they can tell you if anyone has checked the car recently."

Vinnie moved first. "I'll make the calls to PNC. Andy, you get on the blower to Dave Stewart's parents, see if he's run home. If you speak to him, warn him. Casey is one mean bastard."

Marie started to pull herself from her bed.

Marshall shook his head. "Where do you think you're going, miss?"

Marie had her feet on the floor. She was very pale. "I'm coming with you guys."

She looked into Marshall's face with her one good eye. "Don't say

I can't, boss. You know as well as I do, this is probably my last job. I want this one bad."

Marshall knew she shouldn't come, but he needed her analytical brain. "OK, you get your shit together. Any rough stuff, you stay the hell away. I have enough troubles."

Marie beamed. "Yes, sir."

Vinnie and Andy arrived back in the room together. Both looked serious.

Vinnie spoke, "The car that Casey is driving was checked by a section officer in South Yorkshire about two hours ago. The officer is 'unavailable,' so we can't say exactly where.

There was no answer at Dave's parents. We sent a patrol round to check. The fuckin' place is ransacked and there's no sign of Mr. and Mrs. Stewart."

Marshall pushed his hair from his face. "Jesus, Vinnie, Casey's gone mad hasn't he?"

Vinnie knew just how mad Casey was. "We've got to get to Yorkshire and quick. If you take my advice, boss, I say, fuck the protocol and don't tell any fucker we're on our way. This goes a lot further than a fuckin' detective constable."

The four walked slowly along the hospital corridor. Marie was delicate. Vinnie leaned toward Marshall. "What the fuck is she doing here?"

Marshall looked toward Vinnie and Andy. He squeezed Vinnie's arm. "I got enough brawn on this job, Vinnie. I need some brains."

Vinnie looked at Marie and then looked Marshall straight in the eye. "You can say that again, boss."

Dave sat in the plush office, his right knee shaking in a nervous twitch. He was waiting for Ross. He was the only one who could access the safe where the remainder of the files were.

Well, that's what the gorilla in the suit had told Dave when he arrived. That was over two hours ago, and still no sign of Ross.

He was in Sheffield on 'business' and would be back later. Dave felt like he was on a knife-edge. He couldn't take much more.

The music from Ross's club pounded in the distance some three floors down. The place was packed with people having a good time. Dave couldn't remember the last time he felt good. He closed his eyes and let his head fall backward.

He felt exhausted, cheated, and frightened for his parents.

"You thinking of something nice?"

Ross had arrived. Dave was relieved to see him.

"Not in the slightest, Mr. Ross."

Ross could see that all was far from well. "You got a problem, Dave?"

Dave nodded his head. He was unable to speak now. The events of the past days suddenly weighed upon him. The note left at his parents' was the final straw.

His shoulders began to shake. Unable to hide his tears, he covered his face from Ross's gaze. Ross had never seen Dave troubled by anything. He took hold of the young man and sat him in the nearest chair. "Right, mate, just take it easy. Just tell me what I can do for you."

Dave rummaged in his jeans pocket and produced the note. Ross took it and read it swiftly.

Steve Ross seldom showed any emotion. He came from the type of family where to show any kind of feelings was considered weakness. It was fine to show anger, though.

Ross paced his office floor with the note firmly gripped in his right hand. He curled his lip, revealing his gold tooth. His eyes were virtually black. Everyone that knew him well had seen this mood before. They also knew that it meant trouble.

Ross calmed enough to speak. He sat at his desk and smoothed the crumpled paper with his huge hands. The taking of Dave's parents was personal. In life, business is one thing, family is another.

"Let me sort this one, Dave." Ross' voice was ice.

"I'll put my best lads on it right now, but Dave, lad..."

The gangster's face told the story.

Dave looked up at Ross, tears still on his face, the reality slowly dawning in his eyes. "No! Don't say that, Mr. Ross."

Ross was flat calm. "You know they're already dead, Dave?"

Dave couldn't believe, wouldn't believe. Ross had to be wrong. He made mistakes. Everyone does. His voice shook. He took short breaths.

“No, Mr. Ross! They… I mean, Mum and Dad. They’re alive. I know it. I’ll just do as it says in the note. Give them what they want and…”

Ross was shaking his head. “Dave, stop and think. These people, whoever they are, have already killed four times. Do you think that it matters to them?”

Ross handed Dave a very expensive handkerchief. “I’ll tell you what I know; you fill me in on the blanks.”

Dave wiped his eyes. “OK, but we need to get going.”

Ross leaned back and picked up a telephone. He barked some orders regarding the club and how he was not to be disturbed.

“We will, Dave, but first, it was you who did McCauley’s drum that night, wasn’t it? It had you all over it. I take it that’s how you came about these?”

Ross spun around in his chair, tapped a combination into a wall safe, removed the files and dropped them onto his desk.

Dave nodded. Ross continued, “He held files on you and Anne Wallace. Yes, I’ve read them. I’ve read them all. I suppose you thought that you could get him off your backs?”

More nods from Dave.

“What you didn’t know, was that Holmes and McCauley were already trying to blackmail each other over the Bailey job.”

“How do you know all this, Mr. Ross?”

Ross leaned forward.

"When I read this lot, I knew you were in the shit. That's the reason I left you the shooter. Not so you could frighten the life out of Alan Clarke. What's in here, mate, is dynamite, and it don't involve small fry coppers either. When you stole this little lot, you were only minutes away from meeting the man who is now causing all the grief."

Dave was puzzled.

"So, who is it?"

Ross tapped the files with a manicured finger. "There were twenty files here. Take away yours and Anne's, Holmes and Clarke. That leaves us sixteen options. Out of those, five are dead and two are in jail for a very large fraud.

These are the nine that remain."

Ross spread the brown files out on his desk. He held up two files and put the first in Dave's hand.

"The button pusher," he dropped the second file on the first, "the muscle."

Casey checked his reflection. He was an intelligent man. He may not have had a university education like some, but he was no fool. He'd started this job. It would take an intelligent and brave man to finish it.

Walkden was a fuckin' soft bastard.

No bottle;

When it came down to it, only Casey had all the answers. Mind you, hadn't it always been that way? Every time the shit hit the fan, wasn't it him they always called?

*That's how it all got started; back in '74. That's the reason behind all this shit; the IRA bomber case. What a fuck up that was.*

*Clive Williams was a detective sergeant back then. McCauley was just an inspector. The man in charge of the IRA investigation was none other than Detective Superintendent Geoffrey Walkden.*

*Hadn't they all done well? Williams made DI, McCauley a chief superintendent and Walkden was now Lancashire's newest and brightest Chief Constable.*

*Yeah, 1974, what a mess.*

*McCauley and Williams had done the first round of interviews. They thought they were rough, tough boys. They got nowhere with the Paddy, though.*

*He just sat and fuckin' smiled at them. Pissed himself where he sat. Never said a fuckin' word.*

*Walkden wasn't happy. He wanted a result badly. He needed the pip to go with the crown, the next rung on his slippery promotion ladder.*

*Walkden enjoyed watching Casey go to work. Oh no, he didn't get his own hands dirty. He liked to watch. Walkden loved it when the Paddy started to scream. The Irish bastard shit himself during his beating. Not by choice that time, either. He bled all over the fuckin' place he did. Casey had to burn everything. His own work suit, shoes the lot. When Walkden realised the Paddy had snuffed it, he was crying like a baby. Casey wasn't his blue-eyed boy then.*

*Walkden got everyone in the office. He was shaking like a leaf. The big cover up. A death in police custody; Walkden was convinced we would all go down if we didn't play the game.*

*So everyone played.*

*Got away with it too, but McCauley had to be a smart arse didn't he? Kept all the records. All the original notes times and dates. Who? What? Why?*

*No one knew of course, not until that night. The Bailey case was a wrap. Everyone was pissed. McCauley let the cat out the bag then, didn't he?*

*Williams tried to shut him up. He'd known all along, bosom buddies and all that. Of course, McCauley said he'd never use it. Then why keep it?*

*Walkden had a simple answer.*

*Go take it away from him.*

*Trouble was the Chief was trying to fuck too many people at once. Bailey, Holmes, Wallace and Stewart;*

*Stewart was a cool customer alright. He was fucked now, of course. Casey, as usual, had thought of everything.*

*Casey was an intelligent man. So intelligent, he could get away with murder.*

The four police officers sped along the M62 towards Yorkshire. Andy drove whilst Marie slept but groaned occasionally, pain forcing the small sounds from her. Marshall and Morrison were checking Casey's movements in his duty diary against actual events.

They badly needed to contact the officer who had checked Casey's car earlier in the night. He had gone off duty and no one at the local station seemed to know how to get hold of him.

Marie awoke. "We got far to go, boys?"

"About another half hour," said 'Andy.

Marie turned to Marshall. "Found any alibis yet, boss?"

Marshall marveled at the woman's tenacity. "Not a single one. Although we can't put exact times on all the deaths, Casey was either off duty or working alone on those days. In fact, compared to the previous weeks, he's been a very lazy chap."

Vinnie wasn't convinced. "Casey's never been lazy in his life. He's been up to no fuckin' good."

Marshall closed the diary. "All we can do is meet the local guys down at Stewart's parents, and find out what beat this guy was on that checked Casey's car. It's a race from there on in."

The race was definitely on as far as Dave Stewart was concerned. Steve Ross, on the other hand, had completely different ideas.

Ross drummed his fingers on the top of the files. "Do you realise how much this little lot is worth, Dave?"

Dave was impatient. "I don't really care Mr. Ross. I just want to see Mum and Dad safe and sound."

Ross shook his head and looked into the face of the younger man. Ross had befriended Dave, but his eyes were cold and frightening. "I told you Dave, don't hold out any hope. These guys have too much to lose to be identified. Let me deal with it. Let me do it my way and we'll all come out a little richer too."

Dave was getting angry with his benefactor. "Look, you've been good to me, Mr. Ross, and I appreciate that. You helped me in ways no one else could. The only thing I could think about when I was inside was getting revenge. I wanted to see the bastards die."

Ross hunched his huge shoulders and showed the palms of his hands. "And you will, son. Just go with me on this. We do as he says. Make the call. Follow his orders, but instead of putting our arse on the line, we nail his to the fuckin' wall. We make copies of the files and use them to our advantage. This is your redundancy money here, Dave."

Dave stood. He couldn't take any more risks. He had already lost Anne. He couldn't gamble with his parents' lives. "No, Mr. Ross. I just can't do it."

Ross was getting impatient. "Look, use your loaf." Ross handed Dave the phone. "Ask to speak to your mum, then! Tell 'em you won't do fuck all until you speak to her. Tell 'em they got ten minutes to produce her alive and well at the end of a phone, or you go public with the files."

Dave was wavering. Ross was adamant. He pushed the phone

closer to Dave with his ham of a hand. “You know it makes sense, Dave. If you can’t trust me, who can you trust?”

Dave lifted the receiver. He was as nervous as a kitten. He checked the number on the paper. It was local.

It rang four times and then was answered. The voice had a Lancashire accent. Dave didn’t recognise it. He had never spoken to Casey. “Hello David.”

“I want to speak with my mother.”

“In good time, David.”

“No! Now! I don’t think you understand the situation, mate.”

Casey was unmoved. “You’ve been listening to your friend Ross, haven’t you, David?”

The surety of Casey’s voice caught Dave off guard.

“You with him now?

He wants you to copy the files doesn’t he? Has he told you what they are worth to him yet? He‘s a villain, David.”

Casey was about to play his ace. “Don’t think he hasn’t already made his play. He‘s a greedy boy, David. Too rich for our taste; that’s the reason your mum and dad had to be inconvenienced.”

Dave was aghast. Had Ross already tried to sell the files? His mind was spinning. Ross had been in possession of the files long enough to study them. He definitely had enough resources to find out anything that he needed to know to complete a deal.

Dave pressed on with his task. “I want to speak to my mother, now."

Casey's voice, obnoxious and menacing, sent shivers down Dave's spine.

"This is what you will do. You will take the files from that greedy bastard Ross. Get in a fucking taxi and go to Grimethorpe. When you get in the village, find the Working Men's Club, there is a phone box outside. You will get further instructions when you get there. If you're not there within thirty minutes, I'll kill your parents. Even Ross has bitten off more than he can chew this time. If you don't bring the original files, I'll kill your parents. If anyone follows you, or you contact the police, I'll kill your parents. I know what you're thinking, but the police haven't a clue who I am. Once I am satisfied I have the original files, all this will be over. You know a copy is worth zero in court, Dave. I mean, why else screw McCauley's in the first place, eh? You will have nothing on me, or my boss. I'm very well protected, David. You, the law or that two-bit crook Ross has no chance. If you like living, you will forget the whole mess. Forever!"

Dave was shouting, "I don't believe you! I want to speak to my mother now!"

"I don't care if you believe me. Who can you trust, David? Ross? I don't think so. The police? Well, I think you already know the answer to that one. Wallace? He just wants to clear up his daughter's mess."

Dave felt his guts churn at the slight on Anne. His voice became calm and cold.

"I'll be in Grimethorpe in thirty minutes. I'll have the files you want. If my parents are harmed in any way..."

"They'll be fine..."

Dave was sinister, "...in any way. I'll kill you slowly."

Dave dropped the receiver into the cradle. He looked straight at Ross. "Give me the files I need, Mr. Ross. You can keep the rest. I'm sure they'll be worth something."

Ross looked disappointed with his young prodigy. "He turn you against me so easy, son?"

Dave had no desire to lose the argument. "I just want the files, Mr. Ross."

The gangster leaned back in his chair. "Who would you prefer to take on, Dave? Them or me?"

Dave knew he was in the hands of a man who would not hesitate to kill to get what he wanted. If Ross decided to keep or give him copies of the files, there was little or nothing he could do. He pleaded,

"Please, Mr. Ross. Let me do this. Do you really think I'm going to let this bastard go? I promise you will have the files back by the end of the day. You can keep the damn things."

Ross laid a huge palm on top of the papers. "Do you trust me, Dave?"

"No."

Ross smiled. He lifted his hand from the files and gestured Dave to take them. "When this is over, Dave, I'm gonna teach you a lesson."

Dave felt a pang of guilt at his sudden turn on Ross. He couldn't help himself. Who could he trust now? He collected the two files he required. “Thanks again, Mr. Ross… for everything.”

Ross waved away the gratitude. “I’ll get you a car to take you where you need to go.”

Dave shook his head he was going to play this by the book for now. “He said to take a taxi. I don’t know who is on his side, Mr. Ross. Like you said, there’s a lot of money tied up in this lot.”

Ross opened a drawer on his desk and removed a 9mm. semi automatic handgun. The grip and slide were covered in tape. “Here, Dave, take this. It’s clean.”

Dave took the weapon and examined it. He had never fired a handgun.

Ross helped. “It’s a Browning. The magazine is full. Just pull back the top slide and pull the trigger.”

Dave nodded and pushed the gun into his belt at the small of his back. The weapon felt strangely reassuring, the cold metal against his warm skin like carrying a small package of death. “Thanks again, Mr. Ross.”

The two men stood and faced each other. Ross, a hardened criminal without morals or fear; he had and would kill to get what he required. Dave Stewart, on a mission to save his only surviving family, had never killed. Tonight though, he may have to.

Ross gripped Dave by the shoulders. “Make this fucker pay, Davey.”

Casey sat in the dark of the old warehouse. It was cold but he didn't feel it. Come to think of it, he didn't feel too much of anything lately. He surveyed his surroundings. The place was ideal. It nestled near to an abandoned stretch of railway line and a link road. In a fast car, the road would have him on the motorway in less than five minutes.

The old carpet factory was a large dust-laden void. All its machinery stripped away and sold to Far-Eastern competition. Apparently the owners thought it insufficient to discard its workforce. The sale of the people's tools ensured a meagre profit from its demise. Grease marks and bolt-holes were all that was left of the powerful looms.

Dave Stewart's parents lay back to back on the floor near to Casey's own feet. He had bound their hands and feet with electrical flex and used pillowcases for hoods. He should have killed them by now, but he wasn't completely sure if Stewart would fall for the line about Ross.

Now that was Casey at his best. Years of interviewing criminals had taught him to undermine anything the subject thought to be a constant.

Stewart didn't believe he could trust anyone now. He would do as he was told. Once he brought the original files, Casey would be home free.

Irene and Derek were quiet now.

Irene had struggled for a while. She had kept shouting out, being difficult. Casey had kicked her firmly in the face. She had been quiet since.

Some blood had seeped through the white pillowcase, he presumed from her nose. So what? She wouldn't be feeling anything soon.

The old man, Derek, had been more of a problem than Casey thought. He put up quite a fight at the house. Casey smiled as he recalled his adventure. It had been so easy to get in. He simply knocked on the door of the old dears' house. Derek had answered. Casey had pushed the old boy backward into the hallway, and Bob's your uncle!

OK, he'd had to rough them up a little, but hey, this was a big boy's game now.

Casey looked at the couple again. Derek was breathing heavily under his hood. He would be heavy to lift to the car but it was the only way.

Casey would finish the job. He always did. He picked up Derek by the feet and started to drag his bulky frame toward the door of the warehouse. He had only taken two steps when the elderly man kicked out viciously and connected with Casey's gut. The force of the impact knocked him back and caused him to drop the feet of the old man.

Derek thrashed about on the floor in a desperate attempt to free himself. It was a pointless exercise.

Casey was bent double. The blow had knocked the wind out of him. He raised himself to his full height and a sickening sneer appeared on his face. He stood over the bound and hooded figure.

"Well, Mr. Stewart, want to play rough, do we?"

Vinnie Morrison and Andy Dunn stood in the warm, comfortable hallway of Dave Stewart's parents' home. They were in deep conversation with the two South Yorkshire uniformed officers who were protecting the scene.

The local CID were treating the incident as a potential murder enquiry and the two bobbies were reluctant to let Vinnie or Andy inside. The Lancashire crew had decided on the cover story that they were looking for Dave Stewart, as he had failed to honour his bail conditions. The fact that the team contained a detective superintendent and detective inspector, had, so far, gone unnoticed.

Despite the slim cover story, with a little persuasion from Vinnie, the Yorkshire officers talked about what they thought had occurred and what information had been obtained so far.

Marshall was chatting to a dog handler parked outside the house in his van. Man and dog had just completed a search of the gardens in the street.

The usual pleasantries exchanged, Marshall leaned into the open window of the van. The smell of the wet dog caged in the back was eye watering. Marshall examined his notes for the name of the officer who had checked Casey's car on the PNC.

Marshall's manner was as casual as his tired brain could muster. "Do you know a Constable Lincoln, mate?"

The Officer was eating a pie of some kind. Crumbs covered the front of his uniform tunic. Marshall wondered how anyone could eat surrounded by such a stench. The man spoke with a full mouth and a thick accent. "Aye, Dave Lincoln. He's a detached beat bobby aat at Grimey. He'll a gone 'ome na, though."

Marshall looked puzzled, unaware of the local geography, and struggling with the man's Yorkshire twang. "Grimey?"

"Mmm," more crumbs, "Grimethorpe. Tha' knows, its weer t' band comes from."

Between the pie remnants and the accent, Marshall didn't get a word. He felt a tap on his shoulder. Marie Baker attempted a smile. She looked like shit. "Need a translator, boss?"

"I'm afraid so."

Marie introduced herself and found that the dog man was far more helpful when speaking to someone, "we aat a plumb in 'is gob"

Several minutes later, the four Lancashire officers were gathered together and were pooling the information they had gained from their Yorkshire colleagues.

Marshall spoke, "No closer to contacting this PC Lincoln, then?

Vinnie shook his head. "He's not at home; he has a bird somewhere, but no one knows where she lives. We do know the area he was in when he checked Casey's car though. It's about fifteen minutes from here."

Marie piped up.

"This very nice dog handler, err... Bill, has agreed to take us and assist with any searches. Grimethorpe is a small area."

Marshall countered. "Yes, but to find one car without outside help is not going to be easy. I don't want to inform the local control room. You know as well as I do what will happen when they find out we are here, and I don't want anyone back at Preston to know our whereabouts just yet. We need to keep our cover story for the local bobbies that our job is unrelated. If it turns out that Casey has taken Stewart's parents, we get him first, we take him home."

Marshall gestured with his thumb toward the house. "They can have him, when I'm finished with him."

Dave Stewart was having trouble with the taxi. The old car rattled and banged along the small streets of Grimethorpe. The Pakistani driver was new to his trade and didn't know where the hell he was going. Dave was getting more and more irritated. The meter rolled on, but more importantly, another clock was ticking.

Dave checked his watch. There was less than three minutes left of his allotted half-hour. He wiped the condensation from the window of the cab and peered into the darkness.

Then he saw the sign for the club. "Stop! Here, yes here." Dave fumbled for the fare.

"Does tha want me t' wait?" asked the driver in a very strong Yorkshire accent.

"No, pal, you can go."

Dave thrust the fare and a hearty tip into the driver's hand and opened the car door.

He finally stood outside the phone booth. The wind had picked up and it had started to piss down. Dave turned his collar up against the cold and wet.

"Fuckin' brilliant."

Inside, the phone booth smelled like a public toilet. Graffiti covered the walls. Dave didn't give a shit as long as the phone was working. That was his only panic now. He lifted the receiver and heard the telltale purr of a working unit. He rested it back in place and waited.

Casey opened the boot of the Vauxhall car. He had stolen it a couple of hours ago for one solitary purpose. It would probably remain unreported for some time. When it was, the local cops would find it, eventually.

They would also find Mr. and Mrs. Stewart in the boot. Unfortunately, by then it would be too late. The old pair were in a shit state now anyway. It wasn't his fault. The old boy got rough first.

Casey had lost it. He'd done the old man some serious damage. He'd known much younger men who couldn't take a kicking like that. The old man was moaning quietly when Casey put him in the boot.

Casey noticed he'd got blood on his clothes, and made a mental note to dispose of them carefully before he met with Dave Stewart.

He lifted Irene Stewart into the boot and she fell limp on top of her husband. Casey slammed the boot shut. In a couple of hours they would die from suffocation.

Casey walked back into the deserted warehouse and had one last check around. This was not the time to make a mistake and leave something behind. He stripped his coveralls and rubber gloves, bagged them and stored them in the police Rover. He could dispose of them later.

Right, now it was time to ring Dave Stewart.

Marshall and his team were crawling the streets in search of the CID Escort car. The Yorkshire dog handler tagged on behind, the miniature convoy slowly combing the area in the pouring rain.

Marshall checked his watch. It was five am. He was dog-tired. He looked at the rest of the crew. Andy and Vinnie looked fresh. Marie looked bad, and Marshall was starting to feel rather silly for allowing her to come along.

Vinnie was hanging out of the car window. His red hair was drenched. A powerful torch in hand, hoping against all odds to find the car they badly needed for a break in the job.

"We're running out of time, guys," said Marshall, checking a street map and crossing off the ones already searched. "We've only covered about a tenth of the area. At this rate it will be daylight and the cat will be out of the bag."

Marie, as usual, was the one with the ideas. Even in her poor state. It was why Marshall had brought her. She had the ability to rationalise a problem and come up with a workable solution.

She looked over Marshall's shoulder with her good eye. "Well, boss, by all accounts the copper who checked the Escort is a pretty keen guy. Crime orientated sort. He's keen to get on CID from what I gathered."

Marshall still wasn't on her wavelength. "So?"

Marie took the map from her senior. "So, where would a crime orientated bobby be sneaking about in the late evening checking motors?"

Vinnie stopped his search for a second and punched his finger at the map. "Fuckin' commercial property, industrial units, and warehouses, that's where I'd be."

Marie smiled wearily. "Me too, Inspector."

Marshall had no options left. "Let's do this area next then."

Andy increased the speed of the car and made for the Grimethorpe industrial Estate.

Dave's legs were shaking uncontrollably. He wasn't sure if it was due to the cold or his nerves. The phone should be ringing right now. Without the phone call, Dave had no options. He had to wait for the bastard.

A telltale metallic noise came from the unit. Dave grabbed the receiver instantly.

Casey's voice was even and calm, "Don't ask any questions, Stewart, just listen. I hope you have a good memory boy because I'm not going to repeat myself."

Dave was close to exploding with anger but he knew better. "I have a pen and paper. Get on with it."

Casey smiled to himself. "You're a proper little Boy Scout aren't you? OK, from where you are now, take the first road on the right. That's Stiles Avenue. Then you walk a hundred yards or so until you see a small car sales pitch. Turn left and keep walking until the street turns to a dirt track. Stay on the track. That will lead to an old railway line. Follow the line away from the lights of the town until you come to the first tunnel-bridge. Keep walking and stand under the bridge. Hold the files in your right hand. If I as much as feel another person's presence, Mummy and Daddy will be pushing up the daises. Got that?"

"I've got it."

"Good. It won't take more than ten minutes walk David so don't be late."

The phone went dead.

Dave folded the files in two and pushed them into the front of his jeans. He removed the Browning from the small of his back and cocked it. Dave grimaced. "I won't be late mate, trust me."

Dave walked quickly. The rain was beating into his face so fiercely he could hardly hear what was going on around him. He saw the headlights late. A dark saloon car with at least three occupants was headed straight towards him. It was closely followed by a police dog van.

Dave saw a man leaning from the window of the saloon. He was shining a powerful torch at parked cars.

Dave's heart rate went through the roof. He could taste the

adrenaline in his mouth. He bowed his head against the rain and walked as casually as he could.

The car slowed as it reached him. The man with the torch shone it towards Dave, who pulled up his collar even further. Dave's anguish was short lived. The police officers were obviously looking for a vehicle, not a man. The brace of cars sped to the next set of parked vehicles and recommenced their checks.

Dave found the car sales pitch and followed his directions. He had calmed a little now. His heart felt normal again; He was focused on one thing only. Finding his parents alive and well.

The rain pounded against the windscreens of the police vehicles. As the Lancashire car passed Dave Stewart, Vinnie made a comment about the guy being "up to no good."

Marshall was to the point of despair he didn't care about the lone male pedestrian.

Vinnie almost screamed with pleasure, "The fucker's here!"

Parked outside what appeared to be a near derelict building was the Lancashire Police Escort booked out to Rod Casey.

A wry smile came over Marshall's now unshaven face. "Patience is indeed a virtue," he thought.

Andy pulled the car over and killed the engine. The Yorkshire dog van stopped behind and the handler got out, complete with a very large dog that didn't appear to mind the rain at all. He leaned into the open passenger window, rain dripping from his nose just from his brief walk.

Marshall was pulling on his coat.

“Right, Vinnie, Andy, check the Escort. I’ll go with Bill here to check the building.”

“I hope tha don’t expect t’ dog to track in this weather mate.” Bill said who really had no idea of the gravity of the job at hand.

Vinnie and Andy were already getting out of the car to get a closer look at the Escort. The dog handler looked at the two men, who gave the impression of a pair of very angry bare-knuckle fighters and changed his mind.

“Err… Max’ll give it a go though.”

Vinnie slapped Bill’s already soaked shoulder with his powerful hand, nodded toward the disused warehouse and chirped, “Max will search that place a lot quicker than we can, pal.” He pointed at the long-coated German Shepherd. The animal gave the impression of a sawn-off lion, “…and if our fuckin’ man is inside I hope he chews his arse off.”

The dog had already sensed the urgency of his task from the mood of his human colleagues. He danced around the feet of his handler, whimpering in excitement.

The best police dogs are always keen to work, and Max could hardly wait. Marshall stood in the torrential rain and turned to Marie.

“You stay in the car, lady.”

Marie actually seemed grateful for the order. She was dog-tired and in pain. She had long since taken the last of the pain relieving drugs from the hospital.

"OK, boss."

Marshall took the torch that Vinnie had been using and beckoned Bill toward the front door of the warehouse. Within seconds they were examining the small jemmy mark on the door that had been inflicted by Casey hours earlier to gain entry.

Bill tentatively took control. "I'll put the dog in first and see if he indicates anyone."

Marshall nodded his agreement.

The door pushed open without resistance, and Bill unhooked the leash from Max. The dog trembled now with excitement. For Max, the game was about to begin.

Bills voice changed from his deep Yorkshire drawl to a higher pitched, almost feminine sound as he spoke to the dog. "Good boy, good boy. Where is he? Go find him, boy."

Bill now had to physically hold the dog back as Max was at fever pitch. His voice changed yet again as he shouted into the darkened old building. "Police! Anyone inside, stand still, I'm sending the dog!"

Bill released Max, who catapulted into the darkness. Marshall shone the torch at the dog as he padded from left to right. The police dog was trained to search for many kinds of people. He had no way of knowing the good guys from the bad, so if he found a placid person hiding he would simply sit and bark at them. This was the 'indication.' On the other hand, anything that ran or showed aggression got bitten. For Max it was a great game.

The dog stopped suddenly and sniffed at something on the floor. Marshall held the light on the spot. It was a dark stain in the concrete. It was the blood of Dave Stewart's father.

Bill gave Marshall a knowing look. The dog moved on and disappeared out of sight.

Andy and Vinnie joined the pair at the door. Vinnie whispered into Marshall's ear that Casey's Escort was locked and empty. The four men were silent, hoping for Max to bark, the atmosphere painfully tense.

Minutes passed, and the dog returned panting and frustrated. Bill called Max to him and praised him. He ordered the dog "down" and the four men all entered the warehouse.

"He's been in here," said Vinnie, inspecting the floor. "Not too long ago either, I'd wager."

The dog suddenly stood and barked. All four men jumped. It was Marie standing at the door. She stood still and Max sniffed at her. She looked apologetically at Marshall. "Sorry, boss, I'm a nosy female."

Bill ordered Max back to his original position but the dog was reluctant to be still.

He spoke quietly to his trusted companion, "What's the matter, boy?"

The dog's excitement grew. The game was far from over for Max. He padded quickly to the exit and scratched at the door. Bill called him away, mistaking the dog's actions as a desire to go outside for a piss or to get back in the van, in which he loved to ride.

Marie studied the floor. She, like the rest, saw the blood, but as ever she saw more. There were two distinct sets of scrape marks on the floor. She inspected them closely. They both led toward the door. She looked at the scrapings and then at Max. “You are a clever boy, aren’t you?”

The dog whimpered and let out a small high-pitched bark. Bill shouted at him to be silent.

Marie was as excited as Max. “No, Bill, Max is right. Look at these marks, guys.”

The four all studied the black scrape marks. They started at the bloodstain and ended at the door.

Marie was confident. “These are heel marks. Casey has dragged two bodies out of this place,” she pointed at the dog, “and Max here wants to show us where they are.

# WALKING DISTANCE

Dave had followed his directions and was now on a single-track railway line that had high sloping grass banks at either side.

The torrents of rain that lashed at him had made his hands and face numb with cold. Visibility was very poor indeed. Nothing in the way of direct light, only what reflected from the high sodium lights of the nearby 'A' road. The line obviously hadn't been used for a very long time. This was Coal Board property. Once upon a time the coal would have been dragged along this line to a main branch where a train would take it to wherever it was destined. The ghosts of many a Yorkshireman and his trusted pony still sweated and strained along this track.

Dave slowed. He could make out the bridge in the distance. He'd had no time to plan. He'd been working on pure instinct. He stopped and looked at the scene. Under the bridge was total pitch. His man may already be there.

Dave thought it unlikely that he could yet be seen from under the bridge. For the moment he could think in safety. He again checked the Browning and the files. There was no choice; he had to go under the bridge and face whoever or whatever was there. He felt like a child in a nightmare. The total darkness of the bridge was looming in front of him. His heart raced. He could hear the blood in his ears, the howl of the wind and the lash of the rain, nothing else.

He moved away from the centre of the line and walked halfway up the left-hand bank. He could now see the top of the bridge.

There was no one.

Back on the line he walked slowly. Various items of rubbish had been dumped on the line. Old prams and bin liners of goodness knew what. Dave tripped and stumbled his way in the darkness.

He was now less than twenty yards from the entrance to what seemed like the darkest and most depraved place on earth. He could hear water pouring through the roof of the bridge onto some metal object underneath. It would make the chances of hearing the approach of a man impossible. Was anything on his side?

He took each pace with growing disquiet. Despite the freezing rain sweat poured down his spine. Now, for the first time that night, he felt genuine fear. Suddenly there was a flash of movement to his left. With the swiftest movement, Dave drew the Browning and fell to a crouch.

The biggest rat Dave had ever seen pushed its way along the railway line. Dave felt like shooting it. His heart pounded harder than ever. He forced himself to calm, rose to his feet and continued his laborious trek.

Ten yards to go. Dave crouched. The gun pointed at the black void ahead. Each step increased his heart rate. Looking forward, he was blind. Finally he rested his left hand against the stone entrance to the bridge. He made a swift movement and finally stood under the structure. The hammering of the rain indeed obliterated everything other than the loudest of noises.

Dave noticed that steam rose from his clothes, his body heat was pouring from him. He needed a place where he could feel less open. He leaned against the wall of the bridge and felt a little easier. He took the files from under his clothes and held them in his right hand, exchanging the Browning to his left.

Dave didn't know if he could shoot left-handed. Fuck it, he'd never shot a handgun anyway. One way or another, left or right handed, he would soon find out.

Marshall and his team were in poor spirits. They had all expected Max to take them to another building, or at the very least the Escort. Instead, Max sat and barked furiously at an old Vauxhall car parked across the road.

Bill's attempts to dissuade the dog were fruitless. Eventually he had to resort to pulling Max away by the collar. Max was not easily put off, and struggled to make his handler see what he could sense by barking even louder.

Andy sat in the unsecured Vauxhall. "Well, Max has recovered a knock off motor, guys," he said, with more than a hint of sarcasm.

Marie sat alongside him and checked the glove box. Inside, a wallet and a cheque book appeared untouched. "Sloppy thief, I'd say, Andy."

The thump from the boot of the car nearly gave them both heart failure.

Marie gave out a sharp, "Jesus!"

Andy was on his way out of the car. "They're in the fuckin' boot!"

It was firmly locked. Bill ran to the dog van and returned with a crowbar. The officers frantically attempted to open the boot. Andy used his tremendous strength on the bar, and the lid popped open to reveal the hooded and bound bodies of Irene and Derek Stewart.

Andy lifted Irene out first and laid her on the floor. He removed the hood and the gaffer tape on her mouth Casey had thought to add. He put his ear to her face. "She's not breathing! Bill, get on the horn for an ambulance."

Marie took Irene's arm. "She has a faint pulse; we'll do mouth to mouth."

Marshall and Vinnie were pulling Derek from the car. The tough old miner was still conscious. They removed his hood. His face was badly damaged, one eye was completely closed and the remnants of a tooth hung by a thread of gum at the front of his mouth. He couldn't stand.

Marie placed her hand behind the neck of Irene and lifted slightly, opening her airway. She pushed her fingers into the elderly woman's mouth and removed a set of false teeth. Her own injuries forgotten, she began the harrowing task of trying to breathe life into another human being.

Bill jogged over. “Two ambulances en route.”

Marshall surveyed the scene. How much more carnage would this man inflict before they caught him? His voice was distant, “Thanks, Bill, the dog did good.”

Suddenly Marshall came to life. Max was still barking, even though he was in his van. “Listen, Bill, I think our man is nearby. Can Max track him?”

Bill wiped his face, which dripped with the unrelenting rain. “If he can, he’s a miracle worker. There can’t be any scent left in this weather.”

Marshall looked at the two bodies on the floor in the rain. “He found these two, and I’m in need of a miracle today, Bill.”

Marie stood suddenly and backed away from Irene. She turned to her boss and burst into tears. He held the slight woman in his arms, and had to swallow hard himself. He motioned over Marie’s shoulder for Bill to get Max.

She looked up at her boss and smiled through her tears. “She’s breathing, boss.”

Marshall looked into Marie’s damaged face. He could barely control his own emotions. “I won’t forget this, Marie.”

He turned to Bill. “Come on, mate, I need a second miracle now.”

Dave’s eyes were as used to the dark as they were going to get and he could still see the square root of fuck all. The rain fell in buckets on either side of the bridge.

Somewhere off to his left was the hole in the bridge that water poured through. His lack of activity meant that the loss of body heat was taking its toll and he had started to shake. He gripped the pistol hard with his left hand and started on a prayer in his mind.

The light was a shock. It was so bright it rendered Dave totally blind. He raised the Browning in the general direction his mind believed the light had come from. He would have pulled the trigger, but his right leg gave way. A massive explosion went off in his head. Not only was he blind, but now deaf.

Savage pain racked his leg. He had never felt pain like it. He had dropped the files and his weapon. He gripped his right leg. Hot liquid, Dave knew to be his own blood, poured from a wound just above the knee.

Then he could see. A shadow of a man stood over him. A tall man in his forties; he held a police issue Dragon lamp which lit the whole of the underside of the bridge. He also held a sawn off shotgun.

The man smiled. “Can you hear me, David?”

Dave could. Just.

“You have something for me, I believe?”

Dave looked at the floor and saw the files were about ten feet away to his right. He also saw the Browning was about the same distance away to his left.

Casey stepped forward and stamped on Dave’s damaged leg.

Dave screamed.

"Ooops! That hurt, David?" Casey appeared mildly amused. "Now we have to get something straight before you pass out. You see you are bleeding from an artery. See the colour? That's how you tell. You're dying, David, so I can tell you all."

Casey actually seemed to relax. "You see, I am the man who killed that little slut of yours. She did have nice tits, David. I would have had more fun, but it just wasn't a professional thing to do. Now, as for Mummy and Daddy, I have some bad news there too..."

Dave hurt. His leg was pumping too much blood for him to have much strength for long. It had to be now, he knew. His parents were dead. Anne was dead. Why not join them?

The man put more of his weight on Dave's leg. "Did you copy the files, David?"

Dave looked the man in the eyes. Even through his agony, he was going to enjoy this. Dave started to laugh. It was a small laugh at first. It started way down in Dave's stomach. He just couldn't help it. Was it hysteria? He didn't know or care.

Through the laughter, Dave managed to speak, "Who... Who the fuck are you?"

Casey lost his composure. He wasn't expecting this. "I asked you a question, sonny!"

Dave looked down at his leg. His own blood had covered the man's shoe. With the speed of a snake, Dave grabbed the man behind his right knee. He sank his teeth either side of his kneecap.

Casey howled like a stuck pig. In his pain and panic, the shotgun joined the Browning on the deck. With supreme, effort Dave tore at the knee. He tasted blood and felt the cartilage give way. Then he released Casey from his mouth, and with all the strength he had left punched him in the testicles.

Casey fell backward, dropping the lamp and plunging the tunnel into darkness again.

Dave was now free. He flung himself forwards in the direction of the weapons. Casey had struck his head hard in the fall. He had lost his bearings.

Dave had not.

Dave felt the butt of the sawn-off and grabbed it.

Dave clawed his way to his feet. Casey was silhouetted in the mouth of the tunnel. In his frenzy he had gone for the files, and was trying to scoop them up from the floor. Dave thought he looked pathetic.

Then Casey heard the laughter again.

He looked up to see Dave pointing the gun directly at his head. Casey's head cleared very quickly. He needed to buy a little time.

He shouted over the cascading water, "You going to shoot me, David?"

Dave's laugh was close to madness. He nodded his head furiously.

"Oh, yeah."

Casey wasn't convinced. "You haven't the bottle, sonny. You would have finished Clark if you'd had the guts. I'm a copper, David. You gonna kill a copper?"

Dave straightened his arm and closed his left eye.

"This is going to be too quick, but I haven't much time myself."

Dave couldn't see the dog, but he could hear it. He was confused for a second, and then there was no mistaking Andy Dunn's voice.

"Don't do it, Dave!"

They appeared like spectres at the tunnel opening. A uniformed officer with a dog, 'Armless and Marshall. They all held torches, and Dave could once again see his prey clearly. Tears started in Dave's eyes. He had no control now. Andy was walking toward his friend hands raised.

"Come on, Dave. Let us deal with it. Your mum and dad are OK."

The shock was immense. Alive? Dead? Truth? Lies?

It was all Casey needed, the split second of hesitation. Dave was close to blackout from blood loss and shock. Despite his pain, Casey was agile. He leapt on Dave, knocking him to the floor, his head striking the rail and knocking him unconscious, the shotgun useless by his side. With all the luck in the world, the Browning fell under Casey's right hand.

Within seconds he was on his feet. The handgun pointed firmly at the police officers.

Casey looked on the floor for the remainder of the files. He had them all.

"Now just back off, boys."

Marshall was first. "Give it up, Casey. It's all over, and you know it."

Casey was backing away. He wildly fired a shot in the direction of the officers. They fell to the floor for cover. As they raised their heads, Casey had disappeared into the darkness.

Bill stood first and released Max, who had already performed Marshall's second miracle of the day. "Go get him, boy!"

Police dogs always win when they train against a gunman. It cures the animal of the fear of gun noise. In training, of course, it is blank ammunition.

Max caught Casey in seconds. He was trained to go for the arm with the gun.

Casey shot Max three times before he let go.

Marshall sat beside Bill as he wept over his dog. The bravery of the small group of officers stunned him; for what, for the pay cheque? He didn't think so. An ambulance crew was tending to Dave's injured leg, Andy speaking words of encouragement to his wounded protégée. The troops were on the way. A full-scale search for Casey would be underway in minutes. Marshall would have some serious explaining to do later. He didn't care.

As for Casey, he was near to the road now. He waited for the first car. Ideal, a lone female driver; he stepped out straight in front of the vehicle and pointed the gun directly at her.

The woman looked terrified, and screeched to a halt ten feet from Casey.

He screamed, eyes wild, "Get out the fuckin' car now!"

Casey's knee was bleeding badly, as was his arm where Max had held him so valiantly. He was desperate. The woman did exactly as she was told. She looked like a secretary on her way to work.

She stepped out of the saloon and into the rain. "Please don't hurt me," she pleaded.

Casey took hold of her arm and flung her to the floor.

He jumped into the driver's seat. It needed adjustment for his large frame. As he slid the seat backward, a powerful arm appeared from behind. The stiletto knife slipped effortlessly into his throat.

His face held a look of surprise for several seconds. There was little blood.

Ross removed the knife and wiped it clean. The woman quickly returned to the car, and pushed Casey into the passenger seat with surprising strength. Several figures, draped in black and carrying state of the art night surveillance equipment, were appearing from the fields. Ross's men had seen it all.

The gangster got out of the car, holding the files. He straightened his immaculate overcoat.

"Get rid of him, Wendy."

17533117R00267

Printed in Great Britain
by Amazon